SWEET

PERFECTLY IMPERFECT SERIES

prison

NEVA ALTAJ

Sweet Prison

Editing by Andie Edwards of Beyond The Proof
Proofreading by Yvette Rebello
Manuscript critique by Anka Lesko
Stylistic editing by Anna Corbeaux
Cover design by Deranged Doctor

Perfectly Imperfect
Reading Order & Tropes

1. *Painted Scars* (Nina & Roman)
Tropes: disabled hero, fake marriage, age gap, opposites
attract, possessive/jealous hero

2. *Broken Whispers* (Bianca & Mikhail)
Tropes: scarred/disabled hero, mute heroine, arranged
marriage, age gap, Beauty and the Beast, OTT
possessive/jealous hero

3. *Hidden Truths* (Angelina & Sergei)
Tropes: age gap, broken hero, only she can calm him down,
who did this to you

4. *Ruined Secrets* (Isabella & Luca)
Tropes: arranged marriage, age gap, OTT
possessive/jealous hero, amnesia

5. *Stolen Touches* (Milene & Salvatore)
Tropes: arranged marriage, disabled hero, age gap,
emotionless hero, OTT possessive/jealous hero

6. *Fractured Souls* (Asya & Pavel)
Tropes: he helps her heal, age gap, who did this to
you, possessive/jealous hero, he thinks he's not
good enough for her

7. *Burned Dreams* (Ravenna & Alessandro)
Tropes: bodyguard, forbidden love, revenge, enemies to lovers, age gap, who did this to you, possessive/jealous hero

8. *Silent Lies* (Sienna & Drago)
Tropes: deaf hero, arranged marriage, age gap, grumpy-sunshine, opposites attract, super OTT possessive/jealous hero

9. *Darkest Sins* (Nera & Kai)
Tropes: grumpy-sunshine, opposites attract, age gap, stalker hero, only she can calm him down, he hates everyone but her, touch her and die

10. *Sweet Prison* (Zahara & Massimo)
Tropes: age gap, forbidden romance, only she can calm him down, opposites attract, he hates everyone but her, touch her and die, OTT possessive/jealous hero

11. *Precious Hazard* (Tara & Arturo)
Tropes: arranged marriage, age gap, enemies to lovers, grumpy/sunshine, opposites attract, touch her and die, OTT possessive/jealous hero

12. *Title, MCs and tropes—to be revealed*

Author's Note

Dear Reader,

The Perfectly Imperfect is a series of interconnected standalones, where books can be read in any order. However, *Sweet Prison* (book 10, Massimo & Zahara's story) was written as a companion to *Darkest Sins* (book 9, Kai & Nera's story), and I strongly recommend reading the duet in tandem and in the proper order. In this book, I have only reflected on the events that occurred in *Darkest Sins* if they are essential to the current plot because 1) I wanted to avoid repetitions, and 2) this is Massimo and Zahara's story, while Kai and Nera already shared theirs.

If you have not yet read *Darkest Sins*, or have chosen to skip it, your enjoyment of *Sweet Prison* may be greatly impacted, as knowing the events that transpired in the preceding book is crucial for understanding characters' motivations and the intricacies of how their lives and paths are intertwined. Without that awareness, you may find yourself a bit lost in the tangled web of the Mafia world.

Whatever choice you make, I hope you love this book as much as I do.

Happy reading!
Neva

CONTENT WARNING

Please know that *Sweet Prison* features a romance between stepsiblings. Massimo and Zahara (Zara) are not related by blood. The hero is the son of Zara's stepmom, from her previous marriage. If this is not your cup of tea, please consider skipping this story.

It's also important to mention that the age gap between Massimo and Zahara is 17 years.

Neither has an extensive recollection of each other from the period they briefly inhabited the same household following the marriage between their parents. When they first reconnect in *Darkest Sins*, Zara is 18, while Massimo is 35.

Please be aware that this book contains content that some readers may find disturbing, such as gore, violence and graphic descriptions of torture.

Sweet

PERFECTLY IMPERFECT SERIES

prison

PROLOGUE

 Zahara

Nuncio Veronese's Funeral, Boston

(Zahara, age 18; Massimo, age 35)

JUST YOU, NERA.

Massimo's words ring in my head as I hurry along the dirt path toward the parking lot. My vision is so blurred by tears that I can barely see where I'm stepping. I lift my arm and brush the wetness away with my sleeve.

That bastard.

"Zara! Wait!" my sister calls after me.

I quicken my pace. I'm in no shape to talk with her now. The only thing I want to do is curl up in a dark corner and cry in peace.

When he made his approach toward Nera and me, my heart was beating so rapidly that I was afraid I was going to have a heart attack. In a way, I've always perceived Massimo as somewhat unreal. Untouchable. Out of reach. Seeing him here, in front of me, as a real flesh-and-blood entity, almost made me faint. And my stupid heart sang with joy.

Until he crushed it with one simple sentence.

Just you, Nera.

I have no idea what he wants to discuss with my sister. Maybe he wants to lay a claim to our family's properties. That would fit with his cunning methods.

I don't fucking care.

He already claimed the only thing I care about. My heart.

And he squashed it.

CHAPTER
one

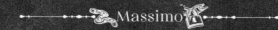

Fifteen years ago
(Massimo, age 20)

"**A**LL RISE."

I adjust my suit jacket and slowly stand up from the defendant's seat. The cuffs of my shirt are too tight, chafing the already irritated skin on my wrists. The motherfuckers who escorted me from county lockup to the courthouse made sure to slap the smallest handcuffs on me that they could.

Judge Collins waddles in. His mass of white hair and beard contrasts with his black attire. I try catching his eye, but his gaze persistently strays elsewhere, almost like it's intentional. I guess he's trying to make sure no one suspects that we actually know each other. It's hilarious, considering how many favors he's received from Cosa Nostra over the decades. He—along with nearly half of Boston's elites, bureaucrats, and top law-and-order brass—was present at the New Year's Eve party where everything went to shit.

I take a deep breath, awaiting the delivery of my sentence.

After my arraignment and pretrial hearing and on my lawyer's advice, I took a deal. A guilty plea to a charge of voluntary manslaughter in exchange for an expected sentence of three years. Maybe four, if the judge doesn't want to look like he's taking it easy on me. With three hundred witnesses, there's no way to deny that I shot the bastard who killed my stepbrother. So I waived my right to a trial and avoided tying up a shitpile of time and money in this clusterfuck, not to mention a potential maximum sentence. This way, with a possibility of parole in about a year, I should be home in no time. Not a bad deal—a handful of years of my life for blowing away the fuck who murdered Elmo. Knowing that I was able to end that piece of shit then and there is also satisfying as hell.

"Massimo Spada, you have pleaded guilty to the charge of voluntary manslaughter as defined by statute and governed by Massachusetts General Laws Chapter 265, Section 13." The judge's voice fills the room, and his eyes finally meet mine. "Justice is blind, Mr. Spada. Every man is equal before the law. Given the gravity of your actions and your obvious lack of regret during the hearing, I hereby sentence you to eighteen years in a maximum security state prison…"

A high-pitched sound, like static on an old-fashioned TV, erupts in my head. It overwhelms the loud murmuring that has suddenly taken over the courtroom.

Eighteen years? *Eighteen fucking years?* No, that can't be right. McBride assured me that four was the absolute maximum I'd get, considering the judge's connection to the Family. This has to be a mistake. There's no other explanation. I turn toward Judge Collins. Stare right at him. Waiting for him to announce that he made an error, all while the ringing bounces off the inner walls of my skull. He doesn't utter another word.

Someone gets ahold of my arms, jerking them behind me. I can vaguely hear my lawyer yammering at me about an appeal. Somehow, over the ruckus happening both inside my stunned brain and out in the room, I still manage to hear the clank of handcuffs locking around my wrists. This can't be happening. God knows I'm not innocent in this or any other crimes I've committed, but he has no right to ruin my life like this! It's a fucking nightmare, and I need someone to punch me in the face so I can wake the fuck up!

I dig my heels into the floor, still glaring at the judge, who's descending the steps after leaving his seat.

No. I will not have the next eighteen years of my life stolen.

"Collins!" My roar explodes over the clamor of hushed voices.

The bastard doesn't even blink. Just keeps ignoring me completely.

McBride is babbling some lawyer crap at me again, his tone almost hysterical. Something about how I'm making this worse, but the words just graze my mind, caught in the ringing in my head that's only getting stronger. Hands, several pairs, grab my arms and push me toward the door on the side of the courtroom. I keep looking over my shoulder, searching for Judge Collins. Waiting for him to put a stop to this madness. Glancing back, every couple of steps, even as I'm being led down the narrow hallway toward the holding cell where I changed into my freshly pressed suit less than twenty minutes prior. My legs seem to be moving on nothing but muscle memory.

"Two minutes, Spada." One of the guards reaches for my handcuffed wrists. "Your transport is waiting."

"Two minutes for what?"

"For you to change your digs." He pushes me into the room and nods to the far corner.

Acid surges up my throat, burning my flesh, as I follow his gaze to the rickety bench.

There, on top of the wooden boards covered in cracked and peeling paint, lies a neatly folded pile of clothes.

Denial. Blind rage. Helplessness. The chaos of different emotions hits me, all of them washing over me at the same time, and suddenly, I can't fucking breathe. Can't move. Can't think. The only thing I can do is stare at the bright orange stack of clothes on that bench, searing my fucking corneas.

CHAPTER
Two

Massimo

Three months earlier, New Year's Eve
Home of Nuncio Veronese (Boston Cosa Nostra Don)

THE SMELL OF DRIED OREGANO AND FRESH PRODUCE tucked away in wooden crates on the shelves wars with the slight scent of mold hanging in the air. There are no windows, and the only source of light is the single fixture hanging from the center of the ceiling, throwing a yellow glow on a disheveled, sniveling mess of a man. Carlo Forino. Two of my guys flank him, keeping him from leaping off the stool his ass is currently planted on.

I flip a chair around and straddle it, hanging my forearms off the sturdy wooden back while I observe this pitiful excuse of a human. Carlo is breathing rapidly, practically hyperventilating, but he avoids meeting my gaze. He knows why he's here. And he knows what's coming.

His labored breaths mix with the subdued tones of a piano drifting in through the closed door. Even though the party is largely happening in the main hall on the other side of the mansion, the sounds carry all the way here, to this out-of-the-way pantry.

"Where's our money, Carlo?" I ask.

"Business hasn't been going well at the bar, Massimo," the man chokes out. "But it's just a bit of a rough patch. I swear I'll pay you guys back. I just need a few more days."

I cross my arms over the top of the chair and cock my head. "Your business troubles don't have any bearing on our deal. The due date was yesterday."

"Next week. I'll have it all next week."

"Alright." I nod and turn to Peppe, who's standing to the left of me. "There are meat shears in the drawer over there. Cut off his pinkie."

"Massimo." Elmo's voice comes from the corner of the room. "Is that really necessary? He said he'll pay."

I look over my shoulder, pinning my stepbrother with my stare. His face has a peculiar greenish hue, and he's fidgeting with his hands. Even in his fancy, tailored tux, he still looks like a kid. Elmo turned eighteen last week, and his father, the don of the Boston Cosa Nostra, figured it was time his son was more involved in the Family's dealings. This "meeting" was supposed to be Elmo's introduction to the less savory side of the business.

Too bad Elmo is not cut out for this life. Much like his father, actually.

"We're not a charity institution, Elmo. You don't want this scumbag to go around telling people *La Famiglia* has gone soft, do you?"

A howling wail reverberates through the room.

"No but…" Elmo's gaze wanders toward Carlo, who, by the sounds of it, has just lost his finger. "Dear God. I… I'm going to be sick."

I squeeze the bridge of my nose and exhale. "Leave, Elmo."

"You know I can't. Dad said—"

"And I said, *get the fuck out!*" If he loses the contents of his stomach in front of our men, he'll lose their respect. And in Cosa Nostra, respect is everything.

I get up and approach my stepbrother, ignoring Carlo's increasingly pathetic wails. Elmo's face has gone so pale it looks translucent. Placing my hand on his shoulder, I squeeze it reassuringly. "I'll talk with Nuncio and make sure he comes to his senses. Have you decided on a college?"

"Yes, but… I don't think he'll let me. He wants—"

"I don't give a fuck what Nuncio wants. Consider the whole thing done. And stop fidgeting with your damn tie." I adjust the bow that was tied askew at his collar. The kid isn't a suit guy, that's for sure. My tailor nearly had a meltdown trying to make Elmo stand still while taking his measurements. "Go, enjoy the party. I'll be there in a bit."

With a deep breath, Elmo nods. "Thank you, Massimo." He taps my chest with his palm and the next second, he's out the door.

I turn around, ready to finish my business here. Carlo is clutching a kitchen towel to his bloody hand, whimpering like a pussy.

Four pairs of eyes trace my path to the shelf where Peppe left the shears tucked between two jars of sun-dried tomatoes. I pull a lighter from my pocket and hold the slightly curved blades of the shears over the flame. "Let me see your hand."

"Why?" Carlo croaks.

"Lots of blood vessels in fingers. Wouldn't want you to bleed to death, right? You die, and who's gonna pay your debt?" I nod to the guys, my handpicked crew of enforcers. "Hold him down."

Carlo tries to fight back, but my men subdue him easily. Peppe grabs the sniveling bastard's wrist and presents the wounded hand to me. Shoving the lighter back into my pants, I get ahold of the unreliable idiot's palm.

"You have three days," I bark.

Then, I press the heated blade to the bleeding stump of his finger, and the smell of burned flesh fills the room.

"Massimo." The pantry door swings open, revealing Salvo. "Elmo said you're here and... What in the hell is that smell?"

"Persuasion. For deadbeats." I step to the side, giving him a direct view of the now passed-out Forino.

Salvo swallows audibly. His eyes are wide as they roam over the blood stains and pause on the severed finger on the floor. "Sweet Jesus."

I shake my head. Salvo and I attended the same prep school and have been best friends since day one. Whereas I've never let the high-society glitter get to me and have been doing this shit for years, he's fourth generation Cosa Nostra and accustomed to all the pomp and circumstance that goes along with money, power, and prestige. His father is a capo, and his grandfather was an underboss in his time. This means that Salvo doesn't usually get his hands dirty or even stoop low enough to witness how the shadier parts of our business are handled.

"What do you need?" I ask.

"Don V. has been asking when you're going to join the guests," he mumbles, eyes still focused on the severed finger.

"As soon as I wash my hands."

"Um... okay."

"Save me a few shrimp before Leone eats them all," I toss at his quickly retreating back.

I enter the great hall, taking in the glitz and glamour that is all my mother's handiwork. The guy in the flashy white suit is still playing the piano, but thank fuck he switched to a livelier tune. The don and my mother are having a pleasant chat with a few of the city's higher-ups on the far side of the room, right next to the elaborately decorated Christmas tree. If there were any doubt, the big grin Nuncio is wearing as he stands just to the left of Judge Collins shows how truly he enjoys all the fanfare and other benefits that being at the helm of the Family affords him.

If the plan had gone as it should have, it would be me in his place. Too bad sometimes shit doesn't go as intended.

I was raised and have been trained to assume the leadership of Boston Cosa Nostra since I turned twelve. While other fathers took their sons to football games, mine dragged me to shady clubs and derelict buildings to meet with our suppliers. Instead of playing video games like my friends, I was learning how to shoot. While other boys my age were leafing through porn magazines, I was sitting with my father in our accountant's office, learning how to launder money. Any time there was a big deal going down, my father brought me with him to witness the deed. Despite my father being the Boston don, I was not pampered like the sons of other privileged Family members. Our blood was definitely not blue.

My father started out as a lowly worker, laboring at one of Cosa Nostra's warehouses. He became a made man at seventeen and spent two decades rising through the ranks until he became the underboss. Then, eight years ago, he took over leadership of the Boston Family. Dad believed that only someone who'd experienced all roles on the ladder of Cosa Nostra would make a good leader. Because only someone with personal knowledge of the plights of the soldiers would act in the best interests of every member of *La Famiglia* and not only the higher-ups. And since he wanted me to succeed him as the don, that meant I had to go through it all, too.

So I did. Collected money from the men who owed us.

And beat the shit out of those who couldn't pay. I can't even count the number of times I got home with bloodstains on my clothes after witnessing how the Cosa Nostra justice was served firsthand. I accompanied the foot soldiers on their rounds around the neighborhood or went with them to retaliate against other crime organizations. I spent more days in a dive bar by the waterfront with the organization's muscle, playing poker and drinking, than I spent evenings with my friends from school. I didn't get to go to my junior prom because I spent the night sprawled on a wooden bench in the back room of a casino while a doc dug a bullet out of my thigh after a drug deal went sideways. Quite a thrill-filled life for a teenager. And I liked it that way.

I never minded my lost childhood because I knew I was being groomed to take over the Family when the time came. But that time arrived too soon. I was barely eighteen when my father died. A decade too early for anyone to even consider me for the role. I was a young pup among seasoned dogs. And those bitches couldn't be taught any new tricks.

At the quickly assembled Family meeting, Nuncio Veronese was voted in as the next don. It was an unexpected turn of events. Until it happened, I was sure it would be Batista Leone who'd take over. Older. More experienced. My father's underboss. I think even Nuncio himself was rather surprised when he ended up as the leader of the Cosa Nostra in Boston.

Veronese had young kids and had lost his wife in childbirth only months earlier. So at that same meeting, a deal for him to marry my mother was struck. They married soon after. A wise move. There's no better way of strengthening your position as a new don than marrying your predecessor's widow and bringing his son under your roof. Considering my age—old enough, just not for sitting at the head of the table—I was relegated to the position of Nuncio's glorified "left hand." A messenger, doling out judgment and discipline on behalf of the new don.

Loud, joyful laughter erupts from the group standing by the Christmas tree, pulling me back to the party. Nuncio probably delivered one of his jokes. Fancy dinners and parties with our investors, public appearances, and fundraising events for the organizations we launder money through are always my stepfather's jam, and he pulls them off impeccably.

The charisma the man has is unparalleled. Nuncio Veronese can talk an otherwise rational person into cutting off their own hand and convince them it's for their own good. They might even have the urge to thank him for it. People always gravitate toward him like he's the fucking sun. Important, powerful people. He plays golf with the chief of police every second Wednesday. Has an open invitation to all influential households in the Greater Boston region. Every socialite and power-hungry member of the Boston elite has attended at least one of Nuncio's summer backyard BBQs. He even managed to get a fucking Massachusetts State judge to come to our New Year's party.

Ever since my father's time as the don, Cosa Nostra has been swinging toward a more "populist" approach and avoiding open confrontations with the law. That's probably why Nuncio was chosen to succeed my father. The Family was convinced they made a good choice.

They were wrong.

Nuncio is not a bad man. And that's his worst fault. He's not fit to be in charge of a Mafia Family because when it comes to the dark side of our business, the side that requires horrid and vile work, he doesn't have the stomach for it. That became abundantly clear shortly after he took over. The first time he needed to kill a man, the poor bastard almost fainted. He couldn't even manage to put a bullet into the head of a snitch, ending up hitting the fucker's shoulder instead. Thank fuck it was only me and him in the room. I had to step in and finish the job. I was Elmo's age then. And it wasn't even my first kill.

Gory stuff aside, I hoped Nuncio would at least persevere in other areas. But he proved himself absolutely incapable of handling the Family's business dealings and finances, too. Can't say he didn't try, though. Within three months of taking over, he funneled all our laundered cash into a big-ass construction project but failed to analyze the risks or calculate the anticipated costs. We lost our liquidity and were left with a half-finished residential block in the suburbs and no money to finish the build. I had to leverage several of my father's connections to find investors ready to buy the units before the gray shell phase was complete. After that fiasco, Nuncio started consulting with me on all investments. By my nineteenth birthday, unbeknownst to the rest of the Family, I was making every business decision in the don's stead.

So Nuncio and I struck our own deal. I do the heavy lifting. Manage the finances. Call the shots on investments. Maim and kill people when necessary. And he puts up with the asinine, pompous bullshit, like hosting a party for people who'd stab you in the back the moment you turned or going to fundraisers and sweet-talking the important people we need on our side. And when I turn twenty-five, he'll make me a capo. Then, his underboss. And when the time feels right, when I'm seen as "old enough" to take over the reins of the Family, he'll step down. If he doesn't, I'll just kill him.

"Hey, Massimo." Brio, the capo running our casinos catches up to me as I'm making my way through the crowd. "Did Boss say anything about the expansion plan I presented last week?"

"Yes." I grab a flute of champagne off a waiter's tray. "He said it's an epic load of crap. At the current revenue level, no expansion for the next two years at the minimum."

"Fuck! I spent weeks working out the details, looking for

suitable locations for the new casino. I even researched..." I let Brio continue his incessant babbling, complaining about the "don's" decision, and take in the people in the room.

It's almost midnight, so everyone is having a good time, more or less wasted on free-flowing champagne. I pretend not to notice the two tiny shapes hiding behind the banister on the second-floor landing. My stepsisters love sneaking out of bed and spying on guests during parties. Mother will have their hide if she sees them.

Nera was three when my mother married Nuncio, and Zahara was still a baby, barely a year old. Both think of my mother as their own. They even call her "Mom." I don't mind. The little brats are a nuisance I simply try to ignore, but Mother loves them like they are her own flesh and blood. I'm glad. I was never a cuddly child interested in hugs and kisses. I'm happy she finally has the chance to be a loving, caring mom to two girls who crave her warmth the way I never did.

My eyes travel to a couple half-hidden by a marble column in the entryway as they murmur suggestively to each other. Looks like Elmo is trying to sweet-talk Tiziano's sister. Christ, she's nearly twice his age and will easily chew him up and spit him out, undoubtedly breaking his heart.

For some absolutely unexplainable reason, I've connected with my stepbrother. Maybe it's because he's the only truly good-hearted person I know, aside from my mother. There isn't a single evil bone in the boy's body, despite being born into a Mafia world and constantly surrounded by snakes. He's everything I'll never be. Kind. Thoughtful, especially about the people around him. And selfless to a fault.

Deep down, I've always wondered what it would be like to have a brother. As a boy, I craved a confidant of my own with whom I could share my worries. How much pressure I felt to meet Father's expectations. The taste of acid in my mouth every time I had to maim or kill a man. And the hollow feeling that eventually set in when that sour taste numbed.

All too soon, that bitter burn no longer lodged in my throat. I got used to it. The job became like any other. But once in a while, a stray thought invaded my mind. A feeling of wrongness for taking lives without being even remotely perturbed about it. On the other hand, I realized I'd stopped feeling the strain I'd been under. And that realization made me even more fractured.

I could never admit those concerns to my father, not without appearing weak. And telling my mother was always out of the question. She still clings to the illusion that her son is a good person. But a brother? Yes, I could confide in a brother. And Elmo is the closest I have to that.

That's probably why I feel this weird compulsion to protect Elmo from the clutches of those who would use him for their own selfish needs. His dreams include college and a normal life. And I'll make damn sure that happens.

Amid the festivities, raised voices ring out somewhere near the front door. My gaze snaps over to the entrance where two, obviously drunk, men are arguing. *Jesus.* I'm looking around the room, trying to spot one of our security guards to throw the idiots out, when fists start flying. One shoves the other, yelling into his adversary's face, and reaches inside his jacket.

I immediately head toward them and out of the corner of my eye, see Elmo doing the same. "Elmo!" I roar. "Get back!"

He either doesn't hear my command or decides to ignore me, thinking he can calm the situation. I'm running full speed, but since he was closer, Elmo reaches the enraged men mere seconds before I do.

My fingertips nearly brush his jacket when I lunge for him to pull him away, just as an ear-shattering boom splits the air.

For a fraction of a heartbeat, the sound of that gunshot is the only thing I hear.

No music. No laughter. Just an earthshaking blast. And then, Elmo stumbles backward, colliding with my chest.

Screams explode around us.

"Elmo!" I yell, wrapping my arm around his body to support him.

The fabric of his tux is wet against my palm, and his blood oozes over my hand. Seeing nothing but red, I let savage rage consume me. Somewhere in the back of my mind, I'm aware that there are too many people here, too many witnesses. A good portion of them are not members of the Family. Including Boston's chief of police.

I don't care.

Not giving a fuck about the repercussions, I reach behind my back and pull out my Glock. With my next breath, an animalistic roar leaves my throat, and I send the bullet flying between the eyes of the motherfucker who just shot my stepbrother.

CHAPTER
Three

Eleven years later
(Zahara, age 14)

"**H**EY, CHECK IT OUT! ISN'T THAT OUR RESIDENT
leper girl?"

Laughter rings out around me. I drop my chin
even lower and gripping the stack of books in my arms, hasten
my steps. The sickening tingle at the back of my neck ratchets
up as I squeeze between the students in the hallway and their
judgmental stares.

I should be used to all of this by now. Teasing. Mean, spiteful name-calling. It goes way back to elementary school. The
questions came first. *What happened to you? Does it hurt?* I tried
explaining that it's just how my skin looks and it's completely
normal, exactly as my mom told me to. Regardless, kids typically stayed clear of me—no one wanted to play with me, and
some didn't even want to look in my direction.

Once I started high school, it got worse. The days of peaceful shunning were no more. *Gross. That looks awful.* Or, the
ever-present... *Don't touch me. I don't wanna catch what you*

got. There was no point in explaining that vitiligo is not contagious. They didn't really care, anyway. And since I always tried to ignore them instead of fighting back, I was an easy target for their insecurities. So they humiliate me. Cause me pain. Both physically and with their words.

Oddly enough, the bullying doesn't really bother me anymore… not much, at least. It's the looks of pity I can't stand. So I try to remain as invisible as possible. Do my best not to attract any unwanted attention. Too bad that strategy doesn't work on Kenneth fricking Harris.

"Brown looks good on you, lep." A mocking smile pulls at Kenneth's lips. He halts right in front of me, blocking my way to the school's main entrance, and plants his hands on his hips. "But I think you must have forgotten to check today's forecast. You gotta be cooking inside that mesh-looking thing. Or is it a mosquito net?"

Another round of laughter echoes through the hallway.

"Let me pass, please," I mumble, staring at the tips of my shoes.

"Of course." He takes a step to the side.

Holding my breath, I dash past him, but as I do, Kenneth yanks on one of my sleeves. The unmistakable sound of tearing fabric follows as the fine threads break.

Tears gather at the corners of my eyes while I stare at the ruined lace in Kenneth's meaty fist. I spent days working on this blouse, modifying the original pattern to make the sleeves long enough to cover my hands. Hours of labor that made my back and fingers ache, and this jerk cared nothing about it.

"Sorry, lep." Chuckling, he throws the tattered material to the floor. "But hey, look on the bright side. It's more suitable for the weather now."

There are over a dozen people around us—all of them the jerkface's cronies—and I can feel each of their gazes on my exposed arm. Gawking at the discoloration on my elbow, my forearm, my wrist. The urge to gouge everyone's eyes out with my bare hands, to scream in their faces to stop fucking gaping, surges inside me.

I don't.

I never do.

Biting my lower lip to keep it from quivering, I scoop the scrap of lace off the floor. Clutching it in my hand so hard my nails pierce my palm, I turn and head down the hallway. I can't make a scene, or my father will hear about it. Then he'd probably transfer me to another prestigious school, one filled with even more stuck-up creeps than this one, or maybe just decide to have me homeschooled. I can still hear his hushed words from his conversation with his underboss last week: *My poor little Zara, I'm so worried about her. She always finds it hard to handle stressful situations.*

Sometimes, I wish I could tell him the truth. That I've imagined him showing up at my school, raising hell, and yelling at everyone who has ever hurt me. Or beating the shit out of that asshole, Kenneth. Too bad something like that would never happen. My father might be the boss of Cosa Nostra in Boston, but he would never cause a fuss because of me. The sons and daughters of his business associates attend this school, and the don would never risk jeopardizing lucrative partnerships simply because some boy "upset" his antisocial, skittish child.

Image is everything within *La Famiglia*, and Nuncio Veronese would never stoop to anything so clearly beneath him. It would simply be easier to transfer me to another school, just as he'd done before. And then, I would feel like an even bigger failure.

I'm hurrying across the schoolyard toward the west side of campus when a hand brushes my arm, and I jump.

"Hey, Zara! Want to come to Dania's to watch a movie?"

I force a small smile and look up at my sister. "No. I... I have to study."

"You sure?" Nera asks. "We could— Oh my God, what happened to your shirt?"

"My sleeve got caught on a door handle," I lie.

"Oh?" Her eyes narrow at my ruined blouse. "Is someone bothering you again?"

"Of course not. I wasn't paying attention to where I was going. That's all."

When I was nine, I made the mistake of confessing to my sister about the teasing I received at school. I told her that a boy from her grade called me a bunch of names. Despite being a tiny eleven-year-old, Nera tracked my bully down during recess and fought him. She earned a bruise on her chin and two weeks of detention. And when we got home, Dad grounded her for "despicable behavior unbecoming of our pedigree" and "bringing shame to the Veronese name."

I will never again put my sister in a position to get in trouble because she feels the need to defend me, just because I'm too much of a chicken to stand up for myself. Thank God most of her classes are in a separate building this year. Now she can't witness the bulk of my encounters with Kenneth.

"You guys have fun. I'll see you tonight." I squeeze Nera's hand and head toward the car waiting for me by the campus gates. It's parked just behind the big SUV belonging to Hannah's dad, and I spot my friend getting into the back of it while giving me a brief wave. I'm glad she's rushing off to her dance class right now and doesn't have time to stop and chat. She'd instantly know that something was up with me, having seen enough of my run-ins with Kenneth the dick twat.

"Miss Veronese." Peppe, my chauffeur nods, holding the door open for me.

Without meeting his gaze, I slip into the back seat.

The drive to our house is about half an hour, and I usually spend that time aimlessly gazing out the window. Now, however, I can't seem to sit still. Although the windows are up and the AC isn't on, a shiver races across my skin, and the fine hairs on my bare arm stand on end. Flashbacks of that scene in the school hallway flood my mind. I'd love to be able to talk to someone about it, just so I could call the shit-for-brains Kenneth a douchnozzle out loud. If my brother, Elmo, was alive I'm sure he would beat the shit out of Kenneth. He wouldn't let anyone touch me or call me names. Or at least, that's what I choose to believe. I barely remember Elmo, but Nera does. And she says he was the best brother in the whole world.

I sigh and reach into my bag for my phone. As I do, my eyes catch on the corner of a violet notebook peeking from between a few others. It's the one I use to sketch my designs for custom clothing.

And to write silly letters to my stepbrother who's in prison.

It all started a couple of years ago, while I was still in middle school. My seventh-grade teacher gave us an assignment to write a letter to a friend or family member living abroad. Initially, I considered addressing mine to an imaginary aunt or cousin, since I don't have any real relatives that qualify. But it felt kind of stupid, writing to someone who doesn't exist. But then, for some reason, Massimo popped into my mind.

My stepbrother was arrested for killing the man who murdered Elmo when I was three years old. I have no memories of him. Neither Nera nor I have seen Massimo since the night Elmo died. Massimo won't allow anyone other than my father to visit him in prison, and Dad hardly ever tells us anything about our stepbrother. Despite us *technically* being family, he is a virtual stranger to me and my sister. But since Mom died, I'm not even sure if that thread is still whole.

Before her death, I asked Mom about the picture she kept on her dresser, the one of her and a guy in his late teens. His hair was dark, just as hers had been. I was curious about the boy, and she told me he was Massimo and shared a couple of stories from his childhood. I liked hearing them, but it made her sad to speak of my stepbrother, so she rarely did. She tried to bury the sorrow of having her child stuck in prison for so many years by showering Nera and me with all her love. Laura Veronese was a warm, affectionate woman, and the best mom anyone could ask for. But even as a kid, I saw the anguish in her eyes. The pain was always there. She died of embolism when I was nine. And even though the doctor said it was a massive clot in her bloodstream, I'm certain the true reason was her broken heart.

People say that it's not technically possible to die from heartbreak, but I disagree. I'm certain of it because that's what it felt like when Dad told Nera and me that Mom was gone. We shut ourselves in my room and cried, clutching at the matching dresses she made for us. Although we had lots of money, and Mom could afford to buy us anything we wanted, she preferred to make most of our clothes herself. That's why I started sewing soon after. It makes me feel closer to her somehow.

With Mom gone, Massimo was the only family member, aside from Dad and Nera, I had left. He wasn't living abroad, but he was *real*. That was why I took a sheet of paper from my notebook and wrote to a stepbrother whom I didn't even know. He might as well have been living on a different planet, which seemed ideal for the assignment.

He must have laughed when he received that letter. I don't even remember all the things I wrote in it. There was something about me claiming a set of fancy pens I found in a box with his name on it in the basement. I think I phrased it as a question first—asking if I could have them—then crossed the sentence out and rewrote it as a statement, so he couldn't tell me *no*. I kind of expected him to write me back, but he never did. Eventually, I figured he must have thrown my unsolicited mail away.

I never intended to keep writing him letters.

With the school assignment over and done with, I forgot all about my unsolicited, and probably unwanted, written word vomit and carried on with life. Until a few months later. Until I was bursting at the seams to spout my frustrations to someone; someone who would not judge or look at me with pity.

Or worse, tell me I was overreacting to what must have been just an accident.

Having juice spilled all over my new dress at Dania's birthday party by a jerk-of-a-boy who laughed behind my back after was not an "accident"! So, once I got home, I wrote to Massimo again and raged about how stupid boys were for three entire paragraphs. Then, feeling better after confessing my troubles, and so he wouldn't think I'm a negative person, I added some nonsense about a field trip and how one of the girls threw up on the bus after eating too much junk food even after the teacher warned her to take it easy. I thought he might find that funny.

But there was no reply.

Still, I kept writing. I penned a letter every couple of months filled with dumb, unimportant things. Like, who came to a fancy lunch at our house and what food was served. Or how the plumber who was fixing our blocked sink ended up flooding the kitchen. I also ranted a lot about school. Math especially. And because I was so proud of my accomplishment, I even sent Massimo a sketch of the first dress I sewed for myself.

Since I've always been too anxious to talk with other people or be open about my feelings, over the last two years, writing to Massimo has become a sort of stress relief. It might sound pathetic, but those letters were the closest thing I had to a friend I could talk to about whatever was on my mind. It felt safe. I knew he would not criticize me or judge me. Because, obviously, Massimo wasn't reading my letters in the first place. He never responded to a single one.

I really need my friend now, as I'm staring at the tattered lace in my hand. My mind starts to buzz with all the things I want to say to him.

"Everything alright, Miss Veronese?"

I look up, meeting Peppe's gaze in the rearview mirror. He might wear a nice navy suit, but there's an unmistakable air around him. A roughness, and maybe even a little danger. He doesn't seem like a plain old driver to me, even if he's been working as one as long as I can remember.

"Yes, all good," I mumble.

When he looks back at the road, I pull out my violet notebook and flip to a blank page, one that follows the sketch I've been working on of a blouse with beautiful lantern sleeves. Fishing out a pen, I start my letter with *Dear Massimo*, as usual. It's not that he's "dear" to me or anything, it's just a common way to start letters, I guess, and I've addressed them all like that so far.

I spend at least ten minutes describing the intricate details of the blouse—starting with the difficulties of getting the pattern just right, then the complexities of the cuffs and the hidden button at the back. After that, I switch to rambling about the fabrics I'm considering for when I eventually sew it, listing the pros and cons for each one.

Then, I let Massimo know about the barbecue Dad threw earlier this week, with most of the *La Famiglia* members in attendance. It was a big event. I write two paragraphs describing the outfits, as well as the gossip I overheard in the fifteen minutes I spent among the attendees.

As the words land on paper, I'm starting to feel better, but the situation with Kenneth is still heavy on my mind. Reeling from the encounter, and without really meaning to dump another pile of my woes at my stepbrother's feet, I add a couple of brief sentences about what happened. I don't go into much detail and finish up by calling Kenneth Harris an asshole who deserves a swift kick in the rear.

I sign the letter as I always do—*Zahara*.

I like my full name, but other than my teachers, no one calls me by it. I'm always Zara to everyone around me. When I was little, I couldn't pronounce Zahara. I tripped over the syllables and ended up saying "Zara" instead. It stuck. I love my name, but at this point, it feels silly to ask everybody to call me Zahara. So I don't bother.

"Peppe"—I tap the driver on the shoulder—"I need to make a quick stop at the post office."

By the time we arrive home, rain is coming down in sheets. I don't wait for Peppe to open my door, just dash out of the car and across the driveway to the front entrance. I don't think he noticed my torn sleeve and I want to keep it that way. If he tells my dad, I'll be accosted and I'll have no choice but to provide an explanation. And I'm not in the mood to make up any more excuses today.

Running inside, soaking wet from my short sprint through the downpour, my eyes fall on a pile of mail on the antique console table in the foyer. Dad must not be home. He always takes the mail straight to his study when he arrives. As I pass by, I notice an unusual-looking white envelope among the typical bland utility bills and bright-colored invitations. It has a printed label of some kind in the upper left corner.

I pull out the envelope to take a better look and almost drop it. It's addressed to me. And the return label is the name of the correctional facility where my stepbrother is serving his time.

Looking around to make sure nobody saw me, I race up the stairs, directly to my room. No one knows I've been writing to Massimo other than our maid, Iris. And I would prefer to keep it that way.

Something tells me Dad would not be pleased if he found out about my letters. Whenever he mentions my stepbrother's name, there's an odd pitch to his voice. It's subtle, but it feels like his tone carries a bit of animosity. At my stepbrother? At the situation? Whatever the cause, it makes him cranky, and I'm afraid he'd forbid me from writing to Massimo if he knew.

I shut my door, then lean back upon its solid surface and take a deep breath. Excitement sparkles in my chest, and my hands shake as I tear the envelope open. Has Massimo actually written back? What might he have said? I wonder if he's asked how we're all doing. Or, maybe, he's told me what his life in prison is like.

When I finally manage to pull the folded pages out, I smooth out the creases while my eyes roam over the contents. Two pages! Both sides of each sheet are filled with graphs and formulas, and random notes in neat male handwriting are squeezed in between.

It takes me a full minute to realize what I'm looking at.

An overview of linear equations—concise explanations of particular aspects, like what they are and how they work, as well as examples.

A small smile pulls at my lips. Last week, in my letter to Massimo, among relaying random everyday nonsense, I mentioned that I was learning about linear equations in my Algebra class. And that, for the life of me, I couldn't wrap my head around the concept.

I guess he's been reading my letters after all.

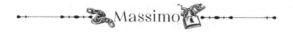Massimo

Maximum security correctional institution, Boston suburb

"Spada. You've got mail."

I lift my head, looking at the correctional officer crossing the yard toward me.

"Take a walk," I tell my fellow con who's sitting behind me on the weight-lifting bench.

The buzzing of the tattoo gun on my left shoulder blade stops, and a moment later, I hear the artist scuttle away. He's a rather skittish guy, but he knows his shit.

Reaching out, I take the envelope from the CO's extended hand. "How's your trouble-making cousin doing, Sam?"

"Good. He's still in rehab, but should be out next week." The guard throws a look over his shoulder. "Thank you," he whispers once his attention returns to me.

"Just make sure he stays away from the Triad's territory when he gets released. The Chinese were very eager to teach him a lesson for dealing on their turf."

"I know. Thanks for putting in a good word for him, Mr. Spada."

I nod. "You made sure no one has messed with my mail?"

"Of course. Everyone knows your stuff is off-limits. Do you need anything else?"

"No. You're free to go, Sam."

I wait for the CO to leave before I rip open the envelope and pull out the folded paper. Another letter from my little stepsister. I'd never admit it to anyone, but receiving her mail has brought unexpected amusement into the doldrums of my present life, even though, most of the time, they contain nothing more than the ramblings of a teenage girl.

Until a few days ago, I never bothered replying. I had more important things to handle than discussing the latest movies I hadn't seen or my stepsister's sewing patterns. And I couldn't care less what the seam allowances were for. I was too busy making and strengthening connections with mob factions through the people incarcerated with me, dodging sneak attacks inside the maximum security pen, and trying not to get killed whenever my back was turned or I closed my eyes for a fucking minute.

Last week, however, half of her damn letter was a tirade about linear equations. The next thing I knew, I was wondering why I'd spent two hours of my time writing out explanations of math problems for my little nuisance. It's been years, but I still remembered that shit. Learning has always come easy to me, regardless of the subject. My high school guidance counselor even tried to convince my father that I should make Harvard Law my postgrad goal. I laughed my ass off when I heard that.

It appears that sewing is once again the main topic of my

stepsister's rhetoric because there is almost an entire page on some shit called *bias binding* and *bound seams*. I shake my head as I try to process that crap.

As I continue reading, the next paragraph catches more of my attention. After citing some of the guests at Nuncio's barbecue party and vividly describing their outfits, Zahara has included quite a few remarks about things she overheard. One in particular spikes my interest—a meeting between Nuncio and a real estate agent. A meeting that Nuncio didn't mention when he came to see me last Thursday.

I tap the edge of the letter with the tip of my finger as I ponder that fact. The secret calls with Salvo provide me the info I need on matters within Cosa Nostra as well as updates on business dealings, but he's not close enough to the don to inform me of the things happening inside Nuncio's house. Peppe's information is more valuable on that front, but as a driver, his access is limited to the staff quarters and the kitchen. He can't tell me what's happening inside the main part of the house or during the parties Nuncio loves to throw so much. That kind of information would be very, *very* valuable, but there has never been a way to obtain it.

I look at the letter again. Maybe now there is. I just need to focus my stepsister's written prattle in a more useful direction.

Whatever scruples and morality I had before I got locked up have been obliterated in this fucking hellhole. Using an innocent girl as an asset to further my designs doesn't bother me in the least. It could work. I'll just need to give her subtle guidance on the type of information she should include in her letters. Anything even remotely connected to my less-than-legal affairs needs to stay out of our correspondence.

I refocus on the letter to read the last paragraph.

It's just a couple of sentences about some guy named Kenneth, a senior in her school. There are no specifics about what he did, and she sounds rather unbothered, her words delivered without even the level of teenage dramatics inspired by linear equations, but I can read her distress between the lines.

After two years of her letters, I've gotten familiar with the quirks of her mind. I might not know what my stepsister looks like, not having seen her since she was a toddler, but I have a really good idea of how she thinks. She may have tried to tell me that whatever happened was "not a big deal," but I'm-sure-as-shit convinced that it was. And regardless of the lack of familial feelings toward her, I won't allow anyone to come after one of mine.

Folding the letter up, I slide it into my pocket, then set off across the yard toward a group of inmates playing cards at a concrete slab.

"Kiril." I lift my chin at the shirtless guy sitting at the head of the table. His torso is covered in tattoos, and he has a brow piercing over his left eye. "Losing again?"

The Bulgarian fixes his gaze on me, then mumbles something in his native language. The rest of his boys drop their cards and leave in a hurry. Taking a seat at the empty spot on his right, I interlock my fingers behind my head.

"Something wrong with the job, Spada?"

"Nope." I shake my head, scanning the yard for potential snitches. "Your problem will be dealt with tomorrow, as we agreed."

"I want it to be painful."

"Your preference has already been noted. Don't worry. Your uncle will be handled with utmost care."

"Good. I owe you one."

I smile. "You owe me much more than 'one.' The way you keep going, I'll have all of your problematic family members taken care of by the time you get out."

A throaty laugh rumbles from his chest. "How the fuck do you do it, Spada? You've been locked up here for what, five years? And you can get shit handled on the outside as if you're there personally."

"Almost eleven," I say. "As for *how*… well… loyalty, of those who know me. Money. A lot of it. And connections. A few favors. But most of all—fear. That's definitely the best motivator."

"Mm-hmm. Remind me not to get on your bad side. Ever." He gives me a good-natured wink.

One of the COs in the guard tower signals the end of recreation time, and the inmates start trudging toward the entrance to Block D—my "Home Sweet Home" for another seven and a half years. Some are keeping to themselves, walking alone with their heads bent low, but most are gathered in larger groups. Keeping to their packs for protection. Trying not to draw the attention of the guards stationed throughout the yard.

This fucking place truly resembles a zoo sometimes.

"I need you to do something for me, Kiril."

"Name it."

"Some pissant has been harassing my stepsister at school." I dip my head in greeting as the leader of one of the smaller gangs in my block passes. "I need you to send one of your nephews to have a chat with the little fucker. Do that, and I'll consider the debt for your uncle paid in full."

"Done. How intensive do you want that chat to be?"

"A few broken bones will suffice."

"Is there a message you want my boys to relay?"

"Yes." I meet Kiril's gaze. "Next time he comes within twenty feet of Zahara Veronese, he'll be eating his food through a straw. For the rest of his life."

Kiril lifts his pierced brow. "I didn't think you cared about anyone enough to trade favors for them. Especially, a *stepsister*?"

"I don't give a fuck about the girl. But I need her focused on something more important than school bullies. Make sure it gets done." I push off the bench. "This punk better find his ass-kicking therapeutic."

Chapter four

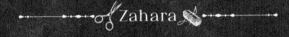
Zahara

One year later
(Zahara, age 15)

A SOFT KNOCK ON MY DOOR PULLS ME OUT OF THE deep, dark pit that is my math homework. "Come in."

"Zara." Iris, our maid, peeks in. "Am I interrupting? I wanted to get your take on the curtains that need to be changed in the parlor."

Her tone is serious, but there is a slight smirk on her face. The one she wears whenever she has a letter for me.

I leap off the bed and dash across the room.

"Sure. Come in." I basically drag her inside and shut the door. "You have it?"

"Yes. I snagged it as soon as I picked up the mail." She pulls the folded envelope from her pocket and hands it to me. "Do you need me to drop off your response today?"

"I'm not sure, yet."

"Okay. I'll be downstairs if you need me."

She turns to leave, but I grab her arm, stopping her. "Thank

Iris is only a couple of years older than me. She's been working full-time for us ever since her mom—our cook—got really sick a few months ago, and Iris ended up dropping out of school. But even before that, it seemed like she was always at our house, often helping the maids with housekeeping or working in the kitchen with her mom. And for the past three years, Iris has been an accomplice in my "pen-pal plan." When I first started writing to Massimo, she was the one who got me the postage stamps. And now, when I can't do it myself, she mails the letters for me. She also diligently checks the incoming mail every day. That way, she's able to pull out and hide Massimo's replies before anyone else has a chance to spot them in the stack.

I'm so thankful for Iris. For being my trusted ally. My friend. Especially since I can't admit to Nera about my letter exchange with our stepbrother. I want to, and so many times I've considered confessing, but I'm too worried she'll go into an "overprotective sister" mode and tell Dad. Nera's concerns for me have been spiking lately, with her bugging me to tell her everything that's happening at school and wanting to know if anyone has been bothering me. I love her, so much, but I see the strain in her. She's carrying enough weight on her shoulders without having to worry about mine, too.

"I told you already, you don't need to thank me." Iris smiles.

I squeeze her arm. "How's your mom? Is she feeling better?"

"No. Not really." Her face falls. "The doctor changed her meds again, and our insurance won't cover the new ones. I may need to find a second job."

I clench my teeth. Life is so unfair sometimes. Iris's dad was a Cosa Nostra soldier, and when he got killed on the job, the Family "compensated" her mother with money. Not that it did them much good. Due to her illness, Iris's mom can't work at all anymore, so Dad hired Iris as our maid. Now, Iris is solely responsible for taking care of her mother and their mountain of bills.

"Wait here," I say and rush to my vanity where I keep my jewelry box. Grabbing one of my cuff bracelets, I bring it to Iris. "It's eighteen-karat gold. Hopefully, you can get enough for it to cover the cost of medicine for a few months."

"Miss Zara…" she chokes out, staring at the bracelet. "No. Your father gave this to you. I could never accept—"

"Please." I take her hand and place the trinket on her palm. "No one could save my mom, but maybe the doctors can save yours. Besides, I hate that blasted thing anyway."

"No. I can't." She tries to give the bracelet back, but I just shake my head.

"You can. And you will. I hope your mom gets better soon."

Iris sniffs and wipes her eye with her sleeve. "Thank you."

"Don't mention it."

As soon as she departs, I tear open the envelope. It's been weeks since Massimo's last letter. Like all the previous ones, it's written on plain white paper, with ordinary blue ink.

For a few moments, my eyes absorb the cursive text, admiring the way Massimo makes every word and letter look so perfect. I've always been amazed by the beautiful, even flow of his writing. There is an elegant uniformity to each stroke. Every capital A has the same little curve. Each T is crossed with an identical horizontal line that always seems to be of a similar length. But my favorite is the uppercase Z. Sharp, boldly written, with a small dash across the middle.

Once I'm done feasting on his penmanship, I start reading the actual words.

Zahara,

I'm glad that school is going well. Education is the only investment that carries no risk. It can never fail, and it can never be taken away from you.

I'm happy to hear you enjoyed lunch at Brio's with your dad.

*You can learn a lot from businessmen like them, so you should defi-
nitely consider joining Nuncio on other such occasions.*

*The new renovation project at the Bay View Casino sounds
very promising. I discussed the details with Nuncio last week, and
it sure seems like there are many variables that need to be handled.
For a project of such magnitude, estimating the final costs is very
difficult. Things can go wrong in two hundred different ways. And
that would be bad. But a skillful project manager can cope with the
unexpected. Sometimes, though, mistakes can get pushed beyond
two hundred and one, and that would just be one wrong thing too
many. I feel very strongly about that.*

*If you'd like to learn more about similar projects, you should
visit your father's friend, Monet. He used to hang out in Nuncio's
study a lot. Maybe you've met him? Bearded guy who's usually wearing a beret? If you haven't, you can find him at Harrison Avenue,
number 4195. I'd love to hear his thoughts on this subject.*

*With regards to your question—No. It's definitely not quiet
here during the night.*

M.

As usual, I need to read the letter several times to decode
it. It took me a while to get used to the way he formulates his
requests—enlacing his letters with subtle hints about what he
needs me to do. A year ago, I would have just gaped at this message, completely baffled by the content. Not anymore. I've had
a lot of practice.

In one of his earliest letters, Massimo asked if I'd seen the
Mission: Impossible movie. He said that in prison, there's very
little privacy, and he wished messages had a way to self-destruct
like in the film. It was an odd thing for him to mention, especially
without further context, but after streaming the Tom Cruise
classic, I finally understood that my stepbrother wanted to write
me something that he did not want others to see.

In letters that followed, he would recommend other movies

to me, never mentioning why he thought I would like them but telling me of his favorite scenes. I'd watch them, of course, trying to figure out what it was he was trying to tell me without actually spelling out the words.

After that, Massimo would point me to more movie scenes, or passages from books, or even real-world events, and I'd scour each to get what he was hinting at, eventually understanding what he needed me to do. Deciphering his code words took a bit longer—sometimes two or three letters and a lot of googling through references before his meaning would sink in. But it did, and now, it's like we formed our own lexicon.

As I turn his latest letter in my hands, excitement flutters in my stomach at each little clue he's written. His creativity never fails to amaze me.

This time, he wants me to stick close to my dad and try to find out more about what he discusses with his capos. That's fairly clear. And he wants to know if the renovations at the Bay View Casino exceeded two hundred grand. But the rest? Hell if I know.

I don't remember a guy in a beret coming over to our house. In fact, I don't think I've ever seen any man—outside of military guys on TV and hipster, artist types—wear one in modern life. I google the location he mentioned, and find that it doesn't exist. Harrison Avenue is a former industrial area that's being redeveloped into a trendy neighborhood with luxury housing, and it has just over a thousand listed addresses. Nothing like the 4195 Massimo indicated.

After reading the perplexing part one more time, I hide the letter under my bed and head downstairs.

Dad is still not home, and Nera is spending the day at Dania's. Most of the staff are occupied with hanging the new curtains in the parlor. Making sure they don't notice me, I turn left into the hallway off the stairs and slip into my father's study.

I'm not certain what Massimo was getting at, but he must have mentioned this room on purpose.

The study is empty, as expected. No bearded guys lurking inside, waiting for me to discuss the business of renovating commercial properties. As I turn to leave, my eyes land on the painting on the wall behind Dad's desk. It's a rendition of a guy whose dark beard hides the lower part of his face. He's wearing a gray coat. And a black beret. Hesitantly approaching the painting, I take in its impressive array of light and color, as well as the ornamental frame that surrounds it. In the center of the bottom edge, there's a little plaque.

Self-Portrait With A Beret
Claude Monet

"Hello, Mr. Monet," I snort, then start feeling around the frame. On the right-hand side, I find a tiny button. I push it, and the painting swings open like a beautiful door to a hidden room, revealing the safe concealed behind it.

After throwing a quick glance over my shoulder to make sure the study door is still closed, I punch in the four-digit code Massimo cleverly relayed in his letter into the keypad. With a muted click, the safe pops open.

After seeing hidden safes revealed in movies, I expect to find money, jewelry, and other loot inside. But it's nothing of the sort. Just a bunch of file folders, stacked and filling the interior nearly to capacity.

No wonder I've never found anything overly useful within the desk drawers. Looks like Dad keeps all his paperwork in here. Massimo either found out the code to the safe somehow, or Dad never bothered to change it.

My hands shake as I leaf through the folders, trying to find anything related to the renovations at the casino. For some reason, this feels different from going through Dad's desk, and I'm kind of bothered by the taste it's leaving in my mouth. The thing is, though, I know that I'm doing this for a good cause.

The Family has been enjoying prosperity and a steady flow of business success over the past decade.

And it's *not* thanks to my father.

It took me a while to understand the true nature of things, and where everything and every*body* actually stands. At first, I thought Massimo simply wanted to stay on top of what's going on around here. But gradually, I realized it was much more than just curiosity. Dad might be the official don of the Boston Cosa Nostra Family, but he's not the one calling the shots, not about the business or regarding Family matters.

It's Massimo.

I may not have actual proof of that, but after analyzing Father's behavior, it's as clear as day.

More than once I've caught Dad changing his stance on a particular topic after he's returned from visiting Massimo. I've also noticed that he hedges rather than give a direct answer whenever he's asked his opinion on important business issues.

Vague responses. Deflections. Clever excuses. *Such an amazing proposition, Brio. Let me think a few days about it.* Or, *That's very concerning, gentlemen. I'll look into it.* Avoidance, until he gets the chance to visit Massimo and receive guidance from his stepson. Sometimes I wonder if Dad ever actually makes any of the decisions that are supposed to rest with the don.

I finally find the folder I'm looking for and scan the stack of papers inside.

Sketches. Receipts for renovation materials. Invoices from the firm that completed the work, which happens to be a Family-run company that's often used to launder money. Clever. Not only can we list the disbursements as business expenses on the casino side, since we're paying out with clean money, but that cash gets pumped into the reno company to cover the inflated costs, and the firm ends up laundering its own funds.

I'm not sure what's driving Massimo's insistence on keeping the overall reno expenditure under two hundred grand, but he must have his reasons.

The final figures on the last page seem fine—just shy of the budget by less than a grand. Good. I slip the folder back into the safe and shut the door, then move my friend, Mr. Monet, back into his original place. This isn't the best time to carefully review the other folders kept within the safe, but I'll do that on one of the nights when neither Dad nor the household staff are around.

These little covert missions I'm doing for my stepbrother are slowly turning into quite an adventure. Apart from his first response where he explained the ins and outs of linear equations to me, all of his subsequent letters contained questions or asked for further information. And with that, for more than a year, he's been using me to spy for him.

And I don't mind it one bit.

Unlike my sister, I like the Cosa Nostra world. The intrigue. The sting of danger. Secret deals brokered under the shimmering lights of lavish parties. Parties that I would love to enjoy, but usually end up avoiding because I simply don't fit in. This world is an entity of its own—it's a complex, intricate macrocosm where only a select few are granted entry. As the don's daughter, technically, I'm already a part of it. But in reality, I'm actually not.

A year ago, I was at a pretty dark point in my life, feeling utterly useless. And weak. Powerless. But now, I'm beyond ecstatic and filled with satisfaction because of everything I've done for Massimo, all without anyone else finding out. I don't feel useless anymore. And I certainly don't feel powerless. So no, I don't give a shit that he's using me apparently without remorse, because I don't feel used. And I'm greatly enjoying the glimpses I'm getting of my mysterious stepbrother and his immoral methods. I can't help but admire him for his devious, manipulative ways. The determination and pure single-mindedness required to achieve what he has, especially considering his circumstances, is mind-blowing.

Ruling the Italian Crime Family from inside prison walls. Unbelievable.

I tiptoe out of Dad's study and dash up the stairs, hurrying to compose my "report." Maybe, I'll also ask Massimo something else about himself. Something that would require more than a single-sentence answer. Maybe, just maybe, he'll be willing to share what he wants to do when he's finally free to walk out the prison doors.

Massimo

Zahara,

Glad to hear you were able to connect with Nuncio's old buddy. He knows a lot of good stuff, so good on you for following through, kid.

I'm happy to know that his old habits haven't changed, and he's still hanging around his familiar stomping grounds. But keep in mind that his neighborhood isn't always safe, so if you visit him again, make sure your timing is well coordinated. I would worry if you went to see him and he wasn't there.

As for your question—I've never actually given it serious thought. I guess, I'd try to find a spot where all I could see is trees and the sky. No walls. Not another soul around. Just silence. I'd lose myself to staring at that openness for hours. And enjoy the peace.

You know, people tend to overlook the small everyday things, not realizing their value until they are ripped away. And I don't mean just the material stuff. Something as simple as being able to sleep without hearing someone near you taking a piss, for example.

Later, I'd find a goddamned whorehouse and fuck my way through every woman in the joint.

PS: What the hell is fusible interfacing?
M.

I sign the letter and throw the folded paper into the rusty metal cabinet next to the bed, the final sentences still burning in my mind.

Yeah, I've got a detailed plan for every step I'll take with regard to the Family business, but I never actually considered what I'm going to do for myself once I finally leave this shithole. I didn't even think about it until now, answering my stepsister's question.

Yup, getting laid sounds pretty good.

Do I miss sex? Of course I do. But the lack of it doesn't bother me as much as it probably should. In the morning, I jerk off, and it's nothing more than handling my body's biological needs before I get on with my day. I don't think about women at all. All my mental energy is directed to my main objective— making sure Boston *La Famiglia* is headed in the direction I want it to go. Nothing else matters. I don't think about anything else. I don't care about anything else. It's as if my existence—can't really call *this* life—depends on fulfilling that purpose. A shrink, if I gave a fuck about some overeducated ass's opinion, would probably tell me that sort of single-minded focus isn't normal, or healthy, for that matter. Good thing I didn't ask. *My way* is the only thing that allows me to survive.

My life, as it was, stopped the moment Judge fucking Collins delivered his sentence.

Jesus fuck, you're so dramatic, the annoying voice in the back of my mind mocks.

I squeeze the bridge of my nose, willing the infuriating asshole to go away.

About a decade ago, I was treated to my first all-inclusive, extended trip to solitary. After a week in the hole, I must have snapped. Bored out of my damn mind, I started talking to myself. The echo off the peeling paint of the walls made it seem like another person was there with me. That's when this fucker showed up to join the lively debate I was having.

No, I didn't suddenly develop a split personality. I just imagined what my alter ego would say if it had a voice and ran with it, filling both sides of the conversation to pass the time. I liked the asshole. He was still me—obviously—but with less fucks to give about most things. It was freeing, in a way. So, I went back and forth in my mind on how I could have avoided the fight that got me thrown into that stinking hole in the first place. Once I got back to my cell, I figured the asshole would be gone to whatever dark corner of my gray matter it crawled out of.

It didn't.

Exactly. You're stuck with me. For good.

Jesus. Get lost!

The shrill ringing of the bell breaks the relative silence, signaling the lunch hour. I wait for the cell door to slide to the side, then step out while my bunkie, a lanky kid in his early twenties, keeps lazing on the upper cot. He got locked up for killing four people in the middle of his college quad, and despite us being cellmates for over three months, he still hasn't mustered the courage to speak with me. Instead, he simply tries his best to stay out of my way. The day he arrived, a fight broke out in the chow hall, and he witnessed me trying to dig an inmate's eye out using an empty yogurt container. This seems to have freaked him out.

Or maybe it's my frequent vocal not-so-friendly chats with the pain in the ass living rent-free inside my head that got it done.

As if.

Fuck off!

It's not like that fight was anything unusual. Shit like that happens at least once a week, either in the yard or the chow hall. Most times, the guards don't even get involved. With so many crazy motherfuckers in one place, it's safer and simpler to just let the cons sort out our issues than for COs to step in to break it up. This place follows a slightly different set of laws than good old Uncle Sam decrees. So, unless the brawl escalates to epic proportions, guards largely ignore what's going on. But when the proverbial shit does hit the fan, they just douse the culprits with pepper spray. We call it "dinner and a show." I quite enjoy the entertainment.

In the dining hall, the main line for chow has already formed. Typically, the room buzzes with a multitude of simultaneous conversations or guys yelling over each other, but not today. Most of the men are shuffling toward their food in silence, or are already seated and eating without uttering a word. The atmosphere feels charged.

"I've been looking for you," Kiril mumbles as he falls in step with me, already holding his lunch tray. "We've got new arrivals."

"I should have guessed. Who?"

"The president of Chelsea Biker Gang and his second-in-command. Armed robbery, and they ghosted a couple of cops." He nods toward the two burly guys standing in the corner, glaring at me from across the hall. "Want me to get you a weapon?"

"No need." I bump his fist with mine in thanks and head toward the food line, keeping my eye on the newcomers.

Survival behind bars is no different from surviving in a jungle. The local animals are segregated into packs. There are small ones and some bigger factions, each ruled by its own leader, all constantly fighting to maintain their place in the food chain. Everyone's place in the hierarchy usually gets defined shortly after their arrival, and it depends on their connections, capabilities, and simply how mean the son of a bitch is. From time to time, a new fish or a dumbass who believes he's some big shit, decides to challenge the apex predator and claim the seat of power for himself. Little do they know, in this shithole, I'm not only the alpha, I'm the jungle fucking king.

As I carry my chow toward the table by the narrow window,

the two biker boys head in my direction. The taller one, sporting a bald head but a full beard, pulls a small switchblade from up his sleeve.

"You Spada?" the shorter guy asks when they reach me, smothering me with his bad breath and revealing a few missing teeth. His buddy stands next to him, gripping his weapon.

I set my tray on the table and smile. "You wouldn't be asking if you didn't already know."

He narrows his eyes and gives a barely noticeable nod. The bearded guy swings, aiming for my kidney.

I grab "Harry's" forearm and slam his hand on the table, making the asswipe howl in pain when his wrist connects with the metal edge. With my free hand, I swipe the tray and strike it against "Shorty's" face, sending beans and pasta flying all around. A punch to the MC president's solar plexus dispatches the foul-mouthed fuck to trail after my lunch until he lands on his back a few feet away, allowing me to focus on his bearded companion, who's still clutching the blade.

I swing at him, aiming for his head, but the scumbag moves and slashes at me, catching my forearm with his knife. Cursing, I grab his wrist with one hand and his beard with the other, then whack his head on my raised knee. Blood explodes from his nose and drips onto the concrete floor right next to where he dropped his steel.

Someone grabs me from behind to pull me away, but I snap my head back, my skull cracking against the motherfucker's, and kick the biker's shin. Shouts come from every direction as the all-out fight consumes the chow hall. It really doesn't take much to entice this crowd to join the fray, and food, trays, and plastic cutlery soar overhead.

"Harry" charges me, once again gripping his blade. I kick his hand away and grab the front of his shirt, then send him flying across the room, where he drops head-first on one of the tables and remains down, unmoving. When I turn around, looking for his buddy, I find Kiril squeezing the dickwad's neck in his massive fist. "Shorty's" feet are dangling off the ground, while the Bulgarian slaps the biker gang leader's face with his free hand.

"I've been a bad boy," Kiril says, his manner as easygoing as always, then smacks the man's face one more time. "And I won't do it again. *Say it.*"

Pain explodes in my shoulder. I turn around and headbutt my new attacker. The fucktard tried to bury a plastic shiv in me. I'm just swinging at the idiot's face when the alarms blast from overhead speakers, accompanied by the spray of white mist. I shut my stinging eyes, blindly sending my fist flying, and feel it connect with the soft tissue just before I succumb to a coughing fit.

Damn COs and their pepper spray.

CHAPTER
five

──────•◦ Zahara ◦•──────

One year later
(Zahara, age 16)

SOFT NOTES OF A CLASSICAL MELODY CARRY ACROSS
the garden, blending with the chatter and laughter of
dozens of guests mingling around the tables. The cherry
tree that overhangs the small platform where the string quartet
is playing is in full bloom, but there isn't even a hint of its sweet
scent in the air. Instead, perfume and cigar smoke suffuse the
area, drowning everything else out and making my nostrils
itch and burn. Like he always does, Dad insisted that I attend
his annual spring cocktail party. As if there won't be another
occasion next month.

And the next.

It's a necessary evil, I guess. A great number of business
deals are conducted at these parties. Relaxing atmosphere, fancy
food, expensive wine… All of that makes people more suscep-
tible, much easier to sway toward a deal they might not be so
inclined to accept in a more rigid business setting.

Tugging the sleeve of my dress down, I pull it over my

wrist and continue watching elegantly dressed women chat and flirt with confident, influential men. Red dresses. Gold. Raspberry-pink. Short. Long, with thigh-high slits. All were chosen to attract attention.

I'm so fucking envious.

So many times, I've dreamed of wearing a gown like I see here. There's a stack of sketches of beautiful dresses with open backs and low necklines hidden under my bed. I occasionally pull them out and imagine the fabrics that would best suit each design. Bittersweet fantasies, because I'd never make these dresses for myself. I don't have the guts to wear them.

People staring at me and whispering words they don't think I can hear always gets to me. It's suffocating. I can't handle it, so I try to stay far away from any kind of attention. Remain invisible to everyone around. Even to the waiter with a tray of drinks who passes by without offering me a beverage. Luckily, that invisibility has a few benefits.

With my eyes downcast, I step away from my hidey-hole near the wall and get lost amid the crowd in the garden.

"Is it true that Donatello is getting remarried?" a woman asks her date as I walk by.

It's true. It's also old news. I drift away from the couple and meander toward the right edge of the lawn where I spied Brio—one of my father's capos—and his wife. Brio runs Cosa Nostra's casinos, and from what I gathered by eavesdropping on the meeting he had with my father last week, there've been some problems in that business. Lingering at the hors d'oeuvres table just behind them, I pretend to be captivated by the selection and load up a small plate while listening in to their whispered conversation.

"The don won't budge," Brio says in a low voice. "We can make a shitload of money, but Nuncio didn't want to even hear about it. Who the fuck cares if the players want to take a few sniffs here and there? It will just make them more amenable to spend their cash."

I raise an eyebrow. Brio seems like he's still hell-bent on getting cocaine into our casinos. Interesting. I wait to see if he'll say more, but another man approaches, and the conversation shifts to the latest football game. Shame. Abandoning my plate and grabbing a glass of mineral water, I head to the other side of the garden.

In addition to the high-ranking Family members, there are also a fair number of people who are not Cosa Nostra present here. A few government officials, most of whom are on the Mafia's payroll. A handful of B-list celebrities. Lawyers, lots of those. As well as CEOs and major shareholders of several big-ass corporations. All of them, in some way, are connected to Cosa Nostra, be it through business dealings or bribes.

I spot a man in a black tuxedo munching on a shrimp cocktail and recognize him as a cardiac surgeon who racked up a huge debt at the blackjack tables last year. The Council—comprised of my father's capos and key investors, and led by the don—decided to forgive what he owed in exchange for his services. Now, he's at Cosa Nostra's beck and call. Indefinitely.

When my father implemented this policy of "recruiting" prominent individuals by wiping out their gambling debts, there was an outcry of epic proportions within the Family. *Forgiving thousands of dollars of debt? Sacrilegious!* But when Brio's cousin was shot in the shoulder during a stupid drunken quarrel, guess who saved the day? The cardiac surgeon. He patched the idiot up and pumped him full of meds through an IV in the back room of the bar. No paperwork. No questions asked. No problems.

The naysayers shut their mouths quite quickly once they realized how convenient it was to have a plethora of useful people in their back pockets. The return on investment of that policy has been good, with the benefits far outweighing the lost revenue from the unpaid debts. The don was then thought of as a vanguard of some kind. No one suspected that the mastermind behind it, and every other profitable business decision in over a decade, is locked up in a maximum security prison and has been there the entire time.

I continue to meander among the guests, catching snippets of their hushed conversations, committing everything that may be relevant to memory. In his last letter, Massimo asked me to keep an eye on my father's second-in-command—Batista Leone. The underboss hasn't arrived yet, which is strange. Usually, the ass-kissing bastard is glued to Dad's hip at these kinds of events.

As I gaze around the garden, my eyes catch on a man in a gunmetal-gray suit standing off to the side, talking with a lady wearing a gold cocktail dress. He's in his early thirties, with dark-brown hair that curls a little at his nape. Salvo Canali. His family is one of the oldest and most respected in Boston Cosa Nostra, so it wasn't a surprise when he was promoted to capo a few years back. On Massimo's order, I'm sure. From what I've gathered, Salvo and Massimo have been best friends since their school days.

It's actually rather hard to find any info about my stepbrother. People rarely mention him, almost like he's been forgotten completely. As if he never even existed. But if they only knew...

Another woman approaches the pair and kisses Salvo's cheek. He's always been popular with the ladies and has a different woman on his arm at every party. That makes me wonder why he's still unmarried. The Cosa Nostra men usually marry young, and Salvo is already thirty-three. Same age as Massimo.

How old will Massimo be when he's released from prison? Around forty, if I've calculated correctly. He'll probably marry as soon as he takes over the Family. My stomach drops and pressure squeezes my chest the instant that realization hits me.

"Zara, my dear." My father's voice rings out behind me, making me jump.

I swallow and turn around. "Um... hi, Dad."

"I'm glad you saw reason and decided to come down." He pats my back, as if he's praising an obedient dog. "Lovely evening, isn't it?"

"Yup."

"Happy that you're enjoying yourself, baby. It's imperative to be seen. To get to know people who are important to *La Famiglia*. Soon, your sister will be married to one of these nice men. And then, it will be your turn."

I can't suppress a shudder. He's already planning on marrying us off. Sadly, it's not uncommon. Most marriages within Cosa Nostra are arranged to strengthen alliances or to ensure a favorable business merger. But I'm barely sixteen, and Nera only just turned eighteen, for God's sake.

"Don't worry." Dad pats my shoulder again, obviously confusing my disgust with anxiety. "I'll make sure we find a sweet, gentle partner for you when the time comes. Maybe Ruggero. The two of you would be a good match."

My gaze follows Dad's to a group of men gathered by the stage where the musicians are playing. Ruggero, the youngest son of Capo Primo, is hunched over, wiping his nose with one of those handkerchiefs that no one has used in the past century. His maroon suit hangs on his short, willowy frame. With his thick-framed brown glasses and unruly hair that he's tried to wrangle with too much gel, Ruggero looks like an escapee from a retirement home crashing someone's Christmas party. And to think, the dude isn't even twenty.

"I disagree," I mumble.

"Why? He'll likely take over Primo's position at some point. Ruggero has been working very hard to learn all the ins and outs of properly laundering money from his dad. And he has a very mild temperament. You'll have nothing to fret about being with him, Zara."

I've never felt the need for violence, but now, as I take in the gently condescending look on my father's face, the urge to punch him overwhelms me. How is it possible that he still doesn't understand me? His own daughter. Just because I prefer to remain on the sidelines doesn't mean I'm a weakling or that I'm terrified of people. He would never comprehend the strength and determination it takes to make myself go to school every morning, to endure the nonstop taunting and tasteless jokes, and to ignore the spiteful bullies.

At least that scumbag Kenneth Harris has graduated, so now I don't have to see his ugly mug every day. I'm thankful he stayed away from me after the incident when he ripped off my sleeve. Maybe the car accident he was in a couple of days later shook a bit of human decency into him. He spent nearly a month in the hospital and when he returned to school, he was sporting a cast on both arms.

"I think you should get back to your guests," I prod.

"You're right." Dad smiles. "Try to enjoy yourself. But no alcohol. We can't have the don's daughter seen behaving improperly." He turns to leave, then halts and reaches into his jacket pocket. "I almost forgot. I saw this today and thought you'd like it. I got a matching one for your sister, too."

A pesky tingling sensation settles in my nose as I stare at the delicate gold chain bracelet in my father's palm. A small vintage-style charm with a ruby at its center hangs off one of the links.

"It's from the latest collection. I thought you'd like the retro design."

"It's lovely," I choke out.

"Glad to hear it." Smiling, he hands me the bracelet and kisses my temple. "Now, go mingle and show them how a well-bred lady behaves."

The crowd closes in around my father as he walks off across the lawn. People flock to him, hoping for a few words with the don, or just to be seen at his side. His ever-present charisma and the power of his position draw them in like a beacon. He always has a joke or two up his sleeve. A perfect compliment for a lady, an approving nod for a man, a radiant smile for anyone seeking his attention.

There are no awkward silences with Nuncio Veronese because he always has just the right words to keep the conversation flowing. He remembers the birthday and anniversary dates for every Cosa Nostra member and has never once forgotten to send a tasteful card or bouquet to show that he cares. How can anyone ever doubt his thoughtful nature? He really is the perfect man for the role he's been playing for over ten years, a role he obviously enjoys wholeheartedly.

My hand closes around the bracelet with such force the charm will likely leave an indent on my skin. Too bad that by maintaining the perfect persona of a benevolent leader, somewhere along the way, the great Nuncio Veronese forgot his other role. Being a loving father to his daughters, not simply acting like one for the sake of his image. Maybe then he would remember that I can't wear most of the jewelry I've always coveted. And certainly none that he buys for me.

Once upon a time, I asked my sister if our dad loves us, and her reply still rings in my ears today. *Of course he loves us,* she said. *But I think he loves the Family more.* Nera has always been more adaptable than me, and she seems to have accepted this situation for what it is. Well, I can't. There are no incremental levels in love. No middle ground. You either love someone and are willing to do anything for them. Or you don't love them.

Therefore, I don't feel even an ounce of regret or shame as I follow after my father, snagging bits of the guests' exchanges along the way. Catching a whisper here, a proclamation made in a low voice there. Collecting the info I'll relay in my letter to Massimo tomorrow morning.

In the past, I dreaded attending these kinds of events and did everything I could to avoid them. Not anymore. I'd never admit it to anyone, but these days, I actually enjoy my father's shindigs. To most people here, I'm invisible, and they have no idea the impact I have on their lives. Granted, it's indirect and hardly life-altering. But still, it makes me feel as if I'm finally a part of this world. *My world.* Long have I wanted to be accepted into it, but I never had the guts to try to make it happen.

Until Massimo showed me the way.

I keep that feeling of fulfillment and purpose close to my heart, letting it wash over me as I weave between the guests, committing to memory every single detail he might find useful.

Batista Leone has arrived, and he's standing next to Dad by the string quartet, speaking in hushed tones in the shadow of a cherry blossom tree. Based on the hardened set of my father's jaw and his furrowed forehead, whatever they are discussing must be serious. I circle to the far side of the stage and stop just behind the cello player. The musical accompaniment is sophisticated and elegant but is a tad too loud, and I have to concentrate to hear what my father and the underboss are saying.

"Brio has a valid point," Leone says as he takes a long sip of his whiskey, making an awful sound as if he's slurping soup. I cringe, disgusted with the man's lack of decorum. "Offering coke at the casinos would bring in dozens of new, well-paying customers each month. Why not integrate these two very profitable businesses under the same umbrella?"

"Because members of the Family are listed as part of the ownership group, Batista. If the DEA got wind of this, we'd all go down."

"We could offer the product only to select clients, those who have proven to be reliable. Do it under the table, so to speak." Leone shifts toward my father, and I'm forced to lean closer so I don't miss the rest of his comment. "Just a few transactions here and there."

"And what if someone talks? Word spreads quickly, you know that."

"We can offer cut-rate prices, conditional on them keeping their mouths shut. With that, there's basically, no risk. Think about it, Nuncio."

My father looks down at his drink, contemplating the idea, and after a few tense seconds, he nods so slightly it's barely noticeable.

I shake my head. He can't actually be considering it, right?

Two other men join my father and Leone, and each lights up a foul-smelling cigar amid raucous laughter. I take a step back. Keeping to the edge of the lawn, I head toward the house, away from the smoke and the scheming Cosa Nostra cronies.

Once in my room, I take a quick shower, then pull the box of Massimo's letters from under my bed. My treasure. There are nearly fifty simple white envelopes inside, so I had to change the hiding place from my closet to an old, rustic wooden chest—shoved as far back underneath the bed frame as I could manage—to keep them safe. All are carefully sorted in the order I received them.

In my latest letter to Massimo, I asked him for dating advice. Not that I'm going out with anyone, or even planning to. I just wanted to see what he'd say. So I lied, mentioning that a boy at school had been hitting on me. Massimo probably found my question stupid. A teenage girl asking a man over thirty, one who spent close to half his life in prison , for dating tips. I'm not sure what possessed me to ask him something so foolish. Or maybe I am, but admitting the truth would only make me feel even more like a fool.

Because the truth is… I wanted to make him jealous.

When Massimo finally started replying to my letters, his words spiked my curiosity. He's this strange, intriguing entity, so close but at the same time so removed, and I wanted to know more about him. And as I got more glimpses of him, of his magnificently cunning mind, curiosity transformed into admiration.

At some point, though, that admiration blossomed into something else.

The way my heart skips a beat every time I receive one of his letters is not just excitement for a new task. When I sneak around, gathering information, it's not because I'm concerned about the overall success of the Family. Not anymore. I'm doing it for *him*. Because this new emotion I'm feeling is something deeper. Forbidden. And I try not to dwell on it.

I unfold Massimo's latest letter and read the last paragraph again. It contains his response to my question about dating.

Guys are pigs, Zahara. Make sure you know his intentions before you start anything serious. Be careful, kiddo.
M.

I stare at the last word.
Kiddo.
He doesn't care if I'm dating someone. And why would he?
It leaves a bitter taste in my mouth, the same dry burn I almost choked on when I read it the first time.
Crumpling the paper into a ball, I carry it into the bathroom and flush it down the toilet.

Massimo

"The return on our Cambridge investments shows a decline." I lower the printout of the quarterly cash flow report. "Why?"

My stepfather shrugs in a seemingly casual manner, but he keeps playing with his pen. I know he hates coming to the prison to see me for our weekly "meetings," although he's never admitted it. "Rental rates have become too competitive, even with long-term leases. We had to decrease ours by ten percent."

"I don't remember approving that, Nuncio."

"I didn't want to bother you with something so insignificant. It's just a few dozen condos."

I lean forward. "You report every single thing to me, no matter how minuscule, *before* making any kind of decision."

Nuncio winces, but keeps his composure. "The vacancy rate throughout the Greater Boston region is high, and I didn't want to risk losing existing tenants, Massimo. The market has been on a downward spiral since last year."

"Then find a way to make our properties more lucrative! Hire some bimbo and run ads of her doing Pilates in one of our condos or some other shit. I want the rent rates up to last year's level, and I don't give a shit if you need to put up a billboard in the middle of Back Bay to get it done."

Nuncio blinks, then quickly jots a note on his notepad. "Sure."

"What about our catering operations?" I ask.

I've invested a lot of money and leveraged considerable connections to get the "eyes- and ears-off" treatment in this fucking place. The guards are paid to kill the camera in the room when I have a visitor, but I still don't take chances. I always use code when discussing illegal operations with my stepfather. Our illicit drug business is referred to as "catering," and each product has its own stealthy label. I even had Nuncio set up a legitimate catering company to act as a front business, eliminating any possible suspicions.

"Steady profit margins there," he says. "The demand for chicken has increased slightly in the last couple of weeks. We may need to find another farm because the current supplier is at maximum capacity."

"Good. It may be prudent to research suppliers in the South. I'll have a word with a friend, and he'll arrange for someone to contact you."

Nuncio stares at me, clearly confused. *For fuck's sake!* How is it that his adolescent daughter got a handle on my coded language from the start, despite my very limited directions through my letters, and this fool can't find his way with a compass and a map?

"South, Nuncio," I clarify. "The small-scale organic chicken farm we considered a few years ago."

It takes Nuncio's brain another second to catch on that I'm referring to a Peruvian drug cartel. We mostly get our cocaine, a.k.a. "chicken," from Colombia.

"Oh. Yes, that sounds good."

"While we're on the chicken... I got word that you're considering adding drumsticks to the casinos' snack menu."

Nuncio's face pales instantly. He leans back and stares at me with wide eyes. Well, well... My little spy was right. He *was* contemplating allowing drugs in my casinos. Even with the rage coursing through my veins, my lips curve into a smile. That girl is a menace.

"I see." I nod. Then, I slam my handcuffed hands on the metal table. "Don't you dare even think about fucking with my business ever again!"

Nuncio flinches in his chair, his body going stiff with tension. Years of having the Family kiss his ring and dance to his tune seem to be getting to him. Every now and then, my stepfather forgets who is actually in charge around here, so he comes up with stupid ideas. And then, he needs to be reminded of the reality.

With my hands clasped and resting on the tabletop, I pin him with my stare. "Don't make me do things I would rather not do, Nuncio."

Beads of sweat cling to his hairline while I continue glaring at him.

Having my stepfather prance about as the head of the Boston Family while I'm locked up is convenient. Once I'm out, he will officially transfer the reins to me. This arrangement is much more advantageous to him than fighting me for what he knows is rightfully mine, and it alleviates the need for me to tussle with other small-minded fools later. But I have no problem removing him from the picture now if he doesn't follow my orders. And Nuncio knows it.

Dropping his gaze to the notepad before him, my stepfather slowly nods.

"Glad we sorted that out. How are the girls?"

"They're fine. I've been looking into potential marriage matches for Nera. Do you want me to choose, or maybe you already have someone in mind?"

"And what does Nera think of the idea?"

"She threatened to go dancing through City Hall Plaza naked if I make an arrangement for her hand."

A small smirk pulls at my lips. I remember her being bullheaded when she was little. "Cease all marriage efforts for now."

Nuncio meets my eyes. "I didn't expect you to care for Nera's wishes."

"Of course I do. We are a family, after all."

In truth—I don't give a fuck. But she is Elmo's sister, and it's only because of that I'm willing to consider her feelings on the matter. At least until marrying her off suits *my* needs. Then, I'll send her marching straight down that aisle, singing and smiling, as she'll be told to do.

"See you next Thursday." I motion with my head toward the door on the opposite wall, signaling to Nuncio that our meeting is over.

I wait until he leaves, then meet the gaze of the CO uncuffing my wrists from the restraint ring welded to the table. He's one of eight guards on my payroll. "I need to make a private phone call."

"Of course." He unlocks the cuffs and lays his phone in front of me. "Knock when you're done."

A moment later he exits the room, shutting the metal door

after him with a resounding clang. That sound still grates on my nerves, even after all these years.

Lifting the phone, I dial Salvo's number. We've been friends since we were kids, long before my mother married Nuncio, a lifetime prior to everything going to shit. He's probably the only man I trust implicitly these days. Things would be a hell of a lot simpler if I could get Salvo to visit me here from time to time. I'd be able to get the latest on Cosa Nostra's dealings without having to wade through Nuncio's moronic crap. But that would broadcast to every Tom, Dick, and Harry that Salvo is still my supporter.

I don't need the Family or anyone else getting suspicious, trying to figure out what I'm up to, so I can't risk bringing Salvo here. He needs to keep his distance from me to maintain the trust of the other capos. None of them is a fan of mine. At times, though, I can't count on anyone but my oldest friend to handle an urgent matter for me. That's when I use a burner phone carried by the COs loyal to me to call Salvo. And this particular issue needs to be handled promptly.

The instant the line connects, I get straight to the point. "Brio and Leone have been hounding Nuncio to include chicken on the snack menu at the casinos. Were you aware?"

"No." The silence stretches for a few heartbeats. "How did you find that out?"

"Doesn't matter. Keep an eye on them. Especially Leone. Did your guy dig up any dirt on him?"

"Not really, aside from the fact that he's banging Adriano's wife."

"Okay. Keep your man sniffing. Especially around Leone, but also the others," I say. "You need to pay a visit to the Yakuza. Remind them about the deal I closed with Tanaka last year while he was locked up in here with me."

"Will do. You're including them in your future plans, then?"

"Maybe," I say, reluctant to share more over the phone. "I'll call you if I need anything else." I pause for a breath but feel the need to add, "I owe you, and once I'm out, you'll be rewarded for sticking by me all this time."

"That's not why I'm helping you, Massimo. You know that." Salvo sighs. "Any news from your lawyer?"

I lean back in the chair and focus on the cracked ceiling. Five more years.

At the start of my prison term, I was optimistic. I had faith that McBride would be successful in appealing my sentence. No dice. Then, my hopes shifted to an early parole after I served the mandatory minimum of three years. But that got denied. And so did my next application. And the next. With every rejection, it became more and more clear that someone was doing their damnest to keep me locked up. Someone with deep pockets and the right connections to make it happen.

Nuncio has been my primary suspect since he stands to gain the most by keeping me in the pen. But I'm fairly certain he doesn't have the balls. It must be someone else. Lately, I've been inclined to believe it's Batista Leone. The snake has many friends inside the courts and the Department of Correction, and he's cultivated that network since before he became my father's underboss. I do not doubt that he knows somebody with the power to deny me parole.

"Nope," I bite out. "Nothing new on that front."

"I'll reach out to my contacts again."

"Alright." I nod, knowing nothing will come of it. He's tried several times already.

"Are you going to tell me who your other source is?"

For a split second, I contemplate keeping my little spy's identity to myself, but then change my mind. I might need them to exchange info at some point. "My stepsister. Zahara."

"You're kidding me!" he chokes out. "How on earth... Isn't she still in high school?"

"That makes her a very clever, resourceful student. She's been getting me whatever I need for a couple of years now."

A pregnant pause stretches across the line. Salvo is very rarely at a loss for words. My admission must have shocked him. I'm not sure why that would be the case. He knows me well enough, he shouldn't be surprised. I don't cling to principles of morality unless they align with my purposes, and I've never been above using anyone—regardless of who they are—to further my business interests.

"Keep watching Leone," I say and cut the call.

Shortly after I return to my cell, Sam drops by with my mail. The rest of the prison population will be getting theirs after lunch, but I enjoy preferential treatment. As I tear open the envelope, I wonder if this letter will include another editorial on sewing. I don't mind those. They serve as nice fillers, camouflaging the important information Zahara slips to me. And I find it funny when she asks what color fabric she should choose for her next project. As if I can tell the difference between *chestnut* and *copper*. It's all fucking brown to me. Nevertheless, I often end up answering the bizarre questions posed by my teenage stepsister. It's beyond idiotic. Still, it's rejuvenating, somehow, to juggle such mundane things every now and then.

In my initial letters to her, which I sent infrequently until I could be sure they wouldn't draw unwanted attention, I steered Zahara to tell me more about what was happening at home. The kind of shit that gave me a better idea of what Nuncio was up to, and what he may not be sharing with me. *Who attended the annual Family meeting that Stepfather likes to host? Anyone new I might not have met? What did everyone talk about, or did it turn into a TED Talk?* Small things that made it seem like I was missing being there. Then, I ramped it up a bit, focusing on broad areas of business. *Is there anyone who doesn't agree with Nuncio's decisions? Do any of the C-level execs visit him more often than the rest?* I figured whatever I could glean had the potential to be useful.

But as time passed, and more letters were exchanged, I realized that my stepsister could become an even greater asset than I previously considered. An asset I'd be an idiot not to exploit to the fullest extent.

So, I did.

About a year ago, I asked if she could find a particular document for me in her father's office without him or anyone else knowing. My goal was to confirm that Nuncio followed my instructions and signed the contract as I ordered him to, but I was also eager to learn if she could pull it off. Lo and behold, not only did she locate what I was after and assure me that the contract had been executed, but she went a step further and relayed other specifics covered in the terms of the agreement—things like quantities and purchase rates.

A week later, she'd figured out my coded message on how to access Nuncio's safe. Ever since then, unaware of my designs for her or the Family, my unsuspecting mole has been providing me with invaluable insights. Because of her, I know the exact details her father "forgets" to mention when he visits me on Thursdays to deliver his reports about our business. Or rather—my business.

My most recent instructions to Zahara included directions for logging onto her father's computer and getting the online statements for our legitimate bank accounts. I want to keep an eye on the finances as much as I can. Unfortunately, I can't do anything about our hidden accounts, the ones that are attached to our illegal dealings. Despite taking every precaution I could to ensure no one fucks with my mail, I still won't risk mentioning anything incriminating on paper. For now, I'll have to take Nuncio's word on the status of those funds.

I open her letter and scan the first paragraph with a furrowed brow. The numbers appear to be completely off—two-digit values when the balances should be in millions. And then, it hits me. She omitted the zeros, just as I often do when I write to her. Clever girl.

The next few sentences are about her friend's engagement party she attended a week prior. I doubt there's anything useful to me in these. Yet, I still read them, every word.

The letter concludes, as usual, with her questions. Sometimes they are about my life behind bars, but more often than not, they are about me. As a person. I ignored them at first or deflected with short, vague answers. Recently, however, I find myself divulging more details.

I mainly told her about the small things I miss the most. (Metal utensils and regular dinnerware. Freedom to shower whenever the fuck I want. Normal street clothes.) My opinion on the Almighty. (I'm not a believer in a supreme, all-powerful force that miraculously impacts our lives.) Justice, and my views on right and wrong. (The rule of law and the principle of righteousness are a two-way street—the moral correctness of any action depends on which side you ask to define them.)

One time, though, she asked me about Elmo. *Do you remember him? Can you tell me what he was like?* It took me hours to compose the response to her. Not because I struggled to recall the facts and anecdotes. I didn't. But because Elmo's death is still a bleeding wound. Back then—as is now—I still blame myself for not getting to him sooner. For not saving him. I told her that, right before I relayed everything I knew and remembered about her brother. Everything, because she deserved to know him, too.

That was the one and only heavy message I sent her. The rest were a subsurface fluff. It felt strange and sort of silly to share those things with someone. Especially my little stepsister. It still feels that way, at times.

You should keep your focus on more important things instead of bitching about missing real forks.

I squeeze the bridge of my nose, hoping it will make the chatty asshole in my head go away. It doesn't. The fucker continues to enjoy his permanent residence, as he has since he showed up.

It's cushy here. Now, grab that pen and tell the girl to keep her ear to the ground. We need to know more if there's talk of chicken on the menu.

Zahara

"Use the other sink." A girl's whispered voice comes from behind me. "You don't wanna catch that *thing* she has."

I roll my eyes. Same old story, every time. I stopped explaining about my vitiligo long ago, so I just leave the bathroom without bothering to respond to these bitches. God, I'm so sick of them. It's easier to handle everyone's cattiness when Hannah is around. Although we aren't particularly close, she never treats me like an outcast. But she broke her ankle last week and won't be back at school for a while. Her family moved her into some fancy treatment facility specializing in sports and dance injuries where she could recover.

As I walk along the corridor to the main door, I keep my head down, my gaze trained no more than a handful of steps in front of me. I avoid meeting the eyes of anyone I pass, as I always do. This time, however, something is nagging me. It's like an itch at the back of my neck. Something deep below the surface that I can't just scratch away.

Nothing about this moment is different from any other—I bear the scorn of my schoolmates, whether they merely ignore me or openly stare as if I'm a freak. The usual. And, like a scared little mouse, I don't look back at them. As usual.

My feet falter. That itch on my nape feels like more than

simple irritation. I stop in the middle of the hall, staring at the tips of my shoes while my mind drifts to Massimo's latest letter, and that one sentence in particular. It was probably nothing more than an afterthought, only a handful of words, but they ring loudly in my head.

You're a menace, kid. Great job.

I certainly have never viewed myself as anything even remotely menacing. Someone like that exudes resolve and courage. Qualities I don't think I possess. But maybe I do. After all, I've been sneaking into private places and spying on some of the most dangerous people in this city. And I've been sending coded messages to my stepbrother. In prison.

All that, and I'm still too intimidated to look a bunch of teenagers in the eyes. Why? Because I don't want to see their contempt, their conviction that I'm somehow beneath them?

Maybe that's why the back of my neck is itching, and the sensation is getting stronger with every second I continue to stare at the floor. Every atom in my body is buzzing in protest, rebelling against that downcast view.

Slowly, I lift my head. My gaze refocuses directly ahead of me, and I take my first step. And then another. Sure feet carry me forward until I walk out of the school with my head held high. And it feels so damn good.

As I approach the campus gates, I notice the absence of the shiny white SUV that usually drives me home. Instead, there's a slick black sports car parked at the curb. With Capo Salvo Canali leaning on the hood.

"Mr. Canali?" I ask when I reach him. "Has something happened?"

"Salvo. Please. I sent Peppe back, told him I'll drop you off at home." In a much lower voice, he adds, "We need to talk."

"Um... okay," I mumble as I drop onto the passenger seat. What on earth could he possibly need to discuss with me? We've never actually spoken before.

Salvo gets behind the wheel and starts the car. Without a word, he pulls into traffic and proceeds to drive, and with every mile, the silence makes me feel more and more on edge. We're almost at my house when I can't stand it any longer.

"What did you want to talk about?"

"Your sanity," he says through his teeth. "Spying on your father for Massimo?"

I stiffen. "I have no idea what you're talking about."

"He told me. I can't believe he'd resort to using *you*, of all people, in such a way."

My hands tighten around the straps of my backpack. I'm certain if I looked at them, my knuckles would be white. The realization that Salvo is one of Massimo's other spies gets pushed aside when the rest of his words register. And the way he said them.

"Why not me?" I ask.

"Why?" His eyes cut to me and then back to the road. "Because you're barely fucking sixteen! I mean, I know what Massimo is like, but this... *Fuck!* That manipulative motherfucker."

"'*Manipulative motherfucker*'?" I raise an eyebrow. "I thought the two of you were friends."

"We are. It's just... I can't believe he'd exploit a child for his devious schemes."

"I'm not a child. And I guess you don't know him very well, then. If you did, you'd know that he'd do anything in his power to achieve his goals. Besides, it can hardly be called 'exploitation' if the other party is fully aware of the situation and has accepted the terms. And I am, and have. So it's simply a mutually beneficial agreement."

Salvo rakes his hand through his hair, shaking his head as if he can't accept my response. He parks in our driveway and turns off the engine, a scowl darkening his face. "Jesus fuck. I thought you were a nice, meek girl who's only interested in making your little dresses."

Yeah. Just like everyone else. Except for the *manipulative motherfucker* who happens to be my stepbrother. He doesn't think me incapable. Or inadequate. I grit my teeth and look Salvo right in the eye. "That just proves you don't know me, either."

Salvo's expression moves between shock and incredulity. Taking advantage of his dumbfounded state, I throw open the car door and step out.

"Please keep your nose out of my business, Salvo," I whisper-yell, slamming the door shut.

As soon as I'm in my room, I grab my notebook and tear out a sheet of paper. I usually fill my letters with a myriad of details—about Cosa Nostra, school, my sewing—enough that I ramble on for at least a couple of pages each time. Now, however, I scribble a single sentence. No greeting. No signature. Just a burning question.

Do you think I'm meek?

Massimo's response arrives three days later. A lone sentence to match my own.

You might be many things, Zahara, but I'm afraid "meek" isn't one of them.

The airy smile hasn't left my face since I read his words.

Chapter
six

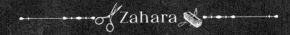 Zahara

One year later
(Zahara, age 17)

THE DOOR TO MY FATHER'S OFFICE OPENS WITHOUT A sound. Nevertheless, I throw another look down the hall to make sure no maids are around, then step inside.

"Zara? Do you need something?"

I startle, gaping at my father sitting behind his massive maple desk. He closes the folder in his hands, the expression on his face is of clear surprise—I barged into his space without an invitation. Well, I wasn't expecting him to be here. I've gotten used to sneaking into Dad's office on the regular to search for whatever Massimo needs. Whenever Dad isn't home, obviously. And today is Thursday. He shouldn't be here!

Every Thursday morning, my father leaves early to visit Massimo in prison. He spends hours at the correctional facility and doesn't return home until late in the afternoon. The routine is like clockwork, and it didn't even cross my mind to check that today was the same before I came down here.

"Um . . ." I throw a quick glance at the imposing grandfather clock in the corner. Just after one. Dad never returns before three. "I'm out of paper for my sketches, so I thought I could borrow some from your printer."

"Sure." He grabs a few sheets out of the tray and offers them to me. "Are you wearing makeup, sweetheart?"

My hand flies up to my face. Over the past several weeks, I've been trying different brands of foundation, fruitlessly searching for one that doesn't irritate my skin. This latest is labeled *hypoallergenic* and *for sensitive skin*, and so far, it's a bit better than the others. There's no rash, but my skin still itches.

"Yes." I accept the paper from him. Going for casual, I comment, "You're back early today."

"Yeah. Massimo is still in the hospital ward and can't have any visitors."

The blank sheets slip from my fingers, falling to the floor. Hospital ward? My pulse skyrockets. I try to draw a calming breath, but it feels as if someone has wrapped their hands around my neck, squeezing tightly.

"Is... is he okay?" Somehow, I manage to form the words.

"Oh sure." Dad shrugs and looks down at the printout he's pulled out. "Just a stab wound to his side. It happens."

It happens? His nonchalant tone communicates loudly that this is a more or less regular occurrence. Dad doesn't sound worried at all. I crouch to pick up the fallen sheets, noticing that my hands shake as I lift the paper. "So... this isn't the first time?" I ask, trying to keep my composure.

"It's a state prison, Zara. There are always skirmishes among incarcerated men, and Massimo is a high-profile individual." Dad motions dismissively, as if he's discussing nothing more consequential than the weather. "He'll be fine."

Anger roils in my stomach as I stare at my father. How can he be so unperturbed? Massimo might not be his flesh and blood, but he's a living, breathing human being. Not to mention, the sole reason for every success my father has experienced and continues to enjoy. Like the countless business connections. The money. The unquestioning loyalty of the Cosa Nostra capos and soldiers. And the respect and adoration of the rest of the Family. Each time one of them bowed and kissed Dad's hand to acknowledge the security and prosperity *he* brought them, they should actually have been thanking and praising Massimo instead. Without Massimo, my father would not have lasted a year as the don. He would have been relieved of his duties, removed, or maybe even "retired." Nuncio Veronese is nothing without my stepbrother. And he knows it.

Maybe that's the reason Dad hates Massimo so much.

"Thank you for the paper," I say with a strained smile and leave my father's office without looking at him.

Back in my room, I head straight for my backpack and pull out my phone. I've never called the prison before, so it takes me a few minutes of googling to find the right number. My fingers tremble as I press the call button and then listen to the ringing on the line for nearly a minute before it disconnects.

Shit. Breath leaves my lungs in short bursts as I hit redial. With every grating buzz in my ear, it's becoming harder to draw in enough oxygen. Finally, after the sixth ring, a rather bored-sounding male voice answers.

"I'd like some information on one of your inmates," I choke out. "Massimo Spada. He's been taken to the hosp—"

"Name?" he drawls.

"Um... Zahara Veronese. I'm his stepsister."

The sound of what I'm certain are two pointer fingers hitting the keyboard drags on for an eternity.

"He's alive."

Dead air replaces the gruff voice on the line.

I stare at my phone. *He's alive.* That's all I get? I wasn't expecting the prison admin to be super forthcoming, but I hoped he'd give me more than a two-word reply, damn it.

Reaching into the nightstand drawer, I grab the notebook

I use to write letters to Massimo and tear out a sheet from the middle. I should probably let him know that Batista Leone has visited Dad an absurd number of times in the last few weeks, but my stupid "report" is the last thing on my mind right now.

With my letter written and in hand, I grab the nearest stack of sketches for my new designs and basically fly down the stairs to look for Peppe.

I can't wait for Massimo's usual response. It could take days. I need to know what's happening. This minute! Speaking with Salvo is my only option; maybe he knows something. But I don't have his number, and there is no way I could ask Dad for it that wouldn't raise suspicion. I also can't just show up at Salvo's home to simply have a chat.

Luckily, I've got an idea.

Salvo's mother complimented my dress at one of the dinners I attended with Dad. The next day, she called, asking if I'd consider making a custom-designed gown for her. I declined. But it appears, I've changed my mind. Why else would I be heading to her house now?

And maybe, just maybe, Salvo will be home.

I find Peppe in the kitchen, munching on snacks.

"I need you to drive me over to Canali's," I choke out.

"Yes, this one would be perfect," Rosetta Canali says while admiring a sketch of a sleeveless gown with a built-in corset and a big bow at the back. "Could you make it in royal blue satin?"

"Blue satin would be great." I nod and leap off the chaise lounge, practically snatching the paper out of her hand. "Okay. I have your measurements, so I'll get started on this over the weekend."

"Wonderful. I'm so excited, dear. You should seriously consider getting into the fashion industry."

Yeah, sure. My dad would be thrilled to have his daughter work as a seamstress for women below her social standing. "I will. Um… Is Salvo here? I'd like to say hi."

"Of course. He's in the study. Let's go and— Oh, there he is." She waves toward the double doors that connect the salon with the library. "Salvo, darling, Zara has changed her mind and agreed to design a dress for me. She even came all the way here so I could look at her sketches."

"Did she now?" Salvo says from the doorway. His face is set in hard, reproachful lines. I don't think he's buying my "I'm just here to make a dress" cover story. He leans on the jamb, partially blocking the exit. "Are you leaving?"

"Yes," I say, then mouth, *We need to talk.*

If it's possible, the expression on his face seems to darken even further. Over the past months, we've been running into each other at various events. Despite my best efforts to avoid him, each time he's found a way to discreetly approach me and lecture me on how foolish I am to involve myself in such a dangerous game. It's annoying as hell. I liked Salvo much better before he found out what I was doing for Massimo—when he was absolutely ignorant of my existence.

"Okay." Salvo nods. "I'll walk you out to the car."

I mumble a quick goodbye to Mrs. Canali and follow Salvo to the foyer.

"Have you heard from Massimo?" I ask as soon as we're out of earshot.

"Not in the last couple of months. Why?"

"Because he's in the hospital ward!" I whisper. "I found out this morning when I snuck into my dad's office to look for something. Only I didn't get the chance because Dad was there. Apparently, Massimo can't have any visitors right now, so my father didn't even go to see him today."

Salvo stops near the front door and grabs my upper arm.

"Are you insane?" he whispers back. "Nuncio might be your

father, but he's also the don. What if someone catches you going through his files and passes that information to the rest of the fucking Family?"

"No one will catch me."

"You don't know that." He cocks his head to the side, studying my face. "You look different."

I furrow my brows, confused by the sudden change of subject. "I'm wearing some foundation."

"Mm-hmm…" He reaches out and sweeps a stray strand of hair off my face. "You look very pretty."

For just an instant, I'm too stunned to respond. Men never give me compliments. What's his deal? Is this a ploy of some kind? Whatever. I have zero mental capacity to analyze Salvo's behavior at the moment.

"If you hear anything, please let me know. Your mother has my number." I step around him and head to the car.

"What did he promise you?" Salvo calls after me. "In exchange for your… *help*? Money? A favorable match for your marriage?"

I don't even bother gracing him with an answer. Men. They all think the world revolves around dicks. God forbid a woman does something because it makes her feel good. Recognized. Worthy. None of the men in my sphere make me feel that way.

Except one.

And right now, I don't even know if he's okay!

Massimo

"Glad to see you up and about, Spada. A few days under the fluorescent lights of the hospital ward has really perked up your complexion."

"Fuck off, Kiril." I nod at the Bulgarian. Pain screams in my hip, the stitches pulling on my flesh as I lower myself to take a seat beside him in the rec yard.

"Owen got you good, I see." He laughs, flashing a gold upper bicuspid. "Is he still in the infirmary?"

"Yup. Severe concussion. He'll live."

"Why the fuck did you get into a fight with that nutcase?"

"He wanted to sit next to me in the chow hall. But the asshole knows I like to eat alone." I squeeze the bridge of my nose. My eyes still sting from the damn pepper spray the COs doused us with. "So, you're catching the chain tomorrow?" The lucky bastard is getting out of here.

"Yup. Four years and eight months in this cage. To be honest, I'm feeling a bit of anxiety."

"You'll get over it. Just make sure you don't suddenly develop amnesia once you're out and forget the terms we agreed on." I pin him with my gaze.

Kiril's crew owns a car wash business with several locations around the state, and they use these to launder money for Camorra. My own laundering channels have been stretched too thin in the past year, so I negotiated an in with the Bulgarians, giving them a cut of fifteen percent.

"I'm a man of my word, Spada." He stands up and offers me his hand. "Looking forward to working with Cosa Nostra."

While we shake hands, Kiril leans toward me. "A new inmate will be arriving next week, and a little birdie told me that the Triad is a bit worried about the reception he'll get," he says in a lowered voice. "Mr. Wang would be extremely grateful if someone could take the boy under his wing."

I raise an eyebrow. "His son?"

"Grandson. The kid got busted for offing a guy who owed them money."

"Tell Mr. Wang that he needn't be concerned for his boy's well-being. And we'll settle the debt at a later date."

I watch Kiril leave, then reach into my pocket and take out

the envelope that arrived this morning. My stepsister's letters are usually several pages long. This one, however, is only a single sheet, with barely a few lines of text.

Are you okay? Dad told me you were injured and in the hospital ward. What happened? I called the prison to see how you're doing, but they just told me you're alive and hung up on me.

Zahara

Rage explodes inside me as I read the last sentence. I can't have anyone in Cosa Nostra suspecting that I'm in any way involved with the Family. Nuncio and my lawyer are the only two approved people on my visitation list for that sole reason. And even though I pay a shit ton of money to make sure my mail remains undisturbed and I can have conversations with Nuncio without being recorded, I don't have anyone in my pocket in the front office. So, my stepsister—with whom I've presumably had no contact for over a decade—calling the prison out of the blue, could raise a serious fucking red flag.

Whoever has been working behind my back, pulling the strings to keep me in here, is high in the Cosa Nostra hierarchy. It's more than likely they have a source inside the prison keeping tabs on me. If anyone even suspects that Nuncio is my puppet, that he isn't actually capable of doing his job, he'd lose the respect and loyalty of the Family and would be immediately removed. My schemes for a bloodless takeover would go to hell in a handbasket.

Another jolt of pain shoots through my side as I rise off the bench and head across the yard. In the corner, scribbling madly in his notebook, is a fresh pumpkin, his head still a little swollen from the welcome beating he received upon his arrival a few days ago. Hence, the name. It's always the same with the new guys—they either crumble into fucking mush or learn quickly how to survive in this pisshole. I think this one might make it; he looks alright, not counting the present state of his head.

I still remember my own hoe check from the welcoming committee. Those three assholes wanted to see if I'd stand up for myself or roll over and play someone's bitch. They jumped me in the shower, two holding me while the third used a pipe on my stomach like batting practice. I was caught completely unaware, and it took two hits to the gut and a kick to the head before I came to my senses. When I managed to break free of the guys pinning me down and get ahold of the pipe, they received my answer loud and clear. My nose never did heal properly from that run-in, and the part of my jaw the doctors had to patch up still stings occasionally. But none of my attackers were left smiling, either. And they haven't since.

My stroll down memory lane ends just as I reach my target. Without a word, I grab the pen from the guy's hand, then brace my stepsister's letter on the wall and jot down a single line of text, right under hers.

Don't you fucking dare call the prison ever again.

I'm halfway across the yard, heading toward one of the guards who "works" for me so I can get him to mail the note back to Zahara, when an unexpected pang of guilt hits me. Stopping in my tracks, I lift the letter and look over my message.

What? The asshole inside my head chimes in. ***The meaning can't be more clear. The kid fucked up! She needs to know just how seriously she screwed the pooch so she doesn't do it again. Or—don't tell me—are you going soft?***

Fuck you! I snap back at my ever-present peanut gallery.

You don't have the luxury to second-guess shit.

76

I know that. So why the hell are these less than a dozen words I wrote bugging me?

With the sentencing appeal denied, the then twentysomething-year-old me accepted that I'd be locked up in this cage for the long haul. For a man in his prime, that pretty much equals death. Over the years I've been rotting away, that reality smacked me in the face again and again, every time my parole application was turned down. Men in these situations have different ways of coping. Some just take it day by day, existing rather than living, pining for the time they'll get their freedom back. While others simply check out, like my first bunkie who was serving thirty years for a double homicide. He hanged himself with a bedsheet barely six months in.

My focus on maintaining control of the businesses and growing the Family's wealth and influence have kept me sane. Everything I've done in the past decade and a half has been accomplished with that sole purpose in mind. I threatened. Maimed. Killed—with my own hands or by my orders—at least a dozen people. Some of those stood in the way of my ultimate goal and needed to be erased from the picture. Others were simply collateral to gain favors and garner IOUs from other influential players, ensuring I'll have the resources and support I'll need when I eventually get released and take back what is mine. I've survived by not giving a crap about people or their feelings. Everyone is either an obstacle that must be overcome or an asset that can be exploited.

Zahara has ended up being a very valuable asset that I am far from done making use of. She's nothing more than that. Once I'm finally free, I'll marry her off to someone who'll offer a business advantage or cement a strategic alliance. I'll do the same with her sister. Both of them are just pawns.

But as I look at my rapidly scrawled response to her letter, that guilt punches me in the chest all over again. She's still just a kid who didn't know any better.

I crumple the sheet of paper and stick it into the back pocket of my pants. Glancing to the left, I spot the pumpkin, still scribbling on his notepad in the corner of the yard. My long steps eat up the distance between us, and then I'm snatching the notebook and the pen from his hands again to write a new reply.

Zahara,
Please don't call the prison again.
M.

CHAPTER
seven

Massimo

Almost a year later
(Zahara, age 18; Massimo, age 35)

THE DARK-BLUE CUBE VAN BACKS UP TO THE OPEN
loading bay door. Every Sunday morning, it arrives to
collect bins of dirty laundry and takes everything to
another nearby correctional center to be dealt with. Keeping
my eyes on the vehicle through the wisps of my frosty breath,
I lean my shoulder on the cold wall of the docking area and
wait for the truck to come to a stop. The driver-side window
slides down, and instantly, a barely audible whistle sounds from
inside the cab.

I grab one of the bins overflowing with mesh bags stuffed
full of filthy shit and carry it to the back of the vehicle while the
stink attacks my nostrils. Stacking the bin in the cargo hold of
the cube van, I throw a look at the correctional officer super-
vising the work. He glances at the other two inmates handling
the bins, then gives me a slight chin lift.

Casually, I head around the truck and lean my shoulder
on the driver's door. "You should have been here a week ago."

"Apologies, boss." Peppe's low voice drifts through the open window. "My brother's shift got changed, so I couldn't take his place last Sunday."

"Make sure that doesn't happen again," I warn.

Peppe is first generation Cosa Nostra. His father was a laborer at one of the Family's warehouses, working alongside my dad. Peppe, however, is more ambitious than his old man ever was. He decided to become a made man by taking the oath and turned soldier during my father's reign. When I got shot the night of my junior prom, it was Peppe who carried my ass to safety, and he ended up being wounded himself in the process. For years, he's been my secret contact within the foot soldiers' ranks.

"What do you have for me?" I ask.

"A guy by the name of Wei Zhao arrived in Block C a few days ago. The Triad wanted you to know that they hold no love toward him and would be immensely grateful if he could be handled. A suicide, if that's possible."

"I'll need a week or two to make arrangements. I don't have anyone reliable in Block C, so I'll take care of it myself. Anything else?"

"The Roxbury brats have been causing a stir, using a location on our turf to move boosted cars. But they've been handled." He pauses, and I can tell that whatever he has to say next, is something that's weighing on his mind. "Capo Armando, though, might become a problem. Since he's been assigned to oversee foot soldiers, he hasn't bothered to come down to speak with our men even once. He seems to be more interested in spending his father's money at the casinos."

I remember Armando. I remember him being a tool. He went to the same school as Salvo and me but was two years behind us. Armando is stupid as fuck, but his father is one of our largest investors. That's why I had to agree to promote the useless son of a bitch. Nuncio informed me Armando's father had

80

asked for it personally. I couldn't risk making any waves among the Cosa Nostra elite at the time, but once I'm free, I'm taking care of that idiot. "I'll see to it that he takes his obligations more seriously from now on. At any rate, he's occupying that position only temporarily."

"I'm glad to hear it." Peppe's head bobs up and down nearly imperceptibly, and then he exhales a long breath. "Motivation is important to people. As is knowing that they're not seen as simply expendable muscle. Men need a leader who values them. They haven't forgotten how it was... before."

I look away, staring at the high concrete wall that surrounds the prison and the electric barbed wire coiled at the top. Everything that lies beyond has been obscured from my view for over a decade. *Yes... Before...* Before I landed in lockup, no local drug deal or internal skirmish happened without me being there. My presence ensured our soldiers' safety because only an idiot would risk opening fire with a high-ranking member of Cosa Nostra in attendance. My men were important to me. Every single one. From my right-hand guy to the lowest courier in the hierarchy. But that was... *before.*

Now... Now I don't give a fuck about anyone or anything beyond the successful execution of my plan. Nothing.

"The man you remember doesn't exist anymore, Peppe. Don't give our men false hope. I'm not the same person I once was. He's gone."

"Or maybe he's simply... lost." He steals a look in a side-view mirror. "The loading is almost complete."

"Yup. Make sure you don't miss your visit next month. I have an errand for Zahara, and you'll need to accompany her." I tap the door with my fist and turn to leave, but Peppe whispers my name and I stop.

"Why are you still using the girl? I'll do anything to get whatever info you need, you know that."

I turn back and pin him with my gaze. Peppe has always

been observant, which is the main reason I positioned him to be one of Don Veronese's drivers—so he could easily monitor my stepfather's movements and overhear conversations en route. But despite his current assurance, I know he could never get me intel from inside the social functions that Nuncio loves to host and frequent. I don't doubt Peppe's willingness or his abilities for a minute. It's simply not in the cards. Not for him.

"She's too young," he adds. "It's too dangerous."

"I don't give a fuck," I snap and head back inside the loading bay. I refuse to give up the ace up my sleeve.

Zahara

Two months later

"Zara!" My sister pounces to snatch the gift box she just handed me out of my grasp. "You can't open it now! Your guests are already arriving and you should open all your presents at the same time, after the party."

I take a step back, squeezing the box to my chest. "They are not *my* guests. I didn't invite any of those people. Dad did. So, I don't care. Your present is probably the only one I'll like anyway."

Nera's smile slips, but she quickly puts on a happy face. "Fine. Let's see if I've chosen well."

Moving a vase of white roses aside, I lay the gift box on the dresser and begin tearing off the wrapping paper. Whatever it is, it's small and rectangular. Is it a new set of sketching pencils? New sewing scissors to add to my growing collection? As soon as the box is completely unwrapped, I almost break down in tears.

"How did you...?" I stare at the limited edition, handheld, electric rotary cutter that I've seen in promo videos. It's the latest and greatest tool for cutting several layers of fabric at a time. "These are only sold in Japan."

"Dania's cousin traveled to Tokyo for work a few weeks ago." She smirks. "You've been babbling about that thing for months, so how could I not?"

"Thank you," I choke out and kiss her cheek.

"He also brought me a fridge magnet. I have it hanging next to the one you got for me in Paris."

I quickly look away, feeling guilty. I got that magnet from eBay. The long weekend trip to Europe with Hannah's family never actually happened. For me, at least. It was a cover story for when I had to personally deliver a secret message to some guy on the outskirts of New York City last month. No one except Peppe, who drove me there and stuck to me like glue during the exchange, knew about it.

The whole thing was an ordeal. Nobody from the other Cosa Nostra Families is permitted into the New York territory without specific permission from their don. I'm pretty sure the guy I met was a local mafioso, though, so somehow Massimo made the arrangements for me. Don't recall the guy's exact name. I was a bit too nervous. Arthur? No, Arturo. And the message made absolutely no sense to me. It was just two sentences.

I have a solution for your problem in Chinatown.
I'll reach out when I'm ready to trade.

I wonder what kind of dealings Massimo has with the notorious Don Ajello? Also, something tells me Peppe is working for Massimo, too, considering he never said a word to anyone about our excursion. He didn't even question me when I told him where I had to go.

"Zara!" The door to my room swings open and Dad steps inside. He's wearing a new black suit and has his hair slicked back, ready to impress whatever bigshot is coming tonight. I have absolutely no doubts about that. "The guests are arriving, and you need to greet them."

I sigh. "I'm coming."

"Good. Now, close your eyes."

Raising my eyebrows, I do as he says. The unmistakable sound of footsteps in dress shoes approaches and moves behind me. Then, something drapes around my neck.

"Don't think I didn't notice you staring at this the other day," he gushes next to my ear and kisses the top of my head. "Happy birthday, baby girl."

When I open my eyes, I'm faced with Nera's shocked expression.

"Please, hurry," Dad says. "It would be incredibly bad manners not to greet the people who came to your birthday party."

The door clicks shut in his wake, and I look down. An exquisite diamond and gold necklace rests over the swells of my silk-covered breasts, sparkling against the beige of my shirt. Yes, it's the one I saw in the jewelry store at the mall when Dad and I stopped to pick up some fabric I ordered. I spent quite a while staring at the elegant piece in the window display while Dad went to use the restroom before we left to meet his associate for dinner.

"I can't believe he did that." Nera rushes behind me to unclasp the necklace. "I'll make sure he returns this and gets you something else."

"Don't bother," I mumble.

"No, I will. And I'll make him apologize. How could he forget you can't wear gold?"

"You'll do no such thing." Taking the necklace from her, I bring it across the room to my vanity and drop it into my jewelry box. Alongside most of my father's previous presents that I also cannot wear. "And you won't mention it to him, either."

"Zara."

"I said no." I take Nera's hand. "Let's see who our dad invited to *my* birthday party."

I snatch a glass of white wine from a waiter's tray while he's not looking and take a huge sip. "If I have to shake another hand tonight, I'm going to kill someone."

"I don't know why Dad insisted on making this into such a big event when it's not what you wanted," Nera mumbles next to me.

"Because his own birthday isn't for another four months, and he's running out of occasions where a guest list of a hundred people or more would be appropriate."

I sigh and glance at the mingling crowd. Being a winter baby means no garden birthday parties, and the great hall is so full, the attendees are nearly tripping over each other. Having so many people this close together is an absolute dream for eavesdropping. However, with Nera at my side, I haven't had many opportunities tonight. Other than a fun snippet that Adriano's wife had her boobs done, which everyone has definitely noticed, I haven't heard anything useful.

On the far side of the hall, standing near the fireplace with Capos Armando and Brio, is Salvo. They appear to be deep in discussion, but every now and then, Salvo throws a look in my direction. I have no idea what his problem is. In the past weeks, I've run into him twice when I went over to take his mother's measurements. Both times he tried to start a casual chat, but I managed to evade him.

"Would you be mad if I take off now?" Nera asks. "I have a paper to finish before tomorrow morning."

"Of course not. I'll make another round through the room and then sneak upstairs myself."

She gives me a quick peck on the cheek. "Text me when you open your presents."

"Yup." I kiss her in return. I can't wait to see all the crystal vases, jewelry, and other meaningless stuff from people who don't even know me.

Once Nera departs, I make my way among the guests, but with the crowd so tightly pressed together, no one is discussing any sensitive subjects. Spotting Salvo heading in my direction, I quickly do a one-eighty and practically run back to my room.

The maids have already brought all of my presents upstairs, piling them in a huge heap on and around the couch. I ignore the elaborately wrapped packages and head to the bathroom but stop when I notice a large unwrapped box among a stack of small gift bags. It's a simple white cardboard box, with just an envelope attached at the top with clear packing tape.

I drift between the rest of the presents and pluck the envelope from the box. Butterflies stir in my stomach as I pull out a plain piece of notebook paper with a single sentence written across the page.

Happy Birthday, Zahara.

It's unsigned, but I would recognize Massimo's handwriting anywhere.

In my last letter, I rattled on for two paragraphs about how Dad has been insisting on throwing a big-ass party for my eighteenth birthday, never dreaming that Massimo would send me a present. Is it a lamp? I hate lamps, but if Massimo got me one, I'll keep it on my nightstand. The package seems large enough for it, and it's rather heavy. By the time I finish lifting the lid, I'm buzzing like a live wire, and my hands are shaking.

It's not a lamp.

Inside the box is a stack of at least ten neatly folded fabrics, each a variation of some sort of brown. My trembling fingers glide over the fine textiles, while my heart doubles its beat with every passing second. Chestnut, dark beige, and russet silk. Copper-colored lace with gold embroidered accents. Super thin cotton in a delicious mocha. Soft and flowy, perfect for summer clothes. How on earth did he get his hands on these?

At the bottom of the box, there is another note. A lone sentence on another unpretentious page.

I hope these cover every shade of brown, so now you can finally stop pestering me about the differences in each letter you write.
M.

I press my hand over my mouth and giggle. I *have* been pestering him. A lot. Teased him, even, for not being able to differentiate the various hues. I get a kick out of his clearly exasperated tone in his replies whenever I write about different shades of brown. Once, he asked me why I always use muted, drab colors, never yellows or oranges, for example. I ignored the question. Didn't want to admit that the bland tints make me less noticeable in the crowd. Fewer people tend to stare at me. Stare at the discoloration around my eyes, more specifically. After all this time, all our letters, not once have I mentioned my skin condition to him. I guess I'm being vain. I want him to think of me as beautiful.

Does he? Think about me? Because I think about him all the time. I imagine our first meeting, in person, after he gets out. He'll rush to me and scoop me into his arms. Tell me he's been dreaming about me. Maybe... maybe he'll even kiss me.

I shouldn't be thinking about my stepbrother like that. It's totally taboo, and I should be ashamed for having these scandalous thoughts bouncing around my mind. While we aren't related by blood, the two of us together would be considered a sin in a conservative Cosa Nostra world. But I like to envision it anyway. And that's not all I envision. I just.... can't help myself.

There've been times when I've gone out with Nera and her friends, and the girls always bragged about their boyfriends. They'd tell stories of what they do with their men. More often than not, I'd end up shocked and red-faced. One time, Dania asked me if there was a guy I liked and offered to help hook us up. I said no, of course. All the boys I come in contact with just seem like stupid kids. I can't even imagine kissing any of them, never mind anything more than that. But I fantasize about kissing Massimo. And I daydream of doing so, so much more.

My mind wanders to the rustic wooden chest tucked beneath my bed. There are at least a hundred letters inside, carefully hidden under a bunch of silk ribbons and scraps of fabric so the maids don't stumble upon them by accident. Every night before I go to sleep, I pull out a few of the letters and read them. Even though I can remember each word for word. The one with the explanation of linear equations is my favorite.

Sometimes, I close my eyes and hold my hand over the flowy characters on the page, imagining Massimo speaking the words. What does his voice sound like? Deep and raspy? Or soft enough to glide over me like a smooth velvet? I don't know, since letters have been our only communication all these years. What does he look like? I wonder, probably for the millionth time. I tried picturing him as a grown-up, an older version of the scowling boy I'd seen in photos. Imagined a man with dark, unruly hair falling across his eyes, but my mind could never make the leap. To this day, I have no idea what my stepbrother might actually look like, but I feel like I know him to his core. And if he really reads all the crap I've been writing in my letters, then he knows me better than anyone else, too. There is only one thing I never mentioned. I couldn't bring myself to tell him about my vitiligo and then know he was just another person who pitied me.

In the beginning, Massimo's letters were infrequent and always way too brief. Curt, vague replies to my questions and more pointed inquiries about the things that were happening at home. With time, though, they got longer, and more personal. The five sentences became ten. Then twenty. Then, a full page.

Although, a large part of each of his messages was still made up of carefully crafted directions for what he needed me to do, or what topic I should be paying more attention to when eaves-dropping on my father's meetings, the way he phrased everything told me more about his interests, his abilities, and how his mind works. With each letter, I've been amazed anew by how cunning he is. Metaphors, code words, hidden clues. If anyone stumbled upon one of his letters, I doubt they'd be able to discern his meaning. It would all seem like nothing more than random rambling or confusing facts. His words were chaos to everyone but me.

A smart, devious man. Never wavering from his ultimate goal.

The man I can't stop thinking about.

His more extensive yet still rather cautious letters have become the warmth that sustains me. Because it is there, between the lines, where I'm learning about the real Massimo. From things he doesn't actually say. Like his trouble sleeping because he's always on alert, expecting someone to cut his throat when his guard is down. How much he misses nature—plants and trees—because all he gets to see are the same concrete walls every day. His affinity for a dry sense of humor. And the guilt he still feels about Elmo's death. He blames himself, even though it was just an unfortunate turn of events, one he could not prevent. He tried, though, and now lives with the consequences of that night. A night I don't remember at all, but I know the truth of what happened because I managed to drag the story out of Dad. I wish I could reassure Massimo. I wish I could take away his pain.

I wish... for something that is forbidden.

CHAPTER eight

Zahara

Four months later

"YOU KNOW NOTHING ABOUT HIM," I SAY. "HOW CAN that be a healthy relationship?"

Nera rolls on her stomach and props her hands under her chin, her eyes sparkling like little gems, the same as they do whenever she speaks about her "stalker." It's plain as day that she's in love with him. In love with a man whose name she doesn't even know, and they've been seeing each other for almost a year.

She stumbled upon him—wounded and bleeding in a dark alley—and took him to the vet clinic where she works to patch him up. When she told me what she had done, I nearly lost my everloving shit. Alone, with a man who had been shot! In the middle of the night! She must have been out of her mind. He could have been a total psycho. But they've been meeting up ever since.

At first, I thought it was just a simple crush that would pass as quickly as it started. As the months dragged on, it became obvious that wasn't the case. I don't recall seeing Nera so happy before, and I'm truly not sure if I should be glad for her or if I should worry.

"Have you ever met someone you can talk to about all the things you can't discuss with anyone else?" my sister asks from her spot on my bed. "Even though you don't know much about them?"

Pain shoots through my thumb as I stab myself with the tip of my needle. A small drop of blood soaks into the beige silk, and I'm nearly hyperventilating, alarmed that she somehow knows my secret. But when I glance up, I see her staring at the ceiling with a dreamy look in her eyes. It was just a rhetorical question, thank God.

"Maybe," I answer, without actually intending to.

"What?" Nera abruptly shoots up in bed. "Who?"

I quickly drop my gaze back to the fabric in my hands. "Don't want to talk about it."

"You know you can tell me anything, Zara."

Guilt threatens to consume me. We've never had secrets between us. Until Massimo. I'm not in any way morally opposed to spying for him, but I do feel bad for keeping my activities from Nera. On the other hand, Massimo has become much more to me than a stepbrother. And because my sister knows me so well, I'm afraid—terrified, actually—that it won't take her long to realize the truth. And condemn me for it.

Did I ever believe it was possible to fall in love with a man sight unseen? To love his mind? His spirit? His hidden nature?

Nope.

But that just underlines how wrong I was.

Because, I am falling in love with our stepbrother.

"Not this time," I mumble, pretending to be engrossed in my sewing.

Nera narrows her eyes at me, but she doesn't pry further, and we segue back into her twisted relationship with her stalker-slash-boyfriend.

"I can't believe it took you guys a year to work up to the first kiss. What are you—twelve?" I say as I lift the bodice of the dress I'm making for her. "You need to try this on. Watch out for pins along the side."

"You're one to talk."

"I guess you're right." I shrug. "I've never even had a boyfriend."

"What about that guy from school? The one who kept following you during lunch."

"Finn? He was just a weirdo." The bodice is a bit too loose, so I unpin the sides and readjust. "Stop wriggling."

"Speaking of weirdos... Have you noticed the way Salvo has been looking at you?"

I frown. "I have no idea what you're talking about."

"You truly are oblivious. I first saw it at lunch after the baptism of Tiziano's son. Salvo was practically devouring you with his eyes."

"The one with escargot on the menu. I remember. Yuck."

"Exactly. The guy is forty."

"Thirty-five," I correct her. Salvo and Massimo are the same age. "He was probably just staring at my face."

"He was. But not because of what you think." Nera sets her hands on my hips and turns me around so I'm facing the oversized mirror.

"You messed up my work," I mumble. "I'll have to redo the bodice again."

"Forget the bodice." Standing behind me, she rests her chin on my shoulder.

Nera is slightly taller than I am, and her hair is a shade or two lighter than my own light brown. Although my nose is narrower and my cheekbones are more pronounced, we look a lot alike. Ignoring the pale patches around my eyes, that is.

"No wonder creepy Salvo can't take his eyes off you," she

says next to my ear. "Can't you see how drop-dead gorgeous you are?"

I sigh. My sister has made it her mission to convince me I'm pretty. She might believe it's true, but I can't. I wish I looked like everyone else. *Normal.*

"Yeah." I turn back around and begin taking the pins out of the bodice. "I need to get started on this if you want it ready for Dad's birthday party next weekend."

"Are you going?"

"Probably." There's no way Dad would let me skip his party, especially since he's back to not-so-subtly insinuating that both Nera and I are ripe to be married. He even hinted that Ruggero would be there, and that it would be a great opportunity for the two of us to get to know each other. Just thinking about it is making me sick.

"Shit, I'm going to be late for my shift at the clinic." Nera shrugs out of the half-made dress and grabs her purse off the chair.

"Have you noticed Dad acting strange lately?" I ask. "He's been distracted, forgetting things. And Leone has been coming over more often than usual. He and Dad hole themselves up in Dad's study for hours."

He also started locking his office door when he's out of the house, something he's never done before.

"Mm-hmm. Some problems popped up at the casinos, but Dad said he's working them out. I have to go." Nera pecks my cheek and rushes out of the room before I get the chance to ask her to elaborate.

Problems at the casinos? The last time I managed to sneak into Dad's office and rifle through the paperwork on his desk was two weeks ago, but I didn't find anything suspicious. There were a few warehouse leases and some brochures for the new condominium block that was just built on the outskirts of Cambridge. That was all.

I'll have to find a way to get inside again and check the documents he keeps in his safe for anything that may shed light on what's going on before I write to Massimo.

One week later
Private property, Thirty miles north of Boston
Nuncio Veronese's birthday party

Laughter and clapping ring out behind me as I rush across the lawn. Dad has obviously started his speech. He usually cracks a few jokes first to warm up the crowd, and then he moves on to flattering the members of the Family. I'd hoped to catch plenty of useful gossip tonight, but Nera stuck by my side all evening, and I didn't get the chance. Dad will be livid when he hears I left his birthday party early, but I don't care. I need to get out of here now after hearing what happened to my sister three days ago.

"Miss Veronese?" Peppe asks when I find him hanging out with the other drivers in a lounge off the attached garage.

"Home, please."

During the past week, I've made several attempts to sneak into Dad's office, but the door was locked every time. The only other way in is through a window that faces the backyard. Dad leaves it ajar sometimes. With all the staff and security guards who typically buzz around the house, I couldn't risk breaking in. Today, all our household personnel were brought to this country estate to help with the party.

I had already written to Massimo this morning, telling him about the bloodbath that decimated Camorra. On Friday, the head of the clan—Alvino—along with half of his crew, had been found dead at an out-of-the-way church outside of Boston. I heard Dad telling Nera about it yesterday when he called her.

Then, he spent a good part of the afternoon shut inside his office and on the phone with Efisio, the guy taking over the Camorra Clan.

Dad's concern over the Camorra news didn't seem that strange at first—any major skirmish inside our territory would be worrisome. Still, I tried everything I could to overhear what they were talking about, but the conversation was much too muted. I figured I'd get a chance to discover the details later, since Cosa Nostra never deals with Camorra, it was likely nothing more than the usual top-dog posturing. Now, though, after finding out Nera was kidnapped by Alvino and that's what led to the carnage at that church, I'm convinced there has to be more to whatever Dad and Efisio were discussing. And there must be a clue or a paper trail hidden in his study.

Something tells me that this situation is critical, so I need to relay every piece of information I can find to Massimo right away. Maybe Salvo has a faster way to contact him? Last I saw, Salvo was in a group with the other capos. With the party in full swing, I might be able to get him alone, but I don't want to turn around and lose the opportunity to sneak into Dad's office. Maybe I could risk calling Salvo? I reach into my purse to grab my phone, but then remember that I left it at home. *Fuck.*

The small display screen above the keypad hidden behind the Monet painting flashes red.

Dad changed the combination on the safe.

I stick my thumb between my teeth, biting my nail. The locked study doors. Changed access code. Dad must have suspected someone inside the house would find out what he's been up to, maybe even been paranoid that whatever it is would reach Massimo. Would he have suspected me? Yeah, as if *poor little*

Zara would ever be capable of doing something so daring. He probably thinks it's a maid or one of the security guards.

I try the digits of the previous combination but in reverse order.

Red light again, damn it.

He must have chosen a number that's important to him, but what could it be? Dad loves birthdays. Maybe he used one of ours? It sure as hell wouldn't be mine. Nera's?

I try it. Nope.

What about his own?

No. Just the mocking flash of red.

"Shit."

I rummage through his desk, moving notes and folders in hopes that he wrote the code down somewhere, but come up blank. A thought strikes me just as I'm ready to give up. *La Famiglia*. It has always been the most important thing to my father. Turning back toward the safe, I enter the date my father took his vows as the new don.

With a barely audible click, the safe door slowly slides open. An unhappy laugh escapes me. It is my birthday after all. My father became the don of Boston on my first birthday.

I've just started leafing through the folders I pulled from the safe when the rumble of a car engine and the squeal of tires come through the window. What the hell? Everyone should still be at the party. It was planned to last well into the night. Quickly, I snap the safe closed and run out of the study just as the front door on the other side of the entry hall flies open.

"Nera?" I choke out.

My sister hovers on the threshold, her makeup smeared all over her face. Her dress is wrinkled, with a big red stain covering the front.

"Nera!" Crying out, I rush across the hall to her.

"I tried calling you." Her voice is hollow and her gaze unfocused. "You... you weren't answering your phone."

"What happened? Is that… blood? Nera, oh my God, are you alright?"

"It must have been a hitman. I tried… I tried waking him but…"

"What? Who?" I cry out.

Her red-rimmed eyes meet mine. "Dad."

No. I reel back as if she kicked me in the chest. *No.* He's okay. He has to be. We have our differences, Dad and I, but that doesn't change the fact that I love him. *He'll be okay.*

"How badly is he hurt? Where did…? Which hospital?" My breath leaves my lungs in short bursts, and I can't seem to form full sentences. Why is she just standing there? We need to be with Dad.

"Zara…" Nera stretches her hand toward me but I swat it away.

"No," I plead. Then, clutching the front of her bloody dress, I bury my face in her neck. "Don't say it. Please, don't say it."

"Dad's gone, Zara."

CHAPTER
nine

Massimo

GLARING STARES.

Hushed whispers.

Dozens of eyes laser into my back as I stride through the gathered crowd toward the white casket at the graveside. Fucking vultures. They might be standing still, but I feel like they're closing in on me. Every nerve, every atom within me is oscillating on high alert. At least in prison, you know who your enemies are, but here, amid the crème de la crème of the Italian Mafia, all bets are off. Some of the faces I don't recognize, but the majority of those present, I remember.

There are more than three hundred people here. The higher-ups are all gathered close to the casket. Men in their Sunday best and women flashing extravagant fucking jewelry. From their attire, you'd think they were at a gala, not a goddamned funeral. Typical. Birthdays and funerals have always been the most elaborately commemorated events in Cosa Nostra. The majority of the foot soldiers stand at the back. The elite do not mingle with plebs; they ignore the men who actually do all the heavy lifting for the Family. It wasn't like that when my father was the don. And it sure as hell won't be once I'm back

Low murmurs follow in my wake as the mourners split, letting me pass while my two guards trail a step behind me. I catch my name whispered a handful of times. Most of the people, however, just stare at my prison uniform and cuffed hands in confusion. With their self-centered lives, fifteen years is apparently enough time to wipe a person from their memories.

The warm, midmorning sun is shining down on the casket spray, wreaths, and floor bouquets set up around the grave site. The bulk of the floral arrangements are white, contrasting with the wall of dark attire surrounding the deceased. It's a beautiful day for a funeral. Unlike the day they laid my mother to rest. I heard it rained, but I was confined to the hole for causing a riot in the chow hall. The day before the funeral, I admittedly lost my shit because the assfucker of a warden denied my request to attend her service.

There's no sadness, no grief, no regret that haunts me as I get closer to the casket. Nuncio never liked me, and I most certainly never liked him. He was simply a means to an end—one of many—a cog that was supposed to help me reach my goal. That's all he was to me. All anyone ever is.

I stop at the edge of the burial plot and let my eyes roam over the people clustered close by. There is no missing Batista Leone; he's off to the side—face stoic and spine ramrod-straight. Salvo is just behind him, wedged between Tiziano and Brio. Our eyes meet, and he gives me a barely perceptible nod. I return it and then take in the rest of the crowd. Several capos and other members of the Family stand with their heads respectfully bowed. Adriano Ruffo is among them, but he's chosen a position a bit further back. Next to him is a short-haired blonde, wearing an obscenely short dress and an elaborate net-like black veil. It must be his wife. But directly across from me, on the other side of the raised casket, are the tops of two women's heads. The enormous flower arrangement is blocking my view of them, but they must be my stepsisters. I take a step to the right so I have a less obstructed sight line.

I recognize Nera right away. She was five the last time I saw her, but with her almond-shaped eyes and soft cheeks, there is no mistaking the girl I often caught sneaking into the kitchen to get cookies. It was all so long ago—in another lifetime.

My gaze shifts to the woman on the left.

And then… and then, I stare.

Like everyone else, she's dressed in black, but something about her captures all of my attention. My eyes travel down her body. She's wearing an elegant blouse with long lacy sleeves that gather at her wrists, and tight tailored pants that accentuate her hourglass figure. The tips of black stilettos peek from beneath the hem of her pants. I look back up, taking in her light-brown hair, partially swept into an updo at her nape while the rest of her locks cascade around her face in soft shiny waves.

That's Zahara, the voice in my head whispers.

Don't be ridiculous. I give him a mental dope slap.

It's her.

No—this beautiful, sophisticated young woman can't be my little spy. She must be one of Nera's friends, offering her support while my stepsister is grieving. This can't be Zahara, can it? All this time, I've pictured her as a gangly teen.

Suddenly, she lifts her head and we lock eyes. A perfect storm explodes inside my mind. Air catches in my lungs, but the damn things won't compress to let it out.

I. Can't. Breathe.

Her eyes go wide with surprise. And recognition.

It is *her.*

The first thing that shoots through my mush of gray matter is: *Where are her pigtails?* Unlike with Nera, I don't remember much of Zahara as a child. She was only a toddler who tended to get in the way, so I stayed clear. But I remember the pigtails.

And for whatever fucked-up reason, I expected an older version of the same.

I can't fucking tear my eyes away from hers. Her gaze holds much more than a mere realization that she's looking at Massimo Spada, a largely forgotten man, standing at the graveside. There's knowledge. Awareness of who I am. Not in the sense of "shadow leader of Cosa Nostra" or "asshole with a chip on his shoulder stuck behind bars." Nope, this is the only soul who has peered deep inside mine. Among more than three hundred mourners here, she's the only one who knows *me*. A man.

My throat suddenly feels very dry. I try to swallow, but can't. The only thing I seem to be capable of is staring at her. The girl.

No, the woman. The woman who unknowingly found a way.

To save me.

From myself.

In my long quest to make every person from my old life forget about me, I've, somehow, almost forgotten myself. But all those things I told her about myself in my letters, things that were supposed to be simple misdirection to hide the real message in my notes, they weren't random fillers. Every single detail was true. And if she hadn't asked, I might no longer remember the answers. In prison, everything that Massimo Spada used to be was stamped out. Forever, I thought. But she brought me back. And now, looking into her eyes, I realize that if it wasn't for her letters, the person who I was—I am—would have been truly lost.

I know you, her gaze says.

More than twenty feet separate us, but it feels like she's right here, next to me.

I know who you are.

She does. Maybe even better than I do.

I know you.

The apprehension and hypervigilance that's weighed me down since I stepped out of the prison van suddenly fade away. Inquisitive looks from the Cosa Nostra members all around don't burn into my back anymore. I no longer feel the need to wrap my hands around their necks and squeeze until they fall limp at my feet. For the first time in fifteen years, I am at peace.

The priest starts talking. The cemetery staff begin lowering the casket. I don't even glance at it. My entire being seems to be bewitched by my little spy. She is so fucking beautiful. I try to take in the rest of her, only then noticing the unusual discoloration around her eyes and on her forehead. A birthmark? Did she have one and I don't remember? Or is it a scar? Whatever it is, it doesn't take away from her beauty. I'm still struggling to breathe because of her effect on me, despite feeling serenity for the first time in years.

Zahara blinks and quickly looks away. Her eyes anchor to the ground as if she's trying to hide from me and in that instant, the blissful peace disappears.

Gritting my teeth, I make myself refocus on Nera, while my higher reasoning slowly kicks in. She's watching me from the other side of her father's casket with trepidation in her eyes. I hold her gaze, clinging to it with everything I have, all to prevent my eyes from sliding back to Zahara. Rapidly going over all the possible solutions for this new predicament we've landed in.

With Nuncio dead, Batista Leone will step in to take over the Family. He's been waiting for that since my father's death. I wouldn't be at all surprised if the slimy motherfucker himself was actually behind Nuncio's assassination. With my parole denied, I'll be stuck behind bars for close to four more years, serving the full extent of my sentence. Rage washes over me anew, and I barely keep my shit together. Patience. And focus. I won't allow anyone to take away what's mine. No matter what.

The priest finishes and a few Family members approach to throw dirt on the casket before leaving the cemetery. Then, the burial staff start pouring soil into the grave. Keeping my eyes on Nera's, I walk around the burial site until I'm standing in front of her.

"Munchkin." I give her a slight nod.

Nera gapes at me for a few heartbeats, then takes a step closer and tentatively wraps her arms around me. "Hello, Massimo."

Her action surprises me. I expected indifference or even plain disregard. But my resolve doesn't waver. The new plan I've concocted revolves around her. She'll probably hate me for it, but I don't give a fuck.

"Let's go, Spada," the guard barks from behind me, yanking my arm.

I take a step back, pulling out of Nera's embrace.

Keeping my eyes from sliding to the left, where Zahara is standing, is a losing battle. I never stood a chance. Is she real or simply a figment of my imagination? My fingers itch to reach out and brush her hand, to confirm she's actually flesh and blood. Why won't she look at me again?

She's scared of you.

Scared? Doesn't she know she's the only person on earth who has no reason to fear me? She knows me.

My point exactly.

Fuck.

"I said, let's go." The guard's grip on my arm tightens.

I force my attention back to Nera. "We need to talk."

"We'll come tomorrow."

"Just you, Nera," I say.

Zahara's body tenses. She tries to hide it, but I spot the look of utter betrayal on her face. I swallow the guilt. This game just got too dangerous, and I won't risk *her* being caught in the crossfire and getting hurt. She's out.

I squeeze my hands into fists, fighting the urge to take another step closer to her. I mustn't. With these fuckers watching my every move, I can't risk showing even an ounce of affection. It would immediately raise the vultures' suspicions.

But I would kill to see her eyes again.

My clever little spy.

My ally.

My... friend.

The restraint I've been holding on to crumbles.

I raise my cuffed hands and tenderly caress her cheek with my knuckles. "Hello, Zahara."

She doesn't even look at me.

"Now, Spada." The guard tugs on my arm, and I let my hands fall away from Zahara's face. Then, I turn around and head toward the prison transport.

Walking away.

Away from the fragile peace that has found me in the most unusual place. Tranquility that lasted barely a few minutes, but I'll remember it for years to come.

The urge to look over my shoulder... to steal just one last glance... just a tiny little glimpse, is ripping me apart. Somehow, someway, I manage to prevail. I can't risk giving myself away. Can't draw attention to her. Someone who shouldn't might easily see.

As soon as I get in the vehicle, the door slams behind me. The thud echoes through the cab like the drop of a heavy granite slab over a tomb. Sealing me inside. With one path forward.

Will she still remember me after the letters stop?

No, that pesky voice at the back of my head admonishes. ***And it's better that way.***

For the first time in years, I agree with the asshole. Forgetting me would be a safer bet. For her.

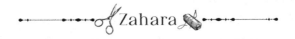

Zahara

Just you, Nera.

Massimo's words ring in my head as I hurry along the dirt path toward the parking lot. My vision is so blurred by tears that

I can barely see where I'm stepping. I lift my arm and brush the wetness away with my sleeve.

That bastard.

"Zara! Wait!" my sister calls after me.

I quicken my pace. I'm in no shape to talk with her now. The only thing I want to do is curl up in a dark corner and cry in peace.

My arms are still covered in goose bumps after coming face-to-face with Massimo for the first time. I didn't expect him to be here. If I knew he was going to be at the funeral today, I would have put foundation. The rash on my face afterward would have been worth it. It might be stupid and vane, but I always saw myself wearing makeup whenever I imagined meeting him. I wanted him to take that first look at me and find me pretty. Instead, I stood silent like a moron because I couldn't think of anything to say. Something else I could have prepared in advance. But I wasn't prepared. Wasn't ready. Years of waiting... longing to meet him at last, and I still wasn't ready.

Saying that he looks different from what I imagined is the understatement of the millennium. I expected a lean guy with an athletic built, similar to the young man I saw in Mom's pictures. So when I noticed the mountain-of-a-man in a prison uniform, covered in tattoos and with his head shaved, my mind blanked. But then, our gazes clashed.

And I knew.

They say the eyes are the windows to the soul, and the moment I saw his—clever, ruthless, scheming—I knew. That terrifying-looking man is my "pen pal." Even without the prison uniform... Even if there were a dozen other men around... I still would have recognized him.

When he made his approach toward Nera and me, my heart was beating so rapidly that I was afraid I was going to have a heart attack. In a way, I've always perceived Massimo as somewhat unreal. Untouchable. Out of reach. Maybe that's why I found it so easy to open up to him. Seeing him here, in front of me, as a real flesh-and-blood entity, almost made me faint. And my stupid heart sang with joy.

Until he crushed it with one simple sentence.

Just you, Nera.

I should have known.

With Dad gone, Massimo doesn't need me anymore. I won't have inside access to whoever takes over the Family. Therefore, I'm no longer of any use to him.

"Zara?" Nera catches up with me in the parking lot. "Are you okay?"

"Yes." I grab the door handle and slip inside her car, dropping onto the passenger seat.

She watches me for a few seconds through the window, then rounds the hood and gets behind the wheel.

"It's just the two of us now." Her voice is soft as she stares at the crowd still lingering beyond the windshield. "Would you like to stay at my place for a bit? I don't like the idea of you alone in that house."

I nod.

Far to the left, the prison transport van has just pulled out of the parking lot and is turning onto the main road. We both follow it with our eyes until the vehicle disappears around the curve.

"What do you think Massimo wants to talk with me about?" Nera mumbles.

"You'll find out tomorrow, I guess."

I have no idea what he wants to discuss with my sister. Maybe he wants to lay a claim to our family's properties. That would fit with his cunning methods.

I don't fucking care.

He already claimed the only thing I care about. My heart. And he squashed it.

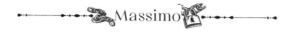

Massimo

I should have noticed that something was off.

As soon as I set foot in the yard, a familiar sensation tingled at the back of my neck, but I was distracted after my first glimpse of Zahara. The impact of that meeting left me feeling like the ground had been pulled from under my feet. Her eyes... I couldn't stop thinking about that look in her eyes, the one of stark, unflinching recognition. Preoccupied as all hell by that, I completely neglected my screaming instincts. I was halfway across the yard when the warning finally registered.

Too few inmates.

Usually, there'd be over a hundred men outside during the rec hour. Everyone from Block D. Just the suckers locked up in solitary or those taking part in an online class would miss their time outdoors. But as my eyes scan the yard, I count barely twenty.

The group of Chinese prisoners I struck up a solid pact with is not in their regular spot. Their bench in the far left corner is empty. The Lenox boys typically play basketball on the court, but they are nowhere in sight. Two of Kiril's guys who've stuck by me after his departure aren't here, either. Basically, all of my staunchest allies in this dump are absent from the yard.

I look up at the nearest guard tower. Normally at this time, there are two COs with guns at the ready against the side railing. Neither of them are there. And no other guards are hanging around inside the perimeter.

Fully alert, but continuing my stroll as if nothing's wrong, I eye the men who are present. What direction will the first strike come from?

Fights and random attacks are a regular occurrence around here. Small skirmishes or all-out brawls, petty squabbles or serious vendettas—they tend to share a few common traits. One, they are rarely premeditated. And two, prison personnel is never involved.

Right now, everything reeks of a setup.

Someone wants me dead.

That's nothing new. Many have tried to off me, hoping to take over my reigning position at the zoo.

But this, this speaks of desperation. Whoever wants my head, wants it bad enough that they've found a way to bring COs into the mix. Or, rather, take them out.

I'm nearly at my favorite pull-up bar by the iron pile where I like to hang out when two guys split off from the larger group by the fence and head my way. Late twenties. Heavily muscled. I've seen them in the chow hall, but we've never interacted. Before now, they kept to themselves and out of my way. If memory serves, both are lifers.

They approach with caution, hands held behind their backs. I move so I'm directly under the pull-up bar and wait. The men exchange a quick look. And then, they charge me. Each wielding a knife.

I jump, grab ahold of the bar, and kick the nearest asshole's chest with both of my feet, sending him flying backward. Leaping down, I land right next to the other attacker, just as he swipes his weapon at me. Not a tiny, easily concealed switchblade, but a big-ass thirteen-inch retractable stiletto. I punch him in the face while he plunges his knife into my left shoulder. The fucker stumbles back, spraying the packed dirt with blood as he shakes his head.

My shoulder feels like it's on fire when I wrench the blade from my flesh. Gripping the hilt, I bury the steel in the shithead's belly, aiming for his liver. He screams and backs up, pressing his hands to the gushing wound with the protruding dagger.

"Spada! Watch out!" someone yells.

I spin around just in time to avoid getting stabbed in the

back and grab the other dickwad's wrist. Squeezing, I enjoy the melody of grinding bones. With my other hand, I grip the front of the guy's shirt and, mentally blocking another jolt of pain in my shoulder, slam my forehead into his ugly mug. Not giving him time to recover, I drive my knee into his midsection and send him toppling to the ground. A cloud of dust rises around us as I drop onto his chest and wrap my hands around his throat.

"Who sent you?" I snarl.

"I don't... know."

I squeeze his neck harder. "I'm going to kill you, and then I'll go after your family! Who was it?"

"I... I swear," he wheezes. "I don't know. The new guard, on the morning shift... paid us off."

"Name?!" I roar into his rapidly purpling face.

Hands grab me from behind, pulling me off the asshole. I try to fight them off, but three COs wrestle me away and start dragging me out of the yard. I keep raging, digging my feet into the ground and throwing punches indiscriminately when I feel a pinch on the side of my neck. My muscles immediately go slack as if they've turned to jelly, and a few breaths later, everything fades to black.

The stench of mold invades my nostrils. I don't even need to open my eyes to know where I am. Solitary confinement. My frequent stopover; a home away from home every couple of months. What does it say when I can pinpoint the hole by its smell?

The screech of metal behind me signals the cell door opening. With a groan, I roll over on the putrid mattress and eye my visitor. My buddy Sam's face floats in front of me, my vision still blurred from the tranquilizer I got spiked with.

"I need you to find a way for me to speak with those two motherfuckers," I croak.

"I'm afraid that's not possible, Mr. Spada." He sets a tray of food on the rusty desk next to the bunk. "They offed each other shortly after they were brought to the infirmary."

"How convenient. Who was on guard at the ward while they managed to get that done?"

"Some new guy. He was transferred here two days ago, but I haven't caught his name, yet."

"Is there a way I can have a chat with him?"

Sam straightens and takes a quick look over his shoulder before replying. "Seems he was in a traffic accident on his way home. He didn't make it."

I shake my head, but not because the fucking thing is still ringing. Though it is.

Alright, someone wants me dead. And when their plan to take me out failed, they quickly covered their tracks.

The fact that they tried isn't what's bothering me. It's the timing.

This scheme was put into place right after Nuncio was assassinated. A coincidence or something more?

You don't believe in coincidences.

No, I don't.

Nuncio's death and the attack on me must be connected. But how? What am I not seeing? And who the fuck would benefit from having my stepfather dead?

There's no trouble brewing between our Family and other organizations, I made sure of that. And business has been booming, so it can't be for money. Power, that's the only logical motive. And if I'm right, it leaves Leone as the suspect. He's the only one who stands to gain substantially with Nuncio out of the picture. Did he somehow get a whiff of who's really been running things in Boston and decided to take me out, too?

Jesus fuck! What if he found out that Zahara had been feeding me inside info?

I leap off the bunk and grab the front of Sam's uniform. "Did anyone read my mail?"

"What?" he chokes out. "No! Of course not!"

"If you're lying to me, I'll fucking end you!"

"I swear, Mr. Spada. Me and Jonas are the only ones who ever touch it before it's sent out to be delivered. The post guy who comes to get it is solid, too. I've known him a long time and I'd vouch for him, honest."

The vise squeezing my chest eases off. *She's safe.* Everyone else can drop dead right in this instant, as far as I'm concerned.

We'll need to stop all communication. Just in case. It will mean no more letters. No more soothing peace for my soul. It doesn't matter. Her safety is the only thing that does. And to make sure Zahara stays unharmed, I'll have Peppe stick to her like a fucking magnet. Protecting her has just become his top priority, with a "fire at will" command to shoot anyone who looks or even breathes at her the wrong way.

I let go of Sam's shirt and gesture toward the door. The sound of his retreating steps resonates off the solid walls, followed by the loud thud of the cell door shutting behind him. I look up at the cracked ceiling, but it's not the crumbling drywall that I see. It's a pair of honey-brown eyes, watching me. Recognizing me. Seeing me.

Chapter
Ten

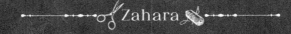

Zahara

Two months later

"Here." I hand Nera a glass of water, still holding her hair back with my other hand.

As soon as she returned from visiting Massimo this morning, she went straight into the bathroom. She's been puking the entire afternoon.

I'm still struggling to wrap my mind around the fact that my sister is pregnant. And that her scumbag of a stalker-turned lover-boy left, disappearing into thin air. If I ever set eyes on the asshole, I'm going to kill him.

"Do you want me to get you some ginger tea?"

"No." She slowly rises to her feet. "I think I'm good."

I lower the toilet lid and sit down while she drags herself to the sink and brushes her teeth.

"I thought morning sickness hits only, well, in the morning."

"I think this is more of a reaction to my conversation with Massimo."

Hearing his name is like taking a sledgehammer right to the chest.

It's been almost ten weeks since our father's funeral. Nera was supposed to meet with Massimo the next day, but when she called the prison to confirm protocol, she was informed that our stepbrother was in solitary confinement and his visitation privileges were revoked for two months. I assume it meant no mail, either, but I'm not certain since I haven't bothered to write. I didn't realize just how much writing those letters meant to me until I stopped. But I'm done.

They say words can hurt you worse than any weapon. It's absolutely true. With three little words, Massimo slashed through my heart, shredding it into a million bleeding pieces. Slicing the silly hope that lay within.

Just you, Nera.

His thoughtless words have wounded me too deeply, and I can't seem to get them out of my head. Like a never-ending nightmare, they fester in my restless mind, displacing my former daydreams. My daytime fantasies of our first meeting, how I imagined it would happen between us. His arms would wrap around me in a tight, tight hug. He'd squeeze so hard, I wouldn't be able to breathe.

God, I'm so stupid! All I can tell myself is, *As if.* I'd laugh at my foolish ass if I wasn't hurting so much. But what makes this whole thing infinitely worse? I still dream about him. Only now, I have an actual face that haunts me in my sleep. Every night, it's him and me, surrounded by people dressed in black. And then, there's that brief, light touch of his fingers on my cheek. Even held captive by the sandman, I can still feel it like a physical caress. My dumb, dumb heart just doesn't want to let it go.

Doesn't want to let *him* go.

Massimo.

"What did he say?" I ask.

Nera looks up and our gazes meet in the mirror. "He wants me to marry Batista Leone."

I stare at my sister in shock. "What?"

"As it happens, all those years, our father was just Massimo's puppet. It's our stepbrother who's been controlling the Family. He called all the shots even before he got locked up. And he intends to keep doing so until he gets released and takes over officially. If I'm married to Leone, it ensures he keeps holding the reins of the Family."

"That's... insane," I choke out. "You can't marry that old pig."

"I have to. It's the only way to keep my baby safe."

"I don't understand."

"Leone is the one who ordered the hit on our dad."

My jaw hits the floor. The filthy bootlicker who followed Dad everywhere like a fucking pup? "I... Are you sure?"

"Yes. And Leone won't hesitate to kill my child if he thinks the baby's existence will pose a threat to him."

"And Massimo wants you to marry the asshole?!"

Nera grips the edge of the sink and drops her head. "Yes. And convince Leone to claim the baby as his. Massimo has some serious dirt on that bastard and he'll use it to keep Leone in check, turning him into nothing but a figurehead. Just like Dad. And I'll be there to ensure everything goes smoothly."

"No!" I spring off the toilet and grab her hand. "You can't do this. You can't. We... We'll run away."

A sad smile tugs at the corners of my sister's lips. "I told Massimo the same thing." She wraps her arms around me, pulling me into her embrace. "But Leone will track us down. I can't risk my baby's life, Zara. I'd rather trade the next four years of my own in exchange for his or her safety. Massimo and I made a deal. I'll marry Leone and do our stepbrother's bidding. And once Massimo is out, he'll let me walk away and cut all ties with the Family."

I bite my tongue so I won't scream at her. How could she be so naive? Massimo will never let her go. He'll just find another role for her and the kid that suits his needs.

"Alright," I mumble into her hair. "We will make it work. And Massimo will keep his promise."

I'll find a way to hold him to it.

Massimo

Anger roils through my veins as the guard escorts me down the hall, toward the visitation room. I thought my orders yesterday were clear—one visit per week. Yet, my stepsister has dared to come today, too.

The heavy metal door opens with a hollow squealing sound, revealing a woman seated at the table in the middle of the room with her back to me.

Glancing at the guard beside me, I give him a look that tells him to kill the camera. His subtle nod makes it clear that he's understood. Before he even leaves, the red light in the corner dies.

The instant that door shuts behind him, my self-control snaps.

"What the fuck is this, Nera?"

My stepsister rises and slowly turns around. But it's not Nera.

It's Zahara.

The fury within me morphs into terror. As I cross the charged expanse between us, the clang of the chains attached to the cuffs on my hands and feet fills the room. The sound reminds me of a funeral march. Hers.

"What are you doing here?" I whisper.

"I heard about the deal you made with my sister." Honey-brown eyes meet mine, and I find myself struggling to breathe. "And I came to make certain you'll keep your word."

For a moment, I can't even remember what deal she's talking about, too stunned by her being here, right in front of me. Talking to me. It's the first time I've heard her voice. So soft. Like a fuzzy blanket. I don't sleep much, and I rarely dream. But I have no doubt her melodic voice will echo through my dreams tonight. Maybe the nocturnal siren will read one of her letters to me. *Bobbins, and stitches, and seams...* I'll gladly spend my somnolent hours listening to nothing more than sewing terms. As long as Zahara speaks them.

"Will you? Keep your word?" Her tone is gentle. But the look in her hypnotic eyes is unyielding.

"Why do you think I wouldn't?" I rasp.

"Because I know you, Massimo. The instant you're out, you'll dispose of Leone and use Nera as a bargaining chip. You'll make her marry one of your prospective business partners, or, perhaps, someone in another crime organization. Marriage within our Family will be out of the question. Especially if her child is a boy."

I blink, at a loss for words. I *was* considering using Nera to strengthen my ties with Kiril. Why am I surprised Zahara figured me out? She's smart. She knows me. Which places her in even greater danger.

"Whatever my future plans are, they are none of your business. Not anymore." I bend to bring my eyes level with hers. "You're out, Zahara."

"It is my business if it involves my sister." She tilts her chin up. "I'm well aware that I was nothing more than a convenient tool to you. One that you used to further your purposes and now have discarded like a piece of trash. But I will not hang back and watch as you do the same to Nera."

My body shakes with barely suppressed rage. Can't she understand that I have to push her away to keep her safe?

I lift my bound hands and seize her chin between my fingers. For years, I've trudged through spilled blood without a second thought, not giving a fuck about anything or anyone. People were nothing but obstacles or pawns. My stepsisters included.

But now, as I stare into Zahara's eyes, I can barely breathe for the myriad of unexpected feelings overwhelming me. Shame and guilt for ruthlessly using her all these years. Horror that my actions may have painted a target on her back. I spent the last two months thinking about her. Day and night. From the moment our gazes met at Nuncio's funeral, the only thing I've been able to fully focus on is her.

"Nera is your family, and you're throwing her to the wolves!" she continues. "Is there a person in this world that you actually give a fuck about?"

"Just one."

Zahara's eyes widen. She sucks in a breath, keeping her gaze glued to mine. A minute passes. I stand stock-still, my face mere inches from hers, marveling at the peace that has once again suffused every fiber of my being.

I've always been a volatile person, and that trait has intensified a hundredfold in prison. My violent outbursts have ensured I spend large stretches of my sentence in solitary. I'm angry. Constantly on alert. Ready to lash out for the tiniest little reason. But now, with her next to me, I just want to close my eyes and enjoy this unexpected bliss.

She's like a bandage over a bleeding wound. A remedy for my madness.

My gaze wanders to her mouth, and my thumb slides up of its own volition, caressing her lower lip. All I need is to lean forward just a little and—

Fuck!

Stepping back, I let go of her face. I must have finally lost my fucking mind in this dump—there is no other explanation.

"You need to leave, Zahara."

"No. I'm not moving from this spot until you guarantee me that you'll keep your promise to Nera. The minute you take over as the don, she and her child are free to walk away."

"And why would I do that?"

"Because if this ploy with Leone goes ahead, you'll still need me. I'll continue being your eyes and ears without anyone ever knowing. Even my sister."

She's right. I need her, but not in the way she believes. Without Zahara, I'm certain there won't be anything left of *me*.

"Absolutely not," I growl. "It's too dangerous."

"If your plan fails, the danger will be even greater. Nera and I will end up in Leone's hands for good. He already planned to marry Nera off into the Albanian faction. I'll probably meet the same fate."

"I will not put you in harm's way, Zahara."

"You had no problem doing it before."

"Before was different. Even if someone caught you going through Nuncio's shit, your dad would never have hurt you. Still, I have regrets. Something else I'll need to live with. But this time, you'd be in the middle of a rabid wolf's den."

"But you're okay with sending Nera in?" She stands straighter, her chin lifting. "My sister and I are a package deal. I'll help you see this through to the end, and you'll set Nera free. If you refuse, I'll convince her to run. We'll take our chances on our own."

"Leone will kill you both when he finds you. And trust me, he *will* find you."

"Maybe. But it's a risk I'm willing to take."

I watch her, standing before me looking so innocent and young. In her alluring silk blouse with her luscious locks tumbling down her back, she reminds me of one of those delicate porcelain dolls my mother had around. She seems fragile, but there isn't even a trace of softness in her steely expression. Only determination and resolve.

Fear explodes in my stomach. She truly means it. If I say no, they will both run, and Leone will chase them. And there's no way I could save her while I'm locked up in this hellhole.

"I swear on Mom's memory, Massimo. We will run."

She'll do it. Accept her terms.

No!

Then you've just signed her death sentence.

I squeeze my eyes shut. "You won't place yourself in even the slightest peril. No calls. No more visits. Only letters."

"Fine," she says, tugging down the cuff of her sleeve. "How are you going to make Leone accept the idea of marriage to Nera?"

"Salvo will come see her tomorrow, and he will bring her some documents. It's all she'll need. Leone will agree to everything."

"Is that it?"

"Yes."

Zahara nods.

"You are not as I imagined you, you know?" I admit. At her questioning look, I add, "No pigtails."

A tiny smile pulls at her lips as her gaze moves up to the top of my freshly shaved head. "You're not as I imagined you, either. No hair."

I chuckle. The sound seems strange. There aren't many things that have made me laugh in the past decade and a half.

"Promise me you will be careful," I whisper. "Please."

"I will."

Charily, I bow my head. "Make sure Peppe comes with you when you move to Leone's. Keep him close."

Her eyebrow arches. "He's one of yours, then?"

"Yes. If things go south, he'll know what to do."

She doesn't argue, doesn't question. We just stand there as I drink her in. Yesterday, Nera told me that Zahara has vitiligo. That's what the skin discoloration on her face is. I'd never heard of the condition before, so I grabbed the phone from Sam to google it, needing to know if it's causing her pain or other ill effects. It doesn't, which is a relief. I can't handle the idea of anything hurting Zahara.

Jesus fuck, I can't believe I placed her into a position where she needed to take so many risks for me. Because of my selfish plans. And she'll be doing it again. But this time, the stakes are much, much higher.

I let the image of her etch itself on my mind because I know it'll be years before I'll see her. Seconds, then minutes pass while we stare at each other in silence, surrounded by the dull gray of cold confinement.

"You should go now," I make myself say.

"Okay." She breaks our locked stare and pivots toward the door, her eyes slowly casting downward.

As she passes me, our arms brush against each other. Without thinking, I reach out and take her hand.

Zahara's sharp intake of breath echoes through the room. She stops. We stand next to each other at the center of the gloomy space—she is facing the door, and I'm staring at the wall on the opposite side. I can feel her heartbeat where the heel of my palm is pressed to the pulse point on her wrist.

"Don't get killed," I whisper.

"Don't kill anyone else," she whispers back. "At least, not in front of witnesses."

A small smile twists my lips. I stroke her wrist one last time and reluctantly let her hand slip out of mine.

Her heels tap on the hard concrete floor.

Walking away.

Taking that peaceful serenity with her.

CHAPTER
eleven

⊶ Zahara ⊷

Letter #159

Dear Massimo,

In your last letter, you were curious about how we're handling all the new things in our lives. No need to worry, Nera and I have settled into our new home. Everything is different but going as well as you can expect.

Her new husband has been under a lot of work stress lately, though. He's not happy with the new direction the management is pressing him to take. But with the aid of well-gathered data, Nera helped him realize that the company stakeholders would not be pleased to learn of his past transgressions, especially of his involvement in the early retirement of the previous CEO. So, after he carefully reviewed the presented documents, he now understands that change is in everyone's best interest, and I'm sure he won't put up any more fuss.

Nera is also adjusting to her new role in the firm. Apparently, there was a personnel issue that came up yesterday that required immediate attention. One of the employees was caught slipping proprietary company info to a major competitor in New York. Upon discovery, management insisted that Nera fire him herself. Shouldn't those kinds of tasks be handled by HR? My sister takes her job responsibilities seriously, but she still spent the rest of the night throwing up in the bathroom.

    Zahara

    PS: Are you still having trouble sleeping?

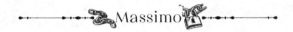

Letter #160

Zahara,

    I understand your sister's unhappiness with being pressured to personally handle the personnel issue, but she knew the stakes when she agreed to take on the job. In business, maintaining the stakeholders' respect is always a concern. They will only remain loyal to the brand if they are continually assured that the leadership is capable of making hard choices and standing firm when required. She'll need to get used to rolling up her sleeves and doing things herself, on occasion. This time, I'm sure it was necessary to make an example of the employee who broke the NDA. Company policy would have required it.

    Nera mentioned that my Balkan friend was very efficient in washing and detailing her car last month. With such prompt and thorough service, she might be tempted to make frequent returns to his establishment in the future. However, she should keep in mind that top-level service commands proportionally high rates. She mustn't throw away her money and should only use that place when the local guy, Primo, isn't available.

    As for your question—the answer is yes. But that's okay. I got used to functioning on three to four hours of sleep a long time ago. Last night, an inmate next door was snoring so loudly that his bunk buddy tried to suffocate the cunt with a pillow. He failed, unfortunately. I might try getting myself thrown back in the hole (that's solitary confinement) one of these days. With the right attitude, the experience is almost like being on vacation. The only downside, the absence of people starts fucking with my head if my trip lasts more than a few days.

I didn't believe the bullshit about humans being pack animals until the first time I ended up in the hole. Did you know that silence has a sound? It's a faint grind, like the creak of wooden boards in an old, abandoned house. You don't hear it at first. But after a while, it feels as if your fucking skull is cracking from how loud it is. Once when my lonely ass was stuck in that six-by-six hole for an extended stay, I started talking to myself, and I don't mean just mindless mumbling. One time, I had a very heated, hours-long discussion with my inner voice, trying to convince the motherfucker that it was not the right time to invest in government bonds. I won.

So, why haven't you sent me any new sketches? Are you on a sewing hiatus? Or are you mad at me because I mistook the dress you designed for Salvo's mother for a bathrobe? You can't hold that shit against me. What do I know of women's fashion? But you... You do. You've got talent. You should follow your passion and open your own shop.

M.

PS: Tell Peppe that I need my laundry done next Sunday.

Letter #207

Dear Massimo,

Batista Leone is not doing well. Last night we had to call the family doctor for an urgent home visit because Batista was having trouble breathing. His blood pressure was through the roof, and at first, we thought it was the result of him spending three days in a row getting wasted at one of the clubs. However, the doc said there are other worrisome health factors.

Nera has been going out of her mind over the possibility of something happening to her husband. She's scared shitless about us ending up alone again. It's still too long until we'll have you by our side. How will we manage?

Nera's work has also been causing her stress. The new chicken supplier from the South wants to renegotiate the rates. They demanded an urgent meeting next Wednesday. I managed to convince Nera to have Salvo attend the meeting in her place. She's in the last trimester of her pregnancy and shouldn't travel.

Just so you know, I'm pretty sure she's pissed about being put in this situation. She may never forgive you for getting her into this mess. To be honest—I won't, either. Even though it was the lesser evil among other, more terrible options. I'm curious if you feel even an ounce of remorse for doing it. Even a little? Even if the end justifies the means? Do you feel ashamed for putting my sister through so much grief? Is there, somewhere deep down inside you, a tiny frisson of self-reproach, perhaps hidden under that loud, ruthlessly cunning, and manipulative persona?

Anyway, I digress…

The C-level execs finally got used to the new management structure and have stopped voicing concerns every second day. That only happened after Nera was successful in expunging the problematic investments our lovely neighbors were allowed to make in the entertainment venues. Hopefully, things will stay calm from now on. Although Brio still makes a cutting remark here and there, no one pays much attention to him anymore. Adriano, however, is once more very insistent on expanding into the hotel market. His voice is heard loud and clear.

Speaking of Mr. Deep Pockets… You know, the more I think about it, the more I'm certain he simply doesn't care about his wife's skanky antics. But for the life of me, I don't understand why someone *like him would choose to stay with a woman like her. The other evening, I saw the two of them during a working lunch at the Villa, and there's no love between them, as far as I can tell.*

Zahara

PS: Do you regret it? Killing the guy who shot Elmo? Would you do it again, knowing the consequences?

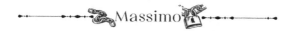

Letter #208 (draft 1)

Why are you interested in Adriano's relationship with his wife? Do you like him? Has that shithead been hitting on you? Because if he has, I'll arrange for one of his own transport trucks to run him over and then back up to plow into him in reverse! There'll be nothing left of that dickwad other than a red fucking stain on the road!

I crumple my letter and throw it in the trash can.

Fucking hell!

Letter #208 (draft 2)

Why does it matter if Adriano's wife cheats on him? If the stupid motherfucker knows it and does nothing about it, he's a fucking sissy. Is there something between you two? If he's laid a—

Fuck. Fuck. *FUCK!*

I flush this goddamned attempt at a note down the toilet.

Letter #208 (draft 3)

Can you find out Adriano's daily routine? See if he likes to take walks during rush hour. Could you get me the day and maybe the approximate time? Please? I'm just curious to know what he does with his free time.

Crumbling the sheet of paper, I stuff it into the loud-fucking-breather's throat. The dickhead shouldn't have walked by my workout bench. Next time he'll know. The fuck.

This is ridiculous, that irritating inner asshole comments. **Maybe you should think about talking to someone. You know, like a professional.**

"I swear, I'll find a way to evict your ass from my head."

Good luck with that.

Letter #208

Zahara,

Even if I knew the consequences of my actions in advance, I'm not sure I could have controlled myself. When I held Elmo in my arms, felt his blood oozing through my fingers... My fingers, that were covering his no-longer beating heart... I knew in my soul there was nothing that could be done for him. And I just lost it.

I was well aware of the countless witnesses to what I was about to do, but that didn't stop me from offing the motherfucker who shot your brother right there on the spot. It was as if I was seized by some animalistic urge. If I was thinking rationally, and with hindsight, knowing that I'd lose eighteen years of my life, I would have waited to kill that asshole until no one else was around. But clearly, higher reasoning wasn't something I possessed at that time. Logic didn't stand a chance as I watched Elmo die.

As for your sister—she knew the deal. I didn't trick her into accepting it, nor lie about what she'd face. So, no. I don't feel bad. I am, however, sorry if that disappoints you. But something tells me it doesn't.

You know me well enough not to be surprised. And you also know that it had to be done, despite it being a bitter pill to swallow. You know our world. How it works. You always have. You've been treading these waters for years, which is completely my fault. And I do regret that.

If I could turn back time and fix my one mistake in the past, I wouldn't change my actions on the day Elmo died. I would use that one chance to stop myself from writing you my first letter. Or I'd burn that letter to ash before it ever got sent. Because the one thing I truly regret in this life is involving you in my mess and putting you in danger. For that, I hope you'll find a way to forgive me someday.

I'm very sorry to hear that Leone isn't feeling well. Let's hope the slimy pig gets better. There is always a Plan B, but I would rather not have to put it into motion.

A friend of mine will reach out to Nera in the near future. Please make sure he is granted the favor he asks of her.

M.

PS: Does Adriano visit often?

Letter #241

Dear Massimo,

Lucia said her first word today. It was "no." I'm not

127

surprised—that kid is a handful. Iris almost had a heart attack a few days ago when Lucia got ahold of my jewelry box and somehow managed to break one of the necklaces Dad bought me. It took me a while to convince her that it doesn't need to be fixed, I'll never wear it anyway. Seeing those trinkets always leaves a sour taste in my mouth. It reminds me that Dad never remembered I can't wear anything other than platinum. I mentioned it to him at least a dozen times, but he still just kept buying gold pieces. He probably thought gold looked more extravagant, and I simply stopped bringing it up after a while.

Lately, I've been thinking about Dad a lot. I spent so many years being angry at him, blaming him for always putting the business first, instead of his daughters. But now, as days drag on without him, I keep remembering the good times. All the piggyback rides he used to give me and Nera. And how he'd let me tie his tie for him, especially after Mom died. He might not have been the best parent... Actually, that's a given, but... I don't know. I think I judged him too harshly. Or, maybe, I just want to remember him as a better man than he was.

Speaking of good times... I'm working on a super cute jacket for Lucia. With puff sleeves and sequins on the lapels. I'll probably use pink velvet. She's going to look adorable! (It makes the hassle I went through with the store's customer service reps after my order was screwed up worth it!) My only worry is that velvet should only be dry-cleaned, and this kid can be a bit of a disaster.

Which reminds me, Peppe says he'll be spending next weekend doing laundry. It wasn't in his original plans, but something happened—not sure what—and I guess it's serious, because he mentioned he'll need to use bleach to handle the stains.

And since I'm telling you about all this cleaning, here's another thing: Nera had to send her car to be washed twice this week. Your buddy managed to remove all the sticky grime, but as you cautioned, he did quote her a higher price on her last visit. The prepaid services package she had has been used up. Since it *was urgent, Nera had to accept the new rate, but she'll probably talk with you about it on Thursday. Maybe there's a way to convince your pal to give her another "friend discount."*

In other news, Batista is getting worse. Remember that Plan B you mentioned? It might be time to start seriously considering it.

Zahara

PS: Why do you keep bringing up Adriano? No, he hasn't dropped by. And he hasn't been here since that lunch, which was more than a year ago. Why are you asking about him so much?

Letter #258

Dear Massimo,

When my jewelry box went missing months ago, I thought Lucia had been playing with it again and must have hidden it somewhere around the house. After a while, I completely forgot about it.

So imagine my surprise when, this morning, a courier dropped off a package for me—a package bearing a logo from a distinguished custom jeweler, The House of Dubois in Paris. Can you guess what was inside? No? Okay, I'll tell you. My old jewelry box. And it contained six necklaces and two bracelets. Stunning pieces that were exact replicas of my old ones, with one exception. These were made of platinum instead of gold.

It was you, wasn't it?

I did not tell you about the necklaces so you'd buy me new ones. But… Thank you.

Zahara

PS: What happened to the original gold ones?

Massimo

Letter #259

Zahara,

I gave instructions for them to be thrown into the Seine. They are at the bottom of the polluted river—a place where items that have caused you harm belong.

I also figured that having the gold pieces around may stir up bad memories for you, and that's not something I want you to experience. I know your father gave them to you, and that might make them sentimental and irreplaceable, but you should only remember the good times with your dad, not the bittersweet moments. I've never been Nuncio's greatest fan, but there's one thing I can tell you about him with absolute certainty. He loved you, although he had a shitty way of showing it more often than not. Focus on the positives instead. You can still take comfort that he chose the jewelry that you like, and now you can enjoy it more fully.

Did you try on the new pieces? I had each one extensively tested at a special lab to ensure they would cause no adverse reactions before they were delivered. It took the bastards four months—almost twice the time Dubois needed to make your jewelry pieces in the first place. Which is why they didn't arrive in time for your 20th birthday as planned.

So... Happy birthday, Zahara.

M.

CHAPTER
Twelve

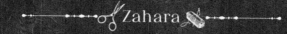 Zahara

Leone Villa

One day following the failed assassination attempt on Nera

I WATCH MY SISTER CROSS THE KITCHEN AND STOP IN front of the magnet-covered fridge. She reaches out and glides her fingers over the one with a picture of an old bridge, then she quickly disappears into her bedroom where Lucia is having an afternoon nap.

Shaking my head, I bring my attention back to what's happening in the yard, directly under the window. Nera's stalker-boy is still there, giving all kinds of orders to the security guards. Hopefully, he won't kill any more staff today. We need all the manpower we have in case whoever tried to assassinate Nera decides to try again.

A shiver runs through my body at the thought of last night's events. The look on my sister's face when she barged into my room where I was sleeping, pleading for help. The sight of the long-haired stranger sprawled out on her bed and covered in blood. The crunch of broken glass under my feet as I rushed across the darkened living room to get towels from the bath-room. The assassin's lifeless body slumped on the balcony. And I know there were more, scattered around the grounds of Leone Villa. Nera mentioned that it was a professional team of hitmen. Her "demon" disposed of them all.

I press my lips together, struggling with the conflicting emo-tions roiling within me. I've despised the guy for a long time for making Nera fall in love with him and then vanishing into thin air for more than three years. He left my sister pregnant and alone. She had me, but it wasn't the same. Her heart has been trapped in purgatory.

But now... now I see that there is more to their story than I thought. Because her stalker-boy almost died trying to save her in the middle of the night. He singlehandedly stopped the team of heavily armed hitmen who had my sister in their sights. And then, this morning, he sliced the throat of Leone's Head of Security for allowing the situation to get that far. And I see how he looks at her—like she is his sun, his moon, and the stars.

Must be nice... to have a man look at you like you're his entire universe.

As I'm closing the drapes, my phone starts ringing. I pull it from the back pocket of my jeans and narrow my eyes. An un-known number. Strange.

Hesitantly, I hit the green button to accept and bring the phone to my ear. "Yes?"

"Are you hurt?"

The phone nearly slips out of my hand. I lean on the wall for support and suck in a deep breath. It's not enough. My head begins to spin.

It's been years since I've heard his voice.

"I swear to God, Zahara, if you don't tell me this instant whether you are unharmed, I'll find a fucking way to get there tonight, just so I can see it for myself! I'm losing my shit over here!" Massimo thunders on the other end of the line.

"I'm alright," I choke out. "How did you find ou—"

"That some assholes infiltrated the house while you slept? Of course I found out!"

"I'm fine. But they were after Nera. She's the one you should be calling."

"I don't give the slightest fuck about your sister right now." His voice drops dangerously low. "Peppe will come get you in twenty minutes. You're getting out of that house."

My hand flies to my chest. His tone is firm and threatening, but I can hear the shaking in his voice. He's not simply worried. He sounds… terrified. For me. Joy and excitement swell within me, spreading until it feels as if a thousand beautiful butterflies are searching for a way out. I've never known Massimo to show concern, never mind be actually worried, for anyone. *Just one*, he said once upon a time when I demanded to know if he gave a fuck about even a single other person. I took it to mean only himself. Dare I hope he meant me? That he cares about me? Just a little bit? Closing my eyes, I try to temper my silly enthusiasm. It's likely he's simply feeling guilty.

"That's not necessary. Nera's stalker-boy has every security guard watching over the house, so you don't have to worry. And you need me here."

"I need you safe! That's an order, not a request."

There is no way I'm leaving my sister, especially now. And I'm not bailing on Massimo. I'm going to see this to the end, no matter the risks.

"Mr. Spada." A muted and nervous male voice comes from Massimo's end of the line. "Someone is coming. I need the phone back."

"Tell me you heard what I said, Zahara!" Hushed, quick words, growled into my ear.

The tang of metal fills my mouth. I must have bitten through my lip.

"I don't take orders from you, Massimo," I whisper. "I'm staying."

"Zahara!"

"I'll mail my next letter in the morning. Take care."

I quickly end the call, but not fast enough, because I still catch Massimo's furious roar across the distance.

Throwing a look at Nera's door to make sure it's still closed, I open the call recorder app on my phone. I installed it a few months ago when I had to contact customer service after my fabric order was messed up, and then, I completely forgot to disable it. Dropping onto the recliner near the window, I hit *Play* on the latest saved file and press the phone to the side of my face.

I keep listening to Massimo's call, over and over, until his voice is so ingrained in my mind that I keep hearing it even after I've turned off my phone.

CHAPTER
Thirteen

·—◦✂Zahara✄◦—·

Letter #294

Dear Massimo,

Still no progress in finding out who was behind the corporate takeover attempt. The temporary staffing Kai arranged from his Sicilian friend's firm is helping to ensure nothing like that happens again. Based on their efforts so far, they're a capable bunch.

As far as other business goes, not much new for me to share with you. Nera is still busy with hiring a suitable replacement to fill the manager position at the Bay View Casino. Kai did not consult with her before firing Lotario on the spot, but though it was a drastic step, it was warranted.

Peppe wanted me to pass on his apologies for not being available to handle the laundry as he was supposed to, but he assured me that it would be taken care of this weekend. Which reminds me—could you PLEASE ask him to stop following me around ALL THE TIME? As soon as I leave my room, he's on my heels, like a puppy. He won't listen when I ask him to back off. I can't even go to the kitchen to get a glass of water without feeling like we're joined at the hip. It's frustrating.

Also, your constant "Leave that house immediately, Zahara" greetings in recent letters are getting old. I'm staying with my sister. Accept it already.

And no, I haven't yet finished that skirt. Lucia caught a bug of some kind and then gave it to me. So, I spent the whole of last week wrapped in a blanket, with a mug of tea pretty much glued to my hand.

Zahara

PS: Have you started the countdown? Just a little over six months left on your sentence.

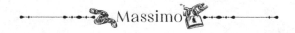

Letter #295

Zahara,

What sort of bug? A flu? A cold? Did you see a doctor and have them check you out?

Why am I even asking? I know you haven't. You can't treat your health so casually, Zahara!

Peppe is following my explicit directions and will continue to do so. That's nonnegotiable, and I consider the discussion finished. Especially with that crazy son of a bitch living under the same roof as you.

I asked around about your sister's stalker-boy and if even half of what I learned is true, that man is seriously fucked-up. He might love Nera and may be committed to keeping the three of you safe, but I still want you to stay away from him.

M.

PS: Yes. 6,387 down; 181 left to go. I've been keeping count since the day I stepped foot in this dump.

PPS: If Mazur ever gives you any trouble, I want to know about it. I'll make sure friends of mine introduce themselves to him, just as they did with your school buddy, Kenneth.

CHAPTER
fourteen

———•ᴥ✄ Zahara ᴥ•———

ALL FOUR OF MY SPOOLS OF BEIGE THREAD ARE GONE. I sigh. Lucia must have taken them to play with. Her newest favorite pastime these days is stealing the bobbins from the basket that sits under my work table and weaving the fibers around and between the legs of the chair and the table, creating a jumbled mess, a sort of net-looking thing. When I asked her about it, she said she was a spider.

I can't believe how fast the little munchkin is growing. She's almost three and such a smart cookie. And on top of that, she has me firmly wrapped around her tiny finger. Or maybe just caught in her pint-sized spider web.

I smile thinking about my niece.

Heading to the living area, I continue my search, collecting the discarded sketches off the coffee table and couch along the way. My apartment at Leone Villa is always a mess. Nera says my stuff spreads as fast as the flu. Zippers, sewing magazines, and partly cut-out patterns litter the floor and furniture. The only stuff I keep organized are things like scissors and needles. Lucia could hurt herself with their sharp points and edges, and I can't have that.

I find my tape measure along with some fabric scraps under one of the cushions, but no reels of thread. I'll have to run out to buy replacements if I want to finish the new dress for Salvo's mother on time. It's probably the tenth I've made for her thus far. She's been keeping me busy, enough that I had to replace Mom's old sewing machine with a new one. Still, my skills are hardly couture for Rosetta to use me exclusively to make her outfits, but it sure seems like she stopped purchasing gowns off the rack. I think that's Salvo's doing. He must be pressuring her to deal with me somehow.

Every time I'm at their house to take Mrs. Canali's measurements or have her try on a dress, Salvo happens to be there. Considering the randomness of my visits, it can't be a coincidence.

I've stayed as far away from Salvo as I could over the years, so why the fuck does he keep insisting we should go out for lunch? There's just something off-putting about him. When he's at the Villa to meet with Nera, I don't leave my room until he's gone. Maybe it's my lack of intimate experience with men, but Salvo's subtle advances are starting to creep me out.

Hopefully, I can avoid him at Brio's party that's coming up next month. I wanted to skip it altogether, but in light of recent developments—specifically, the discovery that Capo Armando is the person behind the assassination attempts on my sister—I need to be there to gather intel about where the rest of *La Famiglia* stands.

Kai has kept Armando locked up in our basement since last night, and from what Nera has told me, he intends to question him. I hope he'll get on with it soon so I can write to Massimo and mail the letter by five. The last thing I want is for it to sit in the collection box the whole weekend. God only knows how I'm going to wrap up that report in a way that wouldn't raise any red flags if my letter were intercepted by a prison guard. It's not as if I can say: *Hey, my brand new brother-in-law just finished cutting the fingers off the guy we've had stashed in the basement, and here's what we learned.*

Hmm, maybe I could use the turkey analogy?

How about: *Kai fowled the turkey that tried to bite off the head of the mommy hen. He finished de-winging and de-legging the beast, and...* No, that sounds stupid. Maybe I should use "pluck" instead.

Spotting a golden strip peeking from under the couch, I reach for it just as I hear the door behind me open.

"I put Lucia down for a nap in your room," I say, rolling up the ribbon I've pulled out. "Did Kai's weird friends finally leave?"

"They did." A raspy male baritone rumbles at my back.

Somewhere in the universe, two neutron stars collide. The force of that impact travels through me. I know that voice. I've been listening to it day and night, playing the two-minute recording of his call on repeat like an obsessed woman. Goose bumps break out across my arms, and all the fine hairs rise as if an electric current just zapped through me. His voice sounds deeper in person. More intense. It's been years since I heard it from only steps away, but I could never forget it. With my breath caught in my throat, I stand up and turn around.

Massimo is lingering in my doorway, his huge form dominating the space, sucking all the oxygen from the room. The perfectly tailored gray suit he's wearing fits him like it's bespoke, accentuating his wide shoulders. The two top buttons of his white dress shirt are undone, revealing hints of the colorful ink on his chest and neck. He looks so polished, so civilized, that for a moment, I find it hard to believe he is the same unscrupulous man who's been haunting me for years. But when my eyes lock with his, I realize it's just an illusion. He is the same vicious predator I've come to know so well. Only shrouded in fancy clothing.

Is this real? Is he? Or is it just my imagination playing tricks?

There are still six months left of his sentence. How can he be here?

I gape at Massimo as he strides across the room, his long steps eating the distance between us way too fast. And once again I find myself battling temporal quicksand. Held captive by my fate but unable to accept it. Years of wanting to be with this man does not mean I'm ready to face him now. I should be used to this feeling. After all, when I went to see him in prison, it took me three hours to psych myself up before I was able to walk through that door.

He stops just in front of me and lifts his hand, then lightly brushes my cheek with his knuckles. "Hello, Zahara."

A shiver runs down my spine. It's as if I'm trapped in a time warp and the scene at my father's funeral is repeating. He *is* real.

"How?" I choke out.

"Salvatore Ajello," he says. "I don't know how that motherfucker managed to pull off what I and the good-for-nothing McBride couldn't do for years, but he did. Ajello's personal attorney arrived with my idiot lawyer this morning, bringing the required paperwork. I was released an hour later."

He's standing so near that his body heat is seeping into me. The blood in my veins turns molten. The breath disappears from my lungs. Bone-shaking tremors rack me inside out, completely obliterating any logical thought.

Massimo's eyes drop to my chest, focusing on the platinum chain and the delicate pearl and diamond teardrop pendant hanging off it. "You're wearing my gift."

"Yes," I choke out, my throat feeling so dry and raw. "I... I have to take it off before I go to sleep, but it doesn't irritate my skin otherwise."

"Good. Saves me a trip to Paris to off Mr. Dubois."

"So... you're a free man." Somehow, I'm able to keep my voice from breaking.

I knew this day would come eventually. And I'm so damn

happy. For him. But I also want to curl into a ball and weep, because this means, whatever this relationship is between the two of us, it's over. He doesn't need me anymore.

After today, I'll lose him.

"Yes." He nods. The tips of his fingers glide over the smooth skin under my left eye, lingering there for a second, but then his hand falls away. "I saw Nera downstairs. Just as I promised, she can leave Cosa Nostra at any time, and I told her so."

I fight my tears, barely keeping them at bay. "And you? What are you going to do now?"

"I'll be summoning the Council and setting up the official takeover of the Family for this weekend. Then, I'm going to focus on finding whoever has been fucking with my life and keeping me in that cage. Once that's done, I'll kill the bastard. Or bastards. Whatever." He glances around the room. "But first, I'll have this house leveled, as well as everything else that belonged to Batista Leone. You should start packing."

Yeah, I guess I should. Whirling around, I head toward my bed where it's pushed into the corner of the room. My legs are trembling so hard, I expect them to fold under me any second.

Holy hell, I can still feel his touch on my face. For just a second—a tiny fraction of a moment—I let those long-suppressed hopes and dreams flare up within me, let myself believe that things between us may have changed. Over the years, he's clearly opened to me. I felt it deep inside my soul. From the day I confronted him in prison, the Massimo I knew transformed into something more. His letters became a lot more open, sharing details about his prison life. His thoughts. His struggles. Even some regrets. And as his letters turned more and more personal, I almost convinced myself that he could have developed some feelings. For me.

A humorless laugh nearly escapes me. I'm still just an idiot who doesn't know when to quit. *Wake up, Zahara! Can't you see he wants you out of his life right away?*

SWEET PRISON

"Kai has an apartment downtown, so we'll move everything there for now," I mumble. "We'll be out of your way by the end of the day."

I have two big suitcases shoved under the bed. Pulling out the larger one, I drag it in front of the dresser and open it right there on the floor. The heat of Massimo's eyes boring into my back is nearly scalding as I start yanking out my clothes and haphazardly dropping everything into the suitcase.

Why is he still standing there? I'm this close to losing my composure, and having him here is making this whole situation a hundred times worse.

I grab a black satin dress off the hook on the closet door and just dump it into the suitcase along with the hanger. It took me almost an hour to iron it last night, but that hardly seems to matter right now. My new lace blouse is next. Then, the cashmere coat. I don't even pay attention to whether anything gets torn or damaged. I just throw in one thing after the other, trying to "pack" as fast as possible because I can't handle being this close to him while I quietly fall apart.

Will I ever see him again?

Behind me, the rhythmic scrape of leather soles on a hardwood floor. Getting closer. My breathing quickens. I pick up my pace, now throwing garments by the armful into the suitcase, while Massimo looms at my back. He's close enough that his next exhale fans across the top of my head. I squeeze my eyes shut, trying to hold myself together.

"I think you misunderstood." The velvety timbre of his voice washes over me, and I try to commit to memory. It might be the last time I hear it.

"Misunderstood what?" I croak.

"You're not leaving with your sister." Massimo dips his head until his mouth is right next to my ear. "You're coming with me."

My body goes utterly still. He's standing so, so close, there's barely any space between us. His stubble lightly brushes my

143

cheek, the rest of him maintaining not much more than the suggestion of distance. Yet still, it feels as if I'm somehow being drawn into his chest. His warm breath wafts over my overheated skin, making me lightheaded while I struggle to process his words.

"Why?" I ask, clutching my maroon alpaca cardigan like a lifeline. Is this simply another one of his games?

He doesn't answer. For what feels like an eternity, Massimo just stands there at my back like some huge immovable statue. My question was simple, so I don't understand why it takes him so long to reply. Perhaps... perhaps he does feel something toward me after all?

"Because I need you, Zahara."

The pounding of my heart skyrockets, becoming so loud it thunders in my ears. Warmth explodes in my chest, swelling and radiating toward my weakened limbs, overtaking my entire—

"I need someone I can trust. Someone who knows what's at stake and who can fill me in on everything I've missed."

The icy grip of winter crushes me, and the joy I felt plummets like a lead balloon. Frost creeps into my bloodstream, supercooling the air in my lungs. Not a spark of the previous warmth remains. *Of course.* Why else would he want me close to him? He's not finished taking over his empire. Not done seizing his due respect and power.

Did you really think there'd be another reason?

I take a deep breath. And then another. At least he's honest. He's always been that with me. But for the first time ever, I hate him for it. I wish he'd lied and said it was because he likes me. I know it's not true, but I'd rather believe a lie right now than face the cold hard truth.

Biting my cheek, I turn around and tilt my head up until our gazes meet.

Dark pools. I had no idea a person's eyes could be the deepest shade of night. His are so dark that I can't distinguish his irises from his pupils. It's like falling into two bottomless black holes, and they are dragging me into their depths.

For most of my life, I rarely met other people's eyes. Largely because I was afraid they'd glimpse the insecurities I tried so hard to hide and would find a way to use them against me. But also, because I didn't want to see what was hidden in their stares. Their unsuppressed opinions of me. How weak I was—for not standing up for myself, for not confronting those who said shit about me. Their convictions that I must be stupid, all because I avoided conflict. Seeing those things in their eyes, made me believe them. I felt small. Worthless. Inadequate. Aside from Nera, who is biased by sisterly love, not a single soul has ever made me feel good about myself.

Until him.

There isn't even a speck of reproach or pity in Massimo's dark gaze as he practically scorches me with his hellish-looking eyes. Trust. Respect. Even admiration. There's something else there, though. A dangerous glint that makes my heart beat even faster. A dark unknown that I can't quite discern.

The way he is looking at me now makes me feel as if I'm brave. And daring. Like I can do anything. Maybe even dance naked through the City Hall Plaza as Nera once threatened to do.

"And what if I say *no*?" I ask. "What if I want to go with my sister?"

Massimo's nostrils flare. His jaw is set in a hard line and the veins in his neck are bulging. He's a rather terrifying sight—towering over me so large and inked and obviously enraged by my questions. If it was anyone else but him, I would have run and hidden by now. But I don't feel threatened by him at all, because even angry, he still looks at me with the same reverence as he did a minute ago.

He fists his hands, which makes his biceps pop inside his

tailored suit. Several seconds pass while he just stares at me. Then, he gives me a curt nod and turns to leave without a word.

I follow him with my eyes as he strides across the room, heading to the door. We both know Nera is the only one getting a free pass. Not me. That was the deal we struck. As the imminent and rightful don, Massimo has every right to make me do whatever the fuck he wants. And still, he is walking away. Respecting my decision. Seeing me as a partner. Traversing level ground.

I have no delusions about the type of person he is. God knows, Massimo is the furthest thing from a saint. He's a killer. A master manipulator who doesn't think twice about disposing of anything or anyone who stands in his way. An unscrupulous, cunning man who used an adolescent girl like a pawn because it served his purpose. But he has never pretended to be something he isn't. Not with me. Is that why I've fallen so crazy in love with him?

"Massimo," I call out.

He's already at the door, but he halts immediately.

"I need half an hour to finish packing," I say. "Then, I'll say goodbye to Nera and Lucia, and we can leave."

Slowly, he turns around and pins me with his dark eyes. "You won't ask where?"

I reach inside the closet and grab a stack of sweaters. "No."

I would follow him anywhere. Even to the depths of hell.

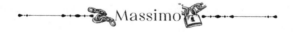

Massimo

The wind blows in my face as I scrutinize the three-story mansion in all its decaying glory. Every window across the structure's facade is dark, all except for two on the ground floor, making the whole thing look sadder somehow. Even in the fading light, there is no missing the peeling paint on the moldings or the rust that has settled on the white iron balcony railings. The damn place looks just how I feel.

"Your childhood home?" Zahara asks next to me.

"Yes." I nod. "One of them. The house we moved to when Dad became the don." My eyes sweep the neglected building once more. "There were always more important matters that needed to be handled, so it kind of slipped my mind to arrange for someone to take care of it. It's been vacant since Mom and I moved out."

I look down at Zahara and find her hugging herself. Shrugging off my suit jacket, I drape it over her shoulders, careful not to touch her unintentionally. That single brief stroke of her cheek earlier is the most I've allowed myself. I shouldn't have done even that, but the temptation to feel her sweet essence, if only for an instant, was too great.

What the hell are you doing?

Yeah... I've been asking myself that question from the moment I asked her to come with me. Actually, I didn't even *ask*. Just proclaimed it like an egotistical asshole, but I think she knew I meant it as a request.

When I arrived at the Leone Villa, my intentions were only to make the necessary arrangements with Nera and then leave. Seeing Zahara was not in the plan. I feared that if I saw her, I'd never be able to let her out of my sight again. My apprehension obviously proved right. The will to walk away dissolved as soon as my eyes found her. Maybe I never had power in the first place. After all, my feet carried me to her apartment while my mind screamed that I might as well be heading to my doom. But resisting seeing her—just once—was never an option for me.

You should have tried harder! She's nothing but a pawn. One whose usefulness has expired, and you need to shed that deadweight off your back.

She was a pawn. But no longer. Somewhere along the way, Zahara became the force that was holding me together. Stepping foot outside the prison gates this morning, my physical form may have technically been free, but it was only after seeing Zahara, that I was finally able to breathe like a truly free man.

Fuck! The girl is twenty-one. Barely an adult. And she's your goddamned family! You need to stop this bullshit and send her away. Now!

I know. But I fucking can't.

Something transpired between us when our eyes met on the day of Nuncio's funeral. What I saw in her piercing stare—her knowledge of *me* and understanding—that... shook me to my core. As if I've been struck by lightning. Something changed at that moment. A huge, fundamental shift in me, like an electric current switching its direction after a sudden surge, heading where it was never meant to be. Set on a very worrisome, forbidden course. Instead of plotting a new way to reach my lifelong goal, every waking second for over three years, I've spent thinking about her. My stepsister.

Days became a battle for survival, not for my life but for my peace of mind, filled with endless waiting. For the time I'd see a CO carrying that envelope to me. I would then fucking inhale every single word she wrote. The parts about business, the ones that were my main interest before, those I skipped in favor of passages she'd penned about herself. Once I'd read the personal sections at least a couple of times, I forced my attention to the Cosa Nostra shit. And after that, I'd spend my days anxiously waiting for her next letter.

I tried to rationalize it, convince myself that it was only a familial bond. Anything else was simply a product of my screwed-up mind after spending nearly two decades in a cage. Fuck knows it's hard enough to remain sane even during a short stint in the pen. I'm thankful as hell I can still count backward from ten. But I didn't expect being stuck in that hole would turn me into a sick goddamned bastard.

One who's fallen for his stepsister.

But that shit stops right fucking now.

I brought her with me because I couldn't face the reality of no longer having her in my life. As a friend. A trusted ally.

Both are in short supply for me at the moment.

She knows me. I need her.

Nothing more.

"Let's have a look inside." I gesture toward the house, pulling myself out of my twisted thoughts.

A couple of white vans bearing the logo of a housekeeping service on their sides are parked on the driveway, not far from the main entrance. I thought I was clear in my instructions this morning that everyone had to be gone prior to my arrival. As we climb the chipped stone steps to the front door, I instinctively reach for the small of Zahara's back.

She's your stepsister. Drill that into your stupid brain. No touching!

I wrest my hand away. It's not that there's anything wrong with a stepbrother laying a supportive hand on his stepsister's back. The problem is, as hard as I try, I can't make myself see her as my stepsibling.

I open the front door and the hinges squeak from lack of use. Drawing a deep breath, I step inside the house that once was my refuge.

And enter chaos.

Halfway up the wide staircase facing the foyer, two women, wearing pale-blue uniforms that mark them as maids with the cleaning service, are polishing the banister. A guy, using an appliance that's threatening to split my fucking head open with its noise, is buffing the marble floors nearby. On the right, through the column-flanked archway to the lounge area, I notice several more people buzzing around—vacuuming the furniture upholstery and dusting the light fixtures. There are more workers in the dining room off the left side of the foyer. A dozen people. Maybe more.

Anxiety surges within me, threatening to overwhelm me completely. I need these people out.

"Mr. Spada." A man around my age, dressed in a pale-blue suit that matches the cleaning staffs' uniforms, rushes toward me with a clipboard in hand. "We are slightly behind schedule. The second floor has been completed. New linens and towels have all been provided, as requested, and—"

"Out," I rasp.

"—groceries have arrived. I had one of my employees put them into—"

I squeeze my eyes shut, trying to suppress the noise and the presence of all these people. But the idiot in front of me keeps talking, spewing some nonsense about the curtains. With every word, my agitation transforms into rage. I take a deep breath, hoping it will help subdue the urge to snap the ignorant prick's neck.

My hair-trigger temper died in the ass during my time behind bars. Typically, being in familiar surroundings and around people I know helped calm me down. Marginally, at least. Since leaving the prison walls behind me, however, I've been hovering on the brink of bashing someone's head in.

"—Oh, and what do you need us to do with—"

My eyes fly open. I grab the front of the bastard's blue suit and lift him.

"I SAID, OUT!" I roar into his face. "EVERY SINGLE ONE OF YOU CUNTS!"

A light touch lands on my forearm. "Massimo, stop."

The haze of red and the madness clouding my mind retreat a little. I release a long exhale, then lower the frantic housekeeping manager to the floor.

"Thank you for the amazing work," Zahara says next to me. "Please gather your employees and leave. We'll call you tomorrow to address whatever is outstanding."

The man nods frantically, then sprints away, gesturing with

his hand and ordering his people to depart. I stand motionless, staring aimlessly ahead, while workers dash past me one by one.

Feeling Zahara's eyes on me every second.

The front door shuts with a loud click. Finally, blissful silence.

"Massimo? What was that?"

"Nothing," I say, furious with myself. "I was always quick to shoot, quick to anger. But I never lost my temper without reason. "I'm sorry if I scared you."

"You didn't. But you did scare them." She places her hand on my forearm again. "Are you alright?"

I look at her, so beautiful and so... calm, even after I lost my shit right in front of her, and some of her calmness seeps into me. The tension in my muscles slowly loosens.

"Nope," I say. "I thought that, once I was freed, things would just go back to how they were. That I'd be back to my old self again. But... I'm not sure that's possible anymore."

"I'm not sure how it could be. You'll have to learn to live with who you are today."

Her palm slides down to my hand, and she laces her fingers with mine. The contact sears my skin—her touch both scorching and soothing.

"Let's go see what the cleaning company has done so we can assess the state of your home."

I let her pull me across the entry hall and into the dining room, clutching her hand in mine as if it's my only hope for survival.

Maybe it is.

The slow drip from the leaking tap in the corner echoes through the illuminated space. The sound rings hollow as drops of water land in the metal sink. Above it, the constant buzzing of a fluorescent bulb. "Lights out" is just a euphemism around here. Although muffled by the distance, the screams coming from somewhere in the adjacent

block still reach me. The heat is brutal; the humidity is even worse, clinging to me with a sticky sheen. The putrid air is heavy, and there's no way to escape its suffocating weight. I turn onto my side, facing the gray wall of the cell, and start counting the cracks in the old paint.

Rusty hinges squeak as the door opens with a clang behind me. Rushed steps, drawing closer. I leap from the bunk and face the man holding a shiv formed from a shard of glass tightly in his hand. The same bald motherfucker who tried to kill me after I got back from Nuncio's funeral is standing in the middle of my cell. Behind him, his bossy short buddy grins, bearing rotten and missing teeth. I swing at "Harry," aiming for his ugly mug, but my movements are too sluggish. It's as if I'm pushing my fist through dense paste rather than fucking air. The bastard smiles. And buries the glass shank between my ribs.

My eyes snap open.

The walls are pale beige, but the paint is peeling in several spots. Half-burned logs molder in the neglected fireplace and a layer of dust coats the once distinguished mantel. The furniture is covered with white sheets.

My home.

I push to a sitting position on the couch and take a look at the laptop I left open on the coffee table. Three in the morning. I dozed off. For a whole twenty minutes.

Last night, Zahara helped me find a renovation company specializing in interior design, and boasting the fastest turnaround times on the market. Then, she contacted them through their website and scheduled a consultation for first thing in the morning. I'm thankful for her help. I'm sure I would have eventually figured out how to do it myself, but I would have wasted hours on that shit.

I thought my main challenge after I got out would be regaining the helm of my businesses. I didn't count on needing to learn how to navigate a much wider world than the one I left behind eighteen years ago. In prison, access to the internet is limited, and online activity is always monitored. Mostly, only educational sites are allowed. I tried to keep up, but at present, I feel a bit out of sync with the times.

As I walk from room to room on the ground floor of the darkened house, the dull tap of my shoes is the only sound in the eerie silence of the abandoned home. I got so used to the nonstop clamor in the pen, that now, all this quiet is a blessing and a curse, and it's making me jumpy in the noiseless dark. The shadows move around me, something I haven't experienced for a long fucking time. I can't be certain if I'm alone or if some asshole is hiding within the shrouded spaces. Glancing outside, I thought I saw someone sneaking through the yard. But did I, or was it a trick of my restless mind and unaccustomed-to-the-dark eyes? My skin crawls with awareness, and a strong premonition of impending doom has me bracing for shit to hit the fan at any moment.

I climb the stairs to the second floor and continue my aimless meandering through the mansion. My head is killing me, from the lack of sleep most likely. Years of getting by on a few winks are taking their toll. Or maybe I'm just getting old. Whatever it is, I'm fairly certain I won't get any more rest tonight. Not in this place that's still so familiar but also not at all. I don't even realize I'm heading directly toward the room where Zahara is sleeping until I'm standing in front of the door at the far end of the hall. Everything is quiet here, too, but the unease I felt on the lower levels has greatly diminished.

Undoing the top few buttons of my shirt, I slide down to the floor, leaning my back on the opposite wall. And then, I just stare at the door before me.

CHAPTER
fifteen

⊶ Zahara ⊷

I DESCEND THE ORNATE STAIRWAY AND TAKE A LOOK around. Massimo mentioned that the temp workers from the staffing agency would be arriving at eight. It's almost time, but he doesn't seem to be anywhere in sight. The small sitting area on one side of the stairs seems empty. I turn in the other direction and head across the enormous dining room that's occupied by a table long enough to seat sixteen people easily. The exterior wall is made up of floor-to-ceiling windows facing the garden. At one point, the view must have been magnificent, especially the winding vines of jasmine spilling from atop the iron arches over a quaint outdoor nook. Currently, however, the grounds are overgrown and filled with weeds.

The far end of the room leads to a small square space that separates the dining hall from the kitchen, which I spot past the open anteroom door. As soon as I cross the kitchen doorway, I stop dead in my tracks.

Standing by another wall made up of big windows, in the brilliant glow of the morning light shining through the glass, is Massimo. He has his back turned to me while he gazes at the backyard. And he's dressed in a pair of gray sweatpants and nothing else.

Every single inch of his upper body is covered in ink. A mix of black and colorful designs wraps over his impossibly wide back, then flows across his broad shoulders and down his muscular arms, all the way to his fingers. It's hard to pinpoint where one image ends and the other starts, as each seems to bleed into the next.

My hand flies to my chest as if that would prevent my wildly beating heart from punching its way out of my ribcage. I haven't had a lot of opportunities to see shirtless men. In school, occasionally, some of the guys would pull off their shirts after soccer practice, and there was that one time I helped Nera clean the blood off Kai when he was wounded, but that's it. Generally, men never held my interest anyway. Men who aren't Massimo, that is.

"Good morning," I croak when I finally find my voice.

Massimo turns around, and I can see that his front is tattooed, as well. "Hey. Sleep well?"

"Yeah, sure," I lie. I barely slept a wink, tossing and turning and thinking about him.

The hours we spent perusing reno companies' sites in the parlor last night, almost left me tachycardic. My heart was racing rapidly the entire time as adrenaline coursed through my system. That stupid muscle inside my chest couldn't deal with his close proximity. Just as it's having a hard time doing now.

Massimo crosses the distance between us with slow, soundless steps. His feet are bare, and, for some reason, that only makes him hotter. "Do you want me to fix you some breakfast?"

I blink. Massimo Spada, the man who'll imminently be crowned Don of Boston Cosa Nostra, is offering to make me breakfast? "Um... I'm not really hungry. I think."

He lifts his hand, and, for a moment, I think he's going to touch my face again, but he just braces it on the doorframe. His deep, dark eyes capture me, while the force of his presence seeps into my bones. Envelops me inside and out.

Unsettling me, all the same.

The few minutes I did sleep last night, I dreamed about him. We were alone in a parlor, and he was holding me tucked closely to his side. The roaring fireplace warmed my skin while Massimo whispered in my ear. Quiet words I have craved for so damn long. How I'm the only one who understands him. His kindred spirit. And how he couldn't wait to be set free, all so he could come to me, and we could be together.

My gaze glides down his sculpted, inked chest, soaking in the sight. There is a faint tingling between my legs that I've never experienced before. Like… an aching need. Oh my God, I'm getting turned on. I press my thighs together, hoping it will make the feeling go away. It doesn't. The ache only gets stronger.

I've never had sex, haven't even wanted to, never so much as had a man touch me down there. But I want Massimo to.

I've been suppressing my feelings for such a long time. This yearning has plagued me for years. And also, the chest-tearing guilt for caring for him as I do, all the while knowing it's wrong. Between my affection and my guilty conscience, there's fear—dread that he'll reject me if he ever finds out. The sheer torment of imagining what people will say when they realize I'm in love with my stepbrother. I'm already a pariah as it is.

Is it really that bad, though? After all, it's not like we're related through blood. How can something that feels so right, be wrong?

"Why do you do that?"

I freeze, while my heart hammers wildly. "Do what?"

"Pull on your sleeve." Massimo cocks his head, lowering his gaze. "You were doing that the whole evening yesterday."

I let go of the cuff immediately. "Just a habit. I… I don't like my hands to show."

"Why?"

"Because people tend to stare."

I didn't think my heart could possibly beat faster than it already does, but as his fingers wrap around my wrist, it nearly bursts inside its protective cage. Breath catches in my lungs as Massimo raises my hand, bringing it up between us for a close look.

"I see why they would do that." His voice turns raspy while he lightly strokes the skin of my palm with his thumb. "You have beautiful hands, Zahara."

A pleasant shiver rushes down my spine from just that slightest touch. And I want more.

I want to feel his touch everywhere. I want kisses... and everything else. To be close to him, and know him carnally just as intimately as I know his mind. I've been such a chicken for so long, too scared to ask for what I want. Not willing to take the risk of giving voice to my desires, all for fear of ridicule. That's not who I'd like to be anymore.

Reaching out with my free hand, I press my palm to Massimo's stomach. His nostrils flare as he draws in a sharp breath. Those stunning eyes peer into mine with such intensity, that my knees begin to shake. He doesn't move a muscle, just watches me while still holding my other hand in his own, cradled in those huge inked fingers.

"Zahara?" A question. His tone conveys confusion as his eyes search for... something.

"Yes?" I bite my bottom lip and slide my palm a little lower.

Warm breath fans my skin as Massimo bends toward me. His nose nudges the hair at the top of my head, and I hear him inhale. This close, I can feel the heat of his body and smell the scent that's purely his. Towering above me, he's an imposing figure, still clutching the doorway with his unoccupied hand. Another deep draw of air, and then he releases his grip on the jamb and places his palm on my hip. Slowly, he starts sliding it down to my ass cheek and—

157

"Jesus fuck!" Massimo abruptly steps back, away from me. The look in his eyes is frantic. His chest rises and falls with jerky movements as he glares down at me. "I'm sorry. I shouldn't have done that."

"It's okay, I—"

"It most definitely is not okay." He grabs the back of his neck with his interlaced fingers and shakes his head. "Shit! What the fuck is wrong with me?" He takes a deep breath and meets my stare. "Goddammit. You're my stepsister. I'm so sorry, Zahara. This won't happen again."

I squeeze the cuff of my long sleeve and look away. Yeah. Of course it won't happen again. As if someone like him would ever be attracted to someone like me.

The ring of the doorbell breaks the silence.

"That must be your household staff. I'll let them in," I mumble and run away.

Sitting across from me and Massimo, the reno company's consultant, Mr. Jeffrey King, looks up from his tablet and smiles.

"I've jotted down all of your requests and I'm happy to say we can take on this project. The timelines might need to stay a little flexible to accommodate all the variables, however, we should be able to finish the job within two months."

I steal a quick look at Massimo. He's leaning back with an arm laid over the back of the couch and glaring at the rep.

"I need it to be done by Thursday."

The man nearly chokes and shifts uncomfortably. "I am truly sorry, Mr. Spada, but the earliest I can have someone here is tomorrow, and it's absolutely impossible to complete the renovation of a house this size in five days. Even if I could bring all of our teams onto this project simultaneously, we will still need at least six weeks."

Massimo's facial expression transforms from bored indifference to a menacing scowl. He leans forward, bracing his elbows on his knees, and gets into the guy's face. "I said, I want it done by Thursday."

"I completely understand your frustration, Mr. Spada, we simply can't—"

Massimo's hand shoots out, and his fingers wrap around King's throat. "I don't think you understand," he growls as he pulls the man toward him.

Grabbing Massimo's knee, I give it a little squeeze. "Maybe they could push it a bit and get it done in a month. Would that work?"

Massimo's hold on the consultant's neck loosens, but he doesn't release him. "No. The Council meeting is scheduled for Thursday evening."

"Then, we'll have the workers overhaul the ground floor first so it will be finished by Wednesday night." I shift my focus to Mr. King. "Is that doable?"

The poor man is tugging on Massimo's thick wrist with both of his hands, trying to free himself, while his eyes flit between me and Massimo. "Absolutely. No problem at all."

"Thank you." I squeeze Massimo's knee again. "Let him go."

The moment Massimo releases the rep, the man scrambles to his feet and hightails it. I wait to hear the telltale slam of the front door, then cross my arms under my chest and turn toward Massimo. He's staring at the floor between his feet but otherwise appears unaffected by what just happened.

"I think we need to talk about the elephant in the room."

His jaw hardens. "I have no idea what you're talking about."

"I think you do. Last night, when you exploded at the cleaning crew, I thought you were merely stressed. Then, this morning, you lost your cool during the staff interviews. And now this."

The fiasco with the job candidates that the staffing agency sent over was epic. Massimo started questioning them about

159

all sorts of bizarre things, including how well they could handle firearms. Saying that most of the people were shocked, is an understatement. And when every one of them withdrew their application and asked to leave, Massimo exploded.

"I sometimes have a hard time controlling my temper. That's all," he says with a shrug.

"Well, you'll have to start managing it better or the capos are going to bury you."

His head snaps up, eyes finding mine.

"You know I'm right," I continue. "No matter how good you are at handling the Family business, if anyone thinks that you're mentally unstable, you're done. All the work you've put in over the years will be for nothing."

He doesn't say a thing, just watches me with a haunted look in his eyes. And I... I just want to embrace him and tell him that everything will be okay. But he was more than clear this morning. He doesn't see me the same way I see him, and there's nothing I can do about that. I can't make him fall in love with me. Still, I've chosen to stay with him regardless.

"Why didn't you tell me?" I ask.

"That I'm royally fucked-up? Would you have agreed to come with me if I had?"

"Yes."

"Why?"

Because I'm in love with you. I can't tell him that, so I aim to redirect. "I'm going to call some of the people who worked for us at Dad's house and ask them to come by. There were a few reliable ones at Leone's, as well."

"No. I don't trust them."

"But you'd trust total strangers?" I lift an eyebrow. "I understand you're being extra cautious, especially with Armando getting killed while locked up in Leone's basement. However, you're aware of what happened this morning. You need to hire people from our world. Those who know to keep their mouths shut. And who can handle *complicated* employers."

"Fine. Only the ones you vouch for, though."

I nod. "By the way, what happened with Armando's body?"

"I had Salvo take care of it." He throws me a sideways look. "What happened with the pantsuit you made for his mother? The one with the green velvet thing on the shoulder. Did she wear it?"

"I can't believe you remember that."

"Remember it?" His lips pull into a smirk. "I had nightmares about the blasted thing. The hidden zipper. The underlining that had to be sewn inside out. You wrote about that damn garment in at least three of your letters. Maybe even four."

I laugh. I'm amazed he actually remembers all those details.

Massimo's eyes drop to my lips. "You should smile more often."

My body goes still. "Why?"

"Because it makes the world seem like a nice place, for a change."

I suck in a breath. Our gazes meet, and, for a scattering of heartbeats, we just stare into each other's eyes. The moment seems to last forever, but even if that was true, it still wouldn't be long enough. We both look away a fraction of a second later.

"I need to head over to the North End," he says, eyes fixed on the unlit fireplace. "It's Saturday, so most of the foot soldiers will be hanging out at their usual watering hole there."

"You're going to talk to them before meeting with the capos?"

"Those coddled old cronies are the ones who need words to be convinced. The men who risk their lives and bear most of the actual burden required for the Family to flourish don't need long speeches. They judge people by their actions. The oath the soldiers took when they joined Cosa Nostra promises their freely given loyalty to the organization. But if a leader wants their respect, that's something he'll need to earn." He looks at his wristwatch. "We should head out now."

I blink. "We?"

"Armando's death wasn't self-inflicted. I'm not leaving you in an unguarded house alone, Zahara."

A mirthless laugh escapes my lips. "No one would ever go to all that trouble just to kill me."

Massimo's hand shoots out so quickly that I nearly miss the movement. He grasps my chin with an unyielding yet gentle grip. The hard lines of his face draw near, and there's a murderous look in his eyes that does funny things to my insides. "You're going to point out anyone who has ever made you feel inferior, and I'm going to separate their heads from their spines."

"It's just… I'm hardly a threat to anyone, Massimo."

A corner of his lips curves upward. "Only because they don't yet realize what you are."

"What?"

He leans in until his face is right in front of mine. "Just point a finger. And see what happens."

Air gets trapped in my lungs as I watch the dangerous glint in Massimo's eyes. He's so close, and I battle the urge to stretch and press my lips to his. The distance between us is so small, that in a fraction of a heartbeat, I could be feeling the heat of his firm mouth on my own. I pull my lower lip between my teeth, biting it to stop myself from succumbing. Massimo tenses. His gaze drops down to my lips and lingers. Then, as fast as if he'd been burned, he releases my chin and straightens.

"We need to make a pit stop at the gas station on the way. I'll go get my wallet."

To celebrate birthdays and weddings, the Family usually prefers high-end restaurants around the city. However, for more intimate occasions, one of the cozy Italian-owned places in North End is usually a go-to choice.

The narrow alley where Massimo has parked his car has nothing in common with the colorful neighborhood I'm familiar with. There are no stores with trinkets in the windows, no happy people laughing as they walk by, and no enticing smells of Italian cuisine. Just a somber-looking taverna at the end of a deserted, dark lane. An old wooden sign above the door, so weathered by the elements that the name of the establishment isn't even visible, is hardly a welcoming sight. The windows of the place are so grimy that even if the light inside was on, I still probably wouldn't be able to see through them.

Standing on a sidewalk before this rather sketchy joint, I tuck myself closer to Massimo. "Are you sure we're in the right place?"

"I'm not certain. Let's check it out." A mischievous grin pulls at the corner of his lips. "Can you whistle?"

My eyebrows shoot up. "Whistle?"

"Yes."

"I guess. Want me to do it now?"

"Please. A long one, followed by two short bursts."

I snort. Then, feeling like a complete idiot, I look at the door and whistle. One long, and after, two short, just like he said.

Nothing happens. Not that I expected anything different. "Now what? Should I try saying *abracadabra*?"

That grin lights up Massimo's whole face, making him look much younger than he actually is. It happens every time he smiles. "Give it a few moments. Everyone usually uses the back entrance."

"Give wha—"

A single low whistle comes from somewhere up above; a second-story window, I imagine. I glance at the upper level but see no one. After another few seconds, an audible *click* from the door makes me jump.

Massimo grabs the somewhat rusty knob and pushes the door open. The hinges protest with a strange, screeching sound.

"Watch your step," he says and walks inside.

As soon as we enter, the door behind us shuts, sealing us in near-total darkness. Only faint light filters in through the dirty windows. The air is so stale that I can almost taste it on my tongue. It takes a few moments for my eyes to adjust to being able to make out the interior. My heart pounds as I contemplate what we've gotten ourselves into. There is a bar to our left and a bunch of tables pushed against the wall on the opposite side of the room. The place looks like no one has been here in years.

Dust swirls in the air as Massimo moves to stand right in front of me. My nose itches from the particles floating around us and the faint smell of mold and... cigarette smoke.

"Scared?" Massimo asks, taking my hand in his.

"No. Should I be?"

I can't really see his face, just a general outline of his body towering over me, but I hear his quiet chuckle. He takes a step back, pulling me with him. More dust rises as he urges me across the room, toward another door that comes into view in the far corner. I sneeze.

"Sorry about that." His thumb brushes my pulse point, setting off a race of goose bumps up my arm. "Two more steps."

The heel of my shoe catches on something, and I stumble forward. Immediately, two thick arms wrap protectively around me.

Warmth. It surges within my body like a current. Massimo's chest rises and falls under my cheek while I listen to the steady beating of his heart. In the span of a thought, though, the rhythm changes, until it sounds like a runaway train. I close my eyes and simply take it in, all the while marveling at the sensuous heat coming from his body. And this sensation of being held in his embrace, even as I know it's only accidental. A stolen moment.

It lasts barely a few seconds, and then he steps away. Leaving me feeling cold without his arms around me.

"Everything okay?" His voice sounds clipped in the darkness.

"Yeah."

I see him nod. He walks up to the door, reaching for the handle in front of him. Another click. Then, a sliver of light bursts through the gap, along with the noise of raucous conversations and ecstatic laughter.

"I know you believe that Cosa Nostra is all about lavish parties and intrigue," Massimo says, sliding the door open and letting out more sounds and smells with every inch. "But it's so much more, angel."

My own silly heart skips a beat. Momentarily, I allow myself to believe that, what must have been a slip of the tongue, actually has a special meaning. That the endearment he casually threw out was just for me. That, maybe, that's how he sees me.

"Come on." Massimo pulls the door back completely and steps aside, revealing a view of total chaos. And life.

Dozens of people—mostly men—are gathered at small round tables crowded around the huge room. They all seem to be speaking at once. The noise is nearly deafening. Two waitresses wearing little white aprons over their short black skirts weave in and out among the seated, setting drinks down and slapping an occasional wandering hand away. At the center of the room, a group of six is playing cards, while several people stand around them. Laughter rings out from the lot as one of the men points to a laid-down hand. Next to the players, a couple of gray-haired old-timers engage in a verbal brawl. Their voices rise and rise as if trying to overcome the levels from the other tables. And in the middle of this all, a dog lies sleeping at the old guys' feet, completely unperturbed by the noise.

The left side of the room has two pool tables, and there's a crowd of about twenty huddled around them. The women seem more interested in flirting with the men than watching or playing a game. A classic jukebox occupies a nearby corner, and a middle-aged couple is dancing right beside it. Off to the side is a small bar top with four stools, yet there's at least double that number of guys jammed in the space, doing shots and yammering excitedly at the woman making the drinks. All in all, it's a typical Saturday evening at a neighborhood pub, but with one major difference: Every single man, including the old guys with the dog, is wearing a gun holster.

One of the men near the table playing cards looks up and his gaze zeros in on us standing at the threshold. It's Peppe. I didn't recognize him without his full suit and tie. His eyes flare in surprise when they register the huge presence standing at my back. Slowly, he straightens and lets out a short, shrill whistle. The conversations and laughter immediately die down, and someone kills the music. Dozens of eyes snap to Peppe, then follow his gaze back to us.

Massimo comes around me and steps inside the room. The sound of chairs scraping the floor fills the sudden silence as almost all of the men spring to standing. A few young guys remain in their seats, not for long, though. The more mature men nearby pull them up by the scruffs of their necks.

Massimo's hand lands on my waist, drawing me into his side as his eyes rove over the hushed crowd. The awestruck eyes of nearly a hundred people stare back at him. The young guys seem confused, throwing quick glances around as if wondering what this abrupt commotion is about. The rest of the men, however, those who appear to be older than their midthirties, don't shift their eyes from Massimo. Based on their expressions, they know who he is.

No one utters a word. The silence is so absolute it's almost palpable. The air itself seems to crack as if charged. Massimo takes one last look at the men gathered in this room, then slowly nods. The motion is deliberate and seems to carry a message.

What is it? Then, every single man who recognized him responds with a nod of his own. Dozens of heads move in unison, their timing is perfectly aligned.

Recognition. Loyalty. Respect. It's written all over these guys' faces. I can see the conviction in their eyes. No doubts, as if the certainty they feel is etched in stone. Regardless of who was in the official position of power all these years, these were—and still are—Massimo's men. I can tell by the way they look at him. The sight is so astounding that it gives me chills.

"It's good to see you all again," Massimo says, then focuses on Peppe. "Eighteen men, split into two shifts. Armed with automatic weapons. I need them at my house within the hour."

"Understood," Peppe responds.

"Good." Massimo's hold on my waist tightens. "I'll see the rest of you again next week."

He turns us around, and a moment later, we're heading once more through the dusty anteroom toward the exit, silence stretching at our backs. Still completely overwhelmed by what I witnessed inside that room, I don't even notice as we step outside of the building.

"You still haven't officially taken over," I say as he opens the car door for me. "Capos won't like that you've commandeered men to be your security detail before you're sworn in as don."

"Those damn cunts can suck my dick. And the security isn't for me."

"Then, what are they for?" I ask as I slide onto the seat.

Massimo squats beside me in the open car door. With his height, his face draws nearly level with mine. The look in his eyes appears almost feral. "You."

My pulse shoots north of the stratosphere—my heart thunders in my chest so wildly it could burst from being so happy and full. Could he be—

"My stepsister's safety will never again be endangered, Zahara."

Crushed. His words obliterate me, grinding my stupid hope into a pile of dust.

I look away, staring through the windshield but not seeing a thing.

"You don't like it?"

I resume picking at the noodles in the takeout container. "It's fine."

Massimo arches an eyebrow at me from the other side of the dining room table. "I can have one of the guys go pick up something else, if you want. I thought you liked Chinese?"

I do. I told him about my favorite foods in one of the letters, just like I spilled nearly everything else about myself.

My hand drifts to the chain around my neck, and I start fiddling with the links, twisting and running them through my fingers. It's one of the platinum necklaces Massimo sent me. I was so damn excited when I opened the package, discovering it was jewelry and that it was from him. My God, the joy I felt, figuring it had to be proof that he does care for me. And he does, just not in the way I want him to. And it's high time I accept it.

"The food is fine." I gesture around the room with my chopsticks. "So, this space is really huge. Maybe you should consider modifying the floor plan?"

"Actually, I was thinking of using it as a meeting room. We can even leave this table and it'd double for formal dining. What do you think?"

"Um… it's your house. Why would it matter what I think?"

A large tattooed hand enters my field of vision. Massimo's thumb lifts my chin, tilting my face up. "Your opinion matters a great deal to me, Zahara. Or I wouldn't be asking for it, would I?"

"I guess?" I mumble, fighting the pull of his magnetic gaze. It's sucking me in, making me wish for things that will never be.

His forefinger lingers at the edge of my lower lip, the contact so light and gentle. My resolve crumbles, and I tilt my head to the side just a tiny bit, causing his finger to brush along my mouth.

Immediately, Massimo withdraws his hand and looks down at his food. "Did you chat with your sister? Where are the lovebirds hiding now?"

"I called her last night. They're at Kai's apartment for the time being. At least until they find somewhere they can keep ducks and horses."

"Mm-hmm. I'd ask *why*, but I don't really care. I assume she's a bit perplexed over your decision to come with me?"

"Very. She questioned me about it."

"And what did you say?"

I stare into my carton of food as if it holds the answer I need. Should I tell him the truth? That I'm in love with him and I want to be as close to him as possible. Even knowing these feelings are one-sided. No, I can't. I don't want him to think of me as pathetic. It's enough that it's how I see myself.

I push the food away and meet his eyes. "I told her that my life is my own and I don't owe an explanation to anyone."

That's not actually true. I simply said I had my reasons and I'd explain everything when we meet face-to-face. There's no point in lying to her any longer. I want to come clean, yet I need to do it when we're alone. I miss when I could tell Nera anything.

"Ah. Then it was you who must have riled her up. Now it makes sense." Massimo smirks.

"What do you mean?"

He takes out his phone and slides it across the table toward me. "Have a look at the email Salvo forwarded to me this morning. It's Nera's goodbye message to him and the other capos."

I open the app and quickly locate the email he mentioned. It's the latest in his inbox. There isn't much in terms of the message content, barely two paragraphs of text. Once I'm done reading, I can't decide if I should laugh or be horrified. Not only had my sister referred to the high-ranking Family members as whiny asshats, but she also told them to smarten up and follow the orders of their true leader. She declared her overwhelming excitement about passing the reins over to Massimo and proclaimed that it was actually he who had made every decision in the last two decades while the rest of them sat on their asses and got rich. With that, she expressed her deepest wish to never see their ugly mugs again and signed off with: *Fuck you all! Nera Mazur.*

I shake my head. As shocking as her message is, I've never been prouder of my sister. "Well, she was definitely fed up with all the crap they kept giving her. Especially Brio. What was the reaction after the bomb she dropped? Specifically, about you ruling from the shadows?"

"My phone started going off at six o'clock this morning. It's hardly stopped since."

"Oh, that's what it must have been. I think I heard it. Were you passing by my bedroom door when they called?"

Massimo's eyes dart away, and he peers intently at something that caught his attention out in the hall. "Yeah. I was… checking the interior access points."

"Are you still having trouble sleeping?"

He looks at me then, his eyes boring into mine. "Nope. Not anymore."

CHAPTER
sixteen

"NO. THE DECISION HAS BEEN MADE, AND I'M NOT changing my mind." I squeeze the phone between my shoulder and my ear and reach for the plate of prosciutto. "The men stay put. It's not up for discussion, Salvo."

The pan sizzles as I drop the slices of Italian ham over the egg mixture. An omelet is the only dish I know how to make, but I'm not letting any fucking stranger come near Zahara's food. Once Peppe gets here, I'll tell him that he's in charge of the kitchen from now on. I'm sure he will be thrilled with his new duty. I just don't trust any of the staff. He better know how to cook or we might have a problem.

"You can't give orders before the meeting with the Council, Massimo."

"No shit?" I grab a plate out of the cupboard. "Well, in that case, feel free to come over and tell them to leave."

A long exasperated sigh comes from the other end of the line. "You know they won't."

Damn right, they won't.

"I'm busy, Salvo. We'll discuss all of your concerns when

you come by this evening. Now, any luck locating my favorite member of the justice system?"

"As I understand, Judge Collins is vacationing at his cabin somewhere in Vermont. He acquired it last Friday and couldn't wait to get away."

"The same day I got released? What a coincidence."

"I've spoken to him on several occasions, Massimo. He was worried that if he took it easy on you, people might suspect his association with us. There wasn't any foul play on his part, no one bribed him. He was just doing his job."

Yeah. The epitome of righteousness, that one. He had no objection to reaching out to Nuncio and hiding behind Cosa Nostra when Irish loan sharks were breathing down his neck.

"Call me as soon as you have his exact location, or if he returns to Boston in the meantime." I disconnect the call and throw the phone on the counter, then carry the plate over to the small breakfast table by the window. As I'm heading over to grab cutlery and a glass of juice, the kitchen door swooshes open.

"Mr. Spada! Oh, I'm so sorry." A maid dashes into the room and turns toward the table. "Please, let me help you set up—"

"Don't touch that plate!"

The girl flinches and freezes in place. "But… I just…"

"Out! Now!"

"Massimo? What's going on?"

My head snaps to the side. Zahara is standing in the doorway, her gaze bouncing between me and the maid, who seems to be on the brink of tears. I don't care about the girl's feelings in the least—she should have known better than to try handling food without explicit permission—except the look of reproach in Zahara's eyes makes me falter.

Clenching my jaw, I point my chin at the door as I address the maid. "You can leave. Peppe is the only person allowed in the kitchen."

Zahara arches an eyebrow.

"And I apologize for yelling," I say through gritted teeth.

The maid mumbles something and rushes past Zahara, who is still holding me pinned with her unwavering stare.

"I appreciate the effort, but that didn't sound like a heart-felt apology to me."

"The girl was going to mess with your breakfast," I grumble. "I've witnessed inmates spiking food with bad dope or other shit too many times."

Zahara's gaze moves to the plate I've set on the table, and a strange look crosses her face. "You made this?"

"Yes. But don't get your hopes up, it's only an omelet. I figured you must be sick of takeout after the last two days."

I watch her as she slowly approaches the table. She's wearing high-waisted brownish-red pants that emphasize the perfect curve of her hips and hug her mouthwatering, round ass.

Purge the mental images of your hands stroking your stepsister's behind. Right the fuck now! And the ones where you strip her of her clothes!

I shut my eyes and shake my head in a useless attempt to do the right thing. When I open them again, Zahara is sitting at the table, bringing a forkful of the omelet to her mouth.

"Tinia has worked for my father for years," she says before taking a bite. "She was not going to *spike* my food."

"Tinia?" My eyes and whatever brain cells are still functioning are transfixed on Zahara's lips. Her pouty mouth is the only thing I'm capable of thinking about right now.

"The maid you just yelled at."

"Right. Well, I'm not taking any chances." I quickly turn around and busy myself with stuffing the dirtied pan into the dishwasher.

"Please tell me it was a joke when you said you're putting Peppe in charge of the kitchen."

"Nope. I don't trust the staff you hired."

"I do, though. Most of them have worked for my family

for years. If it makes things easier, Iris can cook for us. I trust her completely."

"Trusting someone entirely is not wise."

"Well, she's the one who helped me with your letters for all the time I was at Dad's. And she is not going to poison anyone."

I lean on the counter and watch Zahara eat. "You have no qualms?"

"None."

"Fine, then." I nod. I trust *her* judgment. "Salvo is coming over tonight. He should have Armando's tox screen results, so we'll have a better idea of what we're dealing with. But I'm betting your wacko of a brother-in-law is right, and the idiot was offed with cyanide." The night before I was released, Armando set up an ambush for Zahara's sister. Kai, Nera's main squeeze turned hubby now, caught him. The braid-wearing son of a bitch broke the traitorous capo's arms and legs and then dumped him in their basement. When I arrived the next morning, however, we found Armando dead, foaming at the mouth like the rabid dog he was.

"I don't think Nera would approve of you calling her husband a wacko. He has a name, you know." Zahara picks up a piece of prosciutto with two perfectly manicured fingers and brings it to her lips.

My eyes follow the movement like I'm goddamned hypnotized. And then, she licks the tips of those delicate fingers. And I… I almost fucking combust on the spot. *Shit!*

I rest the back of my head in my hands and take a deep breath.

"Why did you shave your head?" she asks.

"Habit." Since my last necessary grooming, my hair had grown almost half an inch, so I got rid of it this morning. "In lockup, grabbing someone's hair was the easiest way to keep ahold of them to smash their face. Or to get in a few stab wounds, maybe even slit their throat."

"You're not in prison anymore, Massimo."

"I know. Sometimes though, that detail kind of slips my mind. I didn't even think about it when I picked up the razor this morning." I glide my palm over the curve of my smooth head. "It's been years. I wonder what I'd look like if I just let it grow."

"Me too," she whispers.

I meet her eyes.

"You're out," she continues in that soft voice that sounds like the sweetest music. "You need to stop looking at every person as if they are the enemy. And you need to let go of your paranoia that someone is going to kill me."

I look away, focusing on the jasmine vines beyond the window. Last night, as I lay in front of Zahara's bedroom door, waiting for sleep to claim me, I thought quite a bit about my unfounded concerns.

There's no logical reason for anyone to want Zahara dead. Hurting her won't gain anyone an advantage.

I know that. I also know that I should stay away from her. But I can't. Can't make myself do it, either. The mere idea of something bad happening to her is making me lose my shit.

Stop finding those pitiful excuses. She doesn't need your protection. You're simply trying to justify your actions, creating a rationale for hovering close to her. It needs to stop.

Sometimes, I wish I could get my hands on the voice inside my head and choke the fucker out. Because the asshole is right all too often.

Damn right, I am.

Fine. No more imagined death threats. No more stupid reasons for keeping her with me all the time.

I grab the carton of eggs off the counter and carry it to the fridge. "I have to go shopping. Only two of the suits my lawyer got for me fit."

Zahara looks up from her plate. "Okay. I'll do my unpacking since I haven't had time, yet."

"Good," I say, aimlessly staring at the contents of the fridge, then I slam the door shut. "That's good."

Like a mindless moron, I head toward the door. Halfway there, my steps falter. I stop. There are nine heavily armed men on every shift. *Is that enough to cover the house and the perimeter of the estate?*

Yes, it is.

I continue, only to pause again at the threshold. *Maybe I should take her with me? Just in case?* There are a lot of fuckers from the reno company on site. Any one of them could pose a danger.

Nope. No more excuses.

I grab the jamb on both sides and squeeze until my hands ache.

Don't.

Do NOT fucking say it.

I grit my teeth. "I don't think it's safe for you to remain here alone. Go get your purse, Zahara."

I love shopping, but I usually do it alone or with my sister. Trying on clothes in front of other people is not my thing. On the few rare occasions when I joined Nera and her friends, I usually ended up standing off to the side, watching them parade about in all sorts of outfits and shoes. I have to admit, though, seeing Massimo as he tries on suit after suit is a sight to behold. Even though this one is still too tight in the shoulder area, just like the previous four.

"Did men shrink in the past two decades or something?" Massimo grunts as he struggles to button the jacket over his chest. The fabric is stretched so tight over his broad frame that it looks like it could burst at any second. The way the sleeves are straining around his bulging biceps is rather comical, too. Not to mention, they are way too short.

"I don't think so." I try to keep my face straight, barely containing my laughter. "I guess you'll have to wait for the ones you ordered from the tailor to be done."

"The motherfucker said he needs three days. I can't go around naked."

A blush creeps up my cheeks just from imagining that scenario.

Yes, please.

"Um… let me see the seams. There might be a way to let them out." I take his wrist, inspecting the hem of the sleeve, then pull his arm up, trying to gauge the presence of extra material at the seam along the side. "I can try, except I'm not sure if it will look good."

"Sir, let me see," the sales associate chirps from her spot by the shelf of folded shirts and rushes toward Massimo. I noticed her ogling him the moment we stepped inside the store. She was all too ready to assist him.

Tall and thin, she's dressed in a bright-yellow sleeveless blouse that ties around her neck, leaving her arms and back bare. I can't stop looking at her flawless skin—there isn't even one blemish on it. The last time I wore a short-sleeved top, I was in elementary.

The associate stops in front of Massimo, right next to me, and reaches for the lapels of his suit jacket.

A pang of jealousy hits me right in the chest. I let go of the sleeve and take a quick step back. Am I a bad person for hating a random, unfamiliar woman just because she looks so perfect? Because *they* look so perfect standing next to each other?

"Get your hands off me," Massimo growls.

The woman tenses and retreats. "I apologize. I was just thinking…"

"You thought wrong." He turns around and stalks into the changing room, slamming the door closed in his wake.

A long sigh sounds on my left. I look at the sales lady as she stares at the closed door Massimo just disappeared behind, adoration clearly written all over her face.

"Your boss is such an intense man." She sighs again. "Any chance I can get his phone number?"

Every fiber of my being stiffens, and I wonder how in hell this woman knows who Massimo is. He might not be the official don yet, but— Oh. She didn't mean "boss" in that context. I guess, she just assumed I'm Massimo's PA.

"Not from me. You'll have to ask him yourself," I mumble.

I shouldn't be surprised. No one in their right mind would think I'm Massimo's girlfriend or anything along those lines. Soon after we stepped inside the mall, I realized the reaction the man beside me could draw from women. He didn't even need to try. Every woman we passed stared at him with lust-filled eyes. With his tall muscular frame, shaved head, and tattoos covering his neck and hands, Massimo is one of those men who command attention simply by walking into the room. Each woman, without exception, gazed at him as if he was larger than life. If I thought he had that effect only on me, I was hugely mistaken.

"I need to stop at the drugstore," Massimo says as he approaches me and lays his palm on the small of my back. "The shower gel McBride got me smells like cat piss."

"I think I saw one down that hallway," I mutter, distracted by his touch.

"Great. Do you need anything?"

"No. I…" We've left the men's clothing store, and his hand is still resting on my lower back. "I can't use regular cosmetics. I usually buy special products for sensitive skin."

"Maybe they'll have some. We'll ask."

"I would need to check the ingredients listed for each. It takes time, and Salvo is coming in less than an hour."

"Fuck Salvo."

We find the drugstore just a few doors down. Massimo heads to the personal care aisle and grabs a random bottle of body wash off the shelf.

"Don't you want to smell it first?" I ask.

"Can't be worse than the one I have at home. Trust me."

I bite the inside of my cheek. "I actually think it smells nice. Lemony."

Massimo stops and looks at me. Maybe I shouldn't have said that. Does he think it's strange that I've noticed his scent?

"You sure?" His eyes glint, yet I can't quite decipher the expression.

"Um... I don't know. I think so. Lemon. Or lime, maybe."

Slowly and without breaking our locked stare, he leans down until our faces are almost even.

"Why don't you check?" He tilts his head to the side. "I can't go around smelling like cat piss."

With my heart rate jumping to double speed, I lean forward and touch the tip of my nose to his neck. As I inhale, his scent fills my nostrils.

"Lime," I rasp. He's still bent down, his cheek lightly brushing mine, so I draw in another deep sniff. "Definitely not cat piss."

"Jasmine." His voice is rough next to my ear.

"What?"

"The way you smell." His lips feather over my earlobe, and a small shiver runs down my spine. "Like jasmine. And peace."

I swallow. A man walks by us down the aisle and catches Massimo's leg with his basket. Still, Massimo does not move. He remains hovering over me, and I feel as if I'm seconds from being snared completely by the magnetic pull of his body. What would happen if I let myself surrender? Would he retreat? I don't want him to move away, so I reach out and grab a fistful of his shirt. Under my touch, Massimo's chest rises and falls in quick succession. Faster than normal. His breath is fanning over my neck, and the faint touch of his stubble tingles against my chin.

Closing my eyes, I lean my cheek on his. "I didn't know anyone could smell like peace."

"Me neither." The faintest of touches lands just below my ear, there one moment and gone the next. "But now I do."

Lips. My heartbeat skyrockets. It was his lips.

"Good afternoon!" A high-pitched voice chirps somewhere behind me. "Can I help you with something?"

Massimo immediately takes a step back, breaking our contact. "Yes. We need cosmetics for sensitive skin."

"Of course. We have products with organic ingredients there, on the left. Or, if you prefer vegan...."

I blindly follow after the clerk while trying to process what just happened, and Massimo trails a few steps behind. Was it a kiss? Or just an accidental touch?

"... and we have amazing foundations with one hundred percent coverage." The lady stops at the makeup counter. "Would you like to try any?"

My stomach feels like it just landed on the floor. I tried every brand of foundation a few years ago, but my skin wouldn't tolerate a single one. I ended up with an awful rash on my face, and Nera threatened to march me to the doctor unless I stopped using them.

"What's *foundation*?" Massimo asks while the woman pulls out various sample bottles and lines them up on the counter next to a magnifying makeup mirror.

"It's a liquid concealer, for the face," I whisper.

"Yes," the lady chirps, lifting one of the containers. "I think this shade would be the best match for you. It's one of the most popular brands, dear. Complete coverage of imperfections is guaranteed, and it lasts the whole day. It's even waterproof. Try it and see how pretty you'll look."

I grit my teeth, trying to ignore the tingling in my nose. My vision begins to blur, and I quickly blink away the tears. The sales lady seems nice and has that motherly air about her. I'm sure she means well, however, her thoughtless words sting nevertheless. Without realizing it, she's making me feel like I'll be ugly if I don't wear the foundation. It's not the first time someone's acted like they have the right to give me their unsolicited advice. It happens far too often.

As I open my mouth to let her know I don't want any of the products, Massimo grabs the bottle from the woman's hand.

"So… this is used to fix problems?" he asks as he looks at the label. "And it works well?"

My gaze drops to the floor. He wants me to buy it?

"One hundred percent," the woman responds.

"Good." He unscrews the lid and thrusts the bottle back at the woman. "Drink it."

My head snaps up. The clerk stares at Massimo, then laughs nervously. "Excuse me?"

"You're going to drink it. Every single drop. Or, I'll force it down your fucking throat."

"Massimo." I grab at his forearm. "No."

The saleswoman isn't smiling anymore. Her frantic eyes are flitting around the store while she clutches the container with shaking fingers.

"Don't even think about calling security," Massimo continues, his voice low and heavy with threat. "I'll kick their asses and then make you drink this shit anyway."

"Please, sir… I-I didn't mean to offend."

"Drink!"

"That's enough!" I snap and grab the damn bottle of foundation from the woman's grasp. The poor thing was already bringing it to her mouth. "I'm sorry. We're leaving."

I tug on Massimo to pull him away, but he isn't budging and continues to glare at the sales clerk. The lady seems to be seconds from fainting, and I wouldn't be surprised if she actually did. Having an enraged six-foot-seven man glaring at you like he's ready to commit murder has to be terrifying.

"Massimo." I yank on his arm again. "Please."

Thank fuck he lets me drag him away this time. I keep my grip on his forearm until we're out of the store.

"You shouldn't have done that," I say as we step inside the elevator. "It happens all the time. It wasn't her fault."

"Well, she won't do it again."

"It was unnecessary. And mean—you scared her."

"You didn't see the look on your face, Zahara. I did." He punches the button for the parking level, then braces his palm on the wall right next to my head. "No one gets to hurt you like that."

"She was just a clueless old lady."

"Clueless old ladies included." He leans forward and seizes my chin with his other hand. "School gossip. Fucking math problems. Thousands of ways how to make puff sleeves. For years, you wrote to me about every little thing but you never once mentioned your vitiligo. Why, angel?"

My breath catches in my lungs. His face is right there in front of me, his eyes searching mine. The urge to step back, to somehow run away and hide from his inspecting gaze overwhelms me. I know he's already seen every discolored spot on my face. The huge pale patches around my eyes. Another on my forehead. Several small ones on the left side of my chin, right where his fingers are pressing. He's not blind, even if he didn't bring them up before now like so many others. Still, his sudden question leaves me feeling raw. And there's nowhere for me to hide here. I'm caged between the elevator wall and Massimo's body, so I have to endure his scrutiny.

"You," Massimo rasps, tilting my chin up, "are the most beautiful thing I've ever set my eyes on. And if anyone makes you doubt how fucking gorgeous you are, I'll make them regret it for the rest of their lives."

A loud ping signals the elevator's arrival at the parking level. I remain rooted to the floor, my back plastered to the cool panel behind me. All I can do is gape at Massimo.

"You got that, angel?"

I nod.

"Good."

He releases my chin and without saying another word, takes my hand and leads me out of the elevator.

He called me beautiful. No... *gorgeous.* Did he mean it? Or was it simply a white lie to make me feel better about myself? Some of his actions confuse me, give me whiplash with the mixed messages he's sending. Like during that... moment in the store. I could have sworn he was going to kiss me before the sales associate interrupted us.

I steal a sideways look at Massimo, observing his harsh profile as I try to keep up with his long stride. The way his body moves—with measured, purposeful motion while he scans his surroundings like a predator on the hunt—is making my heartbeat erratic. He's the hottest man I've ever seen. No, of course he wouldn't have kissed me. I'm just imagining things I wish could be true.

We're between two parked vehicles, heading toward Massimo's Jag where it's tucked away in the back row, when he abruptly drops my hand.

"Get down," he whispers, simultaneously reaching behind his back without breaking his stride. "Now, Zahara."

I immediately sink to a crouch.

Massimo twists to the left, gun in hand. A loud bang explodes in the wide space, followed by the unmistakable shattering of glass. Instinctively, I wrap my arms over my head.

More gunshots. A car alarm starts blaring somewhere, and then another. A bullet hits the white sedan on my right. It's hard to determine where the gunfire is coming from, but I can see bullet casings fall to the ground around Massimo's feet as he returns fire. I count three before the noise dies down.

"Let's go." Massimo grabs my hand and pulls me up. "Quickly."

We cross the distance to his car at a run.

"Stay low," he barks, shutting the passenger door after I get in and rushing around the hood to get behind the wheel.

The tires screech as he backs up and then turns toward the exit ramp. When we pull up to the garage gate, he slows down and opens his door, looking at something on the ground. I lean over to see what it is, only catching a pair of legs before Massimo slams the car door shut and hits the gas.

"Do you know who that was?" I ask.

"Yes. A guy from prison. There was some beef between us, but he got out a few years ago."

"Must have been a hell of a spat to try to kill you now. How did he find you?"

"I'd like to know the answer to that question, too." He reaches out and cups my cheek. "You okay, angel?"

His touch singes my skin, the heat of it spreading through me until it's hard to breathe. Massimo's eyes remain focused on the road as he strokes under my eye with his thumb. Being shot at is hardly a pleasant experience, although suddenly, it doesn't feel so bad.

"Yeah," I mutter. "Sure."

As we make our way toward Massimo's home, his focus keeps bouncing between the road up ahead and the rearview mirror. Is he worried someone is following us? I don't think that's it. He hasn't looked back or glanced at the side mirrors with any wary intent. We're stopped at a streetlight when his brows suddenly furrow and his gaze darts back to the mirror.

"Zip it, asshole," he mumbles. "I'm sick of your constant bitching."

I blink, confused. "What?"

"Sorry. I was just… Nothing. It's nothing." He shakes his head. "Fuck."

For the rest of our drive, I can't help but watch him closely. Massimo says nothing at all. Still, I'm worried about him. I've seen his temper. Never directed at me, of course, though with everyone else, he can't seem to control it. He's ruthless. Abrasive. Impatient. In itself, it's rather strange, considering his meticulous and goal-oriented personality. His tact and ability to make calculated moves. If he fails to maintain his composure during the meeting with the Council, it will not end well. For them, but most importantly—for him.

Massimo

"Any guesses why that guy would want to off you?" Salvo asks as he pours two fingers of whiskey into a tumbler and passes it to me.

"He tried to steal from me on a few occasions. So I took it upon myself to relieve him of one of his possessions."

"In prison? What was it? Money? Cigarettes?"

I take a long sip and relish the burn down my throat. "His spleen."

The leg of the chair I used for my handiwork caused significant gastrointestinal perforation. And that ensured the bastard would have to shit in a plastic bag for the rest of his life. So yeah, he had a grudge against me. Except there is no way he could have known I was out, much less be able to find me in a matter of days. Not without help. As soon as we got back to the house, I had Peppe check the car for bugs. He located a tracking device planted on the chassis.

"Well, I'm glad you made it out without a scratch. Not that I would have expected otherwise." Salvo laughs and sips his own whiskey. "I got a call from our source earlier. Armando's tox screen came back. Cyanide. They can't pinpoint the time of death, other than to give an eight- to ten-hour window."

So, Nera's psycho husband was right after all, just as I suspected.

"The cameras at the Leone Villa didn't pick anything up?" I ask.

"Nothing."

"I bet the fuck who ordered the hit on Nera is behind that, as well. Armando and he were likely working together, but when idiot got caught, he got silenced before he could talk."

Salvo shakes his head. "Armando could be solely responsible for Nera's attempted assassination. He was neck-deep in debt and taking money on the side. He probably got scared Nera was onto him."

I raise an eyebrow. "And then, he somehow managed to get his hands—his broken hands—on a cyanide pill and check out? No. Whoever painted the target on her back with that kill order is behind Armando's death. The question is, who would want Nera dead?"

"You had her break the two-decade-long collaboration with the Albanian cartel. Dushku is a rather vindictive guy. It could be him."

"Vindictive, yes. Stupid, not so much. Endri Dushku would gain nothing but problems from her demise. There are just too many things that don't add up."

"What do you mean?"

Amber liquid sparkles enchantingly as I rotate my glass. It's almost the same warm shade as Zahara's eyes. I wonder if she's asleep already.

"Massimo? What things don't add up?"

I meet Salvo's gaze. How long have we known each other? Almost three decades? I remember breaking into my father's liquor cabinet when we were barely teens, so that seems about right. Other than Zahara and Peppe, he's the only other person I've trusted with my plans. And he went to great lengths to help me handle everything all these years. So, why the hell do I have this feeling that I shouldn't share this particular line of thinking with him?

"Why Armando?" I lift my eyes off the tumbler in my hand. "The only two syndicates that have a grievance against us are the Albanians and Camorra. However, Dushku has his own people who handle his 'issues.' Camorra does, too. So why involve Armando in their plan?"

"To make sure we don't suspect them?"

"Could be." I throw back the remnants of my drink and lean over the dining room table. The surface is covered with the documents Salvo brought with him. "Let's see what we have here."

On the right are the records for our legitimate businesses: cash flow reports for casinos and strip clubs, contracts with all of our vendors, lease agreements for our commercial properties, the construction company purchase orders and inventory logs, bank statements, return on investment analyses, and tax filings.

The other side of the table is covered with accounts of all of our illegal shit: the monthly income spreadsheet for the past three years of backroom gambling at the Bay View Casino, the thick ledger of debtors with the amounts they owe as well as compound interest rates, and also, all the negotiated deals for money laundering and cocaine.

I reach for the revenue printouts for the last twelve months at two of our downtown strip clubs. We're barely sitting in the black; the profits are sliding down. And the expenses have been rising over the past five years.

"We're killing the strip club business," I state. "Have our lawyers get everything ready to have both venues sold."

Salvo gapes at me from across the table. "Tiziano will be livid."

"I don't give a fuck. And he better step up his efforts in his new role or he'll lose his position as a capo. I'll have no difficulty finding someone more capable to replace him."

"New role?"

"Yes. He'll be taking over the casino business from Brio. As it happens, Brio will be retiring and spending his remaining years at his summer home on Lake Massapoag, fishing." *That motherfucker has been messing with my commands for years and needs to be removed from the picture, pronto. Tiziano has always followed orders, he just happens to be a lazy shit.*

"Massimo, I don't think it's wise to make such drastic changes as soon as you take over. Things are going quite fine as they are."

"Which is exactly the problem. 'Fine' is not good enough." I pin him with my gaze. "Or are you questioning my decisions?"

"Of course not."

"Good. I need all the paperwork for the strip clubs ready and the sale contract drafted in the next two days. I'm flying to New York to finalize everything with the buyer at the end of this month."

"So, it's already a done deal?"

"Yes."

"And who's the buyer?"

"Salvatore Ajello," I say.

A look of utter shock flashes across Salvo's face. He obviously thought I'd been keeping him in the loop on all my plans. Yet, despite his loyalty to me over the years, I still prefer to keep delicate matters close to the vest. And starting a collab with another Cosa Nostra Family, allowing them an in within our territory, might be the most delicate one of all.

Historically, the reluctance to do business together is not based in mutual animosity or bad blood. It's pride. And vanity. Stretching way back to when the first branches of Cosa Nostra took root outside of Italy. Since then, an unspoken competition has existed between the dons. A Family may allow another crime organization to occupy the same territory, perhaps even coop-erate with them, only as long as it's not another Cosa Nostra faction.

That's where teaming up with Kiril and helping him rid his crew of duplicitous scum has proved beneficial. Just as I knew it would. The money laundering racket we set up was simply a bonus. The real prize is the connection. The Bulgarians have been collaborating with Ajello for a long while, and Kiril's word bears a lot of weight in New York. Whatever he whispered into the don's ear all those years ago must have piqued Ajello's in-terest, setting us on this eventual path. It's the only reason I can think of why Salvatore kept sending spies to watch Nera and case my turf. He must have been open to considering a potential deal.

"Jesus fuck, Massimo," Salvo chokes out. "You've lost your goddamned mind."

"Maybe. Maybe not. I plan on informing the Council on Thursday, before the vote."

"Then, you're as good as done."

"We'll see." I lean back in the chair and weave my fingers to-gether behind my head. "Now, there's one more thing we need to discuss. Your compensation for your loyalty. You get to re-main as my underboss, of course. But what else do you want?"

Salvo watches me with narrowed eyes. He may have previ-ously said he doesn't expect anything in return, but he is a busi-nessman. There's no way he'll let an opportunity such as this pass without taking advantage of it. Maybe he'll ask to take on the ca-sinos. That'd be fine by me. I'll find some other role for Tiziano.

"The hand in marriage of a Cosa Nostra woman of my choosing," he finally says.

Both my eyebrows shoot up. *That* I didn't expect. "Take your pick. All I need is the name, and we'll set the date and book the church."

"Zara Veronese."

My vision goes red, obscuring everything in the room. I

had no idea I moved until my fist closes on a handful of Salvo's shirt as I shove him against the wall.

"What did you say?" My voice is barely audible as I bring my face to his.

"You said I can choose," he croaks, glaring back at me. "I'm the second-highest-ranking member of the Family. Who could be a better option to marry your sister than me?"

She's not my fucking sister! I want to yell the words at the top of my lungs, but somehow, I make myself swallow them. He's right. She's not my blood, but is still my family member. I have no right to go apeshit because he's interested in her. But regardless, I want to fucking obliterate him on the spot.

He can't have her! the hypocritical asshole roars inside my head.

"Never," I growl.

Salvo gets his palms on my chest and pushes me back. "Zara needs someone who can protect her. Especially with the shitstorm you intend to bring down on us all. Why the fuck didn't you send her away with Nera?"

Because I can't handle even the thought of being away from her. *Because I want to be the one who protects her.*

Yeah, but who's going to protect her from you? From the man who's been using her since she was a child? From her own stepbrother who has been plagued with dirty thoughts about her for the past three years?

Shut up, you dick!

The squatter in my mind has started to sing a different tune. He dogged me with his "she could have been hurt" speech the entire way home from the mall. And more than once, he nearly slipped and showed his own covetous nature. Yet, despite everything, he's still adamant she deserves better than what I can give her.

"Zahara is none of your concern, and she never will be.

Now, get the fuck out of my sight before you lose *your* spleen!" I snarl.

Salvo's eyes flash with surprise. "Is there something between you and Zara? Is that why she's living here, with you?"

"Don't be ridiculous," I snap. "Considering the situation, it is safer for her to stay here than to live alone."

"You were just shot at!"

"And I handled it. No one can keep Zahara safe better than I can!"

Squinting, Salvo glares at me. "If something is going on between you two, it'll cause a scandal of epic proportions. You know how the Family is where women are concerned. Judgmental whispers. Merciless gossip. Ill repute. The rumors and stigma will follow her for the rest of her life. They'll crucify her, Massimo."

I let go of his shirt and meet him eyeball-to-eyeball. "There's nothing between me and my stepsister. Never was. Never will be. And if you even consider voicing that shit ever again, I'll fucking end you."

Salvo adjusts his tie and steps around me, heading toward the door. "Well, I'm glad that I was wrong. Even if she wasn't your stepsister, I can't think of a more wretched match. Just... look at you. Behaving like a savage beast on the loose."

The door shuts behind him with a soft click.

I turn toward the windows that face the overgrown yard and wrap my hands around the back of my head. He's right. Fucking right again. And he doesn't even know the full extent of how fucked-up I actually am.

And where the hell did he get the idea of marrying Zahara? Strategically, it would be a good move for him, but is there more to it? Is there something between them?

Her life is her own. She can be with whomever she wants. Even Salvo. You have no right to feel jealous. Or angry. Betrayed. She isn't yours and never could be.

"Changed your mind already?" I mumble. "A minute ago, your possessive ass was melting down that Salvo wanted to make her his wife."

A lapse in judgment.

"Sure," I snort, pushing away my voice of reason.

My vision snags on the reflection of the Spada coat of arms hanging on the opposite wall. A double-edged sword on a shield. My father had it commissioned when he became the don. I've never related to it more than I do now. Dark thoughts keep circling my mind. I can't believe Salvo asked for Zahara's hand in marriage. And my reaction? A total Neanderthal move.

Scumbag. I am a complete scumbag because, at the moment, I wish I could grab that sword and run it through my friend. Kill him for daring to lay claim to Zahara.

Fuck! I need so much damned therapy.

Salvo probably picked Zahara because it's the most advantageous match since Nera is already married. He'd elevate his position in the Family, something Salvo has always had a boner for. I can understand his logic and ambition, yet I can't get over him wanting someone who is mine. And that alone makes me want to kill him.

When I finally leave the dining room, it's well after midnight. I take the file folders up to my bedroom on the third floor and then descend the stairs back down to the second.

The rapid tick-tick-tick of a sewing machine sounds from inside Zahara's room. Shouldn't she be asleep at this hour? I lean my back on the wall beside her door and listen to the rhythmic noise. What's she working on? An underlining? Or maybe an invisible zipper? I smile. She hates inserting those.

I wait until everything falls silent, until after I'm sure she's finally gone to bed. Then, I stagger to the antique wardrobe in the alcove at the end of the hallway and take out the pillow I stashed within. Laying it in front of Zahara's door, I sprawl on the floor with my forehead all but pressed to the wooden surface. In the dark, as always, my thoughts turn to her.

My Zahara.

Does she sleep naked? Or does she prefer one of those delicate satin nighties? I imagine her in the nude. Curled up on one side of the bed. I imagine climbing under the sheets beside her. My arm would slide around her waist, and I'd pull her into my body until her back is plastered to my chest. And I'd bury my nose in her hair, inhale her jasmine scent. I want it filling my nostrils until the end of time.

My cock gets hard just from picturing her spooned by my body. Safe in my arms. Mine.

Never going to happen.

I roll onto my other side, turning my back to the door. I only last about five seconds in that position before I twist to face the barrier to Zahara's room again.

CHAPTER
seventeen

 Zahara

Four days later

INCESSANT BUZZING COMES FROM SOMEWHERE ON MY left. I extend my hand and pat the nightstand surface until I find my vibrating phone. The screen mocks me with its brightness, showing that it's 6:30 a.m. My movements could hardly be called coordinated as I shut off the alarm and climb out of bed. Grabbing a matching set of black underwear and a bra from the dresser, I head to the en suite bathroom to take a shower.

The reno company will be completing the final touches on the ground floor today and hopefully, everything will be ready for the big meeting tomorrow evening. The high-ranking members of the Family, capos, and investors, will all be voting for or against Massimo taking over the Boston Cosa Nostra. Typically, this vote is nothing more than a formality, but sometimes surprises can spring up. Like when my father was voted in instead of Batista Leone.

It seems the news of Nera's resignation and awareness that Massimo is responsible for the Family's prosperity has spread

Once people realized that he had been handling the business end of things for the past two decades, their reaction was immediate and came down with the force of a tsunami. For days, the house has been under siege by would-be visitors, though Peppe's guys kept everyone at bay. The upper echelon of Boston's Cosa Nostra society appears to be sufficiently pleased. Considering how much their bank accounts grew under Massimo's direction, there's no reason for them to want to change anything.

Unless he loses his temper during the meeting.

The Family loves money. But they value stability more. They would sacrifice future profits in an instant before they let a loose cannon take the reins of their lives. And based on Massimo's recent behavior, I'm worried that may be the exact outcome.

Ever since his conversation with Salvo on Sunday night, Massimo has been doing his best to avoid me. He has spent most of his time holed up in the dining room, which has been remodeled into a huge meeting hall. At the same time, though—metaphorically speaking—he hasn't let me out of his sight.

On Monday, when I went to visit my niece and sister, he wouldn't let me drive myself over to my brother-in-law's downtown apartment. Massimo insisted on taking me there himself and spent four hours in his Jag, parked in an underground garage waiting for me. Nera wouldn't let him up. She's still pissed at him for turning her life into a living hell these last several years. Massimo grumbled and eventually relented, but only after barking at Kai to keep me safe.

Then, yesterday, when I went over to the Leone Villa to direct the movers on how to pack what's left of my things, Massimo insisted on going with me. He had three security guys follow us in a separate car, and all of them hovered over me the entire time I spoke with the packing crew.

He wouldn't even let me go alone to the nearest store last night to buy some damn shampoo. Instead, he went to get it himself after ordering Peppe to watch the place like a freaking hawk. I was instructed not to leave his side until Massimo returned. All in the name of safety, apparently.

I turn toward the shelf built-in inside the shower stall and grab one of the fourteen shampoo bottles lined up there. Each is labeled as either "For Sensitive Skin" or "Contains Natural Ingredients Only." He remembered. Remembered after hearing only once that products with harsh chemicals, alcohol, and fragrances easily irritate my skin. Now, the cupboards under the sink are crammed with bottles of body milk, shower gel, and hair essentials that all bear the same type of labels. All in all, there must be around thirty containers.

After I'm done washing my hair, I leave it to air-dry and head into the walk-in closet. Five minutes later, I'm working the clasp on the tennis bracelet Massimo got for me and exiting my room when I almost trip over a huge male body, sleeping right in front of my door.

"Massimo?"

He leaps to his feet and pushes me behind his back. I'm squished between his massive form and the wall while he snaps his head from side to side to assess the hallway. His left hand is pressed to my hip, but his right is gripping a weapon at the ready. He looks rather deranged.

"Um… There's no one there," I mumble into his back. He's still wearing the gray dress shirt and black pants from the previous evening. "You can put away the gun."

"Sorry," he says in a gruff voice and bends down to pick up the pillow off the floor. "I'm usually more alert when I wake up."

"Why were you sleeping at my door?"

His face darkens. For a few moments, he just sears me with those hellish eyes, then turns and heads down the hall. Well, if he thinks this conversation is finished, he's wrong! He's been acting weird for days, and we need to get to the bottom of whatever it is before he goes nuclear.

I trail after him along the corridor and up the stairs to the upper floor. This part of the house hasn't yet been touched by the renovation company, and it's in a dreadful state. The ravages of time are more apparent here. Cracked door frames and drywall where the house has settled. Faded, peeling wallpaper in some rooms. Carpet that has seen much better days. I don't understand why he hasn't moved into one of the rooms on the second floor, where I am. It's in much better condition.

Following Massimo inside the room he disappeared into, the first thing I notice is the perfectly made bed. The bedding upon it is pristine, with not a crease or a dent in sight. Even the throw pillows are lined up as they were on my own bed when we first arrived here. That was five nights ago, just after the cleaning company left.

"Where have you been sleeping this past week?" I ask. "Because this bed doesn't look like it's been slept in."

Massimo opens an upright dresser in the corner and starts rummaging through it without a word.

"Will you please answer me?"

He pulls out a pair of sweatpants and a T-shirt, then turns around and crosses the distance separating us in three large steps. My heartbeat quickens at having him this close, my fingers ache to reach out and stroke his chest.

"I slept in front of your door."

My head snaps up. "Why?"

"Because I need to know that you're safe." He lifts a stray wet strand that has fallen over my face and tucks it behind my ear. "And, because for some reason, it's the only place in this house where I can actually get some rest."

Air gets trapped in my lungs. He is so near that our bodies are almost touching. I want to close the gap, lean on him, and bridge that divide. Yet I don't dare move a muscle. Afraid to face another rejection. Terrified of hearing him say that he doesn't see me as anything but his stepsister. So, instead, I content myself

197

with simply staring into his dark, enigmatic eyes, bathing in the warmth of his presence.

"Why?" I ask again.

"Being close to you brings me peace."

I bite the inside of my cheek. "There's a couch in my bedroom, next to the fireplace. I can leave the door open tonight."

Something dangerous flashes in his expression, like a burst of flame—there one moment and gone the next. "Please. Don't."

"Why not?"

Massimo dips his head until the tip of his nose almost touches my crown. Almost. He takes a deep breath as if steeling himself.

"I might come in if you do, Zahara. And we both know that can't happen. Keep the fucking door locked." Abruptly, he spins on his heel and marches to the bathroom, leaving me to stare at the softly shut door.

What just happened?

What did he mean?

I grab at the doorframe and lean my shoulder on the jamb, suddenly feeling weak in the knees.

He can't possibly be implying what I think he is.

Or... can he?

"Now, the Uzi." Massimo gestures to the weapon lying on the kitchen island.

Timoteo picks up the semiautomatic and turns toward the backyard. The French double doors are open, revealing the freshly mowed lawn, and at the far end, a makeshift stand with several beer cans lined up along it.

I sigh. "In case you forgot, Timoteo is here to fill the butler position."

The older fellow worked in my father's home for almost a

decade. After Dad was killed and my sister and I moved to the Leone Villa, Nera had several of our old staff transferred to our new home, including Timoteo and Iris. Following Massimo's disastrous interviews when he attempted to hire house staff, I invited both of them, as well as a few others who have always been reliable, to work at the Spada Estate.

"Exactly," Massimo affirms. "Which means the safety of the house should be one of his top priorities."

"I thought maintaining safety was the job of your soldiers."

"It's always good to have additional marksmen on hand. Come on, Timoteo. Fire at will."

The butler lifts the Uzi and aims at the targets. A moment later, five earsplitting bangs explode inside the kitchen. With my jaw nearly on the floor, I watch Timoteo casually return the weapon to the countertop and clasp his hands behind his back. Then, he turns to face Massimo as if waiting for his next gentlemanly command.

I've always known Timoteo to be extremely capable, yet I had no idea he knew how to shoot.

"Very good." Massimo gives him an approving nod. "You're settling into this situation with an unexpected ease."

"I worked at the house when Miss Nera's husband, Mr. Mazur, was in charge of keeping the property and occupants safe," Timoteo declares as if that explanation is enough. "After just three weeks under his oversight, I consider myself well-versed in... handling the challenging requirements of a similar work environment."

"Perfect." Massimo turns toward Iris. "And the new cook?"

"Iris is similarly adept and used to complexities," I interject. "She had to deal with cleaning up the office after Kai 'fired' the previous Head of Security."

"I have to say, I wholeheartedly approve of your choices for my new staff." Massimo meets my gaze. It's the first time since this morning he's done that. "Thank you for managing them and everything else these past few days. I'd like to meet with everyone as a group and go over some house rules."

Timoteo, with Iris close on his heels, rushes past us, probably to gather the rest of the staff, leaving me and Massimo alone in the kitchen.

"Please try not to traumatize them too much."

A small smile pulls at his lips. It's not one of his wicked smirks, but a handsome, flirtatious grin that does funny things to my insides.

"I'll do my best. Although, I'm not making any promises."

His elbow brushes my arm as he passes by me, and I almost jump out of my skin. It's the same effect each of his letters had on me when they arrived. The difference now, however, is *he* is here. In front of me. He's real. It's still difficult to wrap my mind around that fact.

I tiptoe out of the kitchen and hang back by the kentia palm in its massive planter where it's set up by the archway that separates the entry hall from the dining room. Twelve members of the house staff are gathered at the foot of the stairs, all facing Massimo. Timoteo and Iris are at the head of the line, followed by five maids, the gardener, and three undercooks. Tinia is standing at the very end, visibly nervous to be in Massimo's presence. They all have their hands clasped in front of them and are listening intently to what the lord of the manor expects of them. I handpicked each of them, selecting from those who had worked for my family that I knew could be trusted. They didn't need to be told how intricate and demanding working in the don's household could be, however, I still filled every single one in as soon as they arrived. I also hinted that if they experienced difficulties handling Massimo's temper, they should come to me.

It feels strange to be in charge of anything. I've always avoided people in the past, staff included. Now, I'm directing the renovation workers, hiring staff, and even dealing with sales reps while picking out furniture for Massimo's home. So weird, but it's not *bad* weird. Actually, I'm enjoying myself.

"What do you mean, you've never held a gun?" Massimo's growl breaks me out of my thoughts.

I look up, finding him looming over the gardener—hands braced on his hips, looking agitated as hell.

"I... I didn't have a chance to do so, Mr. Spada."

"That's unacceptable. What about you?" Massimo turns toward the maids, who all appear as if they are seconds away from fleeing.

All five women vehemently shake their heads.

"Timoteo will teach you all how to shoot a firearm by the end of the week," Massimo barks. "One of the guys will get you weapons first thing in the morning. Glocks for the men, Baby Desert Eagles for the women."

Timoteo leans to the side and meets my gaze. The look in his eyes asks me: *Is he serious?*

I nod.

He blinks, returns my gesture, and faces Massimo again. "Of course, Mr. Spada."

"Good. Also, your one and only warning: I do not tolerate traitors. Or give second chances. You keep your mouth shut, or I'll shut it for you. Permanently."

I sigh. Well... He did say he wasn't making promises.

Massimo continues barking orders while I watch him from behind the leaves of the palm. Everything about him is fascinating. Like, the dragon designs inked on his massive forearms. Identical in shape and size, the only difference between them is the color—red on his left and black on the right—and the fact that the two seem to be staring each other down. And how the muscles on his back ripple every time he moves. His biceps, stretching the fabric of his T-shirt, bulge beneath short sleeves that look like they've been painted on. And then, there are his sweatpants—riding a bit low, enough to reveal the waistband of his underwear. *Boxers or briefs?*

My hands itch to explore that magnificent body. How would it feel? He's got a warrior's physique. I want to touch, to taste every single inch of it. With my fingers, my lips, and my tongue. Is he a passionate lover? He must be. He can't be anything else with that personality of his. Could he throw me on the bed and fuck me into the mattress? I'd love for him to do just that.

Heat floods my system. The tingling, achy feeling hits my core again. It's been a constant in his presence, running like a current through my veins. But now, as I'm imagining Massimo taking me over and over, it surges, driving me insane.

Shaking my head to regain my composure, my gaze shifts from his waistband to his hand. It's huge—like everything else about him—fingers gripping the back of a chair while he speaks in his deep, booming voice. Would his touch be rough or gentle? Would he pin me down? Would he make me beg for more? I bite my lower lip as I picture those inked fingers wrapped around my throat while he ravages my mouth with his. Whispers... between kisses. Him telling me filthy things. Telling me... Telling me something that I've only ever dreamed of.

I want you.
I need you.
I love you.

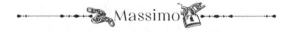

Massimo

I lie in my bed and stare at the ceiling.

The alarm is set, the video surveillance is on. Armed to the teeth, my guys are patrolling the grounds. I just finished my third sweep of the house, confirming everything is as it should be. There are no threats. No intruders in sight. No reason for me to feel so anxious simply because I've decided to stop sleeping in front of Zahara's door.

She's safe and sound. You're just looking for another excuse to head back down, to be close to her. Go to sleep.

I can't.

It's bad enough she found out you've been spending your nights at her door. Not only is it ludicrous, it probably freaked her the hell out.

But what if she needs me? The unknown threat is still out there.

We still haven't figured out who planted that damn bug on my car, the one that led the shooter at the mall straight to me. Salvo thinks it might have been the feds. I don't agree, since McBride picked the vehicle up directly from the dealership and drove it straight to the prison.

Whoever has been plotting against you, wants you dead. If, somehow, they manage to get inside, they'll come for you. Not Zahara. You need to stay put.

As I roll over to my side, my eyes zero in on the door.

Still… What if someone does get into the house? What if Zahara comes face-to-face with a killer and the asshole decides to take her out? She might be struggling for her life while I'm lounging here, a full floor away!

Fuck.

Leaping out of bed, I rush out of the room and down the stairs, cursing myself the entire way. Only once I reach the second floor and plant my butt in front of Zahara's door, can I finally draw a full breath. If anyone dares to go near her, they'll have to come through me. And I might actually get some shut-eye tonight after all.

What happened to the promise you made to yourself to never sleep outside her door again?

I tried, okay?

I swore I wouldn't do it. Even knowing that staying away

from her meant sleep wouldn't come. It's not as if I'm not used to going without.

Even before she found me sleeping by her door, the temptation had been seeping into my bones, getting harder and harder to fight. Knowing she was right there, with only a wooden surface separating us, had been driving me insane. I kept imagining myself walking into her room, simply to watch her sleep. Just so I could be near her. Just so I could feel the peace that only *she* brings to me. When she's by my side, I don't feel like the stark raving mad asshole two decades in prison made me.

That hasn't changed. Being the crazy asshole.

At least I've managed to keep my dirty thoughts in check. Mostly. I've given myself a mental slap whenever reality wanted to slip away. If Zahara had even an inkling of what I'd been thinking, she'd be disgusted. How could she not be?

My thoughts... Lustful, mouthwatering thoughts. Where my hands are on her goddess-like body, tracing every soft curve with my aching palms. Holding her in my arms, her face tucked into the crook of my neck. It's the only place where she'd be completely safe. With my lips, grazing hers, just as I'd fantasized doing since the first moment I saw her.

The moment when she was a bright ray of light, surrounded by so many dark shadows. An angel among a crowd of devils huddled at her father's grave. The only person in this world who didn't feel like a stranger to me.

The only woman who has ever captured my interest. Because of how she saw the *real* me. The one I tried to hide, yet she wouldn't let me, burrowing her way under my skin. I should have known then...

I shouldn't have even...

But like the asshole I am, I still did.

Remembered, what I once told her in a letter. The one where she asked what I would do when I was set free. *I'd fuck my way through a whorehouse*, is what I told her. After almost twenty years without getting laid, a fucking frenzy should've been a piece of cake. Should've easily wiped the daydreams of making love to Zahara from my mind. Something I desperately needed. So, that's exactly where I headed. Had McBride drive me directly from the prison's gate to a Cosa Nostra strip club, where they serve pussy dessert on the side. A goddamned sugar buffet.

And I couldn't get my dick up.

Blonde. Dark-haired. Tall and short. Scantily dressed. Naked. The manager kept bringing girl after girl into the VIP room, and my damn cock didn't even twitch. Not once.

I figured the prison messed me up more than I ever thought, so I left, my broken cock the least of my worries.

That's one problem I no longer need to solve, though. My cock is stone-hard whenever I picture Zahara in my arms. It works just fine every time I imagine her with me. Her delicate skin. Her jasmine scent. Her… honeyed taste.

Jesus fucking Christ. What am I doing? The combative voice in my head is right. I'm turning forty in two months—she's half my miserable age. And if that's not bad enough, she's my *stepsister*! I should feel nothing more than a brotherly affection toward her. Yet there's nothing remotely *brotherly* about my feelings.

I close my eyes, trying to fall asleep, but sleep doesn't come. Tonight, the twenty feet separating us is nineteen too many. Feeling like the sickest creep on earth, I rise from my spot on the floor and slowly turn the doorknob to Zahara's room.

The goddamned door opens.

I fucking told her to keep it locked!

As carefully as I can, without making the slightest noise, I step inside the darkened bedroom.

The carpet covering the floor is thick, muffling my steps as I approach. Moonlight slips through the gap in the drapes, falling onto the bed where Zahara is sleeping. She's curled in the fetal position atop a sea of white bedding. Despite the long-sleeved nightgown, she must be chilly. Especially with her blanket tossed off and bunched at her feet.

For a moment, I let myself stare at her lovely face. It's partially obscured by the sleep-tangled strands of her light-brown hair. Her black nightie has ridden up almost to her waist, allowing me a view of the perfect curve of her luscious ass and shapely legs. My dick is instantly a steel rod.

I don't want to wake her, so I practically hold my breath as I draw closer to her bed. Permitting myself one final, quick look, I lift the edge of the crumpled blanket and carefully pull it over Zahara, high enough to cover her up to her chin. She looks so small. So peaceful. I don't want to leave her.

Looking around, I spot an armchair nestled beside her desk where it's set up beneath a window. It's only steps from her bed and has a direct line of sight. I back away and lower myself onto the seat, all the while fighting to ignore the objections of my painfully hard cock.

For days, I've been trying to figure out what's going on in my head, why I have this obsessive pull toward her. My *stepsister*. I've even gone as far as googling the reasons for my feelings and behavior. This can't be healthy or normal. Hours and hours I've spent combing across various sites, looking at blogs and psychiatric forums covering the issues ex-cons experience as they try to fit back into society.

Who knows if the shit I've read is real, especially since multiple disorders seem relevant to me. Several symptoms hit the nail square on the head. Like the constant hypervigilance. The persistent sense that I'm trapped in a rival gang's territory, just waiting for a shiv in my back. The overwhelming and damn near irresistible impulse to go on the attack, inflicting fear and pain, because for so long it was the only way to keep the cuntfucks in check and myself safe.

The violent urges that I can't seem to control continue to flow through me. They're all I know, all I'm used to. Behind bars, the only way to stay alive is to make sure you're riding at the top. The world around me, I don't recognize and can't fucking relate to. Everyone is a potential threat, a potential enemy. Even Salvo. Despite his loyalty to me all these years.

I just.... don't care anymore. About anything. The fucking Family included. It used to sustain me, like a mental crutch, gave me something to focus on so I wouldn't go nuts in prison. Like a dog with a bone, not letting go of a bite, for if I did, I'd lose the only thing I had.

That drive is still within me. I *will* see my plan to the end. But at the same time... I don't particularly give a shit about it. I want to, though. I want to care, as I did before. Just can't seem to make myself do it. As if something important, something fundamental that makes me... *me*, simply died. I feel so lost. And so fucking angry.

One of the articles I came across during my cyber intro-spection mentioned depression as a possible reason I'm such an irascible bastard. Depression, really? I don't feel apathy or avoli-tion, which is what I thought defined the condition—a general lack of interest in life. Instead, I want to destroy. Annihilate. Burn the fucking world to the ground, the one that dared to move on without me. Spit on the fate that stole half of my life, leaving me to rot in that hellhole. Kill the cocksuckers responsible for that, those still hiding in the shadows. I want to demolish them, rain death on their miserable heads. Slay everyone.

And amid the chaos, the violence, my wrath, there's *her*. My Zahara. My peaceful haven. An angel, offering a hand of sal-vation to a man burning in his own inferno. She's grace, kind-ness, and my last hope. The only thing that keeps me tied to this mortal coil.

I can't taint the only pure thing lighting up my existence. No matter how crazy it makes me, I won't put my hands on Zahara, subjecting her to that stigma for the rest of her life.

Deciding that, though, doesn't make my dick any less hard.

I slide my hand inside my sweatpants and take ahold of my aching cock. Squeezing it to the point of pain that nearly makes me roar into the night.

Yet not a sound leaves my lips. I don't let it. Won't risk waking her up to see me losing my sanity. If this was nothing but a physical urge, I'd have an easier time dealing with the madness. Yet, it isn't. I know it's not. Because, even with Zahara's body completely covered, hidden from my eyes, my mind still conjures up her image. It's not just her sinful curves and ethereal beauty that turn me the fuck on. It's more.

It's the idea of having her tucked into my side, my arms keeping her safe. Of having the right to touch her. Whenever and wherever I want. Of being able to bury my nose in her skin, inhale deeply, having the freedom to breathe her in without reproach. This dark abyss I'm facing, I want us to find a way across—together. I want to tell her all the fears that plague me, things I would never voice aloud to anyone else.

Zahara is the only person who I can see standing next to me for the rest of my life. As a friend. And my lover. *My wife.* God, I've even imagined her pregnant with my babies. A son. A daughter. Mine, all mine. I want to claim her, join in the most intimate and carnal way until we are one. I *need* her like I need the fucking air.

I squeeze my dick again, this time even harder. A punishment for my dirty thoughts. I need the treacherous fucker to go down.

It doesn't work.

It doesn't fucking work.

Letting go of my choke hold, since it's apparent I can't force it to behave, I start to stroke. Imagining what it would feel like to be inside her.

You fucking creep. The voice in my head is brimming with disgust. Even my inner self is appalled by my actions. ***Tugging*** *on your cock in the dark while you watch the woman sleep. One seriously sick bastard, that's what you are.*

"Shut the fuck up," I growl, barely above a whisper.

Closing my eyes, I pick up my pace. My cock is long past the normal point of no return, and every stroke sends a jolt of agony through my starving body. Every cell vibrates with electricity. But the damn thing is still an unbending rod. Swollen and angry. As if my hand alone is no longer enough to bring the release I'm chasing.

Nearly roaring aloud in pain, I squeeze again and open my eyes.

Only to find Zahara sitting up in bed. Staring at me with wide, astonished eyes.

Jesus fuck.

I should get off my ass and walk away. I don't. Instead, I hold her gaze and let her watch me. Maybe this will clue her in on what a twisted son of a bitch I am. Maybe she'll run, never to return to me. I hope she does. Because God knows, I can't walk away from her.

Even though I should.

Zahara

"Shut the fuck up."

My eyelids crack open. I'm a fairly light sleeper and positive that I heard something close by. The room is dark, and it takes a moment for my eyes to adjust to the unlit space. Once I do, the figure sitting near my desk comes into focus.

Massimo.

The silver beam streaming through the opening in the curtains creates an interplay of light and shadow over his impeccably sculpted, shirtless torso. Is this a dream?

His face is tilted up toward the ceiling, however, his eyes appear to be closed and a grimace is marring his flawless features. I don't dare move an inch, pretending that I'm still asleep, while my eyes rove up and down his rapidly rising chest. He's gripping the armrest of the chair with his left hand so hard, I can see the outline of the corded muscles of his forearm. His right hand is somewhat lost in the shadows on his lap, but I can see it moving. There's a telling sway of the bare skin as it glistens in the dim light.

I feel the color flood my cheeks when I realize what he's doing. Transfixed, I watch as he pleasures himself. Right here, in my darkened room. The strange tightness between my legs grips me again, as it does each time he is near. I can't look away. My heart rate blasts into the stratosphere. With every stroke of his hand, the flexing in my core gets stronger.

"Appalled, angel?" he rasps. His voice sounds deeper than usual, his words echo throughout the room.

I swallow, only now realizing I'm sitting nearly fully upright, my eyes locked squarely on him. Yes, I probably should be appalled to find Massimo in my bedroom, jerking his cock mere steps from my bed. But I'm not. I'm so not.

I suck in a breath and meet his gaze. "Don't stop."

Devilish eyes burn through me as he keeps stroking himself inside his sweatpants. Based on the sizable bulge, his dick is huge and fully erect.

He lied. He lied to me after all.

All those things he said… That he sees me as only his stepsister. His assurance that he simply needs to protect a member of his family.

He lied.

As soon as that thought slams into my mind, my heart makes a valiant attempt to break out of my ribcage. It thunders loudly in my ears, and suddenly, all air leaves the room. That devastation I felt for believing his indifference toward me? The despair that gripped me because I thought that there was no chance of him ever returning my feelings? All of that misery was unfounded. A man doesn't come to a woman's room to jerk off if he feels nothing toward her.

He fucking lied!

A mix of anger and elation overwhelms me. On trembling legs, I rise and cross the space between us, until I'm standing at his wide-spread knees. My mouth grows dry. My skin feels clammy. Everything in me brims with barely restrained energy.

"Liar," I whisper. There's no need to elaborate further because I see it in his eyes—he knows what I mean.

"Guilty as charged."

His words ring in my head. I grit my teeth. And then, I slap him across his face. A small retaliation for the hurt he caused me. For making me believe he had no feelings for me.

Massimo doesn't even blink. He keeps stroking his cock, slowly, and without making a sound. His body seems unnaturally tense. A sheen of perspiration glistens on his chest. Is this how a man looks when he pleasures himself? His face is half-hidden in the darkness, though I can clearly see the hard line of his clenched jaw.

That expression doesn't suggest he's enjoying himself. He looks like he's... in pain.

"You said you'd fuck your way through a whorehouse when you got released," I bite out. I hated that awful letter, and my voice nearly breaks as I push out the words. But I need to know—is this simply the reaction of a man who hasn't had sex in years? Or something else completely? Of every male in the universe I might have thought could be turned on by me, Massimo would have been the last.

"Mm-hmm. Drove straight there." His nostrils flare. "And couldn't get my dick up for anyone."

I look down at his lap. He pulls his hand away, revealing the outline of his hard-on, tenting the fabric of his pants.

I can't seem to look away. The anger I've been feeling evaporates, replaced with an onslaught of different feelings hitting me right in the chest. Satisfaction from knowing that it's me who has caused him to be so turned-on. Excitement mixed with bone-shattering nervousness that leaves my mind utterly blank. My fingers are itching to touch him, to assure myself that this is real and not just a product of my imagination, except I don't dare. I'm afraid this is all but a dream, and I don't want to wake up if it is. Because this is Massimo. The only man who has ever made me feel this way. The only one who ever will.

"You have nothing to say?" he growls. "Do you think me vile? A sick fuck who came into his stepsister's room to jerk off?"

My hand is shaking as I hesitantly reach out and lightly stroke his bulge. A guttural, pain-filled moan emits from Massimo's throat. And I whimper. Shaken by both the sound and the power I feel under my palm.

"Why couldn't you... get hard?" I give his cock another gentle brush over his sweatpants. "Tiziano always boasts about having the most beautiful girls in Boston."

"Because none of those women were you, Zahara." His reply is groaned through his teeth.

A swarm of butterflies takes flight inside my stomach as I let every syllable of his growled reply sink in. For years, I've fantasized about him saying things like that to me. In each of those dreamed-up situations, I imagined him softly whispering those words in my ear. I thought I would prefer him to speak like that. I was wrong. This. His growled response, which shows his internal battle—a battle he's obviously losing—is what I needed. A throb, unlike any I've felt, seizes my core, and I feel myself get wetter.

I watch him, this complicated man who turned my life upside down. As a young girl, I wrote to him, hoping he'd step into my big brother's shoes. I wanted a confidant, a protector. Someone who'd tell me that everything would be alright.

Regardless of how tough life got, I wanted him to paint a rosy picture.

He gave me none of those things.

He gave me everything I never knew I needed.

Purpose. Self-confidence. A sense of self-worth.

Without meaning to, he turned me into the person I am today. Strong. Resilient. Capable. The kind of woman I always wanted to be. And *that* woman isn't scared anymore. She's willing to go after what she wants. *Him.* Even when it's scaring the shit out of her.

With my whole body vibrating with need, I slowly sink to my knees on the carpet, right there between his legs.

Massimo's frantic eyes follow my every movement. The tension in his upper body seems to pull tighter. Even in this low light, the pulse point on his neck draws my attention as a slight shiver makes its way through him.

My fingers are trembling as I grab ahold of the elastic of his sweats and carefully pull it down. Massimo's cock springs free, enormous and ramrod-straight. So engorged, it looks almost purple. My hand shakes as I wrap my fingers around his tip and start stroking along his length.

Steel, encased in velvet.

"Zahara." Massimo's deep, rumbling growl breaks the silence. His head is bent, and he's gripping both armrests with wood-splitting force. "No."

"Why not?" I wet my lips. "I don't see you as a brother, Massimo. Haven't you realized that by now?"

His hand shoots out, fisting the hair at my nape. Fire rages inside his dark, smoldering eyes. They blaze through me, igniting my desire. Setting off an inferno neither one of us could escape. "Don't say that."

"Why? It's the truth." I lean forward and press my tongue to the head of his cock.

A violent shudder overtakes Massimo's body, jolting him

as if he was struck by lightning. An intense gratification blooms inside me at the sense of victory I feel. I did that. Me. I may not be experienced, and I'm still feeling nervous that I might do something wrong, yet seeing his reaction to that one single touch, gives me the courage to continue.

I lick him from base to tip, just like I've seen in videos, enjoying the way he responds. Shallow, fast breaths as he nearly bows out of the seat. Tremors rack him while I circle the swollen head with my tongue, building up the tempo, then lick away the drops of salty pre-cum at the slit. Another proof that all his claims of not being attracted to me were nothing but lies. Why was he fighting this pull between us? How would something that feels so good be labeled as something bad? I lick his cock again, relishing having him come undone under my touch. I want more. I want the taste of him to be branded on my tongue, the same way he imprinted himself on my soul.

The tightness and ache between my legs is spiking. I've never felt this kind of overwhelming need as I do now. My panties are completely drenched. Is it the flavor of him, or the fact that I am finally experiencing what I yearned for so long? Getting to know him on a carnal level, having our bodies so in tune with each other.

The silky texture of his stone-hard length scorches my palm as I slide my hand down and gently cradle his balls. When I move closer and seal my lips around his tip, his dick twitches so fiercely that it almost slips out of my mouth. Slowly, I take more of him down my throat while letting my teeth lightly graze his sensitive flesh.

"*Madonna Santa*," Massimo groans, tightening his hold on my hair.

Every muscle in his body is taut, so much so that he remains rigid like a fine marble statue. I let my lips languidly glide up his cock. Feasting on it. He is mine. Massimo Spada is finally mine.

My heart nearly bursts from that thought. I move my mouth to the tip of his cock and suck it, hollowing out my cheeks.

Massimo convulses, and a guttural roar fills the room. Warmth explodes down my throat as he comes in my mouth. I swallow every last drop of his cum. It's a testament. Unequivocal proof. The truth he's been hiding from me behind the facade of rejection.

Evidence of his feelings. For me. And not the sisterly kind.

Still feeling a bit anxious, I get to my feet and stand between his splayed knees. His chest is rising and falling at a galloping rate, while his fingers continue to clutch my hair.

"Massimo?" I caress the side of his tightly clenched jaw with my knuckles.

A low and deep rumble, like a lion's growl, emanates from his throat. The shadows on his bare chest shift when he stands up. His hold on my hair intensifies while he towers over me, staring down at me like a magnificent king of beasts. His other arm snakes around my waist, locking me in a viselike grip and lifting me off the ground. My breath hitches as I marvel at the sensation of being pressed flush against him, and I lose myself in his sultry gaze.

"Are there needles or other sharp shit over there?" he croaks.

I blink, lightheaded and bewildered. "Where?"

He nods toward the antique work desk to the left of us where I've spread out the half-cut dress lining.

"Um... no. I don't think so."

That seems to satisfy him and he gives me another nod, then deposits me right on top of the silky fabric.

His eyes burn into mine as he trails his palms up my thighs, inch by arduous inch. There's so much tension there, in his dark, unyielding gaze. His expression is set in hard lines, his stance so solid, it's like he's become a mountain, not a man.

"So soft..." Low, mumbled words. "I never dreamed your skin would be this soft. Like feathers."

Everywhere he touches sizzles as if singed by flame. He doesn't have a gentleman's hands. His palms are rough, without any trace of softness. Battered skin which endured so much. Just like his soul. But his caress is so delicate as he trails those coarse palms up my legs until his fingers graze my panties. With the hem of my nightgown bunched around my hips, the black lace is the only barrier between my pussy and his touch.

"I've lost sleep on so many nights imagining what you would feel like, angel." Gently, he pushes my legs open. "And your heavenly scent."

Should I be embarrassed right now? Does it make me some kind of hussy if I'm not? That instead of closing my legs, Massimo's words lead me to open them wider. As jittery as I feel over what's to come, I crave it. Anticipate it with every fiber of my being.

I exhale in short, rapid bursts as he drops to his knees and buries his nose at the apex of my thighs. When he inhales, he sounds like a suffocating man who just got his first breath of air.

"Jasmine. Peace," he mumbles into my pussy, breathing in deeply again. "And sin."

Warm breath wafts through the lace of my panties, tingling my sensitive flesh. *Want… Need.* My legs start shaking. And my hands. I lean back and fall onto the surface of the desk, while Massimo keeps nuzzling my pussy with his face.

"I need…" I pant, grabbing his shoulders and arching my back. I don't know what I'm asking for. I just know that I need… more. More of him. I want him to know me inside out. I want us joined completely, so there isn't even a speck of unknown between us. I want to be his in every way.

"I need to feel you… down there," I pant. "I need it so much that it hurts. Please."

Rough palms slip under my ass cheeks, pulling my panties down.

"I'll probably burn in hell for this, Zahara."

The lace slides down my legs, and then… warm wetness… laving my folds. His tongue.

"Dear God," I gasp.

My vision blurs, as if the world has vanished. I'm not in my room anymore. Instead, I'm suspended somewhere in midair, trying to remember how to breathe while Massimo feasts on my pussy as if it's a mouthwatering dessert. He's swallowing my arousal. Licking away every single drop. It's as if my most secret imagination came to life. Years of waiting. Hoping. My chest expands as if my heart suddenly became too large for it. My inner walls clench so wildly, I might lose my mind. *More.* I need more or I'll completely crack.

"Soaked…" he mumbles as he keeps devouring my pussy. "Do you always get so wet, angel? Can any man just milk your juices like this?"

A light press of his thumb on my clit sends my eyes rolling back into my head. Oh God, he's added his fingers now, and he is doing the most sinful things with them. Caressing. Tapping. And… dear lord, pinching while he keeps licking my bud. I'm fighting for air, unable to form actual words. Is it possible to die from pleasure?

"Has any man's touch here felt as good?" Massimo growls into my pussy while the strokes of his tongue turn firmer. More forceful. "I need to know, so I can cut off his filthy, undeserving hands."

His teeth graze my clit, and then he plunges his tongue into my core. Tremors rack my body, incapacitating me completely. I can't move. I can't speak. Can't even breathe. I'm so far gone already, but then, he closes his mouth around my clit and sucks.

I scream, my voice breaking just like my body, and he… for the love of all that is holy, keeps sucking on me. I'm flying, high above my corporeal form. While back on earth, my body is shaking and shattering, each atom returning to the stars.

Wetness trails down my cheeks as I slowly pull myself together.

"Zahara." A low, whispered voice, somewhere close by.

I open my eyes and find Massimo leaning over me, his huge hand cupping my face.

"Angel." A light brush of a finger under my eye. "What's wrong?"

Wrong? I try to respond but only manage a feeble gasp. How could anything be wrong when it was so, so perfect?

"Did I hurt you? You're shaking like a leaf."

"No..." I pant, staring into his eyes. "It... it was the first time."

The corner of his lips curves up. "First time a man ate your pussy like that?"

"No, my first..." I trail off, then draw a deep breath to finish, "...my first... everything."

Massimo's smirk disappears, replaced with confusion that quickly transforms into alarm. Even in near darkness, with only a sliver of moonlight seeping into the room, I can clearly see the color draining from his face. His Adam's apple moves prominently as he swallows.

Jerking his head, he takes the hem of my nightgown and gently moves it down, covering my still trembling core. Why is he acting so strange all of a sudden? Did I say or do something wrong? Is he upset because I'm inexperienced? I can't help it if he's the only man whose touch I've ever longed for.

"Massimo?"

"Hush..." He brushes the back of his hand along my chin and slides his arms under me. "Let's get you to bed."

My weight seems to present no problem to him. Massimo easily lifts me and carries me without breaking a sweat. Once he lowers me to the bed, he pulls the covers up to my neck and takes a seat on the edge.

"I'm so sorry, Zahara." His eyes are downcast, staring at the floor. "I didn't know."

"Didn't know what?"

"That you've never been with a man before."

"Why does it matter?" I'm still shaking all over and can barely form the words.

"It matters, angel. It matters when a sick, selfish bastard almost took your virginity. A man who's twice your age. One who should only be your protector. Who never should think of you... the way I do. I never should have put my hands on you. Tainted you like this. It's sacrilegious."

"We're not related by blood. It's not incest."

"It doesn't matter. If anyone ever finds out... *Jesus*... People will be pointing their fingers at you regardless of consanguinity. In the eyes of the world, I am your family," he clutches the back of his neck. "Fuck! I almost ruined you!"

I reach out to touch his shoulder. "You wouldn't have rui—"

"Yes, I would have," he rasps, sounding defeated. Desperate. "This... us... it can't happen, Zahara. I'm not going to wreck your life by besmirching you with my lust."

I stare at his hunched back, fighting the tears that are threatening to burst free. I know him. When Massimo Spada decides something, no force on earth can make him waver.

"It may be best if I stayed somewhere else. I'll make sure you're still protected. A full security force will stay here with you. You can turn the house into whatever you want. There's staff and the means for you to do it. After tomorrow's meeting, though, I'll move out."

My lips quiver. "This is *your* home. You'd leave it just to get away from me? My presence here is that disturbing?"

Massimo turns around so fast that I flinch. "Don't you understand? I can't fucking breathe when I'm not with you, Zahara!" he growls into my face. "My lungs seize up, and I'm left gasping for air. Everything is a motherfucking wasteland, and

I'm stuck in the middle of it. Choking. Dying. Day after day. I've slept in front of your door just to be close to you. The thought of not having you by my side sends me into a full-blown panic."

He hits his chest with his fist as if trying to dislodge whatever mass has settled there.

"God, I wish I still had the handcuffs they put on me, just so I could use them to chain you to me. I don't want to be away from you, and I never want you to leave me. Do you have any idea how sick that is? Can you comprehend how utterly fucking gone I really am?" He cups my face with his palms. "I will not ruin you. The rest of world can burn in hell, but not you. You're pure. My angel. And this... we... We can't happen. Ever."

I watch as he drags himself away and heads across the room. I'm shocked. Bewildered. Happy and completely devastated at the same time. He feels it, as well. This magnetic pull between us. The yearning. And still, he's walking away. Just because my father married his mother, and that somehow brands this connection between us with an undeniable stigma.

"Don't I have any say in this?" I bite out after him.

Massimo halts at the door, grabbing the frame with his hands. "You don't."

A sob rips from my chest, the physical pain overwhelming. How dare he crush my heart again! How dare he unilaterally disregard our feelings. And all because it wouldn't be socially acceptable?

"I'll pack my shit and leave first thing in the morning," he continues. "It'll be easier on both of us."

I'm so tempted to bury my face in the pillow and bawl my eyes out. Accept the situation like I've always done—without a fight. However, I'm not that timid young girl anymore. The one too scared to lift her eyes off the floor. *He* helped me change her, without ever knowing his impact. I am not dropping my head. I am not letting him walk out of here. I am not allowing him to pull away from me, simply because of this stupid notion that I'll be made a pariah. I don't need saving. Not anymore.

"You're not leaving."

"Zahara…"

"If you do, I'll follow you anyway. So let's just skip the unnecessary packing and unpacking."

The muscles on his arms tighten as he grips the doorjamb. "My self-control is hanging by a thread, angel."

"I know. But practicing will do you good. You'll need your restraint to handle the Council." I turn around, facing away from him. "See you at breakfast," I say in the most casual tone I can muster.

A minute passes. I grip the covers in my hand and wait. Another minute.

He's still here, I know that. I can hear his labored breaths, clear across the length of the room. Is he debating with himself? Why isn't he saying anything? What if the morning comes, and he leaves anyway?

A low whisper fills the silence of the room. "Is an omelet okay?" My heart skips a beat.

"Sure," I whisper back.

CHAPTER
eighteen

Zahara

MY BREAKFAST IS READY AND WAITING FOR ME, JUST as he promised. Just as it has been every day this week.

But Massimo isn't.

I glance around the kitchen and then focus on the setting. The dish is an omelet. Tomatoes. Mushrooms. Shredded cheese. Prosciutto layered over eggs. The plate has been left on the breakfast table, at the seat closest to the window where the bright morning sunrays spill inside. On the right, there's a nicely folded cloth napkin, with cutlery on top. A glass of orange juice is positioned on the left. And completing the setting, in the middle of the table, a small vase with a single sprig of jasmine.

It's all rather sweet, if one disregards the man with a semi-automatic rifle standing in the center of the room.

"Peppe? Is something wrong?"

"Nope. Just following Massimo's orders."

"And those are?"

He throws a quick look at the table. "Watching the eggs."

"Uh-huh. Are they going to attack us?"

The corner of Peppe's lips quivers as if he's going to smile, yet he remains serious.

"Iris went grocery shopping," he says. "I'm not supposed to let anyone get close to your breakfast. If anyone does, I'm to off them, immediately."

I shake my head and cross the kitchen to take my seat, feeling Peppe's eyes on me the entire time. He must be annoyed by Massimo's behavior, too.

"He thinks someone might try poisoning my food," I explain as I eat the first forkful.

"I'm sure that's what he tells himself."

"What do you mean?"

Peppe leans on the fridge, crossing his arms over his chest.

"I've known Massimo since he was fifteen. I've always admired the way his mind works. Unrelenting focus and determination, bordering on obsessive. When he believes something needs to be done, he'll do it, no matter the consequences. And no matter the personal sacrifice. Achieving the ultimate goal is the only thing that matters. And if at some point, an alternate course of action is required, he finds a way to convince himself that it's exactly what he needs to do." He gives the plate in front of me a pointed stare. "Or not do."

"I'm... not sure I understand what you mean."

"He knows it's very unlikely that someone would want to poison you, especially here, but he's convinced himself that is a credible threat. Because it's the perfect excuse."

"Excuse for what?"

"To make you breakfast." He meets my gaze. "I've never seen him care about anyone like he cares about you. To be honest, I didn't think he was capable of it. Which is why he'll do whatever is necessary to make sure you won't end up hurt. The Family tends not to favor... *relationships* between stepsiblings."

I tense. "You know?"

"I have eyes, Miss Veronese. When the two of you are in

the same room, the air itself becomes so charged it would barely need a spark to explode. But maybe, that wouldn't be such a bad thing, you know? To let it detonate. If you are ready to bear the scorn of our world, that is. If you think you can handle it."

"Believe me, I've had plenty of practice in my life."

"Then brace yourself." Peppe nods as he leaves the kitchen. "He'll try to push you away. Might even hurt you believing it will save you from greater heartache. Don't let him."

I eat the rest of my meal in silence, contemplating Peppe's words while staring at the yard beyond the window. With the grass cut and the flowerbeds cleared of weeds, it's finally looking like a garden instead of a wild jungle.

"Is it edible?" Massimo's voice reaches me.

I look up and find him standing in the doorway. His tailor must have delivered his bespoke suits, because the one he's wearing fits him like a glove.

"Yes. Thank you."

"Good. That's good." He shrugs and heads over to the coffee machine. "The Council members will be arriving around seven this evening. We'll hold the meeting in the dining room."

So, we are obviously not going to discuss last night. Does he really believe we can just pretend like it never happened and go back to the way things were?

"Would you mind if I use the lounge area across the way to redo the dress I'm working on?" I ask in the most offhanded tone and pick up my plate to carry it to the dishwasher, which happens to be next to where the coffee machine is. "The fabric I prepared for it is completely saturated with my juices from you eating my pussy on top of it last night, and I decided I want to keep it there."

I never imagined that a person could stay as utterly still as Massimo does when the words leave my mouth. His body becomes so rigid, it's as if he's carved out of stone. The only part of him that appears to still be alive is his eyes. They glare at me with fire. And hunger.

"We agreed; that subject is closed."

I put the plate away and lean my back on the counter. "I don't remember agreeing to anything."

Suddenly, he is in front of me, his body hovering over mine as he grips the edge of the countertop on each side of me. His jaw is clenched, his nostrils are flaring madly. And his eyes, those are glued to my mouth. Is he thinking about how it felt to have my lips wrapped around his cock? Because I am. I remember every second of it. What it was like to have his whole body unravel under my touch. How amazing it felt to have him at my mercy. And then, to have him eat me out on a pile of silk, shattering me into pieces and putting me back together at the same time.

After an endless moment, Massimo reaches out and brushes my bottom lip with his thumb. "Some things are not meant to happen, angel. We are one of those things. And we both need to accept it."

His hand falls from my face. He turns away while my heart withers inside my chest.

"I don't recall you having issues with my decisions when the value of our investments doubled!" Massimo's roaring voice carries beyond the closed dining room door to the little lounge area on the other side of the entrance hall.

Shaking my head, I pull my attention from the sewing pattern I've spread out on the floor. Someone inside that room shouts back, making me tense. It sounds like Brio, but it's hard to tell with the doors shut. Everyone, however, has been so loud that I'm certain the entire household can hear them.

The meeting seemed to proceed just fine until Massimo announced he was getting out of the strip club business and selling off our venues to the New York Family Don. Salvatore Ajello has been a thorn in everyone's side for years, especially after he began to send men to spy on us while Nera was running things as Massimo's proxy. Even knowing that Massimo and the infamous don had some prior dealings, it was still a surprise when he arranged a meeting between Nera and Ajello a month ago. I wondered how he managed to pull that off.

"Oh, you sure about that?" Another round of Massimo's snarling reaches me. His voice is even louder than before. "How about I set up a meeting for you with the Guadalajara Cartel, and you can inform *El Jefe* personally that we'll have to cut the next order by half since Tiziano's girls are tying up a large portion of our cash? You can take Primo with you, I'm certain the two of you will have an amazing time in Mexico."

Everyone starts yelling all at once, insults and threats flying in a cacophonous exchange. I can't even decipher who's saying what. The noise is deafening. It sounds like they are moments away from killing each other. *Shit.*

I swipe Massimo's phone from where he left it on the side table and dash toward the dining room. In a sea of bad ideas, interrupting a Council meeting where the topic on the table is succession is probably the worst, but Massimo needs to snap out of his rampage or this conclave will head downhill, fast. I don't even have a clue what I'll say when I get inside, I just grab the knob and open the door.

As I step into the room, I'm faced with complete madness. The shouting continues without anyone realizing I'm here. Massimo is on his feet at the head of the long black table, his palms braced on the smooth wooden surface. He's leaning forward and shouting at Brio at the top of his voice. Brio—seated to Massimo's left—is sniveling his protests. His face is getting redder and redder with every word, and he's waving his arms and shaking his head like a toddler in the middle of a tantrum.

Next to Brio, Tiziano is slamming his fist on the leather

ledger splayed out before him while exchanging obscenities with Adriano across the table. Adriano is the Family's biggest investor and could probably buy out half of the people gathered in this room. He's always had an air of aristocracy about him, and could easily be the sort of man who sits on his ass and lets others work for him. Instead, Adriano has always been heavily involved, personally overseeing his logistics company's transport of Cosa Nostra drugs across the country. I've never seen Adriano so much as raise his voice at anyone before. Now, however, his normally impeccable appearance is distorted by hand-messed hair and a tie that sits slightly askew.

Primo, who's sitting on Brio's left, is blabbering and pointing between Donatello and Patricio, two other investors in the Family businesses. Salvo is the only person who is silent. He's relaxed back in his chair on Massimo's right, quietly observing the unfolding catastrophe.

"What are you doing here, girl?" Brio's angry voice unexpectedly carries over the yelling.

The shouts suddenly die down, and then everyone is staring at me.

"Um... I just—"

Massimo moves like a predator. In an instant, he's fisting Brio's shirtfront and tie and lifting the older man out of his seat, the twisted material jammed up under the capo's chin. All Brio can do is claw at Massimo's arm while he struggles to breathe.

"Don't you fucking dare speak to her with that tone," Massimo says through gritted teeth right into Brio's shocked face. "Apologize."

Brio's mouth opens and closes like a fish, yet no sound escapes. Massimo tosses him back into his seat like a ragdoll.

"I'm sorry," Brio mumbles as he tries to straighten out his tie.

"I'm sorry... what?"

"I'm sorry for my tone, Zara."

Like a flash, Massimo strikes again—grabbing Brio by the hair and slamming him face-first against the table. He follows that by pressing his elbow to the side of the capo's head, pinning down the now bleeding man. Brio's blood, streaming from his nose, mixes with water from an overturned glass, and the blended liquid soaks the documents spread across the wooden surface and flows toward Brio's mouth and eye.

"She's not 'Zara' to you. Try again."

"I'm sorry, Miss Veronese."

"That's much better." Massimo finally releases the battered capo and looks up at me. "What do you need, Zahara?"

Eight pairs of eyes stare back at me. The room feels supercharged, even though no one is shouting anymore.

"I…" I drop my gaze, focusing on the phone I'm holding. "Your phone rang. It was… it was your lawyer, and it sounded urgent." I swallow, then look up, right into Massimo's eyes. "He might be losing control of some things that need to be handled with finesse. So, I thought you should be made aware."

For a few heartbeats, as his gaze stays locked on mine, his face remains the same angry mask he'd directed at Brio. But then, I notice his facial muscles relax. Slowly, he lowers onto the leather chair and interlocks his fingers atop the table. His entire posture changes, becoming completely at ease.

"Thank you," he says, his tone calm. "I'll make sure to give him a call as soon as I'm done here."

"Okay. Well… I guess, that's all. I'll be going now."

I turn, reaching for the door handle, just as Massimo growls behind me, "Get your ass in that empty chair at the end."

My whole body tenses. He never uses that tone with me. *Shit.* I shouldn't have interrupted their meeting.

"Now, Brio," Massimo continues. "Zahara, please have a seat beside me."

A ball lodges in my throat. And I seem to have lost control of my limbs because I can't move. My gaze remains fixed on the door in front of me. *He can't be serious.* This isn't done. Only capos and appointed members can attend Council meetings.

The dragging of a chair across floorboards breaks the silence. The silence that hangs over the room like a dense shroud. The tension is nearly palpable.

"This is outrageous." Someone's irate mumble reaches me. "The rules—"

"Shut your trap, Tiziano. When you get to be the head of the Family, then you can enforce the rules. But right now, I'll choose which rules I'll honor, and which I won't."

Paralyzed by indecision, I remain rooted in place, staring at a dried paint bubble on the door in front of me.

"Zahara, please." A much softer voice reaches me.

I slowly turn and face the grim expressions in the room. Brio has taken a seat to Primo's left and is glaring at me most vehemently. I bite the inside of my cheek as my eyes glide down the long table, briefly connecting with the judgmental gaze of every seated man until they land on Massimo. He is standing, having pulled out the chair on his left-hand side that was vacated by Brio.

My hands tremble as I take the first step forward, but I refuse to look at the floor as I would have in the past, even with all these powerful men staring at me. All they've ever done is look down on me. Yet, despite the acute pressure of their eyes, the so-familiar urge to hide doesn't hit me.

Another step. And then another. I keep my chin up, gaze connected with Massimo's as I cross the room. I can't believe he invited me to join the meeting. That's unprecedented. He's basically proclaimed me an equal to every man here. Equal to Tiziano, who, a few years ago, asked me to fetch him another drink, taking me for one of the serving staff in my own house. And Primo, whom I overheard telling his wife that, if my father offered their son my hand in marriage, they'd need to find a way to avoid it, hoping that Dad would relent and allow Nera to marry "the darling Ruggero" instead. And to Brio, who once outright asked my dad if I had a speech impediment because I preferred to stay quiet at social gatherings instead of yapping nonstop like other girls my age. They all must be fuming on the inside, and I couldn't be more delighted by that fact.

As I take my seat, Massimo helps slide my chair in and then resumes his place with a slight incline of his head in my direction.

"Now, where were we?" he asks casually, cutting his eyes to Brio.

"You're selling our strip clubs to Ajello," Brio says through his teeth.

"Yes. And in exchange, he is giving us an in with his construction project in Manhattan. We're investing in a premium residential complex fifty-fifty, and splitting the profits in the same way."

Absolute silence descends over the room again while the men stare at Massimo with expressions vacillating between shock and wonder. Salvatore Ajello is known for killing any Cosa Nostra member from outside of his own Family who dares to set foot in his territory. He usually mails the body parts back to their respective don in a bag. Or several. The fact that he agreed to a joint project in New York with another crime family, borders on science fiction or fantasy.

"What's the expected profit?" Adriano asks, seemingly back to his perfectly composed self.

"After the construction is complete and the condos hit the market, he projects sixty-seven point five million in earnings for each side, after tax. Clean, legitimate income we can easily reinvest as we see fit."

"That sounds too good to be true," Brio throws in. "Who will vouch that Ajello will keep his end of the deal?"

Massimo turns toward Brio, his face a mask of barely subdued rage. His jaw is tightly clenched, and the vein on his forehead is pulsing, a sure sign that he's moments from losing his temper.

"Are you suggesting that I've been acting against the Family's best interest?" Massimo's voice is eerily low. He appears ready to kill Brio on the spot. *Shit.*

"I'm just saying that I don't see how this benefits Ajello. Why would he want to let us in? Unless you've made another— *private*—deal with him that you don't want to share with the rest of us."

Oh God. Brio just insinuated that Massimo has been working toward his own concerns and contrary to the Family's. I chance a look at Massimo just as he's reaching behind his back. He always carries a gun.

Under the table, I lay my palm on Massimo's thigh and give it a squeeze. He doesn't seem to notice. *Shit.* I squeeze it again, so hard that my nails almost poke through the fabric of his pants. His body tenses, and for a fleeting moment, he just sits there with his hand suspended behind his back. I look down at the surface of the table and tighten my hold on his leg until my damn fingers hurt. The Council still hasn't voted. He can't outright kill that bastard for insubordination or impudence. Not yet anyway.

Lacking another option, I continue to draw long, even breaths until I feel a soft caress on my fingers. Massimo's hand covers mine. Despite the roughness of his skin, his touch is feather-light. Reassuring. I lift my gaze and find Massimo relaxing back in his chair, his other hand on the table. No gun. *Thank fuck.*

"As a matter of fact..." His voice is nonchalant, the complete opposite of his demeanor from just seconds earlier. "I do have a deal with Ajello."

All eyes are now focused on Massimo, waiting. His gaze slides over every man present and stops on Brio. "Ajello ran into a few obstacles obtaining building permits for a project he has planned in Chinatown. As it happens, the Triad owed me a favor, so Mr. Wang will be happy to assist our new partner in obtaining them."

"I don't remember the Family doing any favors for the Triad," Tiziano grunts.

"Because it didn't. I did," Massimo smirks. "And their debt was significant enough to spark Ajello's interest. Which is why I'm sitting here six months earlier than expected, after he fixed things for me," he says and pins Tiziano with his unrelenting stare. Then, he turns to Primo. "Starting next month, Primo, you'll be laundering Ajello's dirty money."

Outraged cries explode anew, with the men practically losing their shit en masse, but Massimo just continues to chill in his chair, observing this latest flare-up with a serene smile. The entire time, he keeps my hand in his under the table.

"And what are we going to do with our own dirty money?" I whisper.

"The New York Family will take care of it for us, of course."

The yelling suddenly stops, and all heads turn to Massimo.

"Even with numerous shell companies, the businesses we use to launder our money lead back to us. If someone digs deep enough, they'll make the connection," Massimo says. "That risk practically disappears with Ajello in the picture. His infrastructure will add at least three levels of protection, so tracing the source of our cash will be twice as hard. Between the mortgage loans and the interest payments, the inflated prices will be a wash. Throw full concierge services on top, and all the complementary vendors they depend on, and this complex becomes a goddamned license to print money. So, we help Ajello, he helps us. Problem solved."

For almost a minute, no one says a word. They just stare at Massimo.

"You think it will work?" This from Adriano, always the shrewd businessman.

"Like a Swiss watch," Massimo declares. "And if needed, we can always have the Bulgarians 'clean' our extra funds through their chain of car washes. I just need to boot Camorra out of their scheme first."

"And how are you planning to do that?" Brio again.

"By kicking Efisio and his lot out of our territory. That idiot cousin of his, Alvino, dared to kidnap the don's daughter. It gives us grounds for retaliation. I want Camorra out of Boston. If they don't choose to leave, I'll pick them off, one at a time, until our streets are cleansed of their filth."

"That was more than three years ago, Massimo," Brio throws in. "We can't act on it now."

Massimo cocks his head to the side and smirks. "Well, I was out of town for a while and I just found out about that little detail. For me, it's as if it happened last Friday."

"We don't need any skirmishes with outsiders. It's bad for business."

"Let me tell you what's bad for business," Massimo barks and leans forward. "Our competitors thinking they can pull shit like that and get away with it because Cosa Nostra is weak. That era is done. From this point on, every single person in this city will know that no one fucks with our Family. We'll be what we once were—the embodiment of fear and respect. People will tremble when they hear the Cosa Nostra name. And if I need to paint the Boston streets with Camorra blood to make that happen, so be it."

Nods of affirmation from all around the table. Even Brio.

"I'm glad you agree. Then, let's do what we have gathered here to do, shall we?"

I swallow. It's time for the Council to cast their votes. The voting ritual, the oath, and the subsequent swearing of allegiance to the new don is sacred. Massimo's invitation for me to be present at this meeting means the world to me—something he may never realize—but I don't want him breaking any more rules on my account.

Giving his leg another light squeeze, I rise and head toward the door before he can stop me.

"Refreshments await you in the lounge when you're done," I toss over my shoulder and hightail it out of the dining room.

Massimo

The door closes behind Zahara with a soft click. With her exit, the animosity rises within me once again. Ten minutes ago, I almost ruined everything I've been working over two decades of my life for. If she hadn't grabbed my leg and snapped me out of the blind rage that threatened to consume me, I would have probably killed Brio where he sat.

Adriano takes off his black-rimmed glasses and pins me with his discerning gaze. He might be the most unruffled and affable man in the room, yet his word carries a lot of weight. "Old money" talks, as they say. As a majority shareholder in his family-run logistics company, his personal net worth is around ten billion, and more than half of it is invested in Cosa Nostra businesses. Over the years, he's been offered the rank of capo more than once. But he has always declined. If it wasn't for that little fact, I would have bet that he was the one trying to off me so he could become Boston's don. He has the means, for some reason, however, he's never been interested in an official position within the Family hierarchy.

"It's incredibly impressive, and a little mind-boggling, that you were able to steer this Family's investment portfolio and look after business matters from behind bars all these years. And not only did you keep everything afloat, your actions resulted in significant financial gains," Adriano says. "As such, I'm inclined to believe that you'll do an even better job going forward, now that you can be openly involved. You have my vote, Spada."

I accept his decision with a nod.

Donatello and Patricio are next, and neither of them would ever contradict Adriano. They both nod to indicate their support.

I turn toward the other side of the table, leveling my eyes on the capos.

"You have my vote," both Primo and Tiziano say in unison.

Brio remains silent, his gaze focused on his clasped hands on the table. His face is grim, still showing traces of now-dried blood. He really doesn't want me leading the Family—it's plainly obvious—but with the rest of the Council in agreement, he must feel like he has no other option. With his teeth clenched, Brio nods too.

"Salvo?" I turn toward my underboss, still struggling not to punch him in the head every time I look at him. Days later, and I can't seem to shake my ire toward him after he had the gall to ask for Zahara's hand. My friend has been unusually silent for the entire meeting and for reasons I can't explain, it's rubbing me the wrong way. It's just not typical for him to stay out of a discussion. If there's one thing I could always count on, it was Salvo making his opinion known.

"Of course you have my vote, Massimo. I'm glad to see you finally assume your rightful place." He rises out of his seat and comes to stand before me. "My loyalty and my life are yours, Don Spada."

With his eyes downcast, he bends forward and kisses my hand. It's an old tradition. A show of adulation and fidelity to the seat of power, but also, recognition of the protection that will be received from that merciful authority. I was never a fan of it, because it reminds me of a cult. I don't need them to worship me like a fucking saint. It's the last thing I am. And with the changes I have planned, changes that many of them won't like in the slightest, I have no doubts they won't like me in the least. Italians though, and especially mafiosi, do love their ceremonies. So, I patiently sit through the whole ordeal until every man pays his respects.

"Let's move over to the lounge for some drinks, and to discuss how we should approach the issue of disposing of Camorra," I say.

"Now?" Primo asks. "It's almost midnight."

"Yes, now." I let my gaze slice to them. "The vacation is over, gentlemen."

It's almost two in the morning when the last man leaves. Even with Peppe's guys patrolling the grounds and watching the house, I still do a detailed sweep of the upper and lower levels before I climb the stairs to the second floor.

The door to Zahara's room is shut. I press my hand to the wooden surface as if it will help bring me closer to her. It doesn't. I know she's there, right on the other side of this barrier, but the oak beneath my palm has become a literal representation of the obstacles that stand between us.

My whole being is vibrating with the urge to go inside, to simply be near her. The anxiety that has plagued me for the past five hours, ever since the moment she walked out of the meeting room, has twisted me up to the point I can barely breathe. I don't know how to stifle this maniacal *need* I have for Zahara. My self-control has been stretched razor-thin.

And it's not because of sexual attraction. That would be much easier to resist. Zahara *is* beautiful, so beautiful that just setting my eyes on her makes my traitorous dick twitch. Yet it's not only her beauty that makes me crave her. It's *her*. Just... her.

Her spirit.

The fierce fire inside her.

Her boundless compassion and understanding.

She's the only person who makes me feel like myself. With whom I can speak about things I would never voice in another's presence. When she is near me, I feel like the man I once was. The one I want to be again. She's the cure for my madness, abolishing it with her touch and her smile. Just as she did earlier tonight.

And the night before. And the one prior. For days I've been losing my temper with almost everyone who crossed my path. The renovation workers. The household staff. People in public places. With her touch though, a quiet word, a glance, my lunatic self retreats into the ether. Zahara grounds me, like nothing else can. Without her near me, I fear neither the world nor I may survive.

She is the missing piece to my soul. My salvation.

I want her. Want her in every possible sense. As a friend. And a lover. But most of all, as simply... *mine.*

Leaning my forehead on the door, I grit my teeth.

She's not mine.

Can never be.

And that knowledge casts me into utter despair.

Closing my eyes, I bang my forehead on the wooden surface.

I need her. And I don't know how to make that need go away.

Bang.

I want to make her mine. Ignore the fucking scandal. I never gave a shit what people think about me anyway. I'd put up with their contempt and disdain. I would. But in doing so, I'd open her up to stigma for the rest of her life. The Family is ruthless where these types of things are concerned, and Zahara is too pure to deserve their scorn.

Bang.

I need her!

Knowing it's wrong. Knowing she is worthy of better. Doesn't change that I fucking need her! It was easier to resist her before I tasted the forbidden fruit. Now, I can't hold back no matter how hard I try. It's like a beautiful madness has gripped my mind. Tightening its hold on me without mercy. She is all I can think about. My hands on her. My lips on her glorious pussy. I can't get those images out of my mind. I want to, but can't!

Bang. Bang. Bang.

The door swings open, revealing my angel, bathed in soft

light from the floor lamp near the door. So radiant. Dazzling. Gleaming bright. As are the specks of reddish-gold among her luscious strands that have fallen over her lace-covered shoulders and arms. Her hair is the same shade as her knee-length nightie, and the silk clings to her delicious curves. Other than last night, I've only ever seen her in pants and full-sleeved tops.

"What's going on?" she asks, sleepily, and rubs her eyes with her hands. Such an innocent, simple gesture. Jesus fuck, she's so damn young.

"Nothing," I grunt.

"You've been knocking like a maniac, as if the house is on fire, and you say it's 'nothing'?"

Yeah... I wouldn't call that knocking. "Sorry I woke you. I'll go now."

She narrows her eyes. "Is that blood?"

I press my fingers to my brow, just at the edge of my temple. They come away wet and red. I must have split my skin while "knocking."

"It's nothing. Head back inside. And lock the door."

"Why?"

"You know why. Please, angel. I won't be able to walk away until you do."

"Then don't."

My mind blanks. I can feel the tethers of my restraint snap, shredding like an age-worn thread. I grab at the doorframe, squeezing as if it will help anchor me to my spot. Keep me from stepping into her room.

If I do, I won't have the strength to leave.

"Zahara," I whisper. "Shut the door."

"Why?"

The wood cracks under the pressure of my grip. "Because if you don't, I'm coming inside."

Not even a full step. That's the distance between us. A wild storm rages inside me as I take in Massimo standing just outside my door. His whole body is tense, leaning forward with his hands braced on the jamb. I have a feeling that's the only thing keeping him in place at the moment. Every single line of his face is drawn taut as if etched in stone, yet he's staring back at me with eyes that reflect the same tumult I'm feeling.

"You didn't have a problem coming in last night," I say. "But after, you seemed afraid for my mortal soul and acted like what happened between us was a huge mistake. Well, you're not prone to making mistakes, Massimo, and God forbid you should ever repeat one. So no, I'm not closing this door. You'll have to turn around and leave on your own."

Massimo's nostrils flare and he takes several deep breaths through his nose. "Salvo asked me for your hand in marriage."

I stare at him, blinking in confusion. "What?"

"He did. I'll be letting him know tomorrow that I'm... in agreement."

I reel back as if I've physically been punched in the gut. He's giving me away? To Salvo? Like I'm some fucking object he no longer needs? What the actual fuck? Peppe was right; he said Massimo would do anything to keep me from himself. I just never expected this. Not this... this *betrayal*. That's the only word for it. How could he do it? Hurt me like this?

Unless...

I tilt my chin and meet his gaze. His eyes are practically glowing—anger is burning in them. And anguish. Jealousy.

"Fine. If that's your decision, who am I to contradict the don? Good night, *Don Spada*." With shaking fingers, I push the door closed, shutting it right in his face.

I am halfway across the room, barely keeping it together, when a loud bang shakes the walls around me. Nearly jumping out of my skin, I spin around, taking stock of the kicked-open door and the massive man filling the threshold. Massimo's eyes seem crazed and boring into mine.

"Do you like Salvo?" His voice is low, dripping with venom.

I knew it. That *lying* bastard. He was bluffing and never would have followed through on that garbage he just spit out. The last thing he wants is for me to marry Salvo. I can see his lack of conviction written all over his furious face. This is nothing but an attempt to push me away.

"Does it matter?" I choke out.

Massimo takes a step forward, coming inside the room. His hands are fisted at his sides so tightly that his knuckles have gone white, and the vein on his forehead is pulsing.

"Do you"—another step—"like Salvo?"

The nerve of this man. Not only has he just put a hole in my heart, he's now tearing the battered remains to pieces.

I clench my teeth and close the space between us.

"Yes, I like Salvo," I bite out. "I think the wedding should be held next month. We might as well take advantage of the nice weather. I assume he's asked you to be the best man?"

Massimo doesn't say a word, just stares at me with his blazing eyes, so I continue.

"I'm sure he'll make a good husband. After all, you've chosen him for me. Perhaps we'll name our first child in your honor."

"The hell you will," Massimo growls and wraps his arm around my waist.

I knew he was fast, but I'm still shocked when in the blink of an eye I find myself sitting on the desk, with Massimo's palms pressed to the window and gripping the curtain at my back. His face is right in front of mine, his hot breath fanning over my cheeks. If his eyes looked crazed before, they are positively unhinged now. He doesn't even blink as he leans forward and just glares at me. With the lights down low, his irises seem to have merged with his pupils.

"You should have closed that door sooner, Zahara."

In a heartbeat, his mouth slams into mine.

Earthshaking. That's what being kissed by Massimo Spada feels like. Lips—firm and unrelenting—capture mine. Taking. Giving. Consuming.

Our first kiss.

A moment I've dreamed of for years. And it doesn't even compare. My fantasies have nothing on this.

A strange sensation grips my chest. As if a million colors suddenly come to life, eager to burst free. Warmth spreads through my body, lighting me up like the aurora borealis.

The earth keeps quaking. So I wrap my arms around his neck and hold on for dear life because it feels as if I'm shattering, surfing on the seismic waves while he ravages my mouth.

Nothing about us happened in order. His shadowed secrets became mine long prior to our first meeting in the bright light of day. I fell in love with the man long before I saw his face. And I relished the flavor of his cock before I tasted the essence of his lips.

Lips that are devouring me in earnest.

Lips flavored with sweet agony and defeat.

Perfect, perfect lips.

With his hands still clutching the drapes, I miss their strength around me. I let go of his neck, sliding my palms down his arms, tracing the corded muscles. Taut, taut muscles. I try nudging him to wrap his arms around me, but pulling on his biceps does me no good. His limbs are like steel beams, anchored to that curtain. It's as if he's using the gravitational force to keep his hands off me. He doesn't budge, just continues to rain his sweet torment upon my mouth.

A frustrated moan leaves me. I pull Massimo's lower lip

between my teeth and bite it, hard, then pull on his arms again. I'm overcome with the need to have him touch me.

"Fuck," he growls. Then, the hesitant weight of his palm spans the small of my back.

Gingerly, his hand slides along the length of my thigh, dragging up the hem of my nightgown until the tips of his fingers trail the edge of my panties. It's a feathery touch, yet it sends a shockwave up my spine. Goose bumps break out across my skin. I keep kissing him deeply while moving my hands across his shoulders, then down his neck to the collar of his dress shirt. To the first button. My fingers tremble as I clumsily undo the tiny fastener.

Across my hip, rounding to the back, Massimo keeps stroking my skin. Light, tentative movements. They are such a contradiction to the hungry, unyielding way he's devouring my lips. My head is spinning. Is it a lack of oxygen from his kiss or trepidation over what I'm doing? Somehow, I will my hands to slide down to the second button. And then the next. When his shirt is halfway undone, I press my shaking palms to the exposed skin of his chest.

A violent shudder racks Massimo's body. He breaks the kiss but doesn't move away. Under my palms, his chest rises and falls rapidly as he stares directly into my eyes.

"Zahara." His voice is rough, and I can practically feel the vibration roll over my skin.

No one ever says my name the way he does. Like there's so much more behind that word than a simple combination of syllables. And now is no different.

There's a question in his intonation, the same one I can see in his dark, sultry gaze. He won't voice it though, because he knows it's wrong to ask, even though it's obviously tearing him apart. I can clearly see the signs. The tick in his jaw. The stiffness of his body. His furrowed brow. And his fast, shallow breaths.

"I want you to be my first," I whisper, letting him hear in my tone everything I never dared to admit.

Massimo's eyes widen. Elation and anguish war in their inky depths. The conflicting emotions contort his face, but slowly, I see hope win out.

He's on the brink of giving in. Surrendering to this undeniable pull between us.

My nightgown rides higher on my hips as I wrap my legs around his waist and slide my ass forward. Teetering on the edge of the desk, I let his hardness touch my core. He's aroused. Because of me.

Tightening my hold, I draw his cock more firmly against me. Wetness pools between my legs the instant I do.

"Is it really that wrong?" I ask while gliding my hand over the stubble on his chin.

"Fuck, angel," he rasps. His touch leaves my body, hand returning to its twin at the curtain behind my back. "You know it is."

"No one has to know."

"I won't let you be my dirty little secret, Zahara." Growled words. "You deserve better than that."

"What I deserve is to make my own choice." I tilt my face up, bringing our lips into contact. "Please, don't make me beg."

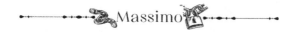

Massimo

Every man has a limit to how much he can bear. The line where sensible thought finally snaps, sending him into absolute delirium. Apparently, mine is Zahara saying *please*.

There's a tearing sound when the drape in my fist rips off its track and plunges to the floor. I slide my hand over her hip again, then once more along the border of her panties, gliding my palm toward Zahara's heat. She sucks in a gulp of air and tightens her arms around my neck, panting. I move to press my fingers to her sweet spot.

"You have no idea what you're doing to me," I whisper, rubbing the soft scrap of fabric between her thighs. She's drenched. "What you've been doing to me ever since you walked out of that visitors' room. Almost four years later and I can still hear the sound of that damn door. It shut in your wake with such finality that I felt as if the prison bars slammed around me all over again. But it wasn't just my body that got locked up in that moment. My fucking heart was caged, as well."

I push aside the wet part of her panties and stroke her silky folds. The way she clutches my shoulders, holding herself right at the edge of the desk to give me greater access, is driving me directly out of my mind. Unable to resist, my lips graze the sensitive area under her ear. "I devoured every letter you sent. They were my lifeline, but also, the source of my greatest fear. I was terrified for you, baby. And I'll forever hate myself for putting you in that position. For sending my angel into the depths of the wolves' den. I will never forgive myself for that."

"It was my decision." Her core quivers under my touch, however, her voice remains steady. Determined. "My choice. Don't you dare diminish it by assuming responsibility for actions that were strictly my own. You can't take that away from me, Massimo."

"So fierce. A lamb who turned out to be lupine." I seize her lower lip with my teeth and bite it. "Do you understand how incredibly remarkable you are, my gutsy little she-wolf?"

She smiles against my mouth. "I learned from the best."

Giving her pussy another light swipe, I break the kiss and meet her gaze. Her honey-colored orbs watch me intently, inviting me to drown in their depths. They sparkle as if thousands of micro-stars are clustered within, their warmth radiating through me.

"I want to make love with you, Zahara. Want to know your

body just as well as I've gotten to know your mind. I'm aching, angel. Starving for you, and it would be my honor and my greatest wish to be your first."

And your only, the deviant voice inside my head growls. *You're mine! No one else can touch what's mine!*

I shove the intruding bastard away and cup Zahara's face in my hands.

"I'll lick and I'll bite each inch of your skin if you'll allow it. With every caress and every kiss, I'll brand you as mine. There's nothing else in this world I want more, but I need to know that you're ready to do this with me."

I'm well aware of her self-consciousness about her skin. She's never so much as breathed a word of it to me, still, I know the worries that circle her mind on the subject. And I, perhaps, can understand better than most that, sometimes, reason flees when faced with fear. I can tell her she's the most gorgeous thing I've ever seen until I'm blue in the face, yet she wouldn't believe a word of it. So what I need to do is show her. Through actions, I'll make her understand just how beautiful she is, how every inch of her is fucking perfection.

Zahara's lower lip quivers. "I... I've never taken my clothes off in front of a man, Massimo. Or anyone, for that matter, in a very long time. I'm not sure I can do it."

"That's okay, baby." I nuzzle her nose with mine. "I'll just kiss you over your nightie."

Her eyes are glued to my hands as I reach for the buttons of my shirt she abandoned. Unfastening the next in line, I wait. Gauging her reaction. Even though she started this, I don't want to assume. "Should I go on?"

"Yes." A trembling... eager reply.

I nod and finish unbuttoning my shirt. Shrugging it off to let it fall to the floor. Next, I bring my hand to the waistband of my pants. Waiting.

"Everything. Please," she rasps, biting her lower lip as her eyes roam over my upper body.

A piece at a time, I continue undressing. Once the last shred of my clothing is off, I stand before her and let her look her fill. Her eyes flash with hunger. She resembles a ravenous huntress, eyeing her prey.

That turns me so fucking on.

Minutes pass, yet she just keeps looking. Taking me in. One endless breath at a time.

"You don't have a problem being naked in front of me?" she finally asks. "Letting me shamelessly ogle you?"

"No. My problem is revealing what hides inside. Even before, it was hard for me to trust people. In my mind, everyone is a potential threat." With my thumb under her chin, I tilt her face up. "Never with you, though. I trust you completely. Without a single reservation. I trust you more than I trust myself. So, please, feel free to ogle. I'm all yours anyway. Body. Soul. All yours, Zahara."

"Why?" she whispers. "How can you trust me but no one else?"

"Because… I love you, baby. With everything in me—good or bad—I've fallen in love with you."

Goose bumps explode all over my body, spreading from my limbs to chase the shivers rushing down my spine. As Massimo's admission washes over me, I suck it in. Each individual sound and syllable. My hand shakes when I reach out and press my palm to his bare chest. Hot skin. Taut muscle. And the wild beating of his heart. I feel him.

"I've been in love with you for so long, I'm not even certain when it happened, Massimo." My voice nearly breaks as I whisper the words. "Is... is this a dream?"

A gentle smile tugs his lips. Without breaking our eye contact, he lifts my hand toward himself.

"Maybe." His mouth drifts over the inside of my wrist. "Only one way to find out."

Tongue. Warm and wet, licking my pulse point. A graze of his teeth as he sucks on my skin. And then, a lightning-fast sharp sting—there one moment and gone just as quickly. But long enough to assure me I'm awake.

Not a dream.

His lips on my wrist, peppering it with kisses. Soothing the ache and exploring as far as they can go. Only up to the fringe of my lace sleeve. Massimo does not rush, does not try to push up the fabric. Languid, tender, he savors me as I am.

Suddenly, I can't stand it. The fabric that's shielding the rest of me from his kiss.

I always sleep in long-sleeved pajamas because I'm more comfortable that way, but in this moment... now... I need my nightie off. I don't want any barriers between us. I want to feel the softness of his lips. His open-mouthed kisses, his licks, and the nibbling of his teeth. I want to feel it all. Everywhere.

"Tear it off," I croak. "The nightgown."

"Angel..."

"Now, Massimo."

He glances up from my wrist, and his gaze collides with mine. His teeth close over the cuff of my sleeve. I suck in a breath just as he jerks his head, and the unmistakable sound of tearing lace echoes throughout the room.

A heartbeat later, his lips are on my wrist again, gliding upward along the inside of my forearm. More ripping fills the silence as he continues to demolish the fabric, section by section. Each destructive tear is followed by more kisses, lazily feathered over the newly exposed skin. He doesn't stop until he reaches my shoulder. And then, he switches to my other arm.

A touch of lips. "So soft." Enthusiastic tearing. "So, so damn soft." A glide of the tongue, followed by a kiss.

My breath leaves me so fast that my lungs are struggling to keep up. My head is spinning. Is my blood crying for oxygen, or is this due to the magic of his lips?

There's no time to contemplate the answer because Massimo moves on to the column of my neck. I stretch, giving him greater access, anything for more of the soothing pressure of his mouth on me. And then, a new wave of tremors racks me as he gently bites my collarbone. My panties are completely soaked already, but I can feel more wetness pooling between my thighs.

The next sounds are of my nightie being ripped right down the middle, followed by the ping of tiny buttons as they collide with whatever surface blocks their path after they are sent flying every which way. Cool air rushes against my overheating skin as the fine silk flutters around me like wounded wings before drifting down to land at his feet. In that split second, I come alive, soaring as high as the clouds, as if a massive weight has been lifted off my back.

Free. I feel free.

"Perfection," Massimo utters in a strangled voice. His fingers are trailing up my arms. Slowly. Deliberately. Over my shoulders and down the valley between my breasts. Then, his palms glide over my hips toward my back.

In a swift move, he pulls me flush with his chest, and his arms wrap around me. He holds me captive in his bearlike embrace so tightly I almost can't draw a breath. His face buried in the crook of my neck, he inhales. A long, deep sniff.

"Can't live without you, Zahara. You're the air in my lungs," he mumbles against my skin. "I need you."

My arms tremble as I cinch them around his broad back,

while his words ring inside my head like crystal. I'm lightheaded as his lips find mine again. Branding. Claiming. Giving.

I tilt my head so my mouth is right next to his ear. "Make love to me," I purr.

The desk legs scrape on the floor as Massimo pushes off and grabs me under my butt. Turning us around, he carries me across the room. I lock my ankles behind his back and nip his lips while he's at my mercy, feeling his stone-hard cock brushing my pussy as he walks. The springs squeak when he climbs onto the mattress, all the while still holding me tight to his chest.

"I'll be gentle," he whispers as he lays me on the bed and hooks his fingers into the waistband of my panties. Slowly, he pulls them down my legs. "I promise."

Eyes as dark as a bottomless abyss never leave mine as he lowers over me, supporting himself on his elbow. His other hand drifts back to my pussy, his fingers resuming those wicked things he does. Stroking. Pinching. Then soothing.

When I finally feel the tip of his cock at my entrance, I'm half-gone with the need to have him in me. I've waited for this for so damn long. I want him. I want everything. Now! But he's gone still again, and his eyes search for something in mine.

"Massimo?"

"I don't have a condom."

"I'm on the pill," I pant. "Please, Massimo, hurry."

He doesn't, though. Carefully, he pushes into me a fraction of an inch at a time.

I know to expect pain during my first time, yet the stress over how much it will hurt isn't even on my radar. All I can focus on is this maniacal urge to be with him as one. One being. One soul. Carnal and cerebral. My body hums, as sensation after sensation overwhelms me, leaving no room for common sense.

"More," I pant.

"No."

"Yes! Please!" I try to grab the hair on the back of his head, but the too-short fuzz just slips through my fingers. *Damn it!*

"Easy, angel. I'm too big, and I don't want to hurt you."

I lift my hips, forcing more of him to plunge inside.

"Fuck, Zahara."

A moan explodes from deep within my chest. Partly from pain, but mostly just elation. I feel so full as my body accepts him. My heartbeat shifts into overdrive, racing so fast that there might be a real danger of my heart exploding. Pure joy. Ecstasy. Rapture. Sheer happiness swells in me.

Massimo mutters almost inaudibly, cursing as he tries to hold himself back. And ultimately fails. The air catches in my lungs as he buries himself inside me to the hilt.

"Baby?" Massimo rasps, his voice sounding gravelly and strained. He braces his left hand on the headboard above our heads while cradling my face with the other.

Our breaths mix. Fast and shallow. In. Out. In. Out. His chest rises and falls in parallel resonance with my own. We are like two perfect halves, finally brought together.

"I never imagined it would feel this way," I pant.

His thumb strokes the side of my chin. "As if we are one?"

"Yes."

Hard lips crash against mine, claiming me once more. I wrap my arms around his neck and my legs around his waist, basically crushing him to me. I'm never letting him go. Never. Massimo Spada belongs to me. No one else. Not to *La Famiglia*. Not to the rest of this world. Only me. He's the very reason my heart is beating. It's his—always been, always will be.

While his mouth devours me at full force, his hips begin to move languidly. He pushes into me with measured strokes, and each slide heightens my awareness of him. He's everywhere—inside and outside—there isn't a part of me that's not connected to him in some way. His cock, sinking deep into my heat. His body draped over me like the most comforting blanket. And his emotions flowing right through me. Directly to my heart. I revel in this new feeling of having him so completely. This man, with his brilliant mind, flawed personality, and indestructible spirit… he's mine. For the first time, he's completely *mine*. And every atom of me feels it.

I press my lips to his arm, just over the eye of the dragon tattooed there, then move on to his collarbone where another creature is inked on his skin. His chin is next. I pepper it with kisses, then bite it lightly while my palms glide down his back—his broad, strong back that I love to admire—before drifting to his arms again. Every inch… I need to touch and kiss every single inch of him.

My Massimo.

The corded muscles of his upper arms flex under my grip as Massimo increases his pace, plunging deeper with each driving thrust. His relentless hammering brings me closer to the edge. Closer to… something. I'm not even sure if I could name it, or what exactly it is. It's primal, though. And epic. And I already know it will forever change me.

As I'm swept higher and higher on the crest of a rising tide, my inner walls start spasming around his cock. I moan, overcome by strange wonder and absolute bliss.

"That's it, angel. God, you're so fucking beautiful," he growls, slamming into me. "Come for me, Zahara."

As if by his command, a faint scream escapes my lips, and I shatter the very next moment. I'm nothing more than a tangle of incomprehensible sensations and numb limbs, like I don't have a physical body anymore. All I can do is hold on to Massimo for dear life, as he keeps sliding in and out, while tremors rock my core.

Sweet kisses. On my shoulder. Collarbone. The scrape of his teeth along my chin. He's replicating the kisses I gave him.

"I love you, Zahara." Words whispered into my lips.

My eyes flutter open, meeting his. The warmth reflected

in those dark orbs reminds me of melted chocolate. I've never seen him look at anyone the way he's now looking at me. The way he always looks at me. Only me.

I sigh. And smile. "I love you too, Massimo."

He holds himself over me, completely motionless, with his cock still buried deep inside my quivering pussy. Every single muscle in his body is so rigid it's like he's made of stone. He's not cold, though. No, the heat from his body warms me like nothing else ever has. I'm reveling in being the focus of his smoldering stare when a deep rumble erupts from his throat.

"I thought my cage was the prison walls, Zahara. But getting beyond them didn't break the shackles that have kept me confined," he says while gritting teeth. His voice is strained, raw-sounding. "You, you are my salvation. And this, this has finally set me free."

Dropping his forehead to mine, Massimo resumes his hard thrusts, leaving me gasping for breath as that unmistakable pressure quickly builds at the base of my spine again. All too soon, another orgasm rips through me, throwing my entire world off its axis. At the same time, Massimo's goes tight everywhere, and an animalistic roar echoes throughout the room. I feel his cock twitch and his hot cum explode inside me. Grabbing his ass, I pull him flush to me so I can feel his sweaty skin and his heart thundering next to mine. And while his body trembles in my arms, his eyes never wander from me.

CHAPTER
nineteen

THE MORNING SUNLIGHT STREAMING THROUGH THE window caresses my skin, its rays falling directly on my chest where Massimo is trailing his finger along the raised ridge of my collarbone. A small smile tugs at his lips just before he lowers his head and kisses the little dip of my throat. I squirm, tickled by his stubble, and giggle.

He quickly pulls away. "Sorry. I'll shave."

"Don't. I like you like this. Rugged. A bit wild looking." I reach out and drag my knuckles along his jaw. "Does this mean I no longer have to eat an omelet for breakfast?"

"Why would it mean that?"

"Peppe might have let me in on how you tend to rationalize things." My eyes find his, and I swallow the nerves that seem to have settled like a lead ball in my esophagus. "You don't need to make up silly reasons and excuses to hover over me, especially because of unfounded paranoia."

"It's not unfounded, angel. The more I think about everything that happened, the more I'm convinced there's a two-decade-long conspiracy against me. One I'm certain was hatched by someone within the Family."

"What do you mean?"

"Well, let's see…" He reaches across me, swiping a handful of buttons off the nightstand. He must have picked them up and left them there while I was sleeping. "It all started with the steep sentence levied by Judge Collins." One of the buttons gets placed on my bare midriff. "It went against the joint recommendation of my lawyer and the DA after I accepted the plea deal. Peppe managed to locate the bastard, so I'll be paying him a visit later today." Another button finds its way to just above my right hip-bone. "Then, we have Leone. Although he was behind Nuncio's shooting, I have a feeling there was more to it."

"You think it had something to do with you? But how?"

"I still haven't figured that out. However, just after I got back from Nuncio's funeral, there were two motherfuckers who tried to off me in the yard. Both of them ended up dead within days, along with the new CO who hired them and orchestrated the circumstances for them to jump me in the first place. I had Salvo dig into the guard's background and see if he could trace the work transfer order, but he came up empty." Massimo drags his finger upward through the valley between my breasts, his touch light and reverent. "The timing of that attack and the fall-out are extremely suspicious."

"There must be some kind of paper trail. Employment re-cords. Financial transactions."

"There's nothing." Dipping, he takes my left nipple between his teeth and sucks gently before placing the next button beside it. "I also can't dismiss the assassination attempts on Nera. Two of them. I'm not buying that Armando was singularly respon-sible for both. My gut tells me he was just a patsy. And getting rid of Nera had nothing to do with her directly. It was another blow against me." The fourth button lands on my other boob. "Just like the ex-con who shot at us in the mall parking lot."

I take in the tiny pearl fasteners scattered over my naked body. The one resting near the tip of my right breast lies just at the edge of a large patch of pale skin. It's the area I'm most self-conscious about. I've always believed it makes my breasts look odd. Not sexy. But that conviction is easy to dismiss with Massimo eyeing that particular globe with an exceptionally hungry look.

"Coincidence?" I ask.

"There's too much premeditation for all of this to be a coincidence. Someone has been going to great lengths to prevent me from taking over as the don." His head dips down once more to lick my breast. Warm tongue circling around the button. Once. Twice. Then, Massimo drags his mouth to my collarbone. His favorite spot, based on how often he returns to it. "Seems like I'm not the only puppeteer in the Family. Someone else is in this game. And he's been pulling strings for years. From the inside."

I glide my hand over the stubble at the back of his head. The spiky strands tickle my palm, and I love it. "You're talking about twenty years, Massimo. Who would invest so much time and effort?"

"Someone very smart, who can afford to play the long game. Someone with a lot of patience." Giving my collarbone one last lick, he leans away and sets the last of the buttons between my breasts.

Did my naked body just become a chessboard?

"I can't help but think there is more than the hunger for power behind it all. It feels personal," he adds.

"But why?"

A furrow develops along his brow, and his narrowed gaze travels over me. "I have no idea. Let's face it, I'm not exactly a likable guy. Every one of the capos could benefit from me being removed from the picture. With the right support, any of them could claim the don's position. However, I just don't see any of those pricks having the fortitude to follow through for this long. And until last week, none of them knew it's been me running the Family all this time."

"Salvo did."

His eyes snap up, finding mine. "Oh, if I could only be so lucky. It would give me an excuse to strangle the fucker, and I'd do it without an ounce of regret. Can't believe the son of a bitch dared to claim you for himself. If he was anyone else, he'd be long dead and rotting in a ditch somewhere. It can't be him, though. Salvo's been helping me from the start. And don't forget that he was my age when I got locked up."

"Then who?"

"For some reason, my mind keeps coming back to Adriano. He has the money and the connections to pull this off. He's been offered a capo's rank several times over the years but has always declined. Maybe that's his strategy, though. What if he's been aiming for the higher seat all along?"

"Adriano wouldn't hurt a fly. He is a businessman, not a killer."

Tiny buttons scatter all around as Massimo grabs my waist and rolls us so I end up on top of him.

"You shouldn't speak so favorably of him, angel. I need Adriano, so I would prefer not to have to kill him because you like him."

I snort and drop my chin to his chest. "I have no idea why you're so fixated on Adriano."

"Because he's the only man I've ever heard you speak nicely of."

A knock at the door saves me from having to respond to that bombshell.

"Miss Zahara," Iris chirps from the other side. "I am so sorry to wake you. The interior designer is here with the sample tiles for the bathrooms, and I can't find Mr. Spada anywhere."

I'm just about to tell her that Massimo is here when he presses his finger to my lips and shakes his head.

"Why?" I whisper, raising an eyebrow.

"No."

I sigh. "I'll be downstairs in fifteen minutes, Iris."

Once I hear her retreating steps, I fix Massimo with my

gaze. "I thought we talked about this and came to a conclusion about our situation."

"We haven't." He cups my face with his palms. "I'd kill for the chance to hold your hand in public and shout to every fucker out there that you're mine, Zahara. But we can't."

"Why not? Is it still about what the Family will think of me? Because if it is, you can rest assured I don't give a shit what their opinions are."

"You say that now. But trust me, angel, when actually faced with it… When you feel their condemnation following you everywhere you go, see them pointing their fingers at you and talking shit behind your back…" He shakes his head as if trying to dislodge an unpleasant mental image. "I'd slice the throat of anyone who dares, of course, yet it wouldn't erase the hurt their vicious words could cause. I loathe the idea of seeing stress and sadness on your angelic face, even for a mere moment, especially if—" He suddenly falls silent.

"If what?"

"Someone wants me dead, Zahara. They've failed so far, but that doesn't mean they won't succeed the next time. I will not let you be ruined because of me before I can eliminate that threat. The pretentious fucks would chew you up and spit you out before my body was cold."

"Nothing is going to happen to you, you hear me?" I bark. "And I don't need to be babied, Massimo. I can handle myself."

"But I want to baby you. Don't you understand? I want you happy, unburdened. But above all else, I need you to be safe. Salvo might be right—by keeping you close to me, I may have painted a target on you, as well." He squeezes his eyes shut and shakes his head again. "The thought of anything happening to you…"

"Nothing will—"

"I'll never consciously put you in danger. I want you with me. Always. Just, don't ask this of me, because I won't do it. There isn't any other way."

I swallow. There is a way. We could run. Leave this place and go to some other country where no one can find us. If anyone could pull that off, it's him. Although, he would have to abandon everything he's worked for over the past two decades. I'd never ask that of him. And in my heart, I'm afraid he might not do it anyway. Not for me. I'm probably stupid for even considering something like that.

"I should go get ready. The interior designer is waiting downstairs." I climb off Massimo and head toward the bathroom.

As I'm passing by the walk-in closet, I catch my reflection in the mirrored doors. Other than a few swaths of my breasts and shoulders covered by strands of tangled hair, my whole body is on display. The room is bathed in morning light, making every mark glaringly visible. It never even crossed my mind to drape a sheet around myself to cover up.

"Admiring yourself, angel?" Massimo smirks as he comes to stand behind me, wrapping his arms around my waist.

I tilt my head, zeroing in on the patches of lighter skin around my eyes, then shift my gaze lower. To larger pale areas on my chest. Then, to a few prominent stretch marks from my breasts growing way too fast when I was seventeen. To a few others on my hips—hips that are too wide to fit the accepted beauty standard.

Slowly, my gaze returns to my face, this time focusing on my eyes. Nose. Lips. My sister has always told me that I'm pretty, but I've never believed her. I couldn't see beyond my imperfections because, deep down, I didn't like who I was inside. Skittish. Scared. Someone who'd rather avoid confrontation than stand up for herself.

Well, I'm not that person anymore.

I meet Massimo's stare in the mirror. His eyes burn with unabashed desire. Judging by his hard cock pressing against my back, he likes what he sees. And, surprisingly, for the first time in my life, I do too.

"I guess I am," I say.

"Good."

His left palm slowly glides up my stomach. It's not as flat as I would like it to be, but the urge to tighten the muscles under my soft curves doesn't materialize.

Massimo's hand drifts higher, squeezing my breast lightly before shifting the locks of my hair resting over the swell to behind my back. Inked fingers glide up my chest and neck to settle on my face, cradling my chin.

"Do you want to know what I see when I look at you?" Words whispered just next to my ear. "Every time I look at you?"

"Yes," I admit.

His lips graze my forehead. Right over the large patch of pale skin above my eye. The spot I've always despised.

"You're perfect. Unique. Flawless. Inside and out." Abandoning his hold around my middle, he lets his right hand move lower. "I could admire your beauty every day, and a lifetime of that wouldn't be enough." He slides his finger across my folds, making me gasp. "I could tell you how gorgeous you are, but if you don't mind, I'd rather express my admiration with my tongue."

I bite my lip. "I don't mind at all."

Massimo

The midday breeze blows through the trees, rustling the leaves. It's so gentle there's no actual sound, yet I can still hear it. After nearly twenty years of nothing closer to nature than a patch of trampled grass in the prison yard, these forest melodies are a welcome intrusion. I stop and take a deep breath of the fresh Vermont air before continuing my stroll toward the rickety dock at the edge of a small pond.

A white-haired, heavyset man wearing a blue-checked shirt and green camo pants is lounging in an Adirondack chair, throwing breadcrumbs into the water. Completely relaxed. He's enjoying the tranquility all around him and doesn't even register the squeak of wooden planks when I step onto the dock.

"You're a hard man to find, Your Honor."

Judge Collins startles in his seat, then labors to rise from it as fast as his girth allows. The bag of breadcrumbs falls from his hand, landing in the water. Immediately, a ruckus erupts from a flock of nearby geese. The birds flap their wings and honk obnoxiously as they attack the remnants of their meal. The previously serene scene transforms into a wilderness madhouse. It's quite a backdrop to the petrified stance of the judge. He still hasn't found the nerve to face me.

"Been a long time since we saw each other last," I add as I walk to the end of the dock and stop just behind him. "Seventeen and a half years, to be exact."

Slowly, an ashen-faced Collins turns around. Despite the day not being overly hot, there's a line of perspiration clinging to his hairline. The bastard has aged. And not in a good way. Or maybe it's being scared shitless that's making him look like he's already got a foot in the grave.

"I-I... It wasn't..." he stutters, eyes locked on the holster peeking out from inside my unbuttoned suit jacket. "I had no choice. I'm s-sorry."

"Mm-hmm."

Pulling the chair toward me and turning it sideways, I step around and sit my ass on the wide armrest. Collins follows my actions with wide, frantic eyes. He doesn't move a muscle, just stands there at the edge of the dock, looking rather comical in his backwoods outfit.

"No other choice." Crossing my ankles, I lean on the solid edge. "So, what was the one you did have?"

He swallows. Loudly. His eyes dart back to my gun. "A max sentence for you or my ties to the Mafia would be exposed."

"I see. Who made the offer?"

"I don't know. I swear. There… I… I received a note. It wasn't signed, and I have no idea who sent it. The instructions demanded a full-term imprisonment, without a possibility of parole. They… they had a list of everything I did on behalf of Cosa Nostra."

I smile. "That must have been quite a list."

"Please. It wasn't my fault. I… I did what I could for you. I took a risk by only sentencing you to eighteen instead of the maximum of twenty years."

Sweat stains spread across his armpits. He looks so old and pathetic, trying to justify how he saved his ass at the expense of mine. Fucking chickenshit. Where's that sense of honor? Of accepting responsibility for your own actions? If you do dumb crap, then have the nerve to stand behind your decisions, at least. Not this cocksucker.

If he had told me that I deserved the punishment, I would have let him go. But this?

This idiot won't get any mercy from me.

"Can you guess who it was? Who could have sent you that note?"

"No. I don't have a clue."

He's telling the truth.

I know. He would have spilled the name the moment he saw me, all to save his worthless ass.

Another fucking dead end.

No shit.

"Well, since there's nothing else you can tell me, I guess I'll take my leave." I straighten and button up my jacket. Collins watches me with a mix of surprise and relief etched across his features.

"I'm… I'm glad you've weathered it rather well. And you seem to be in good shape. Looking good. I… I like the new hairstyle." A nervous grin screws up his bearded face. "If there's ever anything I can do for you… I still have connections and—"

261

"There is one thing."

"Of course. Whatever you need."

I lock eyes with the sanctimonious cunt who played a huge role in destroying my life. "Don't make this harder on yourself than it has to be."

For just a moment, I allow myself to enjoy his confused expression. And then, I slam my fist into his nose, sending the bastard flying backward.

He hits the water like a sinking rock, setting off a splash of gigantic proportions. The geese take flight, filling the air with a cacophony of loud cackles. Between his thrashing and the en masse departure of the local waterfowl, the once calm pond turns turbulent and murky. I step up to the edge of the dock, lowering myself to one knee just as Collins's head breaks the surface. He flails madly, eyes wide and red, as he tries to catch his breath. And all the while, driven by an instinct for self-preservation, the birds circle in the sky over our heads.

"You know the first lesson I learned in the pen?" I smile and lean forward. "To shave my fucking head."

My hand shoots out, grabbing a fistful of his wet hair at the crown. To the tune of resonant honking above, I push Collins under the hazy waters. He struggles, desperately trying to escape from my grip. The birds' loud calls make it impossible for the judge's cries to reach me, but I hear his soundless wail in my head. It reminds me of my own silent screams each time I was dumped in solitary confinement. Cries of fury and terror, while I slowly lost my goddamned mind. And wondered if I'd ever get it all back.

I hold his head under the water until his limp fingers slip from my wrist. Once I let go, his body begins to sink, his face—frozen in horror—barely visible through the sediment he stirred up. And as if straining to see across the murkiness, his glassy eyes are turned toward the sky. Toward the flock of birds still circling, forever out of reach.

Rising up, I shake the water off my hand and head back across the dock. My rental car is parked some distance away, behind some shrubbery along the side of the road. With traffic, it'll take me around four hours to get back home. Which means, just over eight hours—eight hours away from my angel. And I've already started feeling the effects of being separated from her.

Anger. Dread. Shortness of breath.

She truly is the air I need to keep living.

Reaching into my pocket, I take out my phone.

Put that away. You called her an hour ago.

So what? I want to make sure she's okay.

Awww… You are turning into a real softy.

And you're becoming a nuisance. Why don't you fuck off.

Ungrateful bastard! If it wasn't for me, you'd have had nothing to come back to.

Except my sanity. Now, will you please shut the fuck up so I can make this phone call? I can't have a conversation with you lurking and yapping in the background.

Nah, I think I'll stick around. Seeing you riled up is always a pleasure.

Liar.

Says you!

It's not about getting your rocks off. You want to hear her voice, too.

Psst… Did you forget? I hear everything, even when you figure I'm gone.

I squeeze the bridge of my nose. I knew that of course, but I don't like being reminded of the fact.

You're me. I'm you. And I'm not going anywhere, so deal with it already. And call our girl.

You'll keep quiet?

Fine.

Alright. I nod and hit Zahara's number.

CHAPTER
Twenty

Zahara

"**N**O MORE COGNAC FOR TIZIANO," I WHISPER TO THE serving maid while she walks by me, carrying a tray of half-filled snifters.

The girl halts, her gaze darting to the group of men seated at the table in the middle of the parlor. "But, he just asked for another. A double. Neat."

"I know. Bring him a glass filled with flat ginger ale instead. I doubt that he'd even notice the difference at this point. If he does and starts giving you trouble, though, just turn around and leave. I'll handle him at that point."

I follow the server's movements as she makes a brief detour back to the liquor cart before approaching the capos. She then sets their drinks before each man and basically hightails it from the room. My eyes zero in on Capo Tiziano while he tastes his "cognac." He mutters for a moment, likely confused over being handed the wrong drink, but has enough sense not to escalate the matter or draw too much attention to it.

Taking a sip of my wine, I lean my shoulder on the doorjamb and watch the men in the parlor over the rim of my glass. The Council members. Massimo grumbled all day today about having to host this informal gathering over drinks. I had to remind him several times of his own words: *Keep your friends close, but your enemies closer.*

With Judge Collins not being able to shed any useful info, we still have no idea who's been plotting behind Massimo's back. So, this was a necessity. A way to observe all the high-ranking men in a casual environment, maybe get a read on each while their guard is down. *Is one of them a traitor?* Also though, it's a way to play a bit to their massive egos. Capos love to be shown respect by being invited into the don's home. So, while Massimo doesn't like it, he still has to deal with this dog and pony show. It comes with the job description.

Across the room, Primo appears to be in a heated discussion with Brio. Based on the serious looks on both of their faces, they must be discussing finances. Tiziano seems to have forgotten his drink, because he's now wandered over to chat with Salvo, who's been hovering near the corner bookshelf. As soon as my gaze sweeps over the underboss, I quickly look away. The last thing I want is to be snagged in eye contact with him. Over the past hour, I caught Salvo staring at me several times, which gave me the willies. He even complimented me when he arrived tonight, and that felt weird as fuck.

Knowing that the entire Council would be attending this evening, I picked a conservative outfit for myself—simple burgundy pants and a black blouse with a high neckline. It's nothing that I haven't worn before and is the typical attire that previously allowed me to easily blend into the background during various social functions. But tonight, Salvo isn't the only one who's been stealing looks at me. Even though I've kept to myself, picking a spot to stand just next to the entrance, everyone had noticed my presence in the room. Logic tells me that their attention must only stem from curiosity about my being here and nothing else, however, I still feel the need to adjust my neckline and pull down my sleeves to hide my hands every now and then.

Unlike with Massimo, I'm still feeling self-conscious in front of *La Famiglia,* and it's hard to get over that.

"Did you hear what happened to Collins?" Primo asks, his voice loud and a bit tense-sounding. "The poor bastard drowned last week in his own lake."

Brio nods. "Such a tragedy. The man proved himself helpful on several occasions in his day. It won't be easy to get someone else like him into our back pocket again." He looks over at Massimo, who's been talking with Adriano on the other side of the parlor. "Any judges on your 'gambling debts forgiveness' list, boss?"

"Two, actually," Massimo smirks, his eyes meeting mine across the room.

The instant our gazes connect, an electric jolt zaps through my body. It happens every damn time that man looks at me. I might be covered from head to foot, but Massimo's eyes have a way of singeing every shred of clothing off me. As I watch him, he runs his tongue over his lips, as if he can already taste me, and that current of energy zips straight to the apex of my thighs. The things that deviant tongue can do... I feel the blush creeping up my cheeks just from thinking about the possibilities.

"That's new," Brio throws in. "Care to share the names?"

"During our next meeting." Setting his tumbler on the nearby side table, Massimo heads across the room, his eyes still glued to mine.

He stops a step in front of me and braces his palm on the doorframe, a mere inch above my shoulder. We're not touching, but I feel the warmth from his body as if he's a raging furnace. Or maybe that's because the look in his eyes as they peer at me is downright scorching.

"How much longer do I need to endure this crap, angel?"

"At least another hour," I whisper.

"I have way better ideas of how I can spend that hour."

"I'm sure you do." I reach into the bowl of pistachios on the buffet stand to my right and grab a handful. I need something to occupy my hands or I might forget where we are and fidget with Massimo's belt buckle. "Did you discuss the transportation issues with Adriano?" I try to deflect.

"Nope."

"Why?"

"I had... other things on my mind." He looks at the nut I've been trying to crack. "Give me that. Please."

Raising my eyebrow, I drop the pistachios on his outstretched hand.

"Are you bored?"

"Not particularly." I shrug, watching him make quick work out of shelling the pistachios. "What are you doing?"

"Isn't it obvious?"

"That you are stealing my snack? Everyone is watching, you know. Just take the whole bowl and go back to Adriano."

"Mm-hmm... in a second. Give me your hand."

My chest squeezes with emotion while he places the shelled yummies on my palm. When I look up, I find him watching me with a satisfied grin on his face. He doesn't need to say anything for me to know what he's thinking at this moment. Years ago, I mentioned in one of my letters that pistachios are my favorite snack, prattling on for an entire paragraph about how much I hate taking them out of their shells but keep refusing to buy the already-shelled ones. He responded to me with: *we're all a little nuts.*

"Tell the girls not to bring Tiziano any more Courvoisier. In fact, cut him off from all alcoholic drinks. He's becoming too chatty for my liking."

"I did that already," I whisper.

Massimo's grin widens into a full-blown smile. "Of course you did."

He turns around then and heads back to where Adriano is talking with the other investors—Patricio and Donatello. While he walks away, I absorb every single detail about the man who taught me to see the world beyond the obvious shades. His confident, determined stride. That posture of his, tall and commanding. He's not wearing a jacket, so I can see the ripple of his muscles under the gray fabric of his dress shirt. I have intimate knowledge of each rise and valley on that magnificent back because, night after night, I've covered every inch of it in kisses.

When Massimo reaches for the drink he abandoned on the side table, my eyes focus on his hand—fingers strong and inked—gripping the crystal glass. Goose bumps spread along my arms when I recall how it feels to have that rough palm glide down my chest, caressing my skin, and then to have it dip lower, between my legs. He can do such wicked, wicked things with those fingers.

We've only been sleeping together for a couple of weeks, yet it feels like it's been much longer. Massimo knows my body just like I know his. He knows what I like. What I crave. Every sensitive area, every spot on my skin. And I, I know how he likes to be touched, too. When he wants control, and when he's willing to surrender it. Which is never, unless he's with me. But my awareness of him extends past the physical. It's a visceral, living thing, born of trust and secrets shared over a nearly ten-year span. I can anticipate his reactions, read his moods, feel his emotions. That's how I know that his current relaxed stance as he talks with Adriano is just a pretense. An illusion that everyone is blinded by, except for me. Massimo's prison frays might have come to an end but he's still constantly on alert. A wolf who returned to his old pack, ascending to his rightful place as their leader, but remaining vigilant as if he's still surrounded by foes.

As I continue to watch him, I'm suddenly overcome by an urge to wrap my arms protectively around him. To assure him that not everyone in his life is an enemy.

As if sensing my thoughts, he glances away from his drink, his eyes finding mine. There's so much ferocity and determination in that dark gaze. I must be a fool for thinking that I could watch the back of a man like Massimo. Protect him by my own strength. Me, a silly little mouse who still prefers to stay on the sidelines so that people won't stare at her face, the only not-covered part of my skin. But here's a thing about mice... their teeth may be tiny, yet they are sharp. And I won't hesitate, even for a second, to sink mine into anyone who dares to harm my man.

"Miss Zara." Iris comes to stand next to me. "I'm so sorry to bother you. Tinia is crying in the bathroom and won't come out."

"What happened?"

"She was ironing the don's shirt. His favorite one. The one he said he needed for tomorrow morning."

I nod and head out of the parlor, making my way to the staff quarters.

"What's the damage?" I ask as we cross the hall.

"It's completely ruined. I tried to calm her down and reason with her, but Tinia wouldn't stop bawling. She then took the shirt and locked herself in, jamming the door. Says she's never coming out." Iris glances over her shoulder. "She's still terrified of Don Spada, ever since he threw her out of the kitchen when she tried to help him ready your breakfast," she whispers.

Sighing, I come up to the staff bathroom door and gently knock. "Tinia? Could you please come out."

"I can't." Her reply is a whimpering sob from the other side. "The don will be even more mad at me now, and we all know he doesn't give second chances. I'm staying put."

"It's just a stupid shirt." I shake my head. "Just... give me the damn thing. I'll tell him it was my fault, that I burned it."

"He won't believe you, Miss. He—" There's a sniff, and then, the door cracks open and Tinia's puffy, red face comes into view. "The don handed that shirt to me himself, and he sounded very irritated when he said he needed it pressed."

"Don't worry. I'll take care of Massimo." I raise my hand. "The shirt, please."

"Okay." Reluctantly, she passes a wad of black fabric to me. It stinks like singed fibers, with slight melty plastic undertones.

I throw the ruined shirt over my shoulder and reach to wipe away the tears from the girl's face. "Everything will be okay, you'll see. Get your things and go home now. Take tomorrow off."

I'm halfway down the hallway when I hear my name being whispered among the quiet talk.

"If Miss Zara ever leaves, I'm getting out of this house. Screw the job."

"I think everyone would," Iris adds in the same hushed tone. "Let's hope that never happens. Her leaving, I mean. Because, I'm certain the carnage will be a top story on the evening news, after the don goes ballistic and levels the place to the ground."

"He won't go ballistic," I toss behind me. "And, I can assure you, I'm not going anywhere."

Massimo

Silence.

I used to both detest and crave the sound of it. The yelling, the psychotic mumblings. The loud snores that competed with the mind-rattling echoes of things being banged against the iron bars in the dead of night. That neverending clamor used to drive me insane to the point where I'd be ready to beg for just a few minutes of blissful quiet so I could get some fucking sleep. My silent prayer would come true each time I was thrown into solitary. No screams. No pounding. No... anything. Just the sound of my own breaths. As if I was buried alive. Stuck in that hole, it was even harder to fall asleep.

Can't win for trying—a goddammed story of my life.

The barely audible creek breaks the stillness of the dark hallway, making me freeze. The fucking cunts repainted the damn thing but didn't grease the hinges. With slow, gingerly movements, I push the door ajar just enough for me to slip into the bedroom.

Inside, only a small reading lamp is lit, set on the old desk Zahara has been using as a work table for her sewing. She smuggled the lamp from the downstairs library so she could keep working late into the evenings. A small smile pulls on my lips. I hope she resolved the issue with the hidden blazer buttons she was trying to finish this week. Reaching over to the side, I adjust the thermostat controls, turning up the heat in the room. Can't risk my angel getting a cold.

Leaning against the door, I watch her, just as I do whenever she's fallen asleep before I get here.

My Zahara.

The blanket is tangled at her feet, leaving her mouthwatering body in full view, allowing my eyes to freely wander over every inch of her delectable, soft skin. Perfect and magnificent, just as Zahara herself is. I can look at her for the next thousand years and still don't get my fill. She's a vision—more than I ever hoped for. More than I deserve. But she's mine. She is... everything.

It enrages me that there are lowlives in her past who made her feel like she's somehow flawed simply because certain areas of her skin are lighter than others. I recall the way she used to keep pulling on her sleeves and adjusting her hair to have it fall over her face during our first days together. At that time, I didn't quite understand the reason that drove her to hide parts of herself, especially from me. After all, she had shared with me countless details of her life over the years. Her wishes. Her secrets. But not this. None of her letters had ever mentioned her vitiligo. It was only after seeing her in the room filled with self-absorbed men that it hit me. Her need to conceal herself. Why she tried to remain invisible. She'd never tell me outright, but I'm sure it's because of those pricks, and others like them.

What do they know, though, the small-minded, ignorant fools? Zahara is perfect. Just as she is.

It's her heart, not her appearance that makes her unique. Her strength and kindness that make her captivating and irresistible. And yes, Zahara's beauty sets her apart, calls to me, but only because it belongs to *her*.

My love.

That's who Zahara Veronese is.

The plush carpet muffles my steps as I approach the bed, unbuttoning my shirt in the process. Tugging my pants off takes a bit of effort because my cock is hard as granite—a common condition after even a single look at my woman. *Mine*. With a capital M. Knowing that she belongs to me and me alone turns me on like nothing else. As is the fact that she wants me. Accepts me. Loves me.

Once my clothes are finally off, I climb into bed behind her and wrap my arm around Zahara's middle, drawing her tightly against my chest and burying my nose in her hair. Jasmine. Freedom. Peace.

Zahara.

Closing my eyes, I inhale her scent as if it's the only thing that I need to keep me going. To keep alive. To let me rest.

Really? The irritated voice shouts inside my head. ***Your cock is about to explode, and you're just going to ignore it and catch some zees?***

Yes. Go away.

Why?

Because there's more than one way to experience bliss, asshole.

CHAPTER
Twenty-one

Zahara

"**M**ISS VERONESE," IRIS CALLS FROM THE LIBRARY threshold. "Mr. Canali is here."

I pause sewing rhinestones on the hem of the dress and inwardly groan. He just had to drop by while Massimo was away handling the "Camorra issue."

"Don Spada won't be back until six. Tell him to stop by then."

"Actually, I came to see you." Salvo steps around Iris, coming into the room.

Marvelous.

"Thank you, Iris." I pick up another rhinestone and focus back on my work. "What can I do for you, Salvo?"

He approaches the old oak desk where I'm working with long, slow steps and leans his shoulder on the bookshelf. Over the years, while my sister was leading Cosa Nostra, Salvo was an incredible help. Any time there was a problem, he ran interference between Nera and the capos, calming the situation and buying Nera time when necessary. He also took it upon himself to do most of the dirty work, saving Nera from having to deal with nasty things as much as possible. I'm not sure she would have been as successful if Salvo hadn't been there to support her.

Yet, after all that he's done, I've never quite come to like him. Despite his constant, insistent attempts to take me out to dinner, as well as a never-missed opportunity to chide me for putting myself in danger for Massimo's sake, he's remained a perfect gentleman. Even as I consistently rejected his advances. But still… I can't shake the slight unease that washes over me when I'm alone in a room with him.

"For your sister?" he asks, nodding at the bundle of red silk in front of me.

Understandable he'd assume that. Red is Nera's favorite color. But as it happens, it's mine too. I just never wear it. "I don't think you've dropped by to discuss my latest sewing project."

"Why not? I like talking with you. And I'd like to spend more time in your company, if you'd let me."

God, he just won't quit. If I could tell Salvo right now that I'm with Massimo, it would once and for all put a stop to this nonsense. Except, I did promise Massimo we'd keep our relationship quiet. For now.

"We've had this discussion several times. You're a nice guy, Salvo, but I'm not interested in going out with you."

"Yes, you've mentioned that." He leans away from the bookshelf.

With his hands clasped behind his back, Salvo strides around the library, looking over the book-laden shelves and the oil paintings hanging on the walls. When he reaches the fireplace, he halts and cocks his head, observing the winter landscape in an ornate golden frame hanging above the mantel.

"This belonged to my father, you know," he says. "It was in my family for generations, until Dad had to sell it, along with many other art pieces, to cover his gambling debts. Massimo's father bought them all at triple their value. He made a point to mention it whenever his friends came by."

"He wanted to rub your father's nose in it?"

"Of course not." Salvo turns toward me, his eyes flitting around the room. "The Old Spada always insisted that Family should be there for each other. Especially in times of need. A very noble stance for someone who was basically an outsider before he joined said Family, don't you agree?"

"I think, it was honorable of him to help a friend out, having the means to do so," I say. Massimo's father died when I was just a baby, but even to this day, his name still comes up in conversation among certain Family members. Unlike Salvo's father, who is never talked about. Most Italians are very religious, and Mr. Canali killed himself. They see that as a mortal sin.

"It was," Salvo continues. "The Family was smitten with Old Spada and his... unconventional ways. Helping his peers when he could have easily used their misfortune to keep them beholden to him. Granting various members prominent positions within the hierarchy, regardless of their pedigree. As long as he worked hard, any low-born man could earn his spot in the top echelon of our society during Old Spada's reign. He even sent his only son to run around with the foot soldiers, allowing him to break arms and legs as if he was no better than hired muscle."

I narrow my eyes at him. His words seem to be infused with respect and wonder, yet there's a subtle hint of something else in his tone. It sounds almost like... envy.

"Hmm, I think that approach worked out rather well for Massimo," I say. "I've never seen men remain this loyal to their leader, even after he was absent for nearly twenty years."

Something flares in Salvo's eyes, an emotion I can't immediately identify, especially since he looks away at that moment. "Indeed."

"So? Are you going to tell me why you're really here?"

"I wanted to ask if you'd marry me."

I nearly choke. Holy shit! Massimo didn't make up that tidbit about Salvo asking for my hand in marriage when he was trying to push me away from him.

"I can understand your decision to stay with your step-brother." Salvo crosses the room, coming closer. "After all, he has manipulated you for years, ever since you were barely a teenager. He has groomed a nice, timid girl to become his little marionette. One who's more than willing to dance to his tune. And since your sister has a family of her own now, I can see how you would have been left with this conclusion—that you should rely on Massimo as your only remaining so-called family member. He probably even used your naivety to steer you into believing that."

I seem to have lost the ability to speak, too shocked and disgusted by what he's saying.

"Don't let yourself be fooled by his words, Zara. Massimo doesn't care about you. He doesn't care about anything other than his own devious games and the thrill they bring him. It's not his fault. He's just not capable of feeling affection for anyone but himself."

"And you are?" I choke out, revolted. "Will you be my knight in shining armor saving me from the clutches of the big bad wolf?"

"I will." He stops on the other side of the desk and reaches out to stroke my face. "If you'll let me."

I rear back, away from his touch. "Thank you for your gallant offer, however, I have to respectfully decline."

Salvo's expression changes faster than I've ever witnessed anyone's before. One moment, he appears to be a compassionate and understanding man, and the next, his face transforms into a mask of pure rage. His hand, halfway on its journey to my face, quickly redirects. He grabs my wrist with a punishing grip and pulls me toward him.

"Why?" he snarls through his teeth. "I can give you everything! Respect. Security."

"Salvo!" I cry out, trying to yank my hand away. "Let me go."

"I've admired you for years, Zara. You'd be a perfect wife for me."

"You're hurting me, Salvo."

"What did he do to inspire such loyalty, huh? Why won't you let go of that man? He's nothing to you!"

"Because I love him!" I yell.

Salvo's face blanches. He abruptly releases me and takes a step back, dismay and incredulity contorting his features. It lasts only a second, because, as quickly as before, his demeanor shifts. Remorse and what I can only imagine is shame, overtake his face while he runs his hands through his hair.

"I... I'm so sorry, Zara. I had no idea, and I let my emotions get the better of me. Have... have I hurt you?"

"A little," I mumble, rubbing the tender flesh of my wrist.

"Please, forgive me. What I did... and what I said is inexcusable. You know me. I'm not usually like that. It's just... I've loved you from afar for so long, that I simply lost my mind for a moment. Could we please pretend this never happened?"

My eyebrow rises, but I remain silent.

"I swear, I won't ever voice my feelings for you again. Can we just keep all of this—my admission included—between ourselves? Right now, it's a very delicate time for the Family, and Massimo is, of course, my friend. I want to continue helping him achieve all his goals, but if he hears about this, he won't let me."

He sounds sincere. And looks truly apologetic. However, a speck of doubt inside me warns that his outward penitence hides some opaque, deep-seated feelings.

"Fine." The only reason I'm agreeing to Salvo's request is because I'm certain Massimo isn't gonna take this well if he hears about it. And he needs all the support he can get. Including Salvo's. "But touch me again, and I'll introduce you to my favorite pair of scissors. You get what I'm saying?"

To make sure he understands my meaning, I grab the scissors off the table and point the tip at him like a dagger.

Salvo blinks, surprise flashing in his eyes. He cocks his head and looks at me as if he's seeing me for the very first time. "There's more to you than you've ever let on, Zara Veronese."

His tone is strange—a mix of admiration and displeasure tinting his words.

"That applies to most people, Salvo."

"I guess it does." He gives me a respectful nod and exits the library, leaving me with a subtle sense of foreboding that sets all the fine hairs on my neck on end.

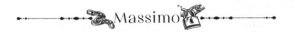

Massimo

The smell of rust invades my nostrils as I trudge between rows of old busted cars, flooding my mouth with fucking acid. It's a stench I became accustomed to in prison. If I had a choice, I'd never go anywhere near another piece of rusty shit. Just my luck that Camorra prefers to hold meetings at their junkyard. The location is remote, and the fact that nothing else is around for miles, makes this an ideal spot in case a meeting happens to go sideways. And with Camorra, that happens quite a lot.

A bunch of barbaric scavengers, all of them.

An animal analogy is actually quite appropriate. Not only for Camorra but for the rest of the underground syndicates, too.

The Cosa Nostra Families are like wolf packs. Well organized and faithful followers of a strict and defined hierarchy. Focused. Territorial. Wary of other packs unless there's an opportunity to claim a limited resource. Where business is concerned, we operate with predetermined and trusted plans, often without deviation, while we chase whatever prey we've set our sights on. And once we've got its scent, we don't let go.

In terms of structure, Bratva is very similar to us. But when it comes to business dealings, you never know what the fuck those crazy Russians are going to do. One day, they could be sitting down with you—drinking and laughing their asses off— and the next morning, they'd be pressing their gun to the back of your head. Very much like bears, whose moods and actions are often defined by how well they slept the previous night.

Predicting the outcome of any given venture involving Bratva is nearly impossible. It could be a giant fucking party or an absolute bloodbath.

And then, there's Camorra. An aptly named "clan" of hyenas. They might look like wild dogs, but they aren't even the same species. While Cosa Nostra and Camorra share the same roots— both originated in Italy—the organizations are very different. Camorra is made up of a bunch of distinct gangs that joined to gain whatever advantage they can. As often as they merge, they split to pursue their own interests, and then join again. There are no rules, and certainly no discipline among their ranks. They make alliances based on whatever drives them at that moment. They take haphazard chances and rarely plan in advance. While with Russians, you might have at least a basic idea of where you stand, with Camorra, you don't have the slightest clue.

Either way, you don't turn your fucking back on any of them.

I walk around the corner, passing the wreck of a bus, and head toward the modular trailer that acts as an on-site office building. It's been set up in a small clearing at the center of the junkyard lot, surrounded by heaps of crushed and decrepit metal.

Just steps from the entrance to the structure and nestled in its shade, two men parked on plastic folding chairs at an aluminum table covered with various dishes of food are stuffing their pieholes. Efisio, the current leader of the Camorra Clan, and his second-in-command, or so I assume. Nearby, eight armed men—each carrying a semiautomatic—are lurking in the harsh rays of the midafternoon sun.

I only brought along Peppe and three additional men, which puts us at two-to-one odds. Not bad.

"You briefed everyone on what to expect?" I ask in a low voice.

"Yes." Peppe nods next to me. "And I have backup at the entrance to this joint."

"I don't think they'll be necessary." I slip my hands into my pants pockets and continue my casual stride.

"Can't believe that's really you, Spada," Efisio exclaims around a forkful of pasta. "I remember when you were just a boy, and your father's soldiers dragged your skinny ass along with them. You've changed, kid."

"So I've been told."

Pulling out one of the unoccupied chairs, I take a seat across from Efisio, making sure I have a direct line of fire at both him and his second.

"It's unfortunate our collab in your casinos was cut short." He reaches for a bottle of fifteen-year-old Sauvignon Blanc, which seems totally out of place here, and fills his glass. "I was looking forward to sharing the profits."

"We've paid out close to double Camorra's original investment. I'd say you walked away with quite a substantial profit from that endeavor, especially considering the length of the term."

"I guess we did. So, to what do I owe the pleasure of this visit, Spada? Do you need another influx of cash? We'd be happy to... lend a helping hand at... your strip clubs."

I quickly glance at Efisio's men, some of whom are leaning on the remnants of an old Cadillac right next to the office building. They seem relaxed, but there's no missing the fact that they are still clutching their rifles in front of them. To make sure I have unimpeded access to my gun tucked into my waistband, I unbutton my jacket and lean back in my chair.

"You have one week to wrap up your business in Boston and get out of town, Efisio."

The older man raises his eyebrows and laughs. "Get a load of this fuckin' guy. You must have had your head scrambled worse than I thought in lockup."

I grit my teeth to stop myself from sending a bullet right into his ugly mug.

"You'll also cease all your dealings with the Bulgarians," I continue. "Kiril and I have already had a chat about that."

"Yah no, you filthy bastard!" Efisio snarls, leaning over the table.

The sound of guns and rifles being cocked ricochets all around us and in the next moment, nearly a dozen barrels are pointed in our direction. One of Efisio's guys is aiming at me, but the rest have leveled their sights on my men. My soldiers, including Peppe, however, are all targeting Efisio. Just as they were instructed to do.

The shrill sound of a ringing phone breaks the precarious silence, interrupting the grunts and heavy breathing that have been the only sounds up to this point.

"I advise you to answer that call," I say.

Efisio snorts, then reaches inside his jacket, never once moving his gun off me. When he takes a look at the screen, his face immediately drains of color. His eyes snap to mine.

"Mirabella?" he rasps into the phone. "Are you alright?"

I don't hear the other side of the conversation, but I see the old man's face paling even more.

"Everything will be fine. Just do as they tell you and you'll be okay." He cuts the line and glares at me with a mix of rage and terror in his eyes. "You motherfucker! She's just a child."

"Your niece is twenty. The same age as my stepsister was when your cousin Alvino kidnapped her with the intent of forcing her to marry him. She was almost killed in the clusterfuck that ensued."

"That was years ago! And I had nothing to do with it."

"I don't give the slightest fuck, Efisio. Camorra dared to come at mine. I do the same, only worse. However, if you agree to leave Boston peacefully, not a hair will be harmed on the girl. You don't, and I kill her. *Capisci?*"

"You wouldn't harm an innocent girl. Alvino was a deranged asshole, but you're not that far gone, Spada."

I brace my elbows on the table and lean forward, getting in his face. "You sure about that?"

His wide eyes bore into mine, searching. And I let him see the truth.

"You sick fuck," he chokes out, gritting his teeth so hard his jaw is liable to shatter.

I stand up and straighten my jacket. "I'm glad we've sorted this all out. I expect you and every member of your clan gone by noon, next Thursday. Do I have your word?"

"Yeah. Now call your men and tell them to let my niece go."

I take out my phone and type a short text. A minute later, a photo arrives—an image of the girl running through a gate toward a two-story house. Lifting the phone, I turn it around to show Efisio the screen. "There. Done."

"I hope you burn in hell, Spada."

"Been there, done that." I give my men a slight nod and head in the direction of the exit. "Enjoy the rest of your day, Efisio."

A sound of pebbles and metal scraps cracking under the soles of our feet follows us as we head across the clearing. The sun is high and it shines on the debris surrounding us, making the stink even heavier. I fucking hate it.

As soon as we round the corner and enter a long alley between two rows of cars, I slip behind the nearest wreck and take out my gun. "Remember, Efisio is mine."

"I doubt he'll try anything," Peppe says as he assumes a position across from me while the rest of my guys spread out nearby. "He gave his word."

"He did. But that was before we released his niece."

"Yes, but—" He doesn't finish because all eight of Efisio's men come into view, guns raised.

Gunfire explodes in the next moment.

The Camorra guys obviously didn't expect to come up on us this quickly, so the first three drop dead even before they get the chance to aim their rifles. The rest scatter, taking cover among the rusted-out vehicles. I manage to hit one in the back before he dives behind a junker of a truck from the last century, but then have to dodge when bullets rain down on me. A piece of shrapnel gets blown off the fender of the car I'm using for cover and flies at my face, nicking my cheek.

My phone starts ringing inside my pocket. If it wasn't for the notes of a classic melody I set as Zahara's custom tone, I might not have been able to pick out the shrill among the gunfire. Typically, my phone is always on vibrate only—at least, ever since Nera's eloquent "goodbye" nearly blew it up. The regular ringing was too reminiscent of the alert sound that bounced off the walls just before the cell doors were unlocked each morning, and I couldn't stand hearing that goddamned screech. But for Zahara, I installed a special ringtone and activated the feature that allows her calls to always ring through, regardless of "silent" or "do not disturb" modes. I never want to miss her calls.

"Zahara." Another bullet whizzes above me. I move to the other end of the car and glance over the hood. "All good there?"

"The designer just called. Apparently, stock is low for the tile I picked out last week, and it'll be a while before they can get more in. So, he wants to know if you'd prefer the same ones in all bathrooms or if— Where are you?"

"Just wrapping up the meeting with Efisio." Aiming at the Camorra goon crouched by an overturned pickup truck, I pull the trigger. "Actually, I was thinking white for the master en suite and, maybe, for the rest of the third floor."

"Massimo? Is that… gunfire?"

"Of course not. Could you ask him to bring us a few new options to look at?"

A round of rapid shots erupts, and the side window to my left explodes, sending shards of glass every which way.

"You lunatic!" Zahara yells into the phone. "Don't have a freaking chitchat on the phone while you're being shot at!"

"Doubting my ability to multitask? You wound me, angel."

"Jesus! Call me when you're done!"

The line goes dead. I look at Peppe, who's crouched less

than four feet away, changing the magazine on his gun. He's shaking his head.

"You think she's pissed at me?"

"Yup." He nods. "Y'know, I've never heard Miss Veronese yell before. With all the shit you've been through, she's gotta figure you're not that easy to kill. But still, she must be truly scared for your life right now. You gonna marry her?"

My head snaps toward him. "That's not your fucking concern."

"That means *yes*. I'm glad. You two are good together. Like opposing forces finally combining into one, and their polarities fusing in harmony. Just like vinegar and oil in mayonnaise."

"You did not just compare my future marriage to goddamned mayo!"

"Don't wait too long to propose, though. Or someone else may snatch her up."

A series of shots spray the side of the vehicle I'm using as cover. I send a few answering bullets in the direction of potential shooters, then duck back down to change the magazine.

"I'm... worried, Peppe. Terrified, actually. She's so delicate. I'm not sure how she'll handle the blowback from the Family. I swear, if anyone even looks at her sideways, never mind says something, I'll obliterate the fucker. Even if it means I'll end up massacring the entirety of Cosa Nostra. I just don't want her hurt, you know?"

"Hurt is what makes us strong, Massimo, and she has already been through quite a bit of it. Give her a chance, and I'm certain she'll surprise you."

He cocks his gun and moves along the line of busted cars, sneaking up on the last of Efisio's men still standing. The rest are scattered among the junk, either dead or on the fast track to meet their maker. However, there's no trace of Efisio anywhere.

Holding my gun at the ready, I step out from the cover the wreck provided me and meander past the fallen Camorra soldiers. Halfway to the office trailer, I spot Efisio. He's slumped on the ground, head bent forward, hand trying to stanch the blood flow from a gaping wound in his chest.

I approach and crouch in front of him. "That was stupid."

The old man laughs, spraying blood from his mouth. "Damn shame I won't be around to witness the finale."

"What the fuck are you yammering about?"

Efisio laughs again, but this time breaks into a coughing fit, spitting out more blood. The stream of it flows down his chin. "So friggin' long in the making. Almost twenty years. I think he's gonna make you beg. On your knees. And I'll miss it. Pissah, ain't it?"

The fuck?!

I grab his blood-soaked shirtfront and snarl into his face. "Who? Give me his name!"

A choking sound leaves Efisio's lips. I lean forward, trying to catch the words.

"I wonder"—he pants, his voice barely audible—"what will feel worse: the bullet he'll put in your head or... his betrayal?"

"Name!" I roar, shaking the son of a bitch.

A small smile forms on Efisio's lips, and then his eyes roll back. Cursing, I straighten and point my gun between his vacant eyes.

"A man who can make me kneel before him hasn't yet been born, Efisio," I bark and pull the trigger.

"Peppe, I have to make a detour," I say into the phone while turning toward the hustle and bustle of Boston's Back Bay neighborhood. "Make sure the remnants of Efisio's clan know that their situation has changed and that I expect them to be gone within the week."

Cutting the call, I slow the hell down and cruise along the swanky street lined on both sides with stores, hotels, restaurants, and every other imaginable establishment steeped in an abundance of elegance and charm. The bulk of the architecture consists of old Victorian mansions, but several modern buildings are tucked in amid the lot. Numerous big names grace the storefronts, their window displays beckon shoppers with the latest fashion trends. I dismiss those immediately as too big and imposing. I'm after something else. Something intimate, inviting, and unique.

This location is ideal, and I find exactly what I need about halfway down the stretch. An old five-story brick building with a couple of good-sized windows on the ground floor and lots of greenery around the arched entrance. It's quaint yet tasteful. Perfect.

Lady Luck must be smiling at me because a car pulls away from the curb right out front, so I scoot my Jag into an empty parking spot and head inside the boutique occupying the lower level. Based on the sign over the door that boasts of impeccable handmade quality and trendy designer styles, the place specializes in haute couture bags and purses.

The older lady behind the counter looks up, her eyes going wide upon seeing me. Obviously, I don't look like one of her usual customers.

"Good afternoon, sir. How may I help you?"

I take a look around, noticing intricately carved, tall wooden shelves. Zahara is going to love them. "I need to speak with the owner or the manager."

"What's this about?"

Reaching inside my jacket, I take out my checkbook and place it on the counter in front of granny. She narrows her eyes at it as if I produced crayons and a coloring book. "I need to know who owns this place because I'm buying it."

"We do." A man who looks to be north of eighty comes out of the back room and stands next to the woman. Her husband, I assume. "And it's not for sale."

I nod and grab a pen from the cup next to the ancient-looking cash register. "Tell you what... This is how it's going to go down. Based on the size of the space and the location, I'd say this place is worth around four or five mill." I write the amount of five million on the check. "I'll triple it," I say while adding "one" at the start of the number, "and you make sure your stuff is out of here by the end of the day. Does that work for you?"

The elderly couple blinks in unison, then, both of them look down, staring at the check I've turned toward them. I wait for them to say something, but they just keep gawking at the digits. Are they counting the zeros? Seeing this sort of reaction to a personally written check is the only reason I still like using the blasted things instead of the Black Amex in my wallet.

"Hey!" I snap my fingers in front of their faces. "Time's ticking, so you better start packing up your shit. I'll have my lawyer drop by in an hour to arrange the paperwork."

"Sir, I..." gramps starts to mumble. "I don't..."

I sigh. Reaching inside my jacket again, I pull out my gun, setting it on the counter right next to the check. "Funeral? Or fifteen million?"

A small gasp leaves the woman's lips before she slams her hands over her mouth. The man just continues to stare slack-jawed at my gun, his face slowly turning a greenish hue.

"Tough choice, I know. The check is real, if you're wondering, and offers slightly better retirement benefits, don't you agree?"

"Indeed," the old guy chokes out. "It definitely does."

"Perfect." I tear the check out of my checkbook and reach over the counter to stuff it into the geezer's front shirt pocket.

Small things. I feel completely at peace as I walk out of the door of this charming little shop. Even the knowledge that Efisio was somehow involved in the decades-long conspiracy against me, proving that there really *is* a plot orchestrated by someone close to me, doesn't seem to faze me. *I can't believe something as* small as purchasing a quaint little boutique would bring me such immense satisfaction in the grand scheme of things.

Fifteen million dollars can hardly be called "small," my inner asshole's voice bites back. The undisguised sarcasm dished out by my alter ego isn't lost on me.

Want me to go back and retract the offer?

Don't you dare!

I smile and get behind the wheel. The shrewd bastard has always been interested in power and financial gain, but it's obvious that even the most devious part of my psyche is fully smitten with my little angel.

Zahara is going to love this place, I have no doubt. Reading all of her letters, it was clear as day that her dream has always been to create her own fashion label. She's been obsessed with designing and sewing clothes for years, but each time I asked why she wouldn't make a business out of it, she shut down. I blame Nuncio for constantly insinuating that this line of work is beneath her. The pompous asshat was never capable of seeing what was right in front of his nose.

I want her to be happy. I want to give her everything she deserves and more. Every single wish she has, I want to make it come true. I vowed that no one would ever again clip her wings or hurt her. Which is why I'll do anything for her, whether she asks it of me or not. Anything, except one thing.

I will not ruin her life.

Because... What if Salvo is right?

What if her feelings for me are simply a product of my manipulations? What if in a few months, or even years, she realizes that? Just thinking of the possibility is throwing me into a full-blown panic.

For years, I exploited this amazing woman to gain a tactical advantage, never realizing what she would become to me. The love of my life. And now, knowing that she's The One, something I felt since the instant our gazes met at her father's funeral, I wish

I had the power to erase the past. Then, I would never have used her. Then, our history would have been built on trust. Then, I wouldn't be agonizing over whether her feelings for me could last. Be real. Without my conduct clouding her judgment. But after what I've done to her, how could they be?

Yet, every fiber of my being hopes that they are.

Am I just an entitled dickhead, or dare I trust Zahara knows her own heart and mind?

I want to shout it to the masses. *She's mine, motherfuckers! All mine!* And she'll forever be that, even if I have to level this all-too-often cruel world, with its bigotry and stupidity, and lay the wreckage at her feet. There's nothing I wouldn't do for her, as long as my actions won't hurt her.

So how could I even consider leading her into the direct line of fire of every single person she's ever known? How could I subject her to their derision and scorn?

I can handle myself. Her confidently spoken words push to the forefront of my mind.

Can she? I know my girl is strong. Her tenacity leaves me in goddamned awe, but at the same time, she's so fragile and softhearted.

…she'll surprise you.

Fucking Peppe. His mayo shit got me caught in wishful thinking again.

This constant tug-of-war between doing what I know is right and surrendering to what I want is driving me nuts. There's no question about what I *should* do. The best thing for Zahara is for me to stay away.

But I can't, damn it! I can't!

Fuck! I smack the steering wheel with my palm.

Just claim her as yours in front of everyone, and whatever happens, fight it with the fires of hell. You've always been a selfish bastard. What's changed?

"I did," I mumble. "Because, for the first time in my life, I care about someone more than my own hide. And what the hell is with you? You've been yapping nonstop about how I'm going to ruin her life, now you're screaming *claim her.*"

Not your problem.

"Don't be a chickenshit. Say it. We both know the truth anyway."

Fine! I'm in love with her, too. There. Happy?

Laughter rumbles inside my chest and then explodes out of me. "You're such a piece of work, buddy."

A startled gasp erupts from a woman passing by my Jag with her dog. She freezes in place and throws a panicked look at me through the open window.

"What?" I bark. "Never seen anyone arguing with themselves?"

Shaking her head, she slowly backs away from the edge of the sidewalk, then hurries down the block, nearly dragging her poor pooch in her wake.

ONSUMMATE INNER PEACE. THAT'S WHAT LYING IN bed, with my body spooning Zahara's, feels like. Despite us being practically intertwined, I tighten my hold around her middle, needing to feel her even closer. I wasn't kidding when I said I wished I could handcuff her to my side. I want her with me. Always. Even now, this absurd urge revs up another degree, and I squeeze her to me harder. She wriggles slightly. Immediately, I loosen my hold and bury my nose in the tangle of her light-brown hair, inhaling long and deep.

Her hair actually reminds me of liquid honey. It shimmers with different shades in the light. At first glance, it might seem like a simple darker hue, however, under intense scrutiny, the golden strands appear here and there. Beautiful. Radiant. Enticing. I've known women who spent good money at salons to get that sun-kissed streaky look.

Highlights. They are called highlights.

Yes. Highlights. But not her.

I know Zahara can't use hair dye because it irritates her skin. She wrote about it in one of her letters. And I remember every detail she ever shared with me. Even things she wrote *before*, when I hardly paid any attention to her inconsequential prattle. Somehow, it all still stuck.

Using the tip of my finger, I carefully push aside a few tendrils that glimmer like spun sugar, uncovering the warm honey tresses hidden beneath. There's even a hint of red in her silky hair. But also, whiskey-colored locks that match her smiling eyes. So many tints, so many layers, it's hard to know what to expect. Just like with my Zahara.

I press my lips to the delicate skin between her shoulder and the column of her neck. So, so soft. The craving to nip it consumes me, drives me out of my mind. I want to bury my teeth in that softness and mark that perfection as mine. The temptation is powerful, but I resist it, restricting myself to only another kiss.

"What time is it?" Her voice is sultry, luscious. The hushed, melodic notes make me instantly hard.

"Still early." My mouth trails down her arm, kissing every inch of the sensual sweetness that makes her who she is.

Does she realize how utterly alluring every part of her is? Her voice. Her skin. Her lush, mouthwatering curves that I can't seem to stay away from. For days, I've been walking around with a constant hard-on, dreaming up ways I could unleash this barely restrained desire upon her.

Just do it. Roll on top and plunge into her pussy in one powerful thrust. Revel in the feeling of your weight crushing her into the mattress, cage her in your embrace. Fist a handful of that glorious hair, pull her head back to get to her delectable throat. Or turn her around and take her from behind. Do it where anyone can see. Mark her! Claim her! Fuck her hard. Unleash the wild brute. Just like you want to.

You mean, like you *want to? Not gonna happen, man.*

Why not? She's given all of herself to you. Why can't you do the same?

Because... she doesn't know you, asshole. She only knows me. This... mild side of me.

We are one and the same. Two sides of the same coin. You can't separate us.

Enough with the psychobabble. I'll never allow her to know that darker part of me. She's pure. Untainted. I could never be rough with her. You, my friend, are reserved only for other people.

Hypocrite. And a coward. That's who you are. In matters of the heart, it's all or nothing. You can't expect her to only love a part of you.

Give it a rest. I won't yield.

Suit yourself. But know this—she's tougher than you think. And by withholding the brutal side of yourself because you don't think she can handle it, you're treating her the same as those bastards in the Family did.

That's not true.

You know it is. Oh, and one more thing. She already knows me.

What?

Silence. The deviant asshole in my mind decided to shut up.

"Get back here and fucking explain," I grumble.

"Explain what?" Zahara twists to face me, spearing me with her questioning gaze. "What do you need me to explain?"

"Nothing. I was just... arguing with myself. I do that a lot."

"Yeah, you told me." She kisses the edge of my jaw. "What was it about?"

A shiver runs up my spine as her long manicured fingernails rake over my chest, leaving red marks across my skin. I close my eyes and take a deep breath. I've been rock-fucking-hard since before I woke up, but now my dick feels like it's gonna explode. I force myself to take another calming breath, all so I can stave off the overwhelming urge to bury myself in her gorgeous pussy in one thrust.

"Stock market fluctuation. He wants me to invest in government bonds, instead." My voice sounds gravelly because I'm barely holding it together. It can't happen!

"Mm-hmm. It must be a riot being in your head. Do the two of you discuss anything else? Or only business?"

Rolling on top of her, I snake my arm around her waist. "Sometimes."

"What's he like? This *other* you?"

"He's a mean fucker." My hand captures her left breast, and I lean down to draw her nipple between my teeth. I won't bite, even though I want to. Instead, I flick it with the tip of my tongue. "Ruthless. Dangerous."

"He sounds fun. Maybe you could let him out to play?"

My cock finds her entrance. Bracing my weight on my elbow, I carefully ease inside. She's so fucking tight I nearly black out every time I slide into her silky heat.

"You won't enjoy his games, angel."

A sharp sting zips up my arms when she buries her nails in my shoulders. It almost pushes me over the edge. Almost.

"How do you know?" she pants.

"Trust me. I just know." With my gaze locked on hers, I slide deeper into her warmth while watching for signs of discomfort. Slowly. Carefully. I push all the way in.

Zahara's rosy mouth parts on a soft moan. Her lips are trembling. I pull out, all the way to the tip, but then slide back in. Painfully slowly. It's the sweetest torment, and I manage to maintain the languid pace as I gently fuck her. The sounds she's making are driving me wild, tempting me to speed up my thrusts. *No, I can't,* I repeat over and over until she finally starts to fall apart in my arms. As her pussy squeezes the life out of my cock, and her body is racked by spasms, I lose it.

I plunge inside. Once. Twice. Hard, powerful thrusts. Bottoming out on every entry. I can't stop. *She's mine! Mine!*

Zahara chokes on her breath, mouth falling open with a silent scream. With my orgasm barreling down on me like a runaway train, I still try to slow down, try to pull away for worry I'm hurting her. My efforts are in vain because Zahara locks her ankles around my waist. I'm not going anywhere. Except to heaven. My restraint shatters, and I fall off the edge.

Mine! The echo of my thoughts thunders across my mind while my angel quivers in blissful glory. I wrap my arms around her while I pump her full of my cum. Marking her on the inside. She's mine. My freedom. My peace. My Zahara.

Both of us are still panting, utterly out of breath, when I dip my head and press my lips to hers for a quick hard kiss. "I'm so sorry I lost control like that, baby. I'll be more careful next time."

"But I liked it." Her eyelashes flutter as she looks up at me. "Loved it."

Yeah, she's likely saying that so I won't feel like a piece of rabid shit. *Fuck.* Going forward, I need to be more subdued.

After another deep breath, I kiss her. This time, much more tenderly.

"Fucking Bulgarians," I mumble as I take a turn onto the side street and almost collide with a semitruck driving in the middle of the road. "Fuck!" I lean on the horn as I swerve around him. "What the fuck is wrong with you?"

I swear, the requirements for getting a driver's license must have loosened over the years because it seems as if no one can follow the rules of the fucking road anymore.

Even though the unexpected meeting with Kiril ended with me getting my point across, I'm still pissed over the shit he tried to pull. Bumping the percentage of his take by three to eighteen? Yeah, not gonna happen. Friend or not—a deal is a deal. And I reminded him of that. With my fist. The crazy bastard just laughed as he wiped blood off his busted lip, then made me throw back a glass of rakia with him.

I'm doubly pissed off because the fucker's antics took me away from Zahara. He called just as she and I got out of the shower, and I left shortly after, prepared to deal with the "urgent matter" Kiril insisted we needed to discuss. I assumed there was a major issue with our money laundering, but instead, he simply felt like riling my ass up. Next time I see him, I might clock him another one just for spoiling my morning with my girl.

I wonder what Zahara is doing now? My foot itches to step harder on the gas pedal so I can get back to her faster.

As I'm pulling up to a red light, the phone in my pocket starts buzzing again. It's been going off for the past five minutes, but with dodging the idiots on the roads, I couldn't answer it before. Cursing, I fish it out, seeing the screen light up with Peppe's name.

"Boss." His tone is urgent. He sounds concerned. "I just got back to the house, and Iris told me that Miss Veronese has taken one of the cars and driven away. She doesn't have her security detail with her."

"What?! Who let her leave?"

"I'm sorry, this is my fault. The men are well aware not to let anyone enter the property, but I did not relay any instructions about stopping her in the event she decided to leave."

"Where did she go?"

"I'm not sure, but Iris says she heard your lady speaking on the phone with her sister, and they mentioned the Public Garden."

I cut the call and hit the gas.

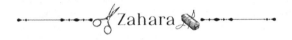

Zahara

"I don't think this is what Lucia meant when she mentioned wanting to see ducks," I say, watching my niece.

Lucia is glaring at the line of cute bronze ducklings following behind their mother along the cobblestone path. Her little fists are propped on her hips like she's ready to chide us all for misleading her. The "Mallard" family has been a kids' favorite feature in the Boston Public Garden for nearly forty years, but it's obviously not measuring up to Lucia's expectations. Her dad is beside her, looking rather lost and confused about what he should do.

"Yeah." Nera laughs next to me as we lounge on a nearby park bench. "Kai promised her we'll have ducks at our new home, but we're still looking for the perfect place."

"If he's going to buy you horses and make sure Lucia has her ducks, it will need to be somewhere outside the city."

"Yup. Likely at least a couple of hours out. If you decide to come live with us, you could probably have an entire floor to yourself."

"That's sweet." I accept a bag of shelled, roasted, and salted pistachios Nera offers and take one of the scrumptious earthy nuts. "Although, as I already told you, I'm staying with Massimo."

"Why? And why him, of all people? Why would you want to live in the same house as—" Her fair complexion suddenly loses more color. "Oh my God. He's making you stay! What is that jackass holding over you?"

I look away, focusing on the sun setting behind the canopy of trees at the edge of the park. It's long overdue, but I owe my sister the truth. Can't keep giving her my vague answers.

"My heart," I whisper and make myself meet her distraught stare. "He holds my heart."

"What?" she gasps, incredulity screwing up her face. "Zara... Massimo is our stepbrother."

"I know."

"That's all you have to say?" my sister chokes out and grabs my hands. "How did this happen? When? Were you visiting him in secret?

"We exchanged letters while he was in prison. For years. The day of Dad's funeral was the first time I set my eyes on him." I look down at my clasped and twisting hands. "You and I, we're quite a pair, don't you think? You fell in love with a guy whose name you didn't even know. And I, well… I fell for a guy without really knowing what he looked like."

"For the love of God, Zara! It's not the same. I, at least, knew what kind of a person Kai was. We met up for nearly a year. Spent time together. Got to know each other, face-to-face. How in the world could you fall in love without meeting him first?"

I sigh. "I fell in love with his mind. He was so cunning in his letters. So devious."

"Oh, he is certainly that! Devious and cunning. He's also an epically arrogant, ruthless bastard."

"Yes, he is. But there's so much more to him. The strength of his will. His strategic mind and sheer determination. All those qualities left me in awe. Every single time. He's so damn smart, Nera. He ruled Cosa Nostra for two decades without anyone ever suspecting a thing."

"You knew? For how long?"

"Yes." I swallow and entwine my fingers with hers. I need to tell her *everything*—now—because I'm not sure I'll have the courage to bring it up again. "I spied on Dad for him. And after Dad died and you took over… then… I spied on you."

"You… spied on me?" Nera's voice is filled with confusion, but more than that, hurt. "For Massimo?"

"Yes."

She starts pulling her hands from mine, but I capture and squeeze her palms harder, then finally gather the nerve to meet her gaze.

"I did it for you. And for Lucia." I sniff. "You may think you know Massimo, but trust me—you don't. He was never going to let you leave, Nera. Your marriage to Leone was just 'phase one' of his plans for you. So, I offered him a deal he couldn't refuse, in exchange for your freedom."

Shock. Disbelief. Anguish. The emotions cross her face. Each, in turn, makes me feel worse than the other.

"I'm so sorry, Nera." I wipe the tears that run down my cheeks. "Please, please don't hate me."

For almost a full minute, my sister simply stares at me. Time drags, it feels like a decade passes in silence. When she closes her eyes and a long exhale escapes her, I expect her to pull away. But she grabs my shoulders and crushes me to her instead.

"I always wondered how the mean donkey-hole knew everything that was happening. I even suspected he had someone planted in our staff who was somehow reporting to him." Her words are muffled by my hair. "I should have guessed. Always knew that my quiet little sister is so much more than she lets people see."

"He's not mean, Nera. Massimo is just… Massimo. And he's never pretended otherwise."

"Hmm. For your sake, I hope that's true." She looks at me pointedly again, as if trying to find more answers. "Dear God, Zara. How did you manage to fall in love with our *stepbrother*? And only through letters?"

"There were a lot of letters," I mumble. "Over the years, about three hundred between us."

"Jesus. And I thought my relationship with Kai started in an off-the-wall way."

"You're not gonna call me crazy? Or tell me that it's just a silly crush and I'll get over it soon?"

Nera leans back, finally releasing me from her assessing stare, and sweeps the loose strands of hair from my face.

"You've never been silly, Zara. Actually, I've often wondered how you're not my *older* sister." She smiles. "So, if you're telling me that you're in love with that raging shitgoblin of a man, I believe you. What the hell do you see in him, though?" Her grin stretches from ear to ear. "Because it can't be his sunny personality. God, I still shiver remembering him laying into me with that booming voice every time I went to see him in prison," she says with an exaggerated shake of her head and shoulders.

I laugh. "Yes, he has a bit of a problem controlling his temper. But if you try to get to know him better, you'll see that he's really not that bad. Sometimes, it's almost like he has two different personas, and he rarely lets people see that other, softer side of him."

"Well, I'll take your word for it, because my brain can't make that leap at the moment."

Lucia's happy squeal resonates from the path, and we both look over, watching her run around the row of duck statues while her dad chases after her.

"Massimo is worried how the Family will react if they find out about us," I say.

"He's right to be worried. You know how stuck-up and conservative those people are. Blood or not, you two are considered siblings. Familial kinship is the most important social value for Cosa Nostra. They will crucify you, Zara."

"Probably."

"Are you sure he's 'It' for you? Because if he's not, and the two of you eventually part ways, no other Cosa Nostra man will ever come near you. You know our world as well as I do. A woman who dares to have a relationship before marriage is frowned upon. I shudder to think what would happen if that woman chose to do so with her own stepbrother."

"Massimo is my soulmate, Nera. He's the other half of me. I can't even imagine myself with any other man because it's always been *him*. And honestly, I don't give a fuck what others might think about me. I'm done hiding, worrying about everyone's opinions, their judgments, their pity. Massimo just sees *me*. Just me. And he gets me. Better than any of those people who've known me all my life." I sigh. "The problem is, Massimo is afraid I won't be able to endure their scorn... or the malice that's bound to follow. But I know I can. And I'm willing to face it all to be with him."

I look at my sister, expecting her doubt to show on her face. There's none, though. Only quiet understanding, and maybe a bit of curiosity shining through.

"He's so harsh with everyone," I continue. "He yells, shouts at the slightest provocation. Except with me. With me, he's always tender and kind. Not once has he raised his voice at me. I love that… How different he is when we're together. But—and don't misunderstand me here—I'm not saying I want him to yell at me… It's just… sometimes, I feel as if he's trying to shelter me too much. As if he's afraid I won't be able to handle him. The real him. Protecting me from himself, kinda like he's protecting me from *La Famiglia*."

It's never more apparent than when we make love. He is so gentle. So careful with me. I love it, but at the same time, it makes me feel fragile. Like I'm too delicate for him to be himself. However, I'm neither weak nor breakable. Not anymore. And I want all of him. The good, and the bad, and hopefully, the naughty. I can take it all. Want it all.

"And can you?" Nera arches her eyebrow. "Handle the real him?"

"Yes. I just wish he'd realize it, too. But I'm afraid he might not."

"ZAHARA!"

I nearly vault off the bench. With my heart caught somewhere in my throat, I jerk my head from side to side, looking around the park grounds. I've been present for an array of Massimo's shouting stunts. The spectrum of intonations and decibels his vocal cords were able to hit in those moments defied logic, but I've never heard this particular quality in his tone. It feels like the ground beneath my feet is quaking from the sheer power of his voice.

"DAMN IT! ZAHARA!"

Frantically searching, I try to locate the source, but it's nearly impossible. The whole park seems to be reverberating with Massimo's thundering voice. On the paths, parkgoers stand frozen, only their heads and eyes swinging around in a panic. Kai, however, with Lucia on his hip while he's shielding her as much as he can with his arm and body, is scurrying toward us at top speed. His right hand is already inside his jacket, clearly gripping the gun in his holster.

"You said Massimo never shouts at you," Nera mumbles next to me.

A small smile pulls at my lips. "He doesn't."

I notice him then. Emerging from behind the trees, eating up the distance with his huge strides as he hurries toward the bench where Nera and I are sitting. The sleeves of his gray shirt are rolled up, revealing the bulging muscles of his inked forearms. When he stops before us, his nostrils flare and his chest rises and falls in quick succession as if he's sprinted through a marathon. The expression on his face is one of outright fury. But the deep wells of his dark eyes look more than slightly terrified.

"Angel," he says as he grits his teeth, all while he spears me with a glare. The tension is rolling off him in waves, but his voice is back to the throaty soft timbre he always uses with me. "Care to explain...?" he continues in that same docile tone.

I'm just about to answer, when—

"WHAT THE HELL POSSESSED YOU TO LEAVE THE HOUSE WITHOUT YOUR SECURITY DETAIL, ZAHARA?"

I barely manage to suppress a grin. "I wanted to visit my sister and niece. As you can see, Kai is here, and we're all perfectly safe."

Massimo throws a look over his shoulder at Kai. For his part, Nera's husband is now right next to my unhinged man, looking rather homicidal himself, even with a giggling toddler in his arms. The sight seems to make Massimo a bit calmer, because his breathing is more even when he turns back to me. "I don't trust strangers with your safety." His tone has reverted to the honeyed quality he reserves for me.

"Kai is not a stranger."

"YOUR BASKET CASE OF A BROTHER-IN-LAW IS ABSOLUTELY INCLUDED!"

His yo-yoing between violent outburst and soothing manner is so comical, I can't hold it in anymore and burst out laughing.

"You find this situation funny?"

"Hilarious, actually," I snort.

"I almost lost my goddamned mind, worried that SOMETHING MIGHT HAVE HAPPENED TO YOU!" He runs his palm over the back of his head. "Fuck. I'm so sorry, baby. I didn't mean to yell at you. It's just... YOU SCARED THE SHIT OUT OF ME!"

I steal a look at Nera, who's been patiently watching this whole exchange. There's bewilderment written all over her face. Then, I glance at her husband.

Kai's forehead remains furrowed as he observes Massimo with caution. "What the fuck is wrong with him? Is he brain damaged or something?" he asks.

"For your information, if there wasn't a child present, I'd brain-damage you, Mazur," Massimo snaps.

"Okay, that's enough." I leap off the bench and grab Massimo's hand. "Let's go home. We've caused enough of a scene."

Massimo broods the entire time I usher him along the paths toward the parking garage at Boston Common. I, on the other hand, am still fighting to keep my laughter at bay, and losing big time.

"I'm glad you're finding my mental breakdown entertaining," he grumbles as he opens the passenger door of the car I borrowed and motions for me to get in.

"Sorry." I chortle. "Where's your car?"

"It's… around. I'll have the guys come back to pick it up," he says and then makes the trek to the driver's side.

He doesn't start the BMW when he slides behind the wheel. Instead, he takes a deep breath and laces his fingers with mine.

"I'm sorry, too. I shouldn't have raised my voice." Taking my chin between his fingers, he slams his lips to mine.

The kiss is hard. Claiming. His teeth are nipping my lower lip while he slides his palm along my chin to grab my neck. Oh sweet Jesus! I never expected a hand necklace to be my thing. As he lightly squeezes my throat, I feel the delicious pressure all the way in my clit. My heartbeat skyrockets. Goddamn! More. I want more. I'm ready to beg, and a small moan escapes me as I lean into his hand, but his fingers are already lifting.

"Sorry, baby." His hold on my neck dissolves immediately. The next moment, his kiss transforms. Becomes softer. Tender. His velvet tongue gently caresses my own. It's a great kiss, and I still enjoy it, yet a small wound breaks open in my chest nevertheless. He's taking it easy on me. Again.

When his lips finally lift off mine, and he leans away, I stare into his stormy eyes. There is so much passion brewing there. Desire. Unsated hunger. This man could devour me with his eyes alone. And I want that! But I also want to feel all of his raw power. Want him to stop suppressing his lustful fire and let us burn.

But it's obviously not going to happen now. His strokes on my chin are already back to the barely-there touch of before.

"We should get going," I sigh.

CHAPTER
Twenty-Three

Zahara

Two weeks later

"HOW WOULD YOU TELL A MAN THAT YOU WANT him to be… rougher with you?"

Iris spins around, the stack of clean towels nearly slipping out of her hands. She stares at me in slack-jawed shock. "Um… rougher? As in…?"

"As in I'm not fine damned china that will break if he squeezes me too hard," I clarify. "Imagine that you're with a partner who's very passionate. A strong, dominant person. That's who he is, and you like him just the way he is. But he does everything he can to suppress his true nature when he's with you. All because he's petrified that you'll get hurt, so he tries to shield you from it. From himself."

"That's beyond adorable."

"It is. It's just…" I sigh. "Shit. I know it sounds stupid. I don't even know what I'm saying."

"You figure he thinks of you as weak?"

"Not exactly. Maybe just 'not strong enough.' That's probably a more accurate assessment." The sash I'm ironing almost tears off the blouse from how hard I tug on it. "I'm not a fucking porcelain teacup!"

"We're talking about Don Spada, aren't we?"

"Who else?" A sad laugh escapes me. "He's absolutely certain no one knows about us."

"Hmm. He stopped sleeping at your bedroom door, but his bed remains untouched. So, I drew my own conclusions."

"Aren't you going to comment on how outrageous it is that I've been sleeping with my stepbrother?"

"Well… it's… it isn't something that's common, Miss Zara. Family is sacred." She looks down at the towels in her hands. "But… I guess, love doesn't care about social rules. One can't simply command their heart. I also know you've been in love with him for quite some time. And that man can't take his eyes off you whenever you're near. The other day, when he was chastising me for allowing you to leave without protection when you went to see your sister, I thought he was going to have an aneurysm."

"Yeah. He yelled quite a lot."

"At you? But… he never does that. He's so different around you. Calm and… more normal."

"I know." I bite my lower lip. "Would you think I'm nuts if I confess that I love his craziness?"

"Mm-hmm. A little?" She giggles. "When Don Spada is in one of his fits, all I want to do is run and hide. I think most people feel the same way because, y'know, they think he's going to off them."

"That's a fair concern."

I set the iron aside and lift the blouse to inspect it. Dark purple, nearly black. High neckline. Long sleeves, with beautiful lace at the cuffs—intricate material that will cover my hands when it cascades down. I was planning to match it with black tailored pants for the party at Brio's tonight. My typical attire.

Except, how can I expect to be seen as strong when I've never been brave enough to attend a Family gathering even slightly less than fully covered? I keep assuring Massimo that I don't care what people will think of me if they find out about our relationship, but I've always feared the brunt of their inquisitive eyes.

I lower my customary blouse and meet Iris's gaze. "Massimo is in his office with Tiziano. Could you please tell him that I need... more time? I'll get ready and have Peppe drive me over to Brio's when I'm done."

"Um... I don't think he'll leave without you."

"Make sure he does."

When the bedroom door shuts after she exits, I throw the shirt back on the ironing board. Spinning around, I head toward my walk-in closet. Most of my elegant clothes are hanging there—sorted by colors, spanning from dark brown to... black. I sigh, glancing at the very few outliers that I made in lighter shades bunched to the side. And at the far end of the rod, hangs a long, gray cloth garment bag. My hand shakes ever so slightly as I lower the zipper, revealing the length of crimson-red silk. The dress I was working on when Salvo paid me that decidedly unpleasant visit and thought I was making something for my sister.

As I carry the dress and lay it on my bed, my stomach churns. But it's not anxiety that's twisting it up in knots. It's excitement. I never imagined that I would even contemplate wearing it in public, much less feeling determined as I do now to go through with it.

I might have been a delicate, too-easily-broken fine china cup once.

But not anymore.

And it's time I show everyone. Most importantly—myself.

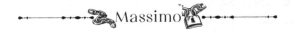

Massimo

"Why the fuck is it taking so long?" I bark into the phone. "If Zahara doesn't want to attend, I'll tell everyone to fuck off and head back home."

"Oh, I'm pretty sure she wants to attend," Peppe drones on the other end of the line. "We're ten minutes out."

"How many men do you have with you?"

"Six. Two in the car ahead of us, and four in another, bringing up the rear. She'll arrive safely."

"Good." I cut the call and look around the huge hall brimming with people. There are over two hundred guests. I actually don't know—or care—what the fuck Brio is celebrating, but this party has become his "unofficial" send-off. Currently, only the Council is aware of his forced "early retirement," but soon enough, I'll make sure everyone in the Family hears the news.

Picking up a glass of wine from a nearby table, I head across the room, checking out the space. I haven't been at Brio's in over twenty years, and back then, his digs were the last thing on my mind. Zahara, however, prefers to stay on the fringe at events like this. We could make ourselves comfortable by the exit to the hallway, where it's less crowded. Or, if she'd rather, we could just hang around near the glass doors that lead to the garden.

I still don't understand why she insisted we must attend tonight. I hate Family celebrations, and she knows that. But more than that, this damn party is a colossal security risk. I made sure to have thirty of my most reliable men positioned around the venue. They all have very clear orders—protect Zahara and watch out for any potential threats. This affair has been designated as a 'weapons-free environment,' except I honestly don't give a shit about Brio's delicate sensibilities or his desire to maintain a bullet-free home. Both of my Glocks are tucked into the holster under my suit jacket.

"Brio has taken the news of his retirement much better than expected," Salvo says as he comes to stand on my left. "I fully expected him to throw a fit."

"He tried. I convinced him of the benefits of accepting the situation for what it is."

"In exchange for monetary compensation, perhaps?"

"In exchange for keeping his limbs attached to his body." I take a sip of my wine. "Peppe tracked the last of Efisio's men who hadn't fled the city by the deadline. Neither of the two idiots could attest to seeing their leader meeting with anyone from Cosa Nostra in the past year. Basically, the same story as with all the others he questioned. It's another dead end."

"Are you sure it's not the Albanians who want you out of the picture? I had one of my guys do some digging. It seems Dushku's business hasn't been doing well. After his dealings with Bratva and then Ajello fell apart, their finances took a serious hit. And now, with us moving on to working with Popov, there are only a few small players left for the Albanians to hang on to as clients."

"Endri is a clever snake. He'll find a way to slither out of this situation."

"Maybe." Salvo shrugs. "You know, I'm somewhat sad we're bowing out of the strip clubs. Many men in this room quite enjoyed blowing off steam with the girls. When's the official handover happening?"

"In a month. I'm meeting with Ajello's underboss tomorrow evening to sign the paperwork. We'll probably—"

The room suddenly falls completely silent. I look around, tracking the surprised gazes of over two hundred guests. They all seem to be staring in the same direction. When my eyes finally land on the source of the commotion, I almost swallow my tongue.

"Fuck me," Salvo mutters beside me.

Under the bright vestibule lights, a vision in red steps into the celebration hall. The upper part of her dress hugs her sublime body, while the long silk skirt cascades over her hips like a waterfall of blood. With each step she takes, the two thigh-high slits shift, revealing her shapely legs. My eyes trail from her shimmering gold heels, up over the flashes of smooth skin, across the tight bodice and the deep V-neckline that plunges to showcase her luscious breasts, to stop at her angelic face. As usual, she doesn't have a stitch of makeup on. But instead of wearing her hair down as she typically does, it's gathered at the crown of her head in a tight, elegant bun.

My lungs contract, and I'm left gasping for air as I watch Zahara glide among the guests. They part like a wave to let her pass. I can't move a muscle. I can't even breathe, absolutely floored by the magnificent sight of her. She walks with sure steps, head held high as if utterly unconcerned by everybody's stares. Their blatant gawking leaves no question—they are seeing her for the first time. In all her regal glory. Through the crowd, she strides like a princess. No... like a fucking queen.

My queen.

Our gazes collide at that moment, and it feels like a wrecking ball just whacked me square in the chest. In a split second, I realize how monumentally wrong I've been to doubt this woman's inner strength. The girl who spent years trying to be invisible no longer exists.

I'm completely absorbed by the heavenly vision before me, so different from the one I already know and love, when a guest—a *male* guest—blocks her path, shuttering my view.

Blind rage erupts within me as I rush across the room, straight for the man who dared to step between me and my angel. I grab the idiot by the back of his suit jacket and fling him to the side, where he crashes into one of the tables, tipping it over.

"You never told me you like red, Zahara," I say, stepping right up to her.

She tilts her head, staring at me from beneath her long lashes. "Actually, it's my favorite color."

My hand lifts as if of its own accord, and I brush her chin with my knuckles. Then, my fingers trail down her slender neck, skimming across her nape where two long ribbons extending from the front of her dress are tied in a bow, their ends draping over her bare back.

"One of those things that needed to be sewn inside out?" I ask, trailing my palm down the length of the silk.

"Yes." Her eyes sparkle like two large whiskey-colored diamonds. "Using the same piece of fabric the bodice was done with."

Around us, people are pretending to be enjoying their drinks, but their baffled gazes don't deviate from us even for a second. They are obviously eavesdropping but can't make heads or tails of our exchange.

"Want to get a drink, angel?"

"I'd love to."

I place my hand on the small of Zahara's back, ushering her across the room to a bar at the opposite corner. Every eye in the room follows us as we make our way. My palm itches to slide lower, to her decadent behind.

Sure. Let's just broadcast to everyone here that you're screwing your stepsister so they can come after her like the damn vultures they are.

"It's called making love, asshole," I mumble under my breath. "And I'm pretty sure she'll kick their butts if they try."

My voice is low, but judging by the handful of perplexed stares, clearly still loud enough.

"Another quarrel with your alter ego?" Zahara whispers, amusement dancing in her tone.

"Maybe."

"Just tell him to shut up."

A laugh builds inside my chest. *You heard the lady. Be gone,* I tell my other self.

My fingers edge the silky smoothness of Zahara's waist-line, and then I let my palm curve over her perfect ass, giving it a light squeeze.

A hush envelops the room again, with only the soulful crooning of the jazz singer somewhere on our right defying the collective deep-held breath. It lasts barely a moment before murmurs and insistent whispers explode from every direction. Fucking vultures. They just can't help themselves.

Not that I'm surprised. The Cosa Nostra views on male-female interactions are very traditional. There's no way a well-bred man would dare lay his hand on a woman's ass without the two being in an official relationship—married or, at least, engaged. The way I'm keeping Zahara pressed to my side would have been more than enough to spark a slew of assumptions that there's something between us. My hand on her ass has blasted those assumptions into a categorical certainty.

I can acutely feel everybody's eyes focused on my hand. The furious muttering gradually becomes louder. It wasn't a conscious act, sliding my hand down to grab Zahara's behind. But keeping it there as we walk across the room, that definitely is. I'm staking my claim. Declaring her as mine—finally. It's a soundless howl that's deafening inside these walls.

I steal a glance at Zahara, worried about her reaction now that the cat is out of the bag. Remarkably, she doesn't seem perturbed… much. Her spine remains straight, and she walks with her head held high. I know her, though. I see the nerves she's trying to hide.

"Want me to kill them?" I ask as we continue traversing among the buzzards.

A playful smirk pulls at her lips. "No. But thank you for the offer."

"You sure?"

"Yes. But I wish they would just stop talking. It feels as if we've landed in a damn beehive."

"That can be arranged."

Changing our course, I guide her to the singer, who's been valiantly trying to be heard over the swarm of noise. Grabbing the microphone from the woman's hand, I tuck Zahara closer to my side while my palm remains firmly planted on her ass cheek. I turn toward the crowd, and they immediately zip their mouths shut, their shocked gazes all zeroing in on me.

"Good." The word ricochets throughout the room. "If I notice anyone, with the exception of the lovely band behind me, using their vocal cords tonight, said vocal cords will be forcefully removed from the throats they currently inhabit. Am I making myself clear?"

A slew of shocked gasps is my only reply. Lots of dumbfounded blinks, though. But no actual words are being uttered.

"I asked, AM I MAKING MYSELF CLEAR?" I roar.

All heads move up and down like a tragic display of bobbleheads. They stay mute as fuck, just continue to gape at me and Zahara.

"And censor your goddamned expressions, because I won't take kindly to any that I don't like," I add. "You'll keep your disdainful and disapproving stares in check, or you'll bear the consequences and my wrath. Consider yourselves warned."

More nods.

"Perfect. Carry on." I throw the mic back to the singer, then glance at Zahara, who's watching me through narrowed eyes.

"You can't forbid people to talk, Massimo."

"No?" I drag my knuckles along the delicate line of her chin. "Well, I just did."

"You're mollycoddling me again."

"I love coddling you, angel. I can't stand the thought that those bastards might say something that upsets you, that they might hurt you with their cruel words. There's no coming back from this now, Zahara. You understand that, right?"

"I do. But what I need you to understand, is that I can handle this. I'm not the meek, frightened girl I once was. Unkind words and reproachful stares don't bother me anymore, and I need everyone to realize that. Including you."

I watch her—so beautiful and fierce—while my heart swells inside its cage like it's trying to reach her. Yes, she is strong. Much stronger than I previously believed. I get it now, though. But if she needs this to affirm to herself and everyone else that she's unshakable, I'll grant her wish.

I stretch my hand toward the singer, who's standing utterly stone-still and in absolute silence. "Give that back."

When she passes me the mic, I wrap my arm around Zahara's waist and turn to face the stunned crowd.

"You are allowed to speak." My voice once again carries across the room. The tone is as insouciant as I can make it, but I let my gaze slide over and pause on as many people gawking at us as I can, clearly telegraphing the aftermath should the subject of their flapping traps piss me off. A swift yet painful death.

As expected, the low whispers restart the moment the microphone is back in the singer's grip.

"Satisfied?" I meet Zahara's honey-brown eyes.

She tilts her head to the side, a small smile curving her lips. "You are incorrigible."

"Without a doubt," I smirk. Then, I lift her into my arms and fuse my mouth to hers.

It's not our first kiss, but it feels as if it is for some reason. Maybe it's because I'm not paranoid about someone walking in on us anymore. It's no longer an issue since practically the whole of Boston Cosa Nostra is gathered in this hall, witnessing me devouring my angel's lips without an ounce of shame or concern for their small-minded sensibilities. And what lips those are… Soft, like the petals of an exquisite flower, and sweet, like the ripest forbidden fruit. Zahara is my paradise garden, and I can no longer restrain myself. I surrender to the temptation to nibble the most succulent lips on this earth, enjoying the faintest panting breaths passing from her lips to my own.

A collective gasp detonates around us, and then the whispering kicks up. Soon enough, the rumble thunders through the room like an earthquake. And I… Don't. Care. Don't give a fuck about anything but my Zahara.

The pounding of my heart, however, has escalated to a breakneck beat. The sound is so loud in my ears that I feel like my entire body is pulsing from the inside out. God, I'm so crazy about this woman. It feels so damn good to at long last be able to claim her as mine in front of everyone. To make sure they all know who this woman belongs to, so no idiot will ever try approaching her again. Next time, I'll kill whoever dares.

Zahara kisses me back, the bold stroke of her tongue leaves me without a doubt about the fervor of her passion. She winds her arms around my neck, her fingers raking through the short hair at the back of my scalp. I haven't shaved it since the day she admitted she wanted to see me wearing it longer. I suck her tongue between my teeth, biting it lightly. She returns the bite. Hard. A metallic tang bursts in my mouth. The taste of blood—harsh and bitter. Such a contradiction to the fresh scent of jasmine enveloping me. The smell of peace that only she could ever give me.

"I need to ask you something," I whisper into her lips.

"Okay."

Reluctantly, I lift my hungry mouth off hers and meet her gaze. "Would you marry this crazy old asshole, Zahara?"

My lungs aren't working. Someone must have shut down my respiratory system, because I can neither inhale nor exhale. The only thing I can do is peer into Massimo's eyes, getting more breathless and lightheaded. The hushed whispers swirling around us explode into a cacophony of astonished shrieks. I barely register them. Am I dreaming? I must be.

"God knows you deserve better, angel," Massimo continues, his tone grave. "But the thing is, I can't let you go. You are mine, Zahara. You've been mine from the moment your knowing gaze landed on my imprisoned ass. There you were, mourning your father, and all I could do was struggle to breathe. Not a day since has passed when I didn't need you. You are the very air in my lungs. I love you, baby. I'm being selfish, but you already know that about me. Please, say yes."

My eyes fill with tears, blurring my vision and his face. I try responding but can't get past the lump blocking my airway. I've fantasized about this moment for so long. I can't believe this is real. Cupping Massimo's rugged cheeks with my trembling palms, I attempt again to push the words out of my mouth. Only a breathless sound escapes me. So I just kiss him. Pouring everything I feel into that kiss.

"You need to say *yes*, Zahara. 'Cause if you don't, I'm liable to kill every man for a hundred miles, just to make sure no one else can have you," he says into my lips.

A shaky laugh bursts from me. "And what about witnesses?"

"I'll get rid of them, too."

"No need for that." I sniff. "Yes. I'll marry you."

Shocked squeals break out behind me, but they're drowned out by Massimo's hurried steps echoing off the hardwood floors as he carries me across the room. I lock my ankles behind his back and chance a look over his shoulder. The top echelon of Boston's Cosa Nostra has gathered in a semicircle at the center of the hall, gaping at our retreating forms in total stupefaction. Among them is Salvo, with a look of great bitterness sweeping across his face. Close by, a stunned Tiziano is practically supporting his wife. Her hands are covering her mouth, eyes blown wide—she's horrified. It's quite a sight.

The urge to laugh overwhelms me. For years, I've done everything I could to remain invisible to these people, never wanting to draw any attention to myself. But now, as I create a scandal that will undoubtedly be talked about for the next decade, for a moment, I'd completely forgotten they even existed. I try to muffle the fit of giggles bubbling up inside me and fail.

"If I'm being completely honest," Massimo grumbles as he kicks a door open. "That's not the reaction I expected to my marriage proposal."

I snort and bury my face in the crook of his neck. "Sorry. You should have seen the expressions on everyone's faces."

"Well, they better get their faces under control before we get back."

Massimo stops at the end of a dark hallway and kicks open another door. The room he carries me into is cast in shadows, a tall floor lamp in the corner the single source of light. Navy drapes obscure the windows on the far side, and all the other walls are lined with intricately carved bookshelves.

"Where are we?"

"Brio's study." Massimo deposits me on the large pedestal desk occupying the middle of the room.

"Why?"

"Because if I have to wait any longer, my cock is going to

explode." He seizes my chin between his fingers and leans in so close his face is but a breath away. His eyes are fierce as they search mine so intently he can surely see the depths of my soul. "I'm going to fuck you now, angel. It's going to be hard. If you think you can't take that, you better tell me right away."

I lift my chin. "Do your worst. Pound me on top of this desk and make me scream your name for everyone to hear."

A feral growl erupts from his chest. His hand slides off my chin and wraps around the column of my throat.

"Zahara." There's a clear warning in his tone, a promise of the most sinful carnal pleasure. "Be careful. My control is hanging by a thread, and the last thing I want is to unintentionally hurt you."

"Then stop handling me as if I'm made of glass." I grab his tie and pull him closer to purr into his ear. "That other you. The one you let out only with others, but never me. The vicious and untamed one. I want *him* to fuck me tonight."

Massimo's body goes still. "We are one and the same, baby," he whispers.

"I know." I grab his chin, mimicking his hold on me. "So don't you dare deny me even the slightest part of you. From now on, I want the whole of you, Massimo. Can you give me that?"

Something flashes in his eyes. Something dangerous. And a little wicked. His gaze remains locked on mine as he unbuttons his pants and slides the zipper down, releasing his hard-as-steel cock. My breathing picks up and turns ragged as he lays his palms on my bare thighs, slowly sliding them higher.

"Apologies for the dress, baby," he rasps. In an instant, a loud rip echoes throughout the room.

A large chunk of red silk sails to the floor, landing by Massimo's feet. He moves his hungry gaze to my chest, pausing on my breasts for a moment, then, continues his downward sweep. The front panel of my skirt, the flimsy scrap that extended off the bodice and barely attached to the long train at the back, the part that created an illusion of two thigh-high slits, has been obliterated. Leaving my bare pussy fully on display.

"This dress wasn't meant to be worn with underwear," I say.

Those devilish eyes glow with unbridled hunger as if my words have unleashed a starving predator. His nostrils flare and his lips quiver on a deep, guttural growl as he reaches out and presses his thumb to my core. I shudder. It may only be a single touch, but it's as if he's set off a barrage of fireworks with it. Needing something to anchor me, I grab the lapels of his jacket, fisting the fabric as I pull him closer to me. The tips of his fingers brush my delicate folds while his other hand finds its way back to my neck to fondle the straining tendons of my throat.

"Zahara," he rasps, sliding his fingers inside my pussy. First one, then he adds another.

My wetness slicks his hand as he pushes in and out. Slowly but with hard, measured strokes. Every plunge stretches my walls, driving me to the edge of oblivion. Throwing my head back, I extend my neck, pressing it more firmly against his palm and reveling in the way his grip tightens.

"Zahara… Zahara… Zahara…" He curls his fingers deep inside of me, caressing my most sensitive spot.

I shudder as wave after wave of tremors racks my body. Instead of abating, the intensity seems to grow as he levels more pressure on his touch. I'm burning up, consumed with fever as electricity sizzles through my veins. I feel everything… and everywhere, completely out of control.

"Yes?" I manage to form the word. It comes out sounding more like a moan.

"Are you ready to take all of me, baby?"

I tilt my chin and nip his ear lightly. "I've always been ready, Massimo."

His answering growl thunders around us as he slips his fingers out. Grabbing my knees, he opens my legs wide and thrusts his huge cock inside me, filling me to the brim.

I suck in a breath at the sudden intrusion. He's so big I nearly faint from the overload of sensation. There's a bit of discomfort, bordering on pain, but all at once, it also feels so, so good. I relish the burn, clenching my inner muscles around him, floating on a new tidal wave of bliss.

Massimo wraps his arm around me, pressing his left hand to the small of my back while he sweeps clear the surface of the desk with the other. Papers, pens, books, and even a few picture frames launch across the room and crash to the floor. Then, he seizes my chin. With our faces mere inches apart, he urges me backward, laying me down on the massive desktop while his body covers mine. As he repositions his fingers along my jawline, I can smell myself on them, feel the slickness of my arousal coating his calloused skin. It excites me. As does the anticipation of more while his other hand glides down along my outer thigh and lifts my leg, moving it over his shoulder. And then, he just looks at me.

"Perfect," he whispers just before he pulls out. A split second later, he's thrusting back in.

He pounds me with such ferocity that the desk skids across the floor with every hard slam of his hips. I'm left holding on to the front of his shirt, clutching the material like it's my only earthly option. He growls. Breathes heavy. He's loud when he fucks. Unrestrained. Unbound. Untamed.

I love it. Love him. Every facet of this complicated man.

His right hand slips to my throat, squeezing it lightly. In that instant, a sense of triumph grips me. Reticent to lose it all too quickly, I clench my fingers around his wrist, making sure his hand stays exactly where it is. And then, with our gazes locked in a silent exchange, I seize his throat with my free hand.

Air leaves my lungs in short sharp bursts, matching the tempo of his movements. I inhale when he plunges in, exhale when he pulls back out. Tangled in an unwavering staredown as we continue to hold each other's throat, he fucks me like a madman.

There is something animalistic in this position. In how I can feel the corded muscles of his neck under my palm. The vibrations while he growls. And he can feel each time I swallow, each time I draw a labored breath. It is as if we truly are as one.

The legs of the desk scrape the wooden floor from the force of his onslaught. I'm fighting for breath, barely managing to get enough oxygen with each shallow draw. Massimo must notice my struggle because his hold on my neck loosens. Not happening. I squeeze his wrist even harder, burying my nails into his skin.

That coil at the base of my spine gets tighter, twisting and twisting until it finally snaps. The release—a galactic explosion—unlike anything I've felt before. I'm spinning, dazed, riding the euphoria of my orgasm when he suddenly lets go of my neck. His cock slides out, and I moan in protest of the loss. But two large hands grab my ass cheeks, lifting my lower body up. Tongue. Warm, wet, velvet. Spears inside my already quivering core. Lips. Hard, demanding. Seal around my clit. Suction. Strong, mind-melting. Teeth, grazing the hypersensitive flesh. And then… a bite. I scream. Careening again over that exhilarating cliff and shattering into a cloud of stardust.

"Heaven," he mumbles into my pussy. "I'm going to lick every last drop of your nectar, baby. And then, I'll make you wet all over again."

He does just that, stroking that masterful tongue of his inside me now. Lapping my inner walls as if he truly intends to lick every drop off me. I grab the short hairs at the top of his head, pulling his face closer, forcing him to reach deeper. Wanting more of his mouth. Then, when his lips close around my clit, sucking on it, I almost faint.

"Jesus baby," he growls as he lowers my ass back down and buries his cock in me again. "Can you see what you do to me? I can't fucking decide if I want to fuck you with my tongue or my dick."

My climax hasn't even ebbed, and I already feel the next one building. A rush of pure elation swells within my limp body, rising higher and higher with each of his frenzied thrusts.

"Zahara, Zahara, Zahara…," he rasps as he pulls my hair free of its bun, fisting the scattered tresses in his hand, and thrusts into me so hard that the desk bangs against one of the shelves, dislodging several books.

"I love…"—he slams into me—"…when you look at me…"—slam—"…like that."

"Like what?" I grab his forearms, trying to hang on.

A wicked smirk pulls at his lips. His cock is lodged deep inside me as he bends until his face is hovering just above mine.

"Like a hungry little she-wolf who can't decide if she'd prefer to eat me, or to be eaten instead." He slides out, only to slam into me again, burying himself to the hilt.

New constellations are born in front of my eyes as he keeps pounding into me while another orgasm overtakes me. I clutch the front of his shirt as strange mewing sounds leave my lips while I ride on the waves of pure bliss.

"Mine!" Massimo roars while rope after rope of his seed fills me.

"Mine!" I echo.

"We'll leave through the kitchen door," Massimo says as he helps me into his suit jacket. A few of the buttons on his shirt are missing, and there are long thin red scratches on his neck. Did I do that to him? I don't remember.

"There's no going back to the party for you, I'm afraid."

"I assumed as much," I smirk. Me returning to the great hall with the entire center panel of my skirt missing and my private business front and center for everyone to see, might be a bit too much. Even for a less conservative crowd. And this one is definitely not that.

Massimo crouches before me, buttoning the jacket up. He barely finished the last fastener when a strange popping sound bursts forth somewhere outside the room.

"What the—"

Quickly, he presses his forefinger to my lips and shakes his head. Then, he pulls one of his guns out from the holster that's stapped around his torso.

"A gunshot," he whispers and cocks the hammer of his weapon.

His steps are utterly soundless as he crosses to the door and cracks it to look outside. Music and laughter immediately bleed into the study, but the sounds are muted as if coming from a distance. Although I didn't pay too much attention to our path here while Massimo carried me, I'm certain we ended up in the furthest part of the house.

"Stay here," Massimo throws over his shoulder and slips into the dark hallway.

Other than the muffled clamor from the party, there's no other noise. Maybe it wasn't a gunshot after all? It didn't sound loud enough to be one. I slide over to the door, peeking through the tiny gap Massimo left when he exited. There isn't much to see in the darkened space, and Massimo's broad back blocks the rest. He's standing at the open doorway to the room directly across the hall.

"What the fuck," he mumbles, and lowering the gun, steps inside.

Throwing a quick glance down at myself to make sure his jacket is covering all my exposed parts, I tiptoe into the hallway. When I reach the threshold of the other room, I stop dead in my tracks.

The body of a woman in a black minidress is sprawled on the floor next to a chest of drawers. Blood is seeping from the hole in the middle of her forehead, soaking the short blonde strands of her hair that are partially hiding her face. She looks somewhat familiar, but with all the blood, I can't place her. Her eyes are open, and they seem to be staring right at me. I want to turn away, yet can't. I've never seen a dead person this close before.

"What happened?" Massimo's agitated tone pulls me from my stupor.

I finally tear my gaze from the body and only then realize there's someone else in the room. A tall, burly man in a gunmetal-gray suit stands over the dead woman. His back is turned to me, and in his right hand, loosely hanging next to his thigh, is a weapon equipped with a silencer. As he turns around, I realize who he is. *Holy shit!*

"Start talking, Adriano," Massimo snaps. "Now."

Adriano thrusts the gun into the waistband at the back of his pants and takes off his glasses. His movements are almost disturbingly casual, especially once he starts wiping the lenses with a small cloth he pulled from inside his jacket.

"I don't see how my personal matters are any concern of yours, Spada."

Personal matters? I look at the dead woman again, and my hand flies to cover my mouth. Dear God. That's Adriano's wife.

"Filippa wasn't a Family member," Adriano continues. "Therefore, her death shouldn't be of any interest to Cosa Nostra."

"But you are." Massimo surges forward, getting in Adriano's face. "Dead bodies have been piling up the last few weeks and disposing of them requires a shitload of work. I certainly don't need to add yours to my count."

Adriano takes one disinterested look at his dead wife. "Don't worry. I will clean up after myself."

I gape at him. Adriano has always been the most gracious among the high-ranking Family members. Calm. Cool. Collected. Outside of the Council meeting I witnessed, he's never argued or lost his temper with anyone, and he certainly never showed violent tendencies. Up until this moment, I'd have sworn he would never harm a living creature in his life. But as I watch him now, discussing the disposal of his wife's body like she's nothing more than an unwanted piece of junk, while appearing utterly at ease and unperturbed by the circumstances, I realize how wrong impressions of people can be. He might appear to be perfectly placid on the outside, yet there's a brewing storm of rage and hatred swirling in his guarded eyes. He just might blow up like a supernova. *Tick-tock. Tick-tock.*

"What about her family?" Massimo asks. "Dead gangsters can be dismissed as the corollary of an internal skirmish, but this is different."

"As I said, I'll take care of it."

The veins in Massimo's neck are bulging, his muscles are straining against his skin, and the look in his eyes is turning homicidal. I don't know what possessed Adriano to kill his wife, but I do know Massimo can't afford to go apeshit and attack Adriano this evening. The man is too important to Cosa Nostra. I know Massimo knows this, except his anger is blinding him right now. That inner brute is taking over. I need to get my man out of here. Now!

"Massimo." I grab his hand and squeeze. "We should go."

His jaw hardens, and his eyes don't shift from Adriano's stoic face. They make quite a sight, these two—both tall and impeccably dressed men but with completely different vibes. Massimo is all glaring, raging fury whereas Adriano is a tightly wound booby trap. Two distinct predators, facing each other, like two cobras ready to strike.

"Please," I urge, squeezing Massimo's fingers in mine. "Adriano did say he's got everything under control. And I'm getting really cold."

Massimo's stance relaxes.

"Peppe has the cleanup crew on standby. Call him." Wrapping his arm around my waist, he pulls me into his side. "Let's go home, angel."

CHAPTER
Twenty-four

Zahara

"**N**o, I am not changing my mind!" Massimo's roars carry all the way to the second floor. The dining room window was probably left open. Or not. His volume frequently hits this peak whenever he's "talking" with Brio. My guess is the soon-to-be-former capo has paid Massimo another visit. Even at a distance, and with hair dryer going, I can still hear the unfolding discussion.

"Are you trying to blackmail me, motherfucker?"

Yup. Definitely Brio.

"Miss Zara." Iris pokes her head into the bathroom. "Peppe says there are major delays on the way to the airport, and he thinks it would be best for Don Spada to leave a little earlier." She winces as another round of shouts erupts on the lower floor. "Also, I just wanted to remind you that the contractor should be here in fifteen minutes to take a look at the roof."

Damn. It took six tries to finally book an appointment with this particular roofing firm. If the tradesmen arrive while Massimo is still having a fit, they'll likely just turn around and leave.

I shut off the blow dryer and glance at myself in the mirror.

My hair is still damp, and all I've got on is Massimo's dress shirt. My immediate impulse is to get dressed and deal with my hair to make myself more presentable before meeting with a capo, outbound or not. The etiquette and proper attire requirements have been engraved in me since I was barely old enough to walk.

Well, things have changed.

"Prepare some refreshments, please," I say to Iris while heading out of the room. "If I'm not done in the dining room when the roofers arrive, find some way to distract them for a little while."

"Sure. Of course. Um… and will you be able to calm the don down before they get here?"

"Yes."

"Oh. That's great. And… how are you planning to do that?"

I stop at the threshold and smirk. "By redirecting his vigor."

As I rush along the hallway and down the wide staircase, several house staff throw surprised looks my way. Some seem amused by my wildly disarrayed hair, but most are perplexed by my choice of outfit. Massimo's dark-brown shirt leaves my bare legs on full display. At least it's long enough to cover my ass and hide the fact that I'm not wearing anything underneath. Not that I would care if it wasn't. Everyone is entitled to their opinions, and I respect that, but I just don't give a fuck what those are anymore.

It feels good. Liberating.

"I can't tell you how *little* I fucking care about the contracts you can secure for the Family, Brio! Schmoozing with the investors and your ability to kiss ass as you did at your party last night is not what this is about. You're still out! If you're bored already, find a hobby. I hear crocheting does wonders for keeping your mind sharp!"

The shouting continues to spread through the mansion like a wave. I glance at the crystal chandelier hanging in the entry hall, then edge along the perimeter of the room. Just in case. That thing might come down any minute.

When I reach the dining room door, I don't even bother knocking. There's no point since no one would hear it anyway. I just twist the handle and step inside.

Brio and Tiziano are on the left side of the long table, hovering in their seats and looking rather stressed. Salvo is across from them, leaning back in his chair and observing the chaos like it's amusing to him. Massimo, meanwhile, is at the head of the table, his lips pulled into an angry sneer.

"And you!" he addresses Tiziano. "Who the fuck authorized you to fire the casino manager at Bay View? I gave you specific—"

Massimo's head snaps up, his eyes darting to the doorway where I'm standing. "Shit, baby. Did I wake you up?"

"Nope." Of course he did. Probably woke up every person on the Eastern Seaboard, along with me, not long after his meeting started. I finally dragged myself out of bed when falling back asleep seemed futile.

Our gazes lock as I casually stride across the vast room, feeling the other men's eyes on me the whole time. Massimo slides his chair back a bit when I reach him, so I use the presented opportunity and straddle his lap.

"The roofing contractor and his men are coming in ten minutes," I say. "Can you wrap this up quickly or, maybe, just tone it down?"

"I can try."

"Yeah, we both know how that usually turns out." My hands drop to his belt, fingers undoing the buckle.

A wicked spark ignites in his smoldering eyes. It quickly transforms into a raging inferno when I flick the button and start sliding his zipper down.

"What are you doing?" The low rumble comes from the back of his throat.

I smile. Then, slipping my hand inside his pants, I pull out his rapidly hardening cock. "Making sure your abundant energy is directed elsewhere, so you can finish your meeting in a more civilized manner."

His eyes don't leave mine for even a second as I lift myself just enough, and then slowly lower onto his straining cock.

Someone behind me clears their airway. "Um, perhaps we should leave?"

Massimo arches an eyebrow. Smirking, I shake my head.

"Stay put," he growls.

I never expected that these shameless actions would be such a turn-on for me. Massimo's dick isn't even halfway inside my quivering center, and I'm already feeling the telltale signs of an overwhelming climax.

"I love your outfit." Massimo glides his hands up my thighs. "Very convenient."

"I kind of thought you might disapprove of me showing up nearly naked in front of your men."

"You can wear any damn thing you want, Zahara. If I don't like how other men look at you, I'll just kill them."

"You're such a romantic."

A corner of his lips curves up. "I know."

He slams his mouth to mine, stealing the moan that rips from my lips when I sink onto his cock completely. The rest of the room disappears. Ceases to exist in this reality. In the back of my mind, I know that *this* is somehow wrong. Disgraceful, even. But I can't bring myself to care. How can I when his hands are on me? Kneading my ass as we keep on kissing. Tugging me closer to his chest. How can anything be wrong when it feels so damn right? I rock, rock my hips with abandon. Utterly lost within this sensation. Feeling whole while Massimo is filling me.

"I didn't know you were into exhibitionism, angel." Words whispered against my lips as he trails his right palm to my chest. Slowly. Reverently.

"Me neither. As it happens, scandalous behavior seems to seriously excite me," I pant. "Are they watching?"

"Yes."

My pussy quivers. I throw my head back and moan. Loudly. Let them hear. Let them see how much he turns me on. Speeding up my movements, I ride him—hard—right there, in front of the Council. In front of the men who'd judge me. Their opinions, though, no longer matter. All I need is to be held in the arms of the man I love. The tremors in my core grow insistent, while Massimo's chest rises and falls quickly under my touch. We're close, but he's holding back his climax. Waiting for me. Waiting to follow me as he always does.

In a lightning-fast motion, Massimo's fingers wrap around my throat. Applying just the right amount of pressure, it's like he hits a button, and I explode. I scream, soaring straight into nirvana, and, a moment later, he chases me with a guttural groan.

Cinching my arms around Massimo's shoulders, I sag down on his chest and bury my face in the hollow of his neck. "Five minutes till appointment time. Wrap this up quickly."

A gentle bite lands just above my exposed clavicle. His massive shirt slipped off my shoulder while I was lost in ecstasy. Then, a kiss follows before he drags his lips across my raised collarbone.

"So, gentlemen, where were we?" His facial hair tingles my skin as he speaks while nibbling the column of my throat. "Oh yes. Tiziano, you'll rehire the casino manager. And, Brio, go sink your feet into the sand. You are all free to leave now, and I have a plane to catch."

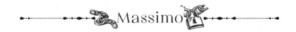

Massimo

New York
Naos, a club owned by Drago Popov

Any kind of construction development is a great opportunity for money laundering. The upfront costs for building supplies are enormous, and in most cases, those expenses can be paid in cash. Dirty cash. When the project is complete and the finished structure is sold, the resulting amount of squeaky clean revenue in your bank account is nothing to sneeze at.

An investment opportunity involving Manhattan properties, where real estate prices have surpassed the previous all-time high after a volatile decade, is a money launderer's wet dream. The projected profits from the residential construction project I'm currently reviewing is nearly seventy million dollars. In terms of initial financing, I can pump at least a third of what I expect to earn to turn our dirty money into cold hard *clean* cash.

"It's acceptable." I close the laptop and slide it across the table toward the man sitting on the other side. "When are you planning to break ground?"

"Next spring, most likely. We anticipate a three-month lead-in will be needed to finalize planning and design, and to get all the legal and permit issues handled." Arturo leans back on the white leather sofa and props an ankle on the opposite knee.

As far as I know, in addition to being the New York underboss, Arturo DeVille also handles Ajello's drug operation. Based on his looks, however, I find it really hard to believe. Drug deals are a messy business, often taking place in remote, dirty locations. Weapons and blood are usually involved. Ajello's right-hand man looks like a fucking fashion model, one who wouldn't know what to do if a gun was handed to him.

Dark hair, perfectly slicked back as if he wasted an hour in front of the mirror just to tame every single strand. A custom-made black suit that shows not a single crease on it. The immaculately pressed black shirt underneath, with the two top buttons undone, offers a glimpse of the gold chain around his tanned neck. He's wearing a fucking cross, like a good Catholic boy. And on his left wrist, a shiny gold Rolex.

"If there's nothing else that we need to discuss, Don Spada, I'll have our lawyer prepare the paperwork. My boss will bring the contract with him when he visits Boston to inspect the venues we're buying."

I raise an eyebrow. "I assumed that you, as his underboss, would handle all the bureaucratic crap."

"Most times, that would be true. In this particular case, however, Don Ajello will take care of it personally. Take it as a statement of good faith, if you will." A waiter approaches to drop off a new round of drinks, but Arturo doesn't even spare him a glance and continues, "This is the first time two Cosa Nostra Families are entering into a strategic alliance of this kind."

I wait for the server to depart before leaning closer. "I don't think it's wise to discuss such delicate matters in front of outsiders, DeVille."

"Normally, I would agree. But as it happens, this place is considered neutral territory, and the staff here are sworn to secrecy. If anyone even breathes wrong, the motherfucker who owns this joint would gut them with a spoon or some shit like that."

"You're not a fan of the owner, I take it?"

Arturo's face darkens. "Drago Popov. He's my brother-in-law."

"I didn't know you were married. Did you get hitched to Drago's sister recently?"

"God forbid." Arturo practically swipes his tumbler off the glass-top table and throws the whiskey back, swallowing it in one gulp. "That hellion should be locked up somewhere, and the key lost where no one can find it. I've never met a more infuriating female in my life. We crossed paths just once, at my sister's wedding, and the nutcase threw a jug of punch at me. And that was after she tried to slice my head off with a flying serving tray."

His phone starts ringing on the table, Ajello's name lighting up the screen. Their conversation is brief, but DeVille's face shows more and more agitation by the time he hangs up.

332

"Duty calls." He stands and offers me his hand. "Looking forward to doing business with you."

Once Arturo leaves, I finish my drink and then take out my phone to call Zahara. The private plane is on standby to take me back to Boston, so I should be home in time for dinner. And dessert.

She doesn't pick up, which isn't that uncommon, since her phone often ends up left forgotten on the nightstand.

I try again as I'm leaving the club, and three more times in the cab while heading to the private airport in Jersey. With each missed call, heaviness settles like a boulder in my stomach. Something is wrong.

You're getting paranoid again, the snarky voice inside my head comments. *She's probably fiddling with those puff sleeves on the new blouse.*

"They are called *lantern sleeves,*" I correct. That gets me a strange look from the taxi driver.

Taking my phone out again, this time, I call Iris. She and Zahara are often hanging out together.

"Zahara isn't answering her phone," I snap the moment the line connects.

"Oh. She must have forgotten to take it with her, Don Spada."

"What?" The bad feeling in my gut intensifies. "Where did she go?"

"Mr. Canali dropped by about half an hour ago. They left in his car. Could be that she needed to take final measurements for Mrs. Canali's latest dress order, because I saw Miss Zara had a sewing pouch with her."

"Who went with her?"

"Peppe. He followed them in his vehicle."

I hang up on her and dial Peppe, but it goes straight to voicemail.

Fuck!

"Step on it!" I bark at the driver while dialing Peppe again. No answer.

Peppe always picks up. I hear my alter ego mumbling in the back of my mind. *Something isn't right.*

"Don't you think I know that?!" I snarl, making the cabbie jump in his seat.

Next, I try Salvo. Three times. But his phone is off, too.

I pull my gun out of my holster and press the barrel to the back of the taxi driver's head.

"If you don't get me to that damn airport in five minutes, you're dead."

Zahara

Thirty minutes earlier

"And this can't wait till tomorrow?"

"My mother is leaving on an unexpected trip in the morning," Salvo says as he slides behind the wheel. "She won't be back for two weeks, and the fundraiser is next month."

As Salvo heads down the driveway, I spot Peppe in the side mirror, getting into his car to follow us. Typically, I'd insist that security isn't necessary, especially since I'll be with Massimo's underboss, but ever since that bizarre conversation in the library, where Salvo confessed his supposed feelings for me, I've been feeling uneasy around him.

"So, you and Massimo caused quite an uproar last night."

I steal a look at him from the corner of my eye. He's got a light grip on the wheel, and the elbow of his other arm is braced in the open window. Whatever bitterness I thought I saw in him at Brio's seems to be gone. "I guess we did."

"Saying that the Family members were shocked would be putting it mildly. It's all everyone's talked about after you two disappeared. The spur-of-the-moment proposal was a particular highlight. But you know what I found especially interesting? Not a single person commented on how fucking outrageous this whole thing actually is. In fact, most seemed thrilled by the idea of their beloved Nuncio's daughter marrying the new don."

My eyes nearly bulge out of my head. I expected everything but that.

"Hilarious, isn't it?" He shoots me a smile. "Don't you just love how Massimo manages to make people take his side without even trying? Even poor Brio… He showed up to this morning's meeting—uninvited—and begged to be reinstated as capo. I just don't understand what it is that has everybody so fucking enthralled with such a psychotic barbarian."

I reel back, aghast at the amount of venom in his words.

"Even you," Salvo continues, "a well-bred Italian girl, so innocent and docile."

He looks at me then. A sly smile still dances on his lips, but his eyes are filled with malice. I can't help but lean back, as far away from him as I can manage.

His smile drops, and with it, all his pretense is gone. "But, really, you're nothing but his slut. Fucking your stepbrother in the middle of our meeting. Your father must be turning in his grave."

The fine hairs on the back of my neck stand up. "Stop the car."

"Did you just want to rub it in my face? Drive home that you don't give a fuck about my feelings? Were you trying to show me that he's still better than I could ever be?"

"Stop. Right now!"

"Sure." He shrugs and steers the vehicle to the curb.

As soon as we stop, I practically leap out of the car and dash toward Peppe's Jeep. He's pulling up just behind Salvo's black Porsche. With Peppe this close, relief hits me like a welcome rain, but in that same split second, awareness slams into me with the force of a hurricane. The stench of garbage overwhelms my senses. The sight of derelict buildings dissolves any notion that this is a peaceful street.

"Miss Veronese," Peppe calls, sticking his head through the open window. "Everything okay?"

"Yup. Changed my mind, though. Wanna go back."

Just as I'm reaching for the handle of the passenger door, the sound of breaking glass fills the nighttime air. I scream and jump back, staring at the red stain spreading across the front of Peppe's white shirt. Shards of the shattered windshield are scattered all over him.

"Peppe!" I cry out, reaching for the door handle again. My fingers barely wrap around it when I'm grabbed from behind and yanked away.

"Shut the fuck up," Salvo growls next to my ear as he drags me back to his car.

"Let go!" I yell, trying to break free, but he's too strong.

Two more muffled gunshots follow. Peppe's body jerks violently each time a bullet hits his chest.

"NO!"

"You're getting back into my car, Zara." The cold bite of steel butts up against my temple. "Shut your mouth and do as I say. You might live through the night if you do."

Icy dread washes over me. The blood in my veins freezes. I can't breathe. Can't move. My eyes are the only part of me left remotely functional. Unfocused and blurred by a sheen of unshed tears, they flit all over Peppe as I slowly drown in the horror before me. A slight rise and fall of his chest tells me he's still alive. Barely. I don't think Salvo has noticed. What do I do? If I try to help, Salvo will just finish the job.

Fuck! What do I do?

"Okay," I choke out. "I'll come with you."

"Maybe there's some sense left in you after all," he sneers and pushes me toward his car. "Move! Quickly."

I wipe my eyes with the back of my hand and shuffle to his vehicle. It takes everything in me to keep my gaze fixed on the shiny Porsche and not look back to check if Peppe is still breathing. I haven't seen anyone else on this street, but I can't lose hope. Someone will find him. They'll call 911. I can't even think about the alternative.

Tears well in my eyes again, making it hard to see. Just steps from the car, my heel sinks into a crack in the sidewalk. I trip and nearly fall.

A brutal grip squeezes my upper arm. "Watch where you're going!" Salvo snaps.

I cry out in pain. His fingers dig into my skin, crushing my flesh practically to the bone.

He pushes me through the still-open passenger door, and I collapse onto the seat in absolute agony.

"Where are you taking me?" I whisper, staring blindly at the road up ahead.

My words are lost in the rumbling of the engine as Salvo starts to drive.

"Why are you doing this, Salvo?"

He doesn't reply.

I don't actually need him to. The truth is as clear as day.

Massimo was right all along. The traitor *is* someone within the Family. Only... he never considered it could be his best friend.

I have no idea why Salvo took me, or what his plans for me are. Whatever his reasons, there's one thing I'm absolutely sure of—this isn't about me. It's about Massimo.

It always has been.

CHAPTER
Twenty-five

Massimo

THE MOMENT THE JET TAXIS OVER TO THE APRON, I LEAP out of my seat and rush toward the airstairs. A group of my men is already waiting by the hangar doors.

"Any trace of them?" I growl.

"No." Joey, one of Peppe's cousins shakes his head. "Neither Salvo nor his mother are at Canali's. Just their staff. Our guys couldn't find anything useful."

"What about Peppe?"

"Some biker found him in his Jeep, pulled over in the slums. He was shot. Three bullets to the chest."

"Is he alive?"

"Yes. Or was when they took him into surgery. He lost a lot of blood. Still waiting to hear if he'll make it."

I press the heels of my palms to my eyes and take a deep breath.

"Do you think it was Camorra, boss? We tracked down everyone we knew of, but maybe there's someone we missed. Could this be retaliation?"

Could it? Definitely probable. The possibility of a gang of Camorra fucks lying in wait and then chasing my people down is very goddammed likely. Is that what happened here? Was Peppe shot while Salvo managed to get away with Zahara? Are they currently safe somewhere, hiding out? Jesus fuck, I want to believe that to be true. But something tells me it isn't.

The phone in my pocket starts vibrating. Pulling it out, I check the caller ID. *Salvo Canali*. I should be feeling a modicum of relief right now. Instead, heart-stopping terror grips me. My guts twist into a tangled mess as I stare at that name on the screen.

"Boss?" Joey mumbles. "You okay?"

"Get back to the house and wait for further instructions."

"Are you sure? We can—"

"NOW!"

With adrenaline pumping through my body, I draw a sharp, impatient breath. Then, swiping right to answer, I bring the phone up to my ear.

"Where. Is. She?" I can barely get the words out, while an icy current zaps down my spine.

"With me," Salvo replies. "Safe and sound. For the moment, at least."

"I'm going to fucking kill you."

The bastard laughs. "Remember the spot we were always sneaking away to when we were kids? Let's play again. Be there in an hour."

The line goes dead.

I move a pine branch to the side and step into a small meadow surrounded by majestic evergreens. Looking utterly perverse at the center of this beautiful glade is an elaborate neoclassical structure. The Canali Family Mausoleum. Three generations of Canalis are buried within its burgundy granite walls, locked behind black art deco doors that are flanked by polished white Ionic columns.

Before this night ends, I'll make sure the fourth generation joins the eternal ranks.

"I'm glad to see you had the good sense to come alone. My don."

Salvo is leaning on one of the columns, arms crossed at his chest. The wrought iron lantern over the entrance casts light on the black Glock in his hand.

I keep my steps slow and measured as I cover the distance between us. Acid churns in my stomach, and the bitter taste of his betrayal tightens my throat. With every ounce of my control, I resist immediately rushing the bastard. Though nothing would give me more pleasure than snapping his treacherous neck.

"Where's Zahara?"

"Inside. Keeping my dad company." He grins.

Red paints the edges of my vision and my ears start to ring. *He has my angel inside the fucking tomb!*

My fingers are itching for my gun, and I'm a split second away from drawing it out when a voice thunders inside my head.

Don't! You'll jeopardize our girl!

Taking a deep breath, I shake the tension out of my muscles, adopting a nonthreatening stance. "Let her go, Salvo. This— whatever this is—it's between you and me."

"Hmm. You've finally wised up. Took you a while. Two decades, almost."

"Never figured it'd be my best friend who'd stick a knife in my back."

The look he gives me is one of undisguised hate. "I was never your friend! The only reason I showed you even a semblance of friendship was because my father made me. The old goat even transferred me into your school, despite me begging him not to."

"Why?"

"So I could get close to the Don's prodigy, of course," he sneers. "Can you fucking imagine how it felt to be compared to you my entire fucking childhood? To a piece of trash who somehow always got top grades, despite missing more than half the classes. And why? Because he was too busy roughhousing with common soldiers and slumming it down by the docks. Our noble prince! The son of a goddamned warehouse worker who wouldn't know what true class is even if it bit him in the ass!"

"You're doing this because I did better than you at school?" I stare at him, flabbergasted.

"At everything!" he yells, eyes bulging from his head. "For years, all I heard was how much better you were. How easily you caught on about the Family finances. And business dealings, how those came so effortlessly to you. And let's not forget the loyalty of our men. All anyone could ever talk about was what a perfect leader you'd be once your time came. You! When it should have been me!"

The casual posture he greeted me with is now gone. Pacing left and right in front of the mausoleum door, he waves his hand in the air like a lunatic. I wouldn't bet against the fact the safety on the gun in his other hand is off. In his fit, he might shoot his foot just as easily as killing me. But there's a more serious danger, and that's the possibility of a stray bullet finding its way through the door. And I can't let that happen. I need to weigh the risks, assess my options, and figure out how to get past him and inside.

"My great-grandfather was one of the founding members of Cosa Nostra in the States," he continues his hysterical rambling. "That's the Canali legacy! By right, my father should have been made don! But this Family had denied him twice his due. First when they picked your old man, and then again, when Nuncio was chosen. It became clear that you, undoubtedly, would succeed him. There was no way we could allow a pleb to take what's meant to be ours, again."

"We?"

An evil smirk pulls at his lips. "It was my father's idea to seize the exceptional opportunity of you being arrested. A few strategically dropped threats and the greasing of several palms later, and you were locked up, where you belonged. After my father died, I simply carried on what he had started."

"Then, why help me? All those years, you aided and abetted as I ran our business. Why the fuck would you do that?"

"You?" He stops pacing and hits himself in the chest with his fist. "I was helping myself! Left to his own devices, Nuncio would have ruined the Family. There would have been nothing left for me to take over!"

I throw another glance at the mausoleum entrance and cautiously reach behind my back. God only knows what might happen to Zahara if I'm incapacitated or dead, but I need to try something. If I can just keep the son of a bitch talking, I might be able to pull out my gun without him noticing.

"So what?" I ask. "You backed my ass, letting me run things from behind bars while you bided your time for an opportune moment, so *you* could take over?"

"Something like that. Laying the groundwork took some time and a fair bit of effort. I had to convince Leone to have Nuncio assassinated first. With him in charge, he could name me underboss, paving the way for my eventual takeover. Due to his health conditions, that wouldn't have taken long. I just needed to get you out of the picture before that happened. Too bad the idiots I hired failed."

The two assholes who jumped me after I got back from Nuncio's funeral.

This fucking guy!

"And you really screwed me by having Nera take the reins, effectively putting a muzzle on Leone. With her in the know, I had to wait to take her out, otherwise, things would look too suspicious. Once she asserted herself as the official leader, that was my chance. I still can't fucking believe the Sicilians failed, all because of that long-haired beast of hers!"

He's spewing bullshit like a fucking geyser, and I can't help but think he's lost his goddamned mind.

"I took another crack at it," he continues, "getting Armando to ambush her. I figured, pinning her murder on him would be a piece of cake. But that good-for-nothing junkie couldn't put a bullet in her head even when I practically delivered it to him on a platter. And then, it cost me three million more to off his fucking ass before he could start singing. Three! That's what I had to pay that greedy De Santi to take the job. Not the usual two. That's a premium rate, Spada, and all because he needed to sneak past his own people to get inside. And for what? Just to take out the trash?"

"You're sick," I spit out, shifting my hand closer to the gun tucked into my waistband.

"No. I'm just driven to make sure I get what I deserve." He lifts his weapon, aiming at my head. "Do you think I'm stupid? Turn around so I can see and lose the piece. Then, get inside."

Fuck.

His gun is aimed at me the entire time as I pull out my Glock and toss it on the grass. If he thinks I can't kill him with my bare hands, he has another thing coming.

I approach the mausoleum and pause at the threshold, but he prods my back with the barrel of his gun. As soon as I step inside the tomb, my eyes frantically search for Zahara. The space is cramped and stifling, shrouded in shadows. Aside from the faint glare of the overhead lantern outside the door, the only light is from a strip of wall washer that illuminates the names of those who are now at rest. It takes a moment for my vision to adjust, but finally, I see her. A small huddled form wedged between two sarcophagi on the floor.

"Jesus, baby." My feet are already moving to her when an earsplitting boom echoes off the walls.

"Take another step, and the next bullet, I'll put in her head."

The sound of a gunshot is still ringing in my ears as my eyes bounce between Massimo and Salvo, trying to decide what the fuck I should do now.

When Salvo dragged me in here, he bound my hands with rope and pushed me between the two stone coffins. It took me over twenty minutes to wiggle the scissors from inside my pouch and slice through the bonds. An atavistic instinct must have had me hanging on to my trusty travel bag that has all my sewing essentials—including my favorite pair of fabric scissors—when Salvo forced me out of his Porsche upon our arrival. Once he ripped the pouch out of my grip and threw it on the floor so he could tie my hands, I remembered what was contained there.

"You have me now," Massimo says as he turns around, positioning himself directly between me and Salvo. Shielding me with his body from the nutcase blocking the exit. "You don't need Zahara anymore. She's in no way involved, so let her go."

"Of course she's involved!" Salvo snarls. "She's yet another thing you took away from me! She was perfect! A nice, cultured Italian woman. Obedient. And loyal. Once I realized what she was doing for you, how much trust you'd placed in her, I knew I had to have her. Just as everything else you considered to be yours. But she fucking rejected me. Because of *you*! Like everyone else, she chose you. And for that, she has to die, too."

Oh God, he's completely bonkers! Desperately, I look around the room, as if an answer to how we get out of this will magically present itself. Maybe if there were someone else here who could save us from this madman. But there's no one. We're on our own.

"Zahara didn't choose me," Massimo says. He's standing motionless at the center of the mausoleum. "I threatened her. I told her I'd kill her sister if she didn't agree to be with me. I love her and couldn't bear the thought of her belonging to anyone else. And she hates me for it."

Salvo cocks his head while his focus shifts to me. "Is that true, Zara?"

I steal a quick look at Massimo, who's now staring at me over his shoulder. There's no mistaking the order in his eyes. *Lie, Zahara,* they say.

I swallow and immediately turn my glare to Salvo. "Yes."

"But you told me that you love him. Was that because of Massimo's threats, as well?"

I nod.

"Well… It does sound like something he'd actually do. Perhaps I will spare you. Killing him and taking his empire… and then the woman he loves? Yeah, that sounds—No. Maybe death isn't the worst punishment for him…" He grins, returning his attention to Massimo. "What if I told you I'll only let Zara live if you admit to the Council that you're not fit for the role of the don? You step down and name me your successor. And then, you leave the country, knowing that I have everything that was once yours. You can die miserably in some fucking ditch, for all I care. 'Cause, that's where you belong!"

"I'll do it!"

Massimo's words thunder across the space. Once. Twice. They echo inside the silent tomb, as if spoken by a chorus of voices. Bouncing off the granite walls. Reverberating through my mind. Over and over again. My lungs constrict as I process his meaning. His choice is *me*. He's choosing me over Cosa Nostra.

Laughter rings out from Salvo once more, but it's not a

happy sound. It's something deranged. And sick. It makes goose bumps break out all over my skin.

"My... my... You really are a goner."

"I'll do anything you want. Anything," Massimo growls. "Do whatever you want with me, but please, let Zahara go."

"Please?" Salvo lifts his brows, then cackles. "Massimo Spada *begging*? That's a first."

"Yes, I am. Please, Salvo."

"Oh, I love the sound of your pleading way too much." He takes a step to the side and levels his gun on me. "I want you to kneel, Massimo. Kneel and beg for her life."

"No," I choke out. He can't do it! He can't!

My insides twist into knots, settling in the pit of my stomach like a giant boulder as I watch in horror as Massimo drops to his knees.

"Please," he rasps. "I beg you. Please, Salvo."

I can't keep the tears at bay anymore. They well in my eyes and slide down my cheeks as I stare at the man I love. I've always been in awe of his pride. No matter what he faced, Massimo has always walked with his head held high, his shoulders back, and his spine locked straight as steel. Now though, he's slumped on the floor in front of this bastard. On his knees. Begging. For my life.

"This is pure heaven." Salvo inhales loudly, like a man sniffing his next line of cocaine. Stepping forward, he points his gun at Massimo's chest. "Now I'm glad that fucker of an ex-con failed. If he'd managed to pop you at the mall, I would have missed this." Manic scorn saturates his expression and his tone. "Hell! It's so damn hard to find competent help these days, right? I mean, I led him straight to you with the tracker, but the dimwit couldn't finish a simple job." His face contorts again as he clenches his jaw. "I bet *your* little helper never let you down," he almost whispers. "Zara! Go wait for me outside. I want to be the only witness to Massimo Spada taking his last breath. It's an image that'll keep me warm at night. Along with you."

"You said you'd let him live!" I cry out, stumbling toward the kneeling Massimo.

"Did I?" Salvo cocks his head. "No, I don't think I did. Out! Now!"

"Zahara." Massimo's voice makes me shudder. "I need you to leave."

Swallowing a whimper, I turn to face him. Dark-as-night eyes bore into mine, and I wonder how they can look at me with such softness, yet hold so much ferocity in their depths at the same time. Massimo has always been a mix of extreme contradictions. And his gaze has never reflected that as clearly as it does now. Rage and calmness. Unwavering resolve and absolute chaos.

"Go," he says. *Trust me*, his eyes add.

Slowly, I nod. "I'll wait outside."

With legs made of lead, I trudge toward the door, keeping my hands behind my back to hide the cut bonds. Every step away from Massimo is an agony I can barely bear, but I urge myself forward.

"She'll learn to obey me, too," Salvo sneers as I pass him. "Very soon."

I exit the mausoleum and press my back to the outside wall next to the door. The tip of my fabric scissors, hidden inside my sleeve, digs into my forearm. It's a useless weapon against a gun, but I kept them with me regardless.

"Any last words, Massimo?" Salvo's condescending voice carries from inside.

"Yes."

The silence stretches, the void ominous in the darkness. My pulse skyrockets as all I can do is madly clutch the scissors to my galloping heart. Waiting. I'm not even sure what for.

In Massimo's eyes, I saw his intent to kill Salvo, but I have

347

no idea how he plans to do it. Knowing Massimo, however, he'll put the bastard through hell first. For all those years of imprisonment. For having nearly half of his life stolen from him. Betrayed by someone he believed to be his friend. What could he possibly say to the asshole who did that?

"Well?" Salvo snaps. "I'm all ears."

"I'LL MAKE YOU PAY FOR PUTTING YOUR FILTHY HANDS ON MY FUTURE WIFE, YOU FUCKING SON OF A BITCH!"

A gunshot exploded when Massimo started shouting. And now the thumps and thuds of a vicious battle reach my ears.

Another loud bang echoes inside, and a part of the column near the doorway splinters, small fragments raining down next to my feet. A muffled whimper leaves my lips as I squeeze the scissors to me like a lifeline. The sounds of the struggle inside amplify my distress.

Rampant grunting. Stuff breaking. Strangled noises. And something decidedly metal hitting the floor.

I have to do something.

Oh God, I *must* do something.

Taking a long deep breath, I push away from the wall and slip across the threshold of the tomb.

Dust hangs in the air, the mites dancing in the beams of scattered light. The floor is littered with bits of stone and shattered statuette pieces that not so long ago decorated the inner sanctum. The scent of gunpowder permeates the air, but there's something else that's smelling up the place, too. Blood.

My eyes snap to the left where the labored breaths and grunts are coming from. Two figures are tangled on the floor. Massimo—thank goodness—has his knee jammed into Salvo's chest, pinning him to the ground. Massimo's hand is wrapped around the traitor's throat, and he's throwing punch after punch at Salvo's face. There is dust and rubble all over his clothes, and the left sleeve of his shirt is torn. I don't see Salvo's gun anywhere.

"Goddamned bastard!" Massimo roars, hitting Salvo's chin. "I'll beat your fucking head into mush!"

As he takes another swing, the underboss manages to land a punch to Massimo's solar plexus. The two of them end up wrestling across the floor, trying to kill each other in a variety of ways. Choke holds. Headlocks. Gut punches. Elbows to the crotch. Whatever they can reach. They roll to the foot of a massive weeping angel statue, which towers above them like a silent witness to this death match.

Both men are dirty and bloody, and Massimo once more appears to have the upper hand. As he winds up for the final strike, though, Salvo somehow manages to slither out of reach and kicks the base of the sculpture.

Breath lodges inside my lungs, and I watch in horror as the winged angel wobbles, then tilts.

"Massimo!" I scream, but my warning comes too late.

The heavy statue collides with Massimo's shoulder, shoving him backward. He falls to the floor amid a thunderous crash of broken stone. And doesn't get up.

My legs carry me toward Massimo's unmoving form before my brain has the chance to register what's happening before me. Salvo, pushing to his knees, drags a huge chunk of a busted wing toward him.

"You're done, Spada." His deranged laugh peals off the mausoleum walls while he raises the heavy fragment above his head.

One breath.

One blink.

A skipped heartbeat.

I swallow my animalistic scream and bury my scissors in the side of his neck. Salvo cries out, collapsing to the side. The piece of the angel's wing slips from his hands and falls to the ground, breaking in half. My hand aches from the force of my grip as I stagger back.

As I gasp and wheeze for air, I stare at the scumbag, almost mesmerized by the spurts of blood that pulse from his wound. I must have hit an artery. He's panting like a dog, his hands shaking while he tries to get ahold of the scissors and apply pressure to his neck.

"Help me." The rasp that leaves his lips is barely audible.

Really? He orchestrated the assassination of my father. Tried to kill my sister, *twice*. And God only knows how many times he tried to murder Massimo. But he wants *my* help?

I never thought myself capable of taking someone's life. Then again, I never thought I could do many things that I've done. So, with my eyes fixed on his, I lift my foot and slam it down on the protruding handle of the scissors, thrusting them further into his flesh.

"That's the obedient, well-bred, Italian girl for you." I spit on his not-yet-cold body, then turn and rush to Massimo's side.

"Hey." Dropping to my knees next to him, I cup his face with my palms. "Look at me."

Massimo's eyelids flutter, and when he finally lifts them, he struggles to focus on me with uneven pupils.

"Baby?"

Some of the weight lifts off my chest. "How are you feeling?"

"A bit lightheaded," he drawls. "Did we just have sex? 'Cause I might have blacked out and want a repeat." He glances around, looking dazed and confused. "Where the fuck are we?"

"Canali's mausoleum. I think you might have a concussion. A severe one."

Massimo's forehead furrows. Groaning, he sits up and presses his hand to the back of his head. "Ouch. Whose idea was it to have sex in a fucking tomb? And why—" He cuts himself off, seeing Salvo's body. "Fuck."

"Yeah."

For a long moment, he just stares at the corpse. Then, his eyes suddenly widen, snapping to mine.

"Jesus fuck!" A viselike hold locks around my waist as he pulls me to his lap, tucking my face into the crook of his neck. "That fucker. I thought he was going to kill you, angel." Practically plastering me to his chest, he rocks us back and forth, back and forth. "When he called and told me he had you…"

"I'm okay," I manage to mumble into his neck.

"And then I saw you curled on the floor… Shit, baby… He pointed a fucking gun at you, and… Oh God—"

"Massimo…"

He buries his hand in my hair, pressing my head more firmly against him while the rocking continues. "I would have died if something happened to you and— WILL YOU FUCKING SHUT UP! I'M NOT SMOTHERING HER!"

"Um… You kinda are," I snort.

"Oh." He stops the rocking but doesn't ease the force of his embrace. "Is this alright? Because I need this, Zahara. Need to feel you, to know you're safe and unharmed, and to—"

"I'm safe. I'm not hurt, and"—I manage to turn my face, just a little—"yes, I can breathe."

"Good." The rocking resumes. "Were you scared? Of course you were. At least you didn't witness the worst of the bloodbath. You didn't come in until I finished him, right?"

"Um… actually…"

"That fucking cunt. I wish he wasn't dead, yet. I want to kill him all over again for threatening you. My sweet, sweet angel…"

I close my eyes and inhale Massimo's citrusy scent, letting it soothe me. We'll have time to go over the specifics of Salvo's death later on. Right now, I just want him to hold me. It feels so damn good to be wrapped in Massimo's arms—

"Zahara?"

"Mm-hmm?"

"Why are your sewing scissors stuck in Salvo's neck?"

CHAPTER
Twenty-six

❧ Zahara ❧

Two weeks later

"CAN I LOOK NOW?" I ASK.

"Nope. Watch your step."

There is a sound of a door opening. Massimo settles his hand on the small of my back, ushering me forward.

I don't need my eyes to tell me that we're somewhere inside, but there's a strong breeze blowing at me from every direction. That confuses me a little. Based on the slight echo of my heels on the hardwood floor, though, I'm guessing that whatever room we just entered is sizable. The combined smell of paint and wood varnish hits me first, yet another scent soon battles for supremacy. It's flowery. Fresh. Jasmine?

"Sorry, baby," Massimo grumbles next to me. "I had the guys bring the industrial fans to clear out the stink, but it's still a work in progress."

Industrial fans? "Will you please tell me where we are?"

Hard, demanding lips crash against mine. I wrap my arms around his neck, spearing my fingers through the short, silky strands. They are not as spiky as they were. He's been letting his hair grow. I'm taking it as a sign of him finally accepting that the life he led for the previous two decades is over and done. My feet leave the ground as Massimo lifts me, and I immediately cinch my legs around his waist. The high slits up the sides of my wide-legged pants fall open, the fabric draping off me, and the breeze from the fan takes no time at all to cool off my bare skin.

Massimo bites my lower lip. "Okay, you can look now."

I open my eyes.

Frames. Enormous ornate wooden frames occupy a massive wall. Gleaming white and accented with a gold leaf finish. Above each is a ceiling-mounted brass picture light, softly illuminating the drawings under the frames' polished glass.

A squeaky whimper escapes me when I realize what they are. Enlarged prints of the dress sketches I've made over the years. Oh God, there's even the very first image I sent to him in a letter, exhibited right there, in the middle of the feature wall.

It's not just the sketches. In front of each frame, stands a sleek and shiny white wrought iron mannequin, displaying the dress depicted in the sketch.

"Oh, Massimo," I whisper, squeezing his neck while I take in the rest of the room.

Vintage shelves, grand cabinets, an abundance of showcase platforms. Comfy seats, decorative mirrors, gorgeous overhead lights. Off to the side, there's a stack of boxes. I can only imagine what this man has hidden away in them. Emotions clog my throat as I look around. No one has ever done anything like this for me.

"I'm sorry if I didn't get every color right. The seamstresses kept pestering me, emailing me photos of various fabrics... As if I can distinguish between the different shades. I mean, *Skobeloff*? What the fuck is that? It sounds like the name of a fancy cake."

I half laugh, half sniffle. "It's bluish green. Similar to teal, but with more vibrant green undertones."

"Shit. I made you cry. I'm sorry. I'll let them know to— YES,

I REALIZE I SHOULD HAVE PICKED TURQUOISE. NOW, ZIP IT!"

"No. No, I'm fine." Cupping his face with my palms, I draw his forehead to mine. "It's perfect. So wonderfully perfect. But... *why*?"

"Because it was your dream. And because you're one hell of a fashion designer, angel. You deserve your own boutique." He carries me across the room, toward the opposite wall where a white satin sheet is covering... something. Shifting me in his hold, he grabs a corner and tugs the cloth away. "And brand," he adds.

I gape at the wide plaque of white and gold cursive letters. Two words. Two words that *do* make me cry.

Zahara Spada

"Oh no! No, no. We're not done." Massimo chuckles as he lowers me to the floor. "We're finished with the setup of the brand. Just not with the actual branding."

I'm barely holding myself together. My vision is blurry as I watch him lower to one knee. There's a mischievous smile curling his lips as he reaches inside his pocket and raises his hand, holding a ring out to me.

"Zahara Veronese, you are the air I breathe and the light that allows me to see. I love you more than anything, and I need the world to know it. You are already my friend. My savior. The love of my life. But now, will you please be my wife?"

"You asked me already, silly." I sniff. "And I said yes."

"Without the ring, it didn't count. So this is a do-over." He lifts the ring higher." It's platinum, of course. So, will you?"

"Yeah," I choke out. "I will."

My hand shakes as he takes it, bringing it to his mouth. That smirk is still tugging on his lips as he wraps them around my ring finger. Wetness pools between my legs as he slowly slides my finger inside his mouth. The sensation is amazing—both innocent and completely erotic. The satiny softness of his lips as they wet my skin while delicately gliding over my finger. And the sharpness of his teeth, grazing it at the same time. As he starts pulling my finger out, his slick tongue strokes the underside, while the edge of his teeth scrapes the top. A perfect combination of rough and tender. Just like him.

"There. All ready." He kisses the pad at the tip.

I'm enthralled as he slides the ring on while taking great care to center the contoured ribbon of diamonds just right. The ceiling lights reflect off the brilliant cluster, arranged with the largest marquise in the middle, and two sets of progressively smaller gems mirroring each other on either side.

"It's a crown." He gently tilts my chin up with his finger. "For my queen."

I bite my lower lip to stop myself from further crying.

"And now, angel..." Hooking his fingers in the waistband of my pants, he slides them down, along with my panties. "Now, I'll make your regal pussy thoroughly wet, before I give it a royal fucking."

A shriek escapes me when he lifts me onto a chaise longue upholstered in white velvet, and then he buries his face between my thighs.

The tip of his tongue circles my clit, the motion fast and ferocious. He positions my legs over his shoulders, then slides his hands under my ass. In one swift movement, he lifts me, bringing me closer to his mouth.

The strokes of his tongue transform into languid, long licks interrupted by sporadic bites as he feasts on my juices. There's something utterly decadent in being sprawled on a vintage sofa while he kneels on the floor and eats me out. I'm certain there wasn't a locking of the door when he first led me in here, which means anyone at all could walk in on us. The possibility of that runs rampant in my mind, exciting me beyond measure. Grabbing his hair, I revel in the tremors rocking my core.

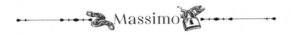 Massimo

My God, the taste of her… It's making me crazy. Almost as crazy as her pulling on my hair does. With fingers anchored in my strands, she tugs my face closer. I swipe my tongue between her folds, inhaling the scent of her. Pure Eden. I'm gorging in a fucking paradise. But my poor cock is stuck in hell because it's been hours since he was inside her.

I lick and stroke, and then take little bites, teasing her delicious pussy. With every touch, she shivers and her body shakes. She's close. So close. I'm tempted to keep torturing my angel just like this, but I don't think I can hold off much longer.

I'm wired. Ready to explode myself. But it's not simply sex that has me so strung out. She said *yes*. The word is still ringing in my head. Still has me awed that she wants to spend her life with me, the crazy fucker.

There are two of us, the ever-irritating voice in my head says. *Noted.*

Mm-hmm. You wanna know what I noted? Not so long ago, you were adamant you'd never kneel before anyone. Well, you're kneeling now, buddy.

Zahara could always bring me to my knees. For her, I'll spend a lifetime kneeling. Now, will you shut up and let me feast on my future wife's pussy in peace. Please.

I like the sound of it in the present sense, rather than the future. Our wife. Tomorrow would make a lovely wedding day.

"Good point," I mumble into Zahara's pussy.

Taking her sweet bud between my lips, I suck on it—hard—marveling over the way she shatters. Breaks apart for me with a mix of drawn-out moans and labored panting. She's so fucking beautiful. So mine. Drinking in the sight of her, I carefully lower her legs onto the fancy sofa and glide my palm over her heated core. Still soaked, even though I've done my damnedest to lap up every single drop.

Aftershocks are running rampant across her body as I stand up and unfasten my belt. She watches me unzip my pants with a wicked smile dancing on her lips. Turning onto her stomach, then rising to all fours, she sends a wink over her shoulder.

"Do your worst," she singsongs, wiggling her ass.

I snap.

Grabbing her hips, I slam into her heat in one powerful thrust, sinking balls-deep. Her passionate screams echo as she comes. I keep pounding her from behind, lost to the world and everything else except my woman.

Mine.

My palm travels up her back, feathering along her delicate spine.

Only mine.

Her pussy grips my cock so tightly that every plunge sends a shockwave through me. Every single one of my nerve endings feels exposed, raw, and on fire. My lungs contract. Heat races across my system.

My air. My love. My peace.

She trembles under my palm as her orgasm hits her. With a guttural growl building in my chest, I increase my tempo, completely losing any sense of reality. Slamming into her tight pussy over and over, I let the roar erupt as I explode into her liquid core.

My Zahara.

Still shaking from the force of my release, reluctantly, I pull out and then lean over to give her right ass cheek a quick kiss.

"Baby? You okay?" I drag my lips to her other cheek and

NEVA ALTAJ

kiss it, too. And then, playfully nip that delectable behind before easing Zahara onto the sofa. "Was I too rough?"

"Never." Watching me with hooded eyes as I rise and tuck my dick away, she sighs. "I just might not be able to walk for a while," she says as a satisfied smile lights up her face.

Sprawled naked on the elaborate piece of furniture I chose for her shop, my angel is nothing but pure temptation. I'll never get enough of her. Will never sate my craving. I might be a free man set to live my life, yet I'm still a prisoner, bound by unbreakable chains. A prisoner of this magnificent woman who has captured my heart. Who has tamed my soul. And there isn't a sweeter feeling. For the rest of my life, I am her willing slave.

Slipping my hand into one of the yet-unpacked boxes, I pull out a length of red mulberry silk delivered from China just a day ago and drape the soft material over Zahara. Can't have my queen catching a cold, can I? Once she's cocooned inside the luxurious, buttery fabric, I lift her into my arms.

"Do you have a number for your nutcase of a brother-in-law?" I ask as I carry her across the room.

"Yeah. What do you need from Kai?"

I stop and look at the love of my life.

"I need him to put me in contact with a friend of his." I crush my lips to hers. "The blond guy who likes to kidnap priests."

EPILOGUE

 Zahara

Two months later

"**W**ELL… I GUESS THIS SUMS UP THE INVESTMENT plans for the next year," Massimo announces and adjusts my position, shifting my hips for another angle that allows him a deeper plunge. "Any questions?"

There aren't any, as usual. Aside from my mewls of pleasure, the only sounds in the grand room are the rustling of papers and hurried steps as the capos scramble to leave as fast as they possibly can. Avoiding all eye contact at the same time. Seems they are still uncomfortable with me attending their meetings.

I'm not quite sure if it's me taking the chair to Massimo's left, which I do every so often, or my preference for sharing his seat that bothers them the most. Of course, the latter involves me straddling my husband and riding his cock in front of everyone while he tries to carry on with the meeting agenda. It's really a toss-up which of us enjoys seeing the barely disguised mortification in their eyes—him or me.

The only person who doesn't pay us any mind is Peppe. He's used to catching us fucking all over the house. As the newly promoted underboss—a position he accepted after being released from the hospital last month—he frequently jumps in to lead the discussion whenever Massimo's train of thought wanders off. It's doubly funny when he acts as if he's not seeing what we're doing, often leaving the capos rubbing their eyes.

"Have a good day, Don Spada." The nervous words come from the direction of the door. "And, uh, my wife wanted me to check if she could book an appointment for this weekend, Mrs. Spada. Would that be okay?"

"Sure." Slowly, I lift higher, feeling Massimo's cock slide almost completely out of me. "Enjoy your day, Tiziano."

The door clicks shut.

"I forgot to tell you," Massimo says, then grips my hips and slams me back down onto his hard length. "We've been invited to a wedding in New York next month."

"Oh? Who's the happy couple?"

"Arturo DeVille. And Drago Popov's sister, Tara."

"Mm-hmm. Are you sure?"

"Yes. Why?"

"The wedding might be delayed. I think someone close to the bride may have died."

"Why do you say that?"

"Tara Popov isn't exactly a common name, and a woman calling herself such emailed me last week, asking for an appointment. She needed a long black gown, complete with a black veil, suitable for a prominent funeral."

"Strange. Arturo called me just this morning, but he didn't mention anyone passing away."

"Maybe he forgot? Or maybe his future wife is simply into black."

"Arturo DeVille allowing his bride to wed in anything other than pure white? Please. That man is the epitome of tradition. Although, the last time I saw him, he was hardly enamored with Popov's sister, calling her a hellion and alleging that she was trying to kill him, if memory serves me right. They must have resolved their differences, or the soon-to-be newlyweds might find marriage a bit hazardous to their health. Mark my words though—if that smug asshole has anything to say about it, his bride will be wearing white."

The End

Dear reader

Thank you so much for reading Massimo and Zahara's story! I would be honored if you could take a few minutes of your time to leave a review, letting the other readers know what you thought of Sweet Prison.

Your reviews are always appreciated. Even if it's just one short sentence, it makes a tremendous difference to the author. The more reviews a book gathers, the greater its exposure in the online store of your choice. And a few words of your honest feedback can help the next person decide whether to give Massimo and Zahara a try.

To leave a review for Sweet Prison on Amazon, scan the code:

WHAT'S NEXT?

The next book in the series is **Precious Hazard**, and it features Arturo (Sienna and Asya's brother) and Tara (Drago Popov's sister). I hope you'll enjoy this story.

Precious Hazard

TARA

My life is perfect just the way it is now,
Without Arturo DeVille in it.
And now, I'm ordered to marry that arrogant,
self-centred snob.

He expects me to be a sophisticated, docile wife,
Who will smile and nod at his every demand.
But it's the last thing I plan to do.

Our marriage vows may say I will cherish and
obey my husband,
But the only vow I'm promising is to
make his life a living hell.
Until he regrets the day he said, "I do."

ARTURO

There are three qualities I expect in a wife:
Obedient. Meek. Respectful.
A woman who will fit into the Cosa Nostra world.

I didn't get a single trait that I wanted in a spouse.
Instead I got everything I never knew I craved.
She surged into my life like an earthquake,
Shaking me to my very core.

My beautiful harbinger of chaos.
My precious hazard.
My wife.

Also, you may want to check out the first book of the Mafia Legacy series—*Beautiful Beast* (book 1 in the second generation spinoff series). *Beautiful Beast* is a loose retelling of *Beauty and the Beast* fairytale. This bedtime story, however, includes a kidnapping and an age-gap romance between Vasilisa Petrova (Roman and Nina's daughter from *Painted Scars*) and Rafael De Santi (the Sicilian, who appears in *Darkest Sins*).

Before the release of Beautiful *Beast*, meet Vasilisa in *Daddy Roman*, a bonus scene available free on my website.

Read the blurb and order *Beautiful Beast* (Vasilisa and Rafael, Mafia Legacy Book #1) through by scanning the QR code below.

ABOUT THE author

Neva Altaj writes steamy contemporary mafia romance about damaged antiheroes and strong heroines who fall for them. She has a soft spot for crazy jealous, possessive alphas who are willing to burn the world to the ground for their woman. Her stories are full of heat and unexpected turns, and a happily ever after is guaranteed every time.

Neva loves to hear from her readers, so
feel free to reach out:

Website: www.neva-altaj.com
Facebook: www.facebook.com/neva.altaj
TikTok: www.tiktok.com/@author_neva_altaj
Instagram: www.instagram.com/neva_altaj
Amazon Author Page: www.amazon.com/Neva-Altaj
Goodreads: www.goodreads.com/Neva_Altaj

Made in United States
North Haven, CT
24 January 2025

64919247R00205